PRAISE FOR WHERE WEAVERS DAIRE

A clever, quirky, and exciting sci-fi and fantasy blend that had me hooked in the first chapter.

— *CITYWIDE BLACKOUT PODCAST*

Exceptionally well written, Gripping, Suspense and action full story! Complements to author on a well written book that is hard to put down.

— *GOODREADS REVIEW*

Just started this book, and already an instant favorite of this year!

I can't wait for the next one and I'm only three chapters in to this one!

— *AMAZON FIVE STAR REVIEW*

It grabbed me from the start and would not let go!

— *BOOKBUB REVIEW*

ALSO BY R. K. BENTLEY

Stuk on the Hollow Series

Where Weavers Daire

When Riders Crosleigh

WHERE WEAVERS DAIRE

BOOK ONE OF STUK ON THE HOLLOW

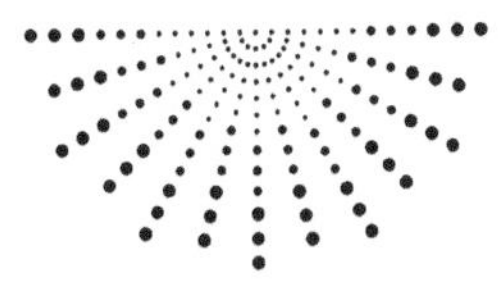

R. K. BENTLEY

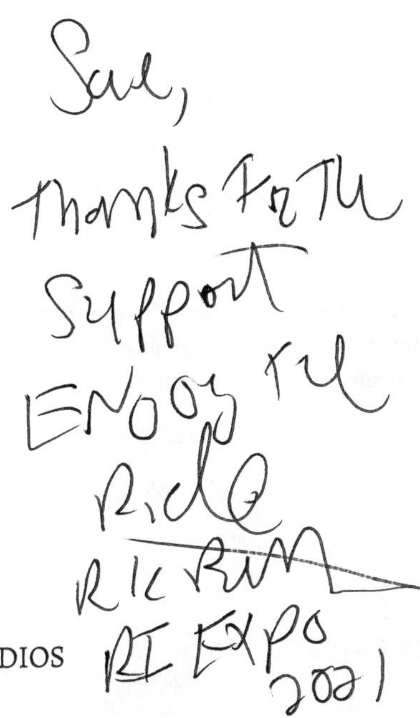

RKB STUDIOS

Published by RKB Studios:

PO Box 9321

Warwick, RI 02889

www.rkbstudios.com

eBook ISBN: 978-1-7325680-0-6

Book ISBN: 978-1-7325680-2-0

Cover by: Damonza.com

Editing by: SLS Editing

❀ Created with Vellum

Dedicated to those who helped me through getting this written.

TABLE OF CONTENTS

PART I

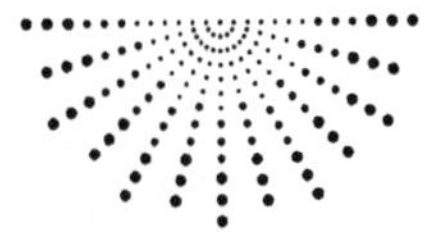

1

FINDERS KEEPERS

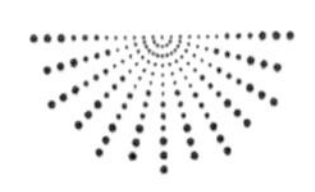

"WARNING: YOU HAVE ONE HOUR OF OXYGEN REMAINING," THE mechanical voice of Melinda Scott's spacesuit whispered through her earpiece.

"I know, I know," the eighteen-year-old grumbled. She counted to five so the urge to unscrew her helmet and hurl it into space abated. She focused on rewiring the derelict ship's electrical systems. "Thanks for distracting me. I forgot which wire is for the thrusters."

Her bubble helmet scraped across the ship's metal frame. A tug from her pliers and a yellow wire presented itself. "Let's try you," she said and twisted the wire's end around a connection point and spun the magnetized screwdriver.

Melinda reached out and gripped one of the six magnetic handholds she had latched across the hull. They led back to a three-foot-long portable battery. It was easy to spot. It broke the wedge-shaped derelict's sleek design. She flipped the bright red lever and tiny bulbs pulsated.

"Yellow is for the running lights." Melinda ignored the spinning vastness beyond. She flipped the lever back to OFF. "Let's try the red wire."

You did all the work, found it, tagged it and after two hours' worth of work, it's all yours. Slow down and focus, she thought.

The one-hundred-twenty-foot-long wedge was full of wiring and avionics along with a laundry list of problems. Backwards wiring. Eroded back-up batteries and three-quarters of the decking was gone. The derelict's stomach-churning rotation was worse. *If you don't slow down, you'll break something expensive,* she thought.

Melinda twisted the red wire. She looked over her shoulder at the exposed pilot's well and its lone occupant. The glassed-in enclosure, long since stripped away, left the frame, the console, and the pilot's body strapped into his seat. Hands floated above his head.

"I know you can't hear me, but don't jettison yourself." She flipped the lever.

The derelict shuddered beneath her and bursts of air shot out into the dark.

"There we go!" she shouted and grabbed Tommy's makeshift control stick. *Stupid pudgy suit fingers. I can barely feel anything.* A simple twist and the derelict's thrusters stopped the spinning.

Melinda tapped on her wrist communicator. "Tommy, tell Mom it's done. I'm gonna need a pickup." The animated icons danced across the two-by-two-inch screen and the transmitters built into the suit's frame did the rest.

Melinda collected the handholds and stowed them in her waist bag. It was full of nine feet of magnetic tether cord, handholds, a stun pistol with extra charges, and a backup video rig. All the items tethered to the inside of her bag, so they didn't float away.

Her magnetic boots attached themselves to the hull of her prize. "Not a bad haul for a second-generation salvage reclamation specialist." She gazed up at the frozen bundles of refuse and rock of the New Welles Asteroid Belt. The outer rings grew fatter with each passing year as starships ignored protocol and dumped their trash. The treasure lay in inner rings.

"Make a note: Pay Tommy for the restoration job on Mom's suit." Melinda stretched. "Thirty-year-old combat spacesuit fits great even if he restricted the military-grade sensor package. The retro bubble helmet is cute, but it fogs easily. Once I get back to the station, I'm swapping this fish bowl for something to cover my neck."

Melinda checked her wrist clock. "Competition is three days behind me." She collected her tools and stowed them in her father's dented toolbox. Magnetized to the hull, it served her well for patching up *Geri's Toy*'s outdated wiring. "After we sell *Toy*, what're you going to—"

The derelict's lights extinguished. Her suit's interior lighting sputtered, and shoulder-mounted torches dimmed. The hiss of free-flowing oxygen disappeared.

"Oh, come on!" Melinda leaned down to spy her feet had separated from the hull. "Some idiot set off an electromagnetic pulse. I really hope that idiot wasn't me! How 'bout I stay perfectly still and get the tether cord out of my bag before the carbon dioxide suffocates me."

A strobe of light erupted from behind and her shadow danced across the hull. "Slow your breathing. Get the magnetic tether. There's a shielded emergency battery pack in the small of your back that should be kicking in." Her inner ear twisted, and the helmet smashed into the deck.

Invisible fingers of gravity took hold and dragged Melinda across the derelict.

“Gravity well!” Melinda's arms flailed for anything to grab onto. “EMP burst too! Some idiot just Space-Cut a ship into the middle of the asteroid belt! Stupid S-Cutting kids!”

The metal frame scraped by until nothing, but the stars filled Melinda's view. She gaped at vastness and her suit's pudgy fingers brushed against something. She clamped down tight until the runaway ride jerked to a stop.

“I should stop complaining, I used to be one of them.” Melinda craned her head to spy the silhouette of the pilot's body. The outstretched hand clenched tight in hers. She looked away; anything was better than the pilot's frozen face. “If the gravity from the event horizon doesn't kill me, I'm gonna strangle the idiot.”

But the gravity released her. The derelict twisted about. The hiss of her oxygen flow restarted, and shoulder torches flared in time for her to see the poor pilot's head.

"Next time, I'll tether myself better." Melinda climbed back onto the derelict, unfurled the magnetic tether cord, and tied one end to the roll bar above the pilot. The other end attached to her utility belt. "Not one word of this to my mom. She'll pitch such a fit."

Melinda picked up Tommy's control-stick shortcut and steadied the ship. "Any cracks?" She studied herself in a two-by-four-inch forearm mirror. A smudge on the helmet's thick glass. Her face was beet red. Her adult diaper unsoiled. Movement in the mirror twisted her around.

The curtain of space parted. A dull shine from beyond stopped Melinda cold. Out of the darkness came a Type-Forty Star Carrier Drive. All seven hundred twenty feet of her.

"That's not the test ship," Melinda said. "What did you get me into, Tommy?"

Fingers of light from the suit's shoulder torches raked across the hull. “If my junior mechanics class was right, drive sections were always two times bigger than the carrier itself.” The liberal use of what were now faded reds and yellows meant it belonged to the Daires. The bulbous rectangle of metal held within its frame engines that were powerful enough to push a star carrier through space. *Toy* was only a hundred seventy-five feet long.

Melinda marched back and found, much to her surprise, the emergency clamp on her toolbox had held. She reached in for a tagging gun. It was used for pieces of salvage that were too big for *Toy*. The one-inch-thick metal spikes had all her information and a nasty virus if someone tried anything funny.

"Warning: Proximity alert." Her earbud buzzed.

Melinda shuffled around. "From where? Oh, I hate inertia."

The derelict and the engine inched towards each other.

Melinda attached her toolkit to the coil. A quick oxygen check said fifty minutes left. She tugged the cord. "If I screw this up, they can't say I didn't try."

The minutes dragged. Melinda used the time to look. The engine's hull was littered with pockmarked tiles, cracked skin, and even the occasional bundle of live wires. The service ladders used by the construction crews and engineers remained intact.

"Just a little closer," Melinda said and de-activated her boots. "I have to plan this just right."

The two pieces of metal silently scraped against each other and Melinda's inertia sent her against the wall. She reached out with one hand while the other held the cord, and, as planned, she grabbed the nearest rung. Several bones whined, and she jerked to a stop. Just as the instructions promised, the tether cord twisted around the closest metallic object.

"Ha!" Melinda hoisted herself up a few rungs until the carriage sat under her. The pilot remained in his seat. "Stay there. I need some back up." She opened her bag and produced three, inert, metal spheres. "Wake up, you three. I've got a job for you."

Several lights gleamed across the sphere's bodies.

"I need a scan of this ship. Bow. Mid-ship and aft. Focus on life signs and power. I'm not moving until you report back." She placed each on the hull and off they rolled.

This isn't Tommy's test ship, she thought and pulled her stun pistol out. *So, what kind of fool jumps an engine mount all the way out here?*

"Mindy," a man's voice surfaced through the static in her ear. "We're five minutes out."

Melinda took a deep breath and said, "Tommy?"

"Yes, indeed. We're in your line of sight. Mom wants to know how're your tanks."

"Tell 'er I have fifty minutes left." Melinda glanced about and saw a glimmer of light move through the murk. A ping in her earbud said it was the salvage hauler named, *Geri's Toy*. "How much time I got left in the pool?" she said.

"Mom says ten minutes at the most, but I think we can push it to fifteen," he said.

You didn't tell her. Why didn't you tell her? Melinda left unsaid and re-adjusted her shoulder torches. "Something just popped in here. The drones are checking now. I need longer."

"What just popped in, Mindy?" Jainey Scott, her mother's voice entered her earpiece.

"Check the drone footage. I'm not moving until they come back with a safe reading. And, before you ask, the Foo Fighter is tied down and tagged." Melinda checked her wrist and three green checkmarks blinked. "Drones say it's clear. What do you want me to do?"

The silence was longer than she expected.

"Proceed with caution." Jainey's tight-lipped response meant she was annoyed.

"The drones found an old airlock on the starboard side. We're going to attach and wait for you," Thomas said. "Good luck."

~

Not the test ship but an engine mount for a star carrier. Not guarded. No defense suites to stop me, Melinda thought. She reached the last rung and re-activated her boots' mag-lock. Carefully, she raised a foot and lowered it. The mag-lock secured itself to the deck. She pulled off a torch. *No power, so this'll have to do.*

The unpainted metal around her gave away the fact it was an addition. A nicely welded section nonetheless, since the rest of the engine section had screws at every foot.

A glimmer had caught her eye, fifty yards away where the torches couldn't reach. "Hello." Melinda pulled her tagging pistol. The darts were nonlethal. Just like all the sharp objects in her toolbox that did a lovely job of reminding pirates of the horrors of an oxygen leak.

Melinda took one step at a time until her torchlight illuminated what floated beyond.

The glimmer belonged to her three drones. They had reformed in a Delta V formation beneath something that gleamed in the low light. It was a tiny shuttle. A bulky hexagon nose with no art, house markings, flags, a name, or paint. Thirty feet long from bow to stern. Too many sharp angles. She floated six feet off the deck. An umbilical tunnel from her undercarriage to the mount.

"Well, what did you find?" Melinda fired one tag dart into the deck and one at the ship. An oxygen level check said forty-five minutes. "No life signs or energy signatures. You three go poke around and keep an eye out. Maybe this is the test ship after all."

~

"Why can't I see her?" Jainey Scott broke the silence in *Toy's* cramped cockpit.

"Then she won't learn anything. Don't worry, she actually listened this time and let the scouts do their jobs." Thomas Scott sat hunched over the control sticks.

"Could've done this on the station." Jainey sighed. "What do you mean this time?"

"Too many civilians and variables involved. And the less they know about this test, the better. Besides, Little Miss Techno-freak will survive." Thomas flipped levers on the overhead panel. The cabin lights dimmed. "She was too eager last time; this time she used the drones."

"And what's going to stop her from hacking through your passwords?"

Thomas' grin in the harsh afterglow of the instrument panel appeared psychotic. "Pudgy suit fingers and using keyboards to hack don't mix."

Jainey snorted and leaned close to the radar dome. "Where'd you find this thing?"

"It dropped into my lap and no one else was using it," he said.

Jainey's silence made him look up into the rearview mirror.

"Think of it this way—some kids get their own ship for their sweet sixteen. Besides, Mindy probably knows it's a test. I proctored her cousin last week." He twisted an ignition key, and *Toy's* engines silenced. "Never heard someone scream that loud inside an empty ghost ship."

"May I remind you that you dropped a derelict into the middle of an asteroid field with no doctors in sight and you haven't run a radar sweep in an hour."

"We have enough medical stims and gauze." Thomas flipped a switch and the radar domes refreshed with an updated return. "No one else for an hour in any direction. Welcome to the shallow end of the pool."

"Shallow end? She nearly got sucked in."

"The shallow end has just enough current where we learn if she can function without a net. I designed and field-tested this scenario. Mindy isn't in here sobbing and shitting herself. She knows the safe words if she gets in over her head. She can't get inside but found the test ship. So far so good. You can suit up if you want, just don't interfere."

~

Melinda finished her walk around. The ship's portside airlock was the only way in. No access to the umbilical tunnel. She hauled herself up onto the airlock's ledge. *Let's make sure someone didn't booby-trap it.* She thought and plucked a spare screwdriver out of her bag. She flicked it and breathed a sigh of relief when it didn't get roasted.

Melinda popped off the control panel and twisted wires. The exterior airlock lights blazed. The hatch's pressure seal broke and the doors peeled back. Nothing so far. Stun gun in one hand, she pulled herself through the lock with the other. The inner door opened into a narrow corridor. The painted red arrows on the wall led her to the cockpit.

The top of her helmet scraped the overhead console. "Gahsakes, who designed this ship?" She stomped her boots on the deck and tapped her wrist. "Melinda Scott, Salvage License Number One Three Charlie Hotel Echo, if anyone's here, identify yourselves. Repeat that message until you get a response. Start a salvage log."

Melinda tapped a console button. "Cockpit controls are unresponsive." The deeper she ventured, the wider the ceiling and walls became. "No stasis pod or a crèche. No human ice cubes. Flat-screen monitor and desk in mid-cabin." At the desk, she wiped off the dust of a leather-bound tome. "Got a spell book. Can't read the inscription. Maybe an arch mage?"

On the rear cabin's back wall, a cloak with long quills woven into its fabric hung on a hook. Shoulders and elbows made of mismatched metal. Collar and the wrists of thick, striped fur. The coat's garishness wasn't what grabbed her attention; it was the mask sewn into the hood.

"I remember you from history class and Aunt Freda's attic." Every mask had a house sigil. This one didn't. Glassy electronic eyes under a furrowed brow. High, accented, red cheekbones and a wide sneer of black teeth. "A nameless, houseless Necromancer's cloak."

Melinda's pudgy suit fingers tapped the mask. She waited for a long moment, transfixed. She picked up the cloak and shook it. Its quills lived up to their cursed reputation. A jingle chimed through the vacuum. "No boogeyman. No cheap scare. Nobody home."

~

Stupid thawing process, Spence MacGregor's fogged brain thought. His arms and legs refused to move. He breathed in and let it out. *You're still in the stasis pod. Body needs to thaw. Focus on your aura. Can't flick spells if your aura isn't focused. Don't panic . . . can almost feel my fingers.* He cracked open an eyelid and jolted awake.

Through the frost, a black EVA suit stood less than three feet away. Cloak in hand.

Spence focused, and a half-assed stun spell spooled up on his left pinky. *Let's not panic, the* You Can't See Me *spell on the stasis door is still working. Can't pillage what you can't see.*

The EVA suit dropped the cloak back on the hook. Clomped up to the mid-cabin when the blasted stasis door dropped. The straps across his body retracted and the pod bed tipped his limp body forward. Inertia and zero gravity did the rest. *Stupid inertia. Stupid stasis pins and needles.*

The cloak blossomed forth and enveloped him. Its innards spewed forth tendrils of energy. Tendrils that seared the long hair off his gangly body. The pins and needles disappeared, and his limbs warmed. *Thanks for the haircut,* he thought.

Spence grabbed the nearest handhold and the cloak sealed itself. Warm-up screens flashed across the mask's lenses. "Rebooting. Please wait," a computerized voice crackled across his earbud.

~

Melinda measured the flat screen on the mid-cabin's wall. A colorful waterfall of wires ran from the screen and disappeared underneath the flooring. "I know where you're going once we get home," she declared.

The flat-screen responded by turning itself on.

Melinda jerked back. Lines of code spread across the screen. "What do we have here? A state of the art and illegal Crosleigh Operating System. No more hand me downs! New gear!" The code was so inviting. She reached out, curiosity building. "What else are you wired into?"

A stray jingle froze Melinda's fingers. She twisted round at the cloak.

The wide-eyed, smiling, death mask stared back.

Melinda winced at the chill creeping down her shoulder blades. She twisted a knob on her chest plate. The bowl's fog disappeared. "It's just inertia. You moved it after all."

The jingling of quills spiked. They twisted, and the mask tilted up. Glass pupils dilated. Teeth snapped. Arms and legs stretched forth from its body. For that moment, the cloak was a perfect mix of science, magic, and myth. Bony fingers wrapped around ceiling handholds and pulled itself out of the rear cabin. An outstretched, crooked, finger beckoned.

Melinda tapped her wrist to reopen a coms channel. "Tommy, you still there?"

"Right here; you have about ten more minutes," he said.

Melinda gaped at the oncoming figure. "I think it's time for me to get out of the pool."

~

"Why is she using the safe word?" Thomas tightened his headset. "Repeat your last?"

"I think it's time for me to get out of the pool." Melinda's calm tone jerked him upright.

Thomas pulled a keyboard close and a flurry of rapid strokes brought none of the video monitors to his left to life. He restrained himself from hitting them since that would accomplish nothing. "Mindy, I know you brought your extra video rig. Turn it on."

One of the screens refreshed and several darkened shapes blurred about until Melinda's face appeared. She pointed the camera lens away from her and focused it on a moving object.

"Where in gahsakes are you?" He jerked back at the sight of the death mask. "I need you to sit tight, Mindy."

"What's going on?" Jainey butted in.

"Change in plans." Thomas twisted the ignition keys. The deck plates shook from *Toy's* engines spinning up. "Don't move, Mindy. I need to dock with the ship, and then you can run."

"Port side only." Melinda breathed deep. "It's not what I think it is, is it?"

"Not over the coms." Thomas brought the sensors on next, followed by the floodlights. "Jainey, strap in." He throttled up and twisted the control sticks. "This is why I planned ahead. So, stuff like this doesn't happen."

~

"It hasn't touched me yet. What's the big deal? It might be friendly." Melinda stumbled back into the pilot's seat.

"It's a Necromancer, Melinda, not a fuzzy alien!" Thomas hissed.

"A Necro-what?" Jainey's voice screeched.

The cloak reached the mid-cabin; the jingling of its quills rose as it closed the distance. The flat screen filled with snow and pictures that barraged Melinda's eyes. An unfamiliar man laughed in her ear and said, "I found you."

She blocked out the snow and focused on the jingle. *Sounds are coming from the quills,* she thought.

Its teeth pulled back. Several languages spewed forth until two words: "Melinda Scott."

Melinda gaped. "And it knows my name. Mom?" she whispered.

"What?" her mother's curt reply came.

"New plan," Melinda said and pulled her stun pistol.

~

What little girl carries? Spence thought and flicked a disarm spell. Four stun rounds were disabled before leaving the barrel. *Not so hard—*

The spell corkscrewed around the fifth round. *Why do I taste iron?* A punch to the gut sent him hurtling into the back wall. The thrust spell he'd spun up bolted towards her.

~

The spell twisted out of control. Its tentacles danced across the flat screen and cracked it. It lunged past her and impacted with the pilot's console. An explosion buffeted the seat.

The death mask spun about, one eyebrow cocked higher than ever.

Melinda looked down the stun pistol and shrugged. "Completely understand why they put expiration dates on those rounds." She pushed herself out of the seat. Kicked. Pulled. "C'mon, momentum, don't fail me now!"

The maw of *Toy's* sleeve appeared, and Melinda heaved herself across.

~

Oh, you didn't just do that! Spence raged and twisted across the cabin, down the corridor, and pulled to a stop at the wide-open hatch.

A boarding sleeve's floodlights polarized the lenses. He fired a thrust spell to cross the expanse and readied a simple lasso spell. *Remember to aim for her ankles,* he thought.

~

"Melinda! What type of plan was that?" Jainey howled.

Melinda arced across the hundred-foot sleeve. Almost there. Her helmet scraped against the airlock's ceiling. She grabbed the nearest handhold to stop and said, "I'm in! Decouple us!"

"I'm working on it!" Thomas' voice crackled. "Mindy, I need you to retract the sleeve!"

Melinda kicked back towards the doorframe and hit the bright red button. "Gahforsaken boots aren't latching onto the decking." The airlock outer door closed. Through the porthole, Melinda gaped at the quills flooding *Toy's* docking sleeve. Furry arms blossomed forth, and gnarled hands gripped the sleeve's handholds. It closed the hundred-foot length in a blink.

Melinda gaped at the angry visage. "Get us out of here!"

~

The airlock door broke the spell's connection and Spence's finger burned. *Too many mid-level spells. You're going to collapse!* he thought.

"Warning: Ship is departing," the mask said. "Insufficient oxygen for pursuit."

"Next time." Spence grabbed a handhold. His ship's engines start-up reverberated through the deck. It jolted forward, the errant sleeve still attached, and twisted out into the dark.

~

The shuttle with *Toy's* docking sleeve still attached pulled away just as something gripped Melinda's right leg.

The outer door's green pressurized telltale lights flared red.

"What?" Melinda twisted around, and her bubble helmet bounced off the deck. This time her fingers found nothing.

Toy's airlock door cycled open and out she went.

2
RUNAWAY

"SHE'S GETTING AWAY!" JAINEY'S VOICE SAID IN THOMAS' EAR.

"Not for long," he said and twisted *Toy's* control sticks. "I need you to suit up."

The snub-nosed salvage hauler came about without slowing. Thomas fired the maneuvering thrusters and lined up the silver gleam of the shuttle in the middle of *Toy's* targeting HUD. The crosshairs locked on and the distance to target clicked away at a good pace.

He eased off the thrusters and inched the in-system drive throttles ahead to one quarter. The rumble of the engines actually soothed, all things considered.

The distance to target on the HUD stopped advancing.

"You need me to what?" Jainey's voice barely said over the rattling of the deck plates.

The shuttle jerked away, but Thomas eased *Toy* to starboard. He nudged the throttles to three quarters ahead.

The distance to target clicked down by one kilometer then another.

"Suit up," Thomas said. He reached out and twisted dials, so the communication array was refocused on the dim smudge behind the target. "Mindy, if you can hear me, I need you to let go. We're right behind you."

"What is she hanging on to?" Jainey's voice said.

"I don't know, but whoever is flying that ship doesn't have a clue," Thomas said and twisted the control sticks.

The engine dials were still in the green and nowhere near in the red. "Thank you, Geri, for sinking enough money into *Toy* to outrun almost anything pedestrian," Thomas said. "Computer, best guess on where they're going?"

One of the dash monitors refreshed with a dotted line right towards free space.

"Zoom out, what else is out here with civilization?" Thomas said.

The monitor refreshed with a sole circle blinked in the middle of the screen: STUK'S HOLLOW, 75% CHANCE OF DESTINATION.

"Count me down to the Stukari Border," Thomas said and reached back to the dials for the defense suite. "I'm spooling up the defense suite. There's gonna be a bump."

Jainey's head popped into view. "You want me to what?"

Thomas eased his hands away from the defense suite toggles. "I said, suit up. We've got enough power to overtake them. I need you suited up to grab Mindy and slice whatever she's got herself wrapped up in," he said.

"She can let go," Jainey said.

Thomas chanced a look at her. "Oh, you didn't get re-certified, did you?"

"My certifications are perfectly fine," Jainey huffed.

"Mindy gave your group a certification drill and you didn't get to the suits in time, didn't you? She has to stop ending the class with an emergency decompression." Thomas sighed and eased back to half ahead. "What is he doing?"

Jainey squinted through the port hole. "Re-establish communications with her."

"I can't. It's either on her end or ours." Thomas stabbed a few buttons on the overhead control panel to boost his signal. "Mindy, if you can hear me, wave your arms. I can't hear you."

Ten seconds later, the smudge waved about.

"Ten-second delay. Her satellite communications must've taken a hit when she bounced off the ceiling," Jainey said. "You go, I'll fly."

"We switch seats, we'll lose her," Thomas said. "Computer, I said count me off."

"*Toy* isn't a strike fighter. Don't overburden her. Where're they headed?" Jainey said.

"The Hollow," Thomas said as the shuttle twisted to starboard and a burst of speed jerked them out of sight.

"This was part of your test?" Jainey said.

"No. This wasn't part of the test." Thomas pulled *Toy* to port as the smudge re-appeared.

"It what?" Jainey said.

"This wasn't part of the test. The engine mount wasn't part of the test. None of this should be happening," Thomas said and got the smudge back in his sights. "They're using maneuvering thrusters only, so it means the main drive system is too cold. It keeps stalling out. That was a stall. The next time they do that, it may ignite, and if we can't get them in time, we're really screwed."

"What did you get us into?" Jainey grabbed his harness. "I knew it. The whole let's go on one last salvage run was the stupidest idea ever, but I just knew it."

"Either suit up or take your station, but don't distract me. I'm trying my damnedest to make sure this guy doesn't know we can overtake him. So, strap it or suit up," Thomas said and inched the throttles back up to a full ahead. "Maybe they don't have line of sight or a rear camera. Whoever it is doesn't know you have to cold start the drives. Now if Mindy can get back on board and stop it, we're good, but sooner or later, we're hitting the border and the flight plan I didn't file doesn't cover going into free space, and the last time I checked, we're all still banished. We need to get that ship because I need to know who else is on board."

"It could've been anyone's cloak," Jainey said.

"No. I know the difference. It's a Necromancer cloak. I need to know who," Thomas said and rolled *Toy*. "Six months ago, I was on a milk run and the engine mount just popped up in front of me. Exactly where we found it. Now, it's back and Mindy found someone on board. She passed her test six months ago in Gunna's junkyard. I have no idea who, what, when, or how but right now, the evidence is on board that shuttle."

Jainey silence drew a look from him. "What?" he said.

"You're red teaming me?" Jainey seethed.

"Red teaming your House. Freda is in on it. I just can't prove it. Officially," he said.

"How is my sister involved?" she said.

"She missed her last six-month check in," he said. "I had an entire squad of First Contact Marauders hunt her and the rest of her little sewing circle down. She acted like it was completely normal, but I got a data stick from her I can't read. I'm pretty sure you can."

Jainey waved a hand to slow him down. "The evidence is behind us," she said.

"Part of the evidence is behind us; the rest of the evidence is speeding away with Mindy and our sleeve," Thomas said and keyed the com channel. "Mindy, I need you to let go of whatever you're tangled up on. Wave once for able, wave twice of unable."

The computer beeped and intoned: "Fifteen minutes until border crossing."

The smudge waved twice.

"Swell. It's not the sleeve she's stuck on. Must be something else," Thomas said.

"I couldn't touch my toes in that suit. If something is wrapped around her ankle." she said.

"Then, I need you to suit up. I'm going to overtake them. We'll grab Mindy and cut through whatever she's snagged onto," Thomas said.

"Cut her with what exactly?" Jainey said.

"My weapons trunk is stowed. Combination is your wedding anniversary," Thomas said.

Jainey stared at him. "And you want me to do what? Throw a sword at her in Zero G?"

"If it's a spell, yes. One of my blessed swords can latch onto whatever is wrapped around her and you just let it go. Swing by and pick up Mindy," Thomas said. "I've done it before."

"You've done this before?" Jainey said.

Thomas scowled. "Freefalling through atmo to our certain doom, but the maneuver has still worked. How I married Dor, actually."

"Ten minutes until free space border crossing. Recommend raise shields and House Colors," the computer said.

"And the defense suite?" Jainey said.

Thomas reached back and flipped three toggles. "Spooling them up. Get your passport handy just in case. Explaining this is going to be a mess."

"And explaining to me why you're red teaming me will take a bit more than just Freda's involvement." Jainey pushed herself out of the cockpit.

~

"Okay, Mindy. We think something is wrapped around your leg. If it's a spell, I've got something in my truck that will get rid of it. We're going to come up alongside you and Jainey will cut you free. Once you're free, we'll swing back around and pick you up. Turn on those gahforsaken shoulder strobe lights and just wait. You got me?"

Ten seconds later, the smudge waved once and several other shakes.

"Yeah, I know. It sounds crazy, but it'll work. I've done it before," he said.

The smudge waved about.

"Oh, you mean your mother in the suit and not me?" he said.

The smudge waved once.

"Don't worry about her. She'll be fine. Just keep an eye on us," Thomas said.

"Doesn't instill a lot of confidence." Jainey's voice said. "You're not going to tell her?"

"I've been broadcasting directly at her and at the ship. If they've broken through our communication lines, I don't want to give them any warning," Thomas said.

"Five minutes until free space border," the computer intoned.

"Ten seconds," Thomas said. "I'm going to punch it. Bring you alongside her, slice whatever it is, let go of it, and Mindy will just float on by."

"You're sure you've done this before?"

"Unfortunately, yes." Thomas tightened his harness. "Computer, execute."

The throttles pushed to the fire wall by themselves. The deck plate rattle returned, and the G-Forces pushed Thomas back into his seat.

"Matching speed to target," the computer said.

The throttles eased back along with the G-Forces and the ships paralleled each other.

"I'm going to grab her," Jainey said.

"No, cut whatever it is. Don't grab her. They'll know and pull away. I'm not losing both of you." He wheezed. "Cut whatever it is. Just cut it."

"There's nothing there!" Jainey said. "I'm not cutting her."

"It's attracted to whatever spell is there. Let go of the sword and just let it do its job. Do not overthink this." He blinked away tears to see the monitor. "Plus twelve seconds. Thirty more and we must power down. We're too close to the border."

"She's right there!" Jainey said.

"And she'll be in pieces if we just bring her on board without untangling her."

"The sword isn't doing anything," Jainey said.

They know, Thomas thought. *You're compromised. Those trunk locks are supposed to be unpickable. Unless you know the locksmith.*

"Ten seconds to the border," the computer whined.

"Computer: full stop and keep us on the Stukari side of the border," he said.

The throttles pulled back to negative thrust and *Toy* quaked.

Thomas jerked forward then back.

The deck plate shaking stopped, and *Toy*'s forward thrust dropped to zero.

The shuttle jerked at an angle. Her main drive fired up and was gone along with Mindy.

~

Geri's Toy disappeared from Melinda's sight.

Slow breaths. Slow breaths, Melinda thought. She looked down and spied silvery remains of a spell around her ankle. *Need to get yourself re-oriented. Get back inside the ship and power down the engines before the idiot burns off the rest of the fuel.*

Melinda reached out and grabbed the remains. *Targeted my limbs. Smart.* She thought and pulled herself along until the sleeve's body appeared. Her fingers tightened around an errant ring.

~

Can I go back to the stasis pod? Spence would've asked if his tongue wasn't lolling about from the damn stasis fog. Instead, he pushed back into the cockpit.

Spence's tongue may not have worked properly but his arms did. *No air. Need a keyboard.* He thought and grabbed the nearest keyboard to hunt and peck his password into the main computer. Several error messages appeared on the cracked flat screen and the stars twisted to port.

~

Melinda climbed through the sleeve. *If it's still attached, the hatch is still open, too. Just like in Zero-G Class just without the safety net and spare oxygen tanks,* she thought.

A sudden up thrust tugged the sleeve hard. It ripped and one of the thruster nozzles appeared. The ice buildup said it was cold. *Trying to cold start the main drive system. Idiot. Ignore it and get back inside. Panic much, much, much later,* she thought.

The maneuvering thruster fired off a burst. Melinda's fingers betrayed her, and she skipped down the sleeve. She grabbed the last ring and took a chance to look around to see why she didn't feel the hull. The blackness of space answered her question.

You've done this before. Ignore it! Melinda thought and looked towards the hatch. A blemish hurtled towards her. She pulled in close and the asteroid punched through the sleeve. Another burst and the hull re-appeared to try to smash her face, but the fish bowl was sturdy enough.

"Warning: shuttle has now left Stukari Controlled Space," the helmet said. "Now entering uncontrolled space. Recommend: Raise shields, spin up weapons and fly House Colors. ETA to Leighton Controlled Space: Two hours current speed. Forty minutes of air left."

"Onboard computer?" Melinda wheezed.

"Ship's onboard computer isn't accepting requests at this time."

Melinda put one hand in front of the other. *This was so worth getting reamed out by Jainey for not detaching properly. Perfect lifeline.* She ignored another radical course change and pulled herself through the hatch.

~

“No, no, no.” Spence retyped. “Shut down the engines, not spin them up!”

The computer had ignored the standard start up sequence and tried to run up the main drive. If the computer's operating system was compromised, it narrowed the options to just one: Wipe the hacker's access and turn off this wild ride so he could reload his mask presets!

"Warning: Cabin has no atmosphere. Hatch is ajar," the mask warned.

Spence pushed forward and twisted the hatch controls.

The deck shuddered, but the wall-mounted indicator lights glared red for negative.

"Warning: hatch still ajar," the mask said.

Spence's left hand twitched and jerked him into the wall. *You forgot to finish the spell.* He thought and flicked a finger to complete the spell. The hatch indicator lights changed to green.

~

Melinda tore open the hatch control box and pulled three levers down. The hatch formed a good seal and the environmental systems pumped oxygen throughout the ship.

"Warning: thirty-five minutes of oxygen left," the helmet advised.

"Explosive decompression in ninety seconds," a sexless voice warned from the cockpit.

Oh, no you aren't. Melinda thought and pulled herself up through the crawl space. She floated back up into the Pilot's Well and came face to face with the Necromancer.

~

Spence's gnarled hands delved into the mass of quills, found the four seals and twisted them counterclockwise. The hood loosened, and the coat depressurized. He pulled back the hood and took a deep breath of stale air.

"Computer! Authorize, MacGregor, Spence. De-activate decompression protocols." He croaked and fanned the stale air about. "Need to find the head." The familiar cramped surroundings that were untainted by scavenger's greedy mitts. Here's hoping that little hellion hasn't left any other surprises behind. "Everything exactly where I left it—"

The EVA Suit re-appeared in the cockpit as if on cue. Gloved hands twisted off her bubble helmet and the dark copper-toned hellion waved the remnants of his spell. "I think this belongs to you," she said.

~

Melinda ignored the shimmering aura blue pupils, the exotic olive skin and dark crew cut. *Talk him to death while you reload,* she thought.

"Who. Be. You." Her old tongue greeting would've been nicer, but now wasn't the time.

"Spence MacGregor." He pulled the round out of the quills and chucked it at her. "Stun round? Who uses these anymore?"

"Simple: it hurts." Melinda grabbed the floating round and stuffed it back into her bag. She grabbed an extra clip. "Stop that timer."

"Computer, full stop and wait for further instructions." Spence pushed off to get clear of the rear-cabin. "What did you do to my ship?"

"Do what?" Melinda mag-locked her boots to the deck. The thrusters spun hundred-eighty degrees. She stood upside down while he remained stationary. "Unbelievable."

"Explosion decompression in thirty seconds," the voice droned.

Spence pointed at the cracked flat screen. "What else did you touch?"

"Me? Your ship is taking a hissy fit and yer blamin' me?" She disconnected the rainbow wires from the flat screen. "Credit where credit is due, I didn't do all this. Try it now."

Spence cocked an eyebrow. "That's it?"

"I don't feel like getting explosively decompressed. Do it!" Melinda said.

Spence repeated his request. The stars stopped spinning and the shuttle rolled right side up. The flat screen lit up with several confirmation windows. "Confirmed." A soothing woman's voice and engine reverb through the deck plates ceased. "Standing by."

Melinda flicked the remains of his spell across the cabin. "And this is yours, mage boy."

"Weaver. Not a mage." Spence pointed. "You shot me first then..." He eyed the cracked flat screen. "Did you touch that?"

"Uh huh. It turned itself on," Melinda said.

~

Not good. This doesn't explain why my center of gravity feels funny. Spence thought and pulled back the floor panels. The rat's nest of wires ran under the floor and into the rear cabin. "I need complete control in thirty seconds or we're all dead."

"That, I can do." Melinda followed the rainbow wires into the rear compartment. "Gotcha." She pulled back the flooring and gaped. "Holeeee."

Spence floated over her. The wires ran under the floor and into six-dozen rectangle-sized six by six-inch metal enclosures. All blinking, clicking and whirring away happily. "Gahsakes."

Melinda whistled. "I've never seen a House Server Farm this big. Who'd you piss off?"

"That's big? Those are the size of my hand," he said.

"Somebody's hacking your screen. Which makes no sense." Melinda took a deep breath. "Oh, did you feel that?"

"It's not a monitor. Computer, give me a location fix," Spence said.

"Negative." The sexless voice returned as did the engine reverb.

Spence dropped to the floor, narrowly missing Melinda. He grabbed her fishbowl as it rolled by and handed it back. "Gravity?" He hand-cranked down the blast shields. The cockpit flooded with light. Not from a sun but from a planet. And it's getting closer!

He climbed into the pilot's seat, but the gaping hole in the panel left him cold.

"There's a backdoor they must have used." Melinda called out and the several sparks blew across the floor. "Higher functions aren't responding." She carried her fishbowl under her arm. "If I touch anything else I'll make it worse. I didn't do this I swear."

"I know." Spence strapped himself into the pilot's chair. "Computer: re-adjust our trajectory! Prepare to deploy air brakes and control surfaces."

"Negative," the computer replied.

He glared at the closest speaker. "And why the gahsakes not?"

"General Order One: You. Must. Die." A warm male voice jerked Spence around. Left hand extended with a stun spell, but they were alone, the targeting spell in his pinky said so.

Melinda pointed to the screen. An erratic group of pixels tumbling across the fractured screen. It resembled a man's face. "Why do I know that voice?" she said.

"Wallace." Spence growled.

"Stukari?" Melinda gulped.

"Yes, it's me and it's time for you to die, Weaver." The pixels jumbled about. The coding degradation only made Wallace Stukari look more deranged than he really was. "I wish I could be there to see it happen, but we have places to destroy and people to explore."

Spence patted down the cloak and found a pocket he sought. He pulled out a spell book and Melinda's nose wrinkled.

"I didn't miss that lovely smell. The one on the desk?" she said.

"It's a decoy." Spence spun the book. "Keep talking and I'll keep thinking, Wally."

"You should've surrendered when you had the chance, you know." Wallace's lopsided smile sneered. "Instead, look where it's gotten you: floating, dead and alone in space."

Spence stuffed the book back into the pocket and grinned. "Not dead, yet." He twisted the seals on the cloak. "Ready for a little trip?"

Melinda laughed. "As opposed to the last one?"

A flurry of sparks blew across the floorboards. "Fifteen seconds to decompression."

Spence tugged on the harness. "Computer, what about your crew's self-preservation?"

"Negative. You. Are. Not. Crew," the computer blurted out.

Melinda twisted her fishbowl back into place then tapped her wrist. "Hear me?" her static filled voice came through his earbud.

Spence nodded and found the ejection levers under the armrests. Reading those misspelled manuals is about to pay off. "Stick close. I surrender, Wally," he said.

"Negative. Decompression in five seconds," the computer said.

"Five more than I need." Spence pulled the levers. Explosive bolts at the chair's base popped and the seat collapsed in on itself. Now flat on his back, restraints locked his limbs and chest in place. The remains of the chair's body encased him in a twelve-foot-long escape pod.

A thud later and the escape pod rushed out into the vacuum along with any of the remaining atmosphere.

~

For emergency use only, Melinda thought and gripped the escape pod's rear handhold painted in yellow and red hazard colors. She chanced a look back to see the tiny shuttle speed away. It disappeared across the curvature of the bright yellow world. She slapped her control console and the fish bowl tinted. "Gahsakes," she croaked.

"Warning, you have thirty minutes of oxygen remaining," the suit told her.

The escape pod's retro rockets fired, and the bright marble stopped spinning.

"Atmospheric entry in forty seconds," an unfamiliar woman's voice said in her ear.

"She's with me. I linked the mask to the escape pod computer," Spence said. "There should be enough space for you in the parachute compartment."

Isn't that where the parachute goes? she thought and pulled open the compartment to find it empty. *We're going to have to ditch.* "I've got thirty minutes of air left at best," she said.

"I'm going to try something else. Conserve your oxygen," he said.

Easy for you to say. Melinda leaned over the edge of the pod and shivered at the darkened world below. *Hurtling through the atmosphere to my death with a proper view is really,* she laughed. *Feels like I'm a sock in the dryer of the Universe. An awfully dark dryer for a lost sock. Where're the cities? Where're the lights?*

Instead, a vast mountain range spread across the middle of what could have been one of the largest continents and rose second by second to meet the stars. Vague outlines of forests dotted the landscape that threatened to spread past the horizon. Rare oases were oddly lit from the ground as if the trees were producing the light by themselves.

With the oases just a memory, Melinda kept an eye on the falling altimeter. She nearly missed a piece of the pod dart away from the ship.

"Alert: Escape Pod Distress Beacon deployed." The woman's voice rang in her ear.

"No ships in the area?" Melinda said. Toy *can't move that fast, can she?*

"Negative," the woman said.

Spence growled. "Does the planet we're about to land on at least have a name?"

"It's Stuk's Hollow," Melinda said. *The one place you can't go. Tommy is gonna kill me.*

3

A LONG LEASH

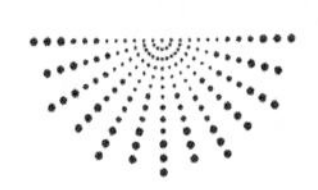

"WHAT WERE YOU THINKING?" JAINEY PULLED OFF HER HELMET ONCE the inner airlock door cycled shut and the telltale lights glowed green. "I got trussed up for nothing?"

"No. Someone picked my locks. All of my gear is completely useless." Thomas closed the lid to his trunk. "Wait. If they went after the trunk, what else..."

"What?" Jainey said.

"I spooled up the defense suite." Thomas pushed himself out of the airlock and across the secondary deck. Through the cramped hallway to the closet he had labeled *Toy's Weapons Bay*.

The door swished open and the two iron kegs latched onto the floor were silent. The silence from their tiny monitors meant nothing had been spooled up, but no spells were cooking to explode.

Thomas stared at the kegs. *What's wrong with this picture? Mindy isn't on board. You've brought the ship to a dead halt and your defense suite is cold as a witch's tit. What's wrong with this*— He stopped and pointed to the wiring. He followed it out the door and bumped into Jainey.

"Now what?" Jainey said. "We need to get Mindy."

"Following my nose," he said. "And we will. I need to know what they did to *Toy*."

"Who did?" Jainey said.

"Someone picked my locks and spun down all my defense weapons. Someone who knew how to pick the unpick able. And right now, our defense suite is cold."

"You said you spun them up," Jainey said and *Toy's* interior lights extinguished.

The emergency lights above Thomas flickered to life and coated the bulkheads in urine yellow. The glow tabs that lined the sharp corners of the auxiliary engineering console next to the airlock pulsed a green tint.

He closed his eyes and counted off. *One, two, three, four, five, six.*

"What are you doing?" Jainey said.

Eight, nine, ten. "Waiting for those expensive shielded back-up generators to kick in," Thomas said. "Stay here, I need to fix something."

"It can wait." Jainey's voice rose.

"Not if we can't get the mains back up." Thomas pointed to the airlock door. "The only thing keeping that closed is the seal. Guess what happens when we can't seal the door properly after whoever just cut our power decides to slice it open because they're too lazy to open it manually?" He pulled himself up the ladder into the mid-cabin and gripped a wall handhold to stop. "Don't touch anything. I need to bring the back-ups on first then the mains."

"I ran this ship before you were born. Tell me what's wrong," Jainey shouted.

"Once I know what's wrong, I will." Thomas pushed off and floated through the darkened common area. The glow tabs that lined the edge of the dining area table gave way to stars she had lined the walls with when she was six. Their fading light guided her towards the rear cabin. No artificial gravity well meant it's a small ship. He grabbed a handhold on the ceiling and spun around to face the floor. Small ship meant one or two-man boarding crew.

"What happens when they kill us and go after you?" Jainey echoed over the racket.

"You honestly think I'm going to let anyone through those doors?"

Thomas pulled off the floor plate and pushed it against the magnetic strip on the wall. One click later and his hands dove into sea of wires and tape. "Next time, Mindy, promise me to hide the surge protector at eye level." He pulled out a length of wire and an acid smell filled his nose.

Thomas ceased the gag reflex his lungs demanded. He held up the mangled body of the surge protector.

"Oh, gahsakes did this?" he said. "I need five minutes and we'll be up and running!"

"Take a look outside before you panic," Jainey called out.

Thomas pulled himself up into one of the ceiling domes and hand-cranked back the blast shield. Through the pockmarked glass, the vastness of space didn't greet his eyes but instead, the smooth underbelly of a scout ship. Any of her painted markings had long lost their luster, but the Stukari Imperial Taxation sigil remained as always, a shining beacon.

Thomas groaned. "Tax collectors. I'd rather be boarded by pirates."

~

Ten minutes later, the double thud of a sleeve's arrestor hooks attaching themselves to *Toy*'s side jolted Thomas' attention to the brightening light beckoning through the outer airlock window.

The outer airlock doors cycled, and two men dressed in blue and gray jumpsuits that could have only come from the design-deficient brain of a bureaucrat floated across the sleeve until they locked their boots onto the deck. The shorter of the two was in charge; he was walking, writing, and talking at the same time to the taller one.

The old man that strolled up behind them sent shivers up his spine. Dressed in slacks, sweater, and sandals. He strolled across the deck, a cane in one hand, tapping as he went. Thomas didn't see an aura of a mage but knew he was a war veteran, a hero, and if the scuttlebutt was right, this man, Zi Stuk was warming the Stuk throne while Jer, his brother, was away on House business.

"Missus Scott," the short one started. He was three decades her senior. TODD was stitched onto his breast pocket. "Your missing airlock sleeve has already been noted. Several fines have been levied against you for not being kindly pilots and offering the use of your sleeve. These fines will be added to your bill. Do we understand each other?"

"Yes, we do," Jainey said.

"If there are any recording devices active, they will be de-activated, and you will be fined. Do we understand each other?" Todd said.

"Completely. All of our personal recording devices were turned off before your arrival, Inspector Todd." Jainey nodded. "If you'll follow me, our passports and paperwork are ready."

Inspector Todd didn't hesitate or stumble; he must have had others who had taken the time to read his nametag. "That won't be necessary. Zephyr has more pressing matters to attend to."

"Mister Scott." Zi Stuk stepped forward and jerked Thomas' head up with the tip of his cane. "I have little time. Did you or did you not say this would be easy?"

"Yes, I did say that." Thomas raised his hands over his head.

"Didn't you say there would be no room for error?" Zi said.

"Yes, I did say that as well," Thomas said.

"And did you or did you not say Melinda was perfect for this operation?" Zi said.

The taller inspector cleared his throat. "If I may… wait, what operation?"

"You may not." Zi snapped and turned his gaze to Thomas. "Did you or did you not?"

"I did, and Mindy did except for—"

"Yes, except we should be taking in that engine mount and not chasing that itty-bitty ship. Which, by the way, where is it?" Zi snapped.

"I haven't had time to check my contacts since we lost sight of the ship. But my and Vernon's covers are still intact." Thomas nodded to the taller inspector. "Per your orders, we've been testing Stuk daughters for the last twenty years. We'd expanded to the Hollow's war orphans, and it was bound to catch someone's attention as planned."

"Whose attention would that be?" Zi said.

"Anyone interested in the lost Wailing Seas throne," Vernon offered. "I did advise you this was a bad idea. Our House changeover is three days away."

"The changeover has nothing to do with it," Thomas said. "Mindy adapted and passed."

Zi lowered his cane and closed the distance between them in a blink of an eye. "You told me she was ready. You said there was zero chance of failure."

"And, she didn't fail." Thomas lowered his arms. "This isn't some trial by fire that the mages used to do. This was designed simply to make sure she was competent and able to adapt. There is no pass or fail. Melinda's a natural-born spacer. I think she spends more time in a suit than out of it. The last three kids pissed themselves when I dropped the ship out of S-Cut."

"Is there a reason you're red teaming my and Jainey's house?" Vernon said.

"On my orders," Zi said. "Six months ago, Thomas had evidence he tripped over someone's operation. We think *Toy* passed by a defunct S-Cut off-ramp and by accident, activated it. Mindy's Foo Fighter was rigged and triggered it again. Twice is too much of a coincidence."

"I don't understand," Vernon said. "If the off-ramp works, that means we don't need out-system drives. We can use S-Cut system to travel from coil to coil."

"Yes, we could, but none of the Houses have authorized it. I've been quietly back channeling and anyone who knows about it is on this ship," Zi said.

"You're worried about someone trying to get off the Hollow without getting authorization first," Vernon said.

"The Hollow has been a non-contact planet for nearly thirty years. Authorized carriers only. This could change things and we're not prepared for it. Our infrastructure isn't ready," Zi said. "If we let someone leave who isn't authorized, we risk going from non-contact to quarantine. And no one wants that."

"All of which we can figure out once we get across the border," Thomas said.

"What about this cloak?" Zi said. "How did it get in the shuttle with her?"

"I don't know. She may've trigger something inside. I haven't had time to scrub her video footage. It was a good idea. I'll use that next time in my simulations," Thomas said.

Zi snorted. "A good idea. It could've killed her. We have any evidence of the encounter?"

"There're many things out here in the dark that will kill even us," Thomas said and tapped a button. A three-dimension video of the Necromancer appeared. "It's good to be prepared."

Zi turned to Vernon. "You told me my lands were cleansed of those abominations!"

"I stand by my report." Vernon tapped it for emphasis. "Maybe it's from another coil."

Zi glanced between them. "She did actually shoot it point blank in the chest, didn't she?"

"It was a stun gun," Vernon muttered.

"We don't know if it's he, she, or an it. Most of them aren't that bad," Thomas said.

Vernon growled and Zi silenced the impending argument with a tap of his cane.

"Let's ignore the fact my grandniece has aim like my sister and move on." Zi smiled. "By the way, where exactly is Mindy?"

"Not here," Thomas said quietly.

Zi's smile vanished and Vernon dropped his head into his hands.

"Excuse me," Zi managed.

"Mindy isn't here right now, but I'm sure if when she's available, she'll be more than happy to talk to you," Thomas managed before the old man's hand was around his throat.

"Where. Is. She," Zi seethed in the oldest tongue Thomas could understand.

"The shuttle," Thomas managed. "On the shuttle. I had a problem and had to break off."

Vernon tapped his slate. "Sir, he's right. Her life signs aren't on board, but they are on board the shuttle we picked up before we jumped out of S-Cut."

Zi released Thomas. "What've you done?"

"You mean what you did. Per your orders, he used Melinda as bait and she got herself into trouble like she always does," Jainey broke her silence. "All because my sister missed a check in and you find some mount that just happens to be there."

"On the same day," Thomas wheezed.

"What?" Jainey said.

"I was coming back from her check-in and the mount just appeared out of S-Cut," Thomas said. "It wasn't alone then, and it wasn't alone now."

"You said it was abandoned," Zi snapped.

"I didn't know who I could trust. I started with you and worked my way down. It took me six months to get to Jainey's side of the House and—" a man's intelligible voice shouted across the sleeve and Vernon shouted back.

"Stop jawing and hurry up. Some kids are screwing around on the other side of the belt."

"Saved by those pesky teenagers," Vernon said. "Oh, Inspector Todd, I hear those nasty teenagers you warned me about are creating havoc." He nodded to Thomas. "Anything else?"

"Yes, you at Zi's side until this is over," Thomas said evenly, and Zi turned around and shouted back a few words.

The outer and inner door sealed. The red telltales flared to green. Thomas held up a hand before Vernon to speak. The double thud of the arrest hooks vibrated through the deck. The light dimmed from the window and Toy was once again silent.

"We need a forty-eight pass to get on the Hollow. A guide, because I've been gone for too long, and plausible excuses for us being here because my flight plan didn't cover any of this," Thomas said to Zi.

"You think I still have that much power on the Hollow?" Zi grumbled.

"If not, then you know someone who can. We've wasted enough

time here. She's low on oxygen and the leash I've got her on is a bit too long even for me," Thomas said.

"You used her as bait and now you're worried about her?" Jainey said.

"No, I'm worried what other trouble she can get herself between now and when we pick her up," Thomas said and turned back to Zi. "Once I get on the ground, I can rally whoever else is still loyal to me. After that, I can get back in forty-eight hours, I swear."

"Why're you even worried about me?" Vernon said.

"It's your House I'm worried about more than you. Besides, you swore fealty to Zi. If you pop, you won't even get off a shot," Thomas said.

"I think I know just the man for the job," Zi said. "Wallace."

"He most certainly does." A man's voice twisted Thomas to the airlock's inner door where a middle-aged man dressed in tan slacks, white button shirt, and jacket emerged. A weathered face with slicked-back, blond hair said a wannabe lord but the closer he approached, the sharper the lie became. Charming, artificial, blue eyes distracted people from the burden of a faceplate so real it fooled even Thomas even with the vague scarring around his chin and forehead.

He strolled across the deck without a pair of clumsy mag boots. "Mister Scott? Lord Wallace Stukari, I hear you're looking for guide." A wicked smile crossed his face and a wink made Thomas' blood pressure boil.

I should've known Wally, Thomas thought through gritted teeth. "You."

"Stowed away when we weren't looking." Jainey laughed.

"Me, and no, Zi has me on retainer." Wallace's fingers waggled hello and produced a cake from behind his back. "I brought cake for the birthday girl." He passed by Thomas and looked up the ladder. "Mindy! C'mon out, we got presents!"

"I'm going to kill you," Thomas seethed.

Wallace's odd look didn't help Thomas' raging heart. "What are you talking about?" He stopped at the floating image of the Necro-mancer cloak. "Home movies?"

No one will ever find your body. Thomas thought and restrained himself. "You did this."

"Yes, I brought the cake and presents. Odd, I couldn't find any of her friends." Wallace smacked the image projector and the Necromancer image re-focused. "Where did you get this?"

That's it. Thomas thought and grabbed Wallace's shirtfront. "Where is she?"

Vernon winced at the violation of personal space but said nothing much, to Thomas' relief.

Wallace's head swiveled from the Necromancer image to Thomas. "Can we focus on the real problem? Where's Spence MacGregor and Miss Scott?"

~

The dull vibrations of the engines hadn't been noticeable until Melinda figured out why she could hear the helmet's voice in her ear. "Warning: you have four minutes of oxygen left."

The altimeter clicking down had increased. "How we doing?" she said.

"Fuel Cells: depleted. Impact in five minutes," the woman announced.

"I need you to pull the hatch back and release the restraints on my mark. Melinda, stay where you are," Spence said.

"Warning: survival rate is currently eighty percent and rising," the woman said.

"Chances your structural integrity will hold without the parachute?" she needled.

"Forty percent."

Spence sighed. "Better than it was fifteen minutes ago. Melinda, wait for my signal."

"You haven't been talking to my brother? This is something he'd pull." Melinda untangled herself and gripped the sides of the parachute bay. "I knew these stupid hazard lights would come in handy someday." She tapped her left wrist and the confines of the parachute container pulsed in shades of white and red. "Ready when you are."

~

Spence cracked his knuckles and flexed his fingers. "If it helps, I've done this before." He pulled the hood down over his head and the cloak pressurized. His spell book remained until the quills reached out and ate it. The fabric shifted about until he felt the book against his chest. *Oh, I take back most of the bad things I said about you.* "Open the hatch."

The hatch doors pulled back and the rush of wind buffeted Spence. The mask's sensors warmed up and he was shocked to see the ground rush beneath at five hundred feet. "I said look for signs of life?" he said.

"Per orders, course to find life and land within one point five kilometers," the mask said.

"There's nothing but sand down there!" Spence yelled.

"The hatch can always be closed," the mask countered.

Just because you're rusty doesn't mean you get to take it out on her. "Pull back the gloves."

"As you wish." The gloves rippled away from his digits.

Spence gripped the release lever and pulled; the remaining restraints released his limbs. He took a deep breath, pulled back his extremities, and dropped out of the pod.

The dark world spun around him. It should've been easier than in daylight; there was no sun to blind him.

Instead, a HUD formed across the mask's lenses. A spinning artificial horizon line appeared along with an altimeter.

The audio dampeners silenced the howling wind until the only thing Spence could hear was his heavy breathing. Several icons flashed across the mask's lenses that stated the atmosphere might be breathable. His body tumbled about; his stomach twisted while he pushed his arms and with a flick of the fingers, the world shuddered around him.

A nudge is sometimes all you need. You spin up too soon, too fast and yer a smudge all over the deck. The artificial horizon stopped spinning. The ground and the sky righted.

"Tag the shuttle and the landing zone." Spence spun ninety degrees and caught sight of it hurtling through a cloudbank. "Melinda, I'm drafting behind you." The anti-rotation spell on his left hand spun down to be replaced with a levitation spell.

The thrust spell to his right hand. The wind picked up and across the sky, he soared. The cloudbank swallowed him, his view obscured until a half-circle icon that represented his radar appeared in the right lens.

"Warning, incoming object. Impact in, ten seconds, nine, eight, seven," the mask said.

"That's the escape pod," Spence said.

"Negative, object is fixed and stationary," the mask said.

A wireframe outline hurtled towards him. The cloudbank parted and even in the dark, Spence couldn't have missed the head of the two-hundred-foot statue rocketing towards him.

The escape pod didn't miss it either.

It crashed through the statue's left arm and continued its course. The weather-beaten appendage disintegrated at the elbow and the remains showered onto the ground.

No. No. No. Spence thought and focused on the thrust spell. "Melinda: jump!"

The lights from her suit bounced out of the ship and he dove towards the hazard lights.

~

Melinda dropped like a stone. Her stomach rushed to her ears.

She ignored the plummeting altimeter and focused on keeping her stomach down. Her suit tugged hard.

"I got you, hang on." Spence's voice rang in her ears.

Three meters became five, six then four, three, two, one. Her feet brushed across something. She picked up her feet and rolled across the ground until she slammed against something.

Melinda breathed a sigh of relief.

"Warning: you have ten seconds of oxygen left," the helmet said.

Melinda spun the fishbowl around and fresh air tussled a stray strand of curly hair. "That shouldn't have worked—" She pulled off her communications carrier cap and threw up. A lovely scent wrinkled her nose. It wasn't from the remains of her lunch but the familiar scent of black art defense candles.

Melinda wiped her mouth and sat back. *Wait. What candles? Stupid defense candles. Wait what happened to the—*

The ground quaked and the screech of metal on stone echoed out into the night, followed by a brief spray of sparks.

That coulda been you. Melinda wiped her eyes from the dust-filled air.

The something she had rolled into was lined with defense candles.

She tapped her wrist and the suit's hazard lights ceased rotating. She tilted her shoulder torches around to bask this seven-foot-long by five-foot-wide and high object made of iron.

What's a Stuk Resurrection Chamber doing out here? Melinda thought. The old tongue etchings were easy to translate: "Announce yourself and be welcomed into my House. So decrees His Imperial Majesty Clarence Stuk the First bids you welcome, Meylandra Stuk."

The air sizzled. A subtle wind pushed against her. Warmth surged through her limbs. Heal Spell never felt so good. Melinda pulled herself upright.

Spence staggered up, still buttoned up and collapsed against the chamber.

Melinda steadied him and said, "You look horrible."

"High Spells. This planet. Aren't helping." Spence's altered voice sent chills down her spine. He followed Melinda's tapping finger. "Announce yourself and be welcomed into my House. So decrees His Imperial Majesty Clarence Stuk the First bids you welcome, Spence MacGregor of the Cross." The air sizzled. "Thank you, Clarence." The plate's electronic eyes narrowed. "Re-check your readings next time to make sure the atmosphere is breathable."

"Checked it on the way down." Melinda twisted her shoulder torches up. "What did we hit on the way in?" She gaped at the statue and its missing arm. "I'm blaming you for that."

~

We landed. Unharmed. And the statue hasn't tipped over, Spence thought and resisted the urge to unbutton the suit.

"Those spells must take all the fun out of crashing," Melinda said. She ambled towards the statue and twisted out of her suit piece by piece.

Spence opened a private channel to the mask. "What can you tell me?" he said.

"Prolonged exposure to the atmosphere could be toxic," the mask stated.

Spence's fingers twitched, inches from the hood's pressure tabs. "Define prolonged!"

"Hundreds of years," the mask said. "Nothing within five hundred yards. I recommend using the breach pod's sensors to extend my range. Repairs required due to someone's aim."

Spence twisted the pressurization locks on the cloak's seam. The hood sagged, and he pulled it back. A gust of sand welcomed his eyes, followed by a chill to his nose. The hum of the wind felt welcoming, the absence of noise brought a smile to his lips.

Spence stared up at the foreign stars above. "Welcome to Stuk's Hollow," he said.

The cold night air laughed back at him until it eased back to nothing but a whisper.

Oh, really? Spence listened and re-joined Melinda. "We're going to make camp at the breach pod. Get those defense candles and line them around us for protection. Let's not wander."

Melinda struggled out of her chest plate. "Don't have to tell me twice."

4
HOUSE BUSINESS

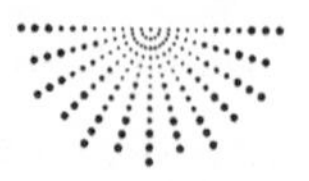

WHA? THOMAS THOUGHT AND STARED DOWN INTO THE SOULLESS, BLUE eyes of Wallace's plate. "Don't change the subject. We all know MacGregor's been missing for years!"

"Not anymore." Wallace thumbed to the image. "That's his cloak. Where is he?"

"Don't you mean where's Mindy?" Jainey said.

"We know where she is, right next to him or at least she was. Thirty years of back channeling to find him and she finds him out here. What are the odds?" Wallace said. "I need to scrub the rest of this video and a secure line."

"It could be any cloak," Zi said.

"No, you've done a good job of burning them out of this coil. It's his. I know that plate anywhere," Wallace said.

"And of course, you would know. Wouldn't you?" Vernon said.

Wallace's pearly white smile wasn't nearly as hospitable as it looked. Thomas had learned many things when dealing with Lord Wallace Stukari. The teeth only came out when he encountered resistance. Others drew their personal dagger for such an offense, Wallace brought his teeth.

"Mister MacGregor and I were thick as thieves when we were children. It kept us alive long enough to be useful. So, yes, I do know a great deal about him. The Necromancer's cloak belonged to his father's father. They smashed in the MacGregor plates and burned down their House to send a message. I built him a new one," Wallace said. "Why her?"

"What?" Thomas said.

"Why Mindy and why now?" Wallace growled. "Doesn't make sense. All the way out here? Miss Scott, I need to borrow secure line from you, immediately."

"No," Jainey said.

"What?" Thomas said.

"Be reasonable," Zi said.

"I am being reasonable," Jainey said. "Mindy is my concern and you're worried about your childhood friend that no one has seen in thirty years."

"What do you want?" Wallace said.

"You're going to find Mindy and then you're free to do whatever you please," Jainey said.

"That sounds perfectly reasonable," Wallace said.

Jainey laughed. "You're going to agree with me that easily?"

"I like this suit. It took me years to find the proper tailor. It hides things in plain sight. My suit and your ship are alike in many ways. Geri scoured the junkyards to find the right manual to put her back together and she does exactly what she is supposed to do. She has little nooks and crannies that hide things. I like all my parts in one piece and that assault shotgun behind your back will ruin what's taken me years to craft," Wallace said. "So, yes, I will find Mindy for you but first, I need a secure line to contact another ship to come pick us up."

"We can't go with this one?" Jainey said.

"Because Thomas' flight plan didn't cover any of this, we bounce across the border like this and everyone will know. We won't even land and they'll probably blow us to bits. I may have been off planet for years, but my contacts still remember my name. Unlike some people in this ship who shall remain nameless," Wallace said.

"He does have a point," Thomas said quietly. "Wait, Jainey is coming with us."

"No. She's staying on board. As planned," Wallace said and looked about. "Your back up just jumped out of S-Cut. Freda has you on a short leash."

"How can you tell that?" Vernon said.

Wallace tapped his plate. "This burden comes with a lovely array of sensors. I'd like to call in a shuttle from the surface and then we'll be going."

"What are you doing?" Thomas said to Jainey.

"I'm not getting involved," Jainey said. "This is what got my husband killed and I'm not going back to the old ways."

"Says the woman who's been hiding behind a desk for thirty years because—" Wallace didn't finish the sentence. Jainey chambered a round of the still invisible shotgun.

"That's enough from you," Jainey said evenly. "Back stabbing *stukarree*."

Wallace grinned without his teeth. "See, coming out of her mouth, it's a compliment and not a swear."

"Everything is fine. But you just had to get your little buddy back, didn't you. Did you think of any of the repercussions for the rest of us?" Jainey spat.

"They won't be coming after you or using you. In fact, I'd like to hear why you're so scared. You and your sister are practically running this place, but why are you running?" Wallace chanced a step away from the group, but Jainey advanced. "This doesn't have anything to do with the House changeover, does it? What else is going on around here because I haven't heard a peep?"

"Oh, don't give me that. You know exactly what's going on," Jainey said.

The double thud of arrest hooks vibrated through the decking and the airlock telltales changed from green to red.

"I've been on retainer with Zephyr for almost thirty years, trying to get Mister MacGregor back. I severed all my connections to the Hollow per that retainer. I've only stepped foot on the Hollow once to get Thom and Mindy out when they got banished to Gunna Space Station. Do you understand what I'm telling you? I don't know what's going on." Wallace raised his voice. "And whoever is coming through that lock had better be with you."

The outer doors cycled. The telltales burned green and the inner doors parted.

"We don't want him or the Cross back," Jainey said.

"Who said anything about the Cross coming back? The Cross is dead. The operating system and network it used is burned out. Nothing can bring it back." Wallace slowed. "Unless, someone... what've you and your sister been doing? Who've you been talking to?"

"It's House business," a woman's voice said from the inner lock. She was a dull shape and the shadows drew around her too close to be a coincidence.

"Hello, person who has the lovely defense cloak," Wallace said.

"Hello, Wally," the woman said and snickered. "Do we really need to the shotgun?"

"I do," Jainey said.

The woman looked back and forth between the group. "Where's Mindy?"

You don't know either, Thomas thought and eased up.

"You two honestly don't know?" he said.

Wallace's head jerked to Jainey. "Can she please lower that?"

"It's House business." Jainey repeated. "It's none of your concern. You lost her?"

"I know where she went. She's perfectly fine," the woman said.

"On the Hollow isn't perfectly fine," Jainey said.

"Can we get back to the Cross because he's been dead for thirty years?" Wallace said.

"I thought he was on our side," Vernon said.

Everyone laughed.

"So, you're all scared of a know-it-all show off?" Vernon said and much to everyone's look, he laughed. "He's harmless and dead."

"Some of us have doubt," the woman said. "Don't we, Thom?"

Jainey scoffed. "You trusted her over me?"

"She's on the list, you're not," Thomas said. "Wrong side of the war, Auntie Jainey."

Jainey laughed, cackled even. "Excuse me?"

"You were on the wrong side of the war, hon," the woman said.

"Since when?" Jainey said.

"Since forever." Thom and the woman said.

Zi cleared his throat. "Your marriage did stop it, after all. If Missus Scott no longer wishes to help, I'm sure Mister Stukari can give us a ride to the Hollow."

The woman beckoned. "Your chariot awaits."

"I can wait for the next one," Wallace said.

"If you're going to call Panya Stukari, she owed me a favor and is on the other side of the docking clamp," the woman said.

"Vernon, be a dear and check to see if she's telling the truth," Wallace said.

"Why would I lie to you, Wally?" the woman said.

"Why me?" Vernon said.

"You're a good judge of character. If you see a feisty five-foot-tall aviatrix, we'll know she's telling the truth," Wallace said.

Vernon turned towards the inner airlock door then stopped and pointed at Wallace. "I'm expendable."

Wallace clapped. "You're faster on your feet than I expected. This is a good thing. Well, what are you waiting for? Go check."

Vernon turned and stopped, again. "You can't just compliment me and expect me to do it."

"Vernon, go check," Zi said.

Vernon edged past the woman. "I'm doing it because he told me too."

"Whatever makes you sleep at night," the woman said. "Now, where's the trust, Wally?"

"Because you haven't properly introduced yourself. I can barely see you behind that defense cloak you have on, and I can't see anything past that sleeve, so you tell me why I don't trust you and the umpteenth time, don't call me that name," Wallace seethed.

"Wait, what do you mean you can't see past the sleeve?" Vernon's voice squeaked.

Something growled in the room and it wasn't Thomas' stomach.

"Sorry. I had to make sure," the woman said.

"Of what?" Wallace snapped.

"We had an incident. I needed to make sure none of you were compromised," she said.

"Compromised?" Thomas said. "Wait. The surge protector. My trunk. The Weaver."

"What are you talking about?" the woman said.

Thomas dropped the bent surge protector onto the table. It mag locked itself, so it wouldn't float away. "This surge protector should be attached to the defense suite line. Instead, someone crushed it with their bare hands. If we had restarted the defense suite, the power overload would have blown us up. My footlocker full of weapons was picked and every single defense sword I have is dead. If it wasn't, Mindy would be here. Instead, she's with the Weaver. Who was probably supposed to kill her."

"One attempt I'd believe but not three in one day," Wallace said. "Someone went to an awful lot of trouble to make sure it looked like an accident."

"And with us watching, no less," Zi said.

"Excuse us, we need to watch the rest of that tape," Wallace said and pulled Thomas out of the room.

~

"There he is." Wallace pointed to the fuzzy picture.

"That's a smudge," Thomas said. "Since when does this station scrub video?"

"Geri knew what he was doing. The station closest to the airlock was used to scrub the video. Scrub it and bounce out the airlock during reconnaissance missions." Wallace tapped away on the keyboard attached to the auxiliary engineering station across the hall from the airlock. "Find the right instruction manual and you could have a fleet of these ships. Innocent looking on the outside but, on the inside, communications gear for decoding After-Action Reports."

The audio dropped out at the cloak got closer.

"What happened to the audio?" Thomas said.

"Anti-psychotics filters kicked in." Wallace pointed to two dials vibrating back and forth. "I think it's coming from his table."

"Table?" Thomas said.

"Yes, that video screen is a war table. Some audio is playing but..." Wallace twisted a few dials. "There we go." He picked up a pair of hand phones and handed them to Thomas. "Take a listen."

Thomas put one to his ear and twisted the other one so Wallace could listen. "That's you," he said. "And they're both alive."

"It does sound like me." Wallace twisted the dials and the audio cleared itself up.

"You going to tell Pan he's alive?" Thomas said.

"Not until I see his face. I give her any sort of false hope and I'll lose whatever credibility I have with her," Wallace said. "Why my voice of all things?"

"Why hack his table? What's it do?" Thomas said.

"The short version is: it's classified. The long version is: it's what Houses used to use to calculate their growth to make sure they weren't going to run out of supplies."

Thomas snorted and said, "It's a calculator."

"A calculator doesn't start or end a war." Wallace twisted dials and the audio replayed. "Something about hacking his table. It's my voice, and she keeps him in view to make sure."

The console beeped several times and a paper table rolled out of a slit.

Wallace stretched the tape across the console. IDENTITY CONFIRMED: MACGREGOR, SPENCER. OUTSTANDING HOUSE WARRANT. WANTED: ALIVE.

"Outstanding," Wallace said and pressed a red button. The screens snowed over, and the video disappeared.

"What'd you do?" Thomas said.

"Scrubbed the console's databanks of the video. Older consoles like these had several sub routines built in to upload their data once they got within range of the transmission station. Which we're nowhere near," Wallace said.

"So just erase the codes," Thomas said.

"Any attempt to erase the codes and the console implodes. The erasure I did isn't permanent so once she gets back to Gunna, it'll upload," Wallace said. "We've got a three-day head start on everyone else. What did she mean when you trusted Freda instead?"

"Six months ago, I tripped over something and the mount just appeared out of nowhere," Thomas said.

"Right, but an engine mount just jumps in and out. That's no cause to go to Freda Stukari unless there's something else going on," Wallace said. "Six months ago, you were out here?"

"Yes," Thomas said. "Why?"

"I had a lead on something that just up and vanished in front of me." Wallace scratched his chin.

"A lead on what?" Thomas said.

Wallace paused the video and pointed to the blurry picture of Spence. "Someone called me and told me I could pick him up at abandoned Knoll Dry Dock just past the Roost."

"That's on the Hollow. You just said you hadn't been there in years," Thomas said.

"I fibbed a little," Wallace said. "By the time I got there, whatever had happened was all over and no sign of him except a dry dock big enough to hold that engine mount. So, what made you call Auntie Freda?"

"I saw *him*," Thomas said.

"Saw who?" Wallace said.

"*Him*," Thomas said.

Wallace chuckled. "The Cross is dead."

"I know but I saw *him*," Thomas said. "Hanging on for dear life and the engine mount jumped out only for it to take *him* with it. I think he found Spence and tried to bring him in, but somebody miss-wired the mount and it jumped."

"That's a lot of what ifs," Wallace said. "But I'm pretty sure it was *him* who called me."

"For the sake of argument, let's say he did find the Weaver," Thomas said.

"After being missing and declared dead for thirty years," Wallace said. "You bring in the Weaver and they'd forgive you for almost anything."

"He's got a crew together," Thomas said.

"Like he always does because he's got intel on something big," Wallace said. "You think he found something and never reported in?"

"He would've written up something, but not if he can't get a signal out," Thomas said.

"He finds the mount. Finds Spence and tries to get help but instead, something goes sideways. The mount jumps, finds you, and jumps out. Meanwhile, no one on the ground knows," Wallace said.

"That's a lot of ifs. But so far, it's been that kind of day," Thomas said. "But, if we got this video."

"Sooner or later, so will they," Wallace said. "I think my role as uninterested negotiator may be needed."

"You're sounding like my wife." Thomas chuckled and lowered his voice. "I don't trust Zi."

"On that subject, we completely agree. He's on the outs. The House change up is in three days, and I haven't a clue who's going to be in charge," Wallace said.

"Always looking for an in," Thomas said.

"No, always looking to be useful. Once you stop being useful, everyone forgets your name. Which reminds me, do you have anyone on the ground or is it just going to be me calling in favors," Wallace said.

"I still have people. They're in deep," Thomas said.

"Which means they're useless without blowing their covers," Wallace said.

"Most of them took positions with other Houses, but they're all front line," Thomas said.

"They'll be on babysitting detail then." Wallace nodded. "That might actually work. They can slip away without being noticed."

"We all need to act like the world isn't coming to end and quietly get ourselves off *Toy*," Thomas said.

"Yes, before Auntie Jainey does anything rash," Wallace said.

"It's an act," Thomas said.

"That assault shotgun of hers with the cursed iron rounds isn't an act," Wallace said. "You think it's that bad?"

"What?" Thomas said.

"You think it's that bad?" Wallace said.

"Freda doesn't leave Homeworld unless it's that bad and if we both got a call from him that something was going on," Thomas said. "That and Vernon hasn't come back yet."

"Was she close to him?" Wallace said.

"Who?" Thomas said.

"Freda," Wallace said.

"She used to be front line recon and then switched over to support after the war," Thomas said. "I brought her in. She didn't have anything on her when she came in."

"That would be a 'yes,'" Wallace said.

"How do you know?" Thomas said.

"Nobody willingly takes a slot with your aunt's House and no one is ever that clean to pass all the exams. My application for Lordship was on the docket for years because of my rebellious youth," Wallace said. "Either she knows something is going on."

"Or he did that thing where he reaches out and talks to you," Thomas said.

"In your dreams which I can't stand." Wallace nodded "Your House. Mine. Hers. That's three. His makes a fourth. Three-quarter majority. I think it's time to go. Bring your gear."

"Useless as it is. Need to find someone to do the blessings and cursing when we land," Thomas said. "And find out whoever bled them dry."

Wallace shut down the station. "We're not landing. We find them and get off the planet as fast as we can. The longer we're on the ground, the bigger the target we are. Bring the footlocker anyway, it'll be good evidence," he said and stepped back into the airlock bay. "We'll be ready to leave in a moment."

"Happy now?" the woman said.

"No. Not really." Wallace extended a hand and twisted down his tongue. "Lord Wa Stuk of House Stukari. And you are?"

The air around the woman brightened and the hood of camouflage cloak revealed a lovely bald dark copper skinned woman. She gripped his open hand. "Lady Freda Leighton of House Stukari. A pleasure to meet you."

"I accept your gracious gift of transport to Stuk's Hollow and accept your sister's request to find her missing niece," Wallace said in the same tongue.

"We will stay here and let you work. Zephyr, you are more than welcome to join them. I'm sure you have business that needs tending to," Freda said.

"I'm what?" Jainey said.

"We are staying here," Freda said. "It's more than time for her to take her rightful place."

"And if they refuse?" Zi said.

Freda's smile melted. "Then you can tell them that the same Houses they turned their backs on thirty years ago are in complete agreement." She handed him a letter with a wax seal on the back. "This letter will cover the particulars. We've been trying to send it to them, but the messenger network is down. There are some things we can endure but infantile behavior and stupidity isn't one of them. The Hollow was once the crown jewel of this coil and it will be again. We don't expect you to deliver to them. Once you see a messenger, give them the letter and you're free to be on your way."

"And if they refuse?" Zi repeated.

Freda's smile returned, much like the one Wallace had given Vernon. "They'll figure it out."

~

Panya Stukari met them at the sleeve with Vernon. The five-foot six-inch, olive-skinned aviatrix was gussied up in a camo green jumpsuit, boots, goggles, leather helmet and fur-lined gloves. Hair tucked under a hat so not to get in her way. Her blue eyes glared up at Wallace and Thomas. "I should've known it was you two," she growled and thumbed to Vernon. "He a peace offering from the last time you screwed me over, Wally?"

"I didn't screw you over. I merely found out the semi-precious gems I paid you with weren't as semi as I was led to believe," Wallace said. "I did pay you immediately in person and an extra twenty percent for the trouble."

"Uh huh." Pan eyed Thomas. "And you look guiltier than normal. Where's Mindy?"

"She's meeting us down on the Hollow for the House changeover," Thomas said.

"You along with everyone else. I've been shuttling people around for the last three days," Pan said. "Well, let's get a move on. We're wasting oxygen."

Once she was out of ear shot, Vernon snorted, "Smooth. Peace offering?"

"You can't lie to a lovely woman. I'll have to remember that if there is a next time," Wallace said.

"It's the truth," Thomas said and pushed his trunk onwards. "From a certain point of view."

"Remind yourself of this moment when you're jailed for crimes against the crown and there's nothing to do but stare at four blank, gray walls for years," Wallace said and ventured across the sleeve and found the cramped cabin of Pan's ship to be slightly bigger than he remembered. The bucket seats that lined the walls were mostly empty, so he chose one on the port side. Vernon and Thomas sat down on either side of him while Zi chose one on the starboard side.

"I just want to remind you we're going on a hunch and whatever video you two watched," Vernon said. "He'd better be worth it."

"He is," Thomas said.

The inner airlock door cycled. The cabin pressurized, and the deck plates shuddered at the engines spinning up.

All of them pulled on the headsets so they could have a private conversation if need be.

"Why?" Vernon continued.

"Because, that cloak, his gift, his plate, all of him is a leftover from a war no one wants to remember. So much so they set a trap for him and got him indentured for thirty years. We need to get to him before they do," Wallace said.

"What's the difference between you and them?" Vernon said. "And what if it's a trap?"

"Unlike our friends who shall remain nameless, I'm not going to wrap a blind contract around his neck," Wallace said turned to Thomas. "And as one of our friends is fond of saying, if it's trap, always remember Rule One."

"And what's Rule One?" Vernon said.

"Get yourself out of it," Thomas, Wallace, and Pan said in eerie unison.

5

SLEEPING DRAGOONS LIE

You must tell her sooner or later, Thomas thought and unbuckled himself from the seat.

He climbed up the ladder, passing through the empty cabin to the cockpit.

The view ports of the shuttle were bigger than he expected. The cockpit was a four-seater, Panya and her co-pilot in front two seats. The engineer seat on the port side was empty along with the communications seat on the starboard. The designers had opted for a curved high ceiling for tall folk unlike what *Toy*'s designers had done.

He settled into the empty communication seat. The wall of screens was dark. Several access codes were needed to even unlock the station. There was a non-descript port off to the side. It was for a House key. The same one around his neck.

"You missed this, didn't you," Thomas said to her.

Panya looked over her shoulder and grinned. "Haven't stopped flying for three days. Give me a stick and rudder any day. Don't worry about my defense genies. I'll check them once we land."

"I'm not," Thomas lied. "I see you found someone to fly with you."

"He's on loan," Panya said. "Once the Houses rotate, I've got a line of free recruits waiting to train. I was about to announce it, but there's a queue. It's going to be a while."

"That's what I wanted to talk to you about. Can I use your com station? I need to type up an After-Action Report?" he said. "I didn't see it on my way in, but is there a brig seat on this ship?"

"You've got control," Panya said.

"I've got control," her co-pilot said.

Panya unstrapped herself from the pilot's chair and eased her way back to the engineer seat. "What you going to need a brig seat for?" she said.

"I have no idea what's down there waiting for me. Once we get into the atmosphere, I'll need you to open the vents and let my buggers wake up," Thomas said.

"You think it's going to be that bad?" Panya said.

You have no idea, he thought. "This is Mindy we're talking about."

Panya crossed her limbs and settled back into the high-backed chair. "What did Mindy find exactly?"

"Her test went a little sideways and got herself tangled up in a runaway shuttle. I need to make sure once we're on the ground, I'm not flat on my back while my augmented blood is re-learning how to breathe whatever toxic crap they used down here during the war," Thomas said.

Panya chuckled. "I almost believed that, too. What happened to getting yourself out of it?"

"I need to make sure someone is there to debrief her when she gets herself out of it," Thomas said.

Panya snickered. "Uh huh. And you want to re-activate that lovely augmented blood to do what, exactly?"

Gahsakes, you're just as infuriating as Jainey is. Thomas closed his mouth before responding. "Wait, are you just reading off the psych eval questionnaire checklist?"

Panya tapped her nose. "You pick up things quick. There are twenty-five more questions to answer before I sign off on your re-activation. And Wallace is right, you cannot lie to a lovely creature such as myself. So, what else is going on, Mister Scott?"

"I am following up a lead," he said.

"This pertains to me or my family because you haven't looked me in the eye since you got on board," she said.

"I have too," Thomas said.

Panya laughed. "No, you've been staring at my forehead. This isn't about Mindy. It's about this lead, then?"

"Yes," Thomas said.

"And you need the chair for who, you or this lead?" she said.

"Myself," he said.

"You're telling me everything once we pick her up," Panya said. "It's in the cabin you just walked through."

"Thank you. Now, which button turns off the transmitter on this station?" he said.

Panya frowned. "Why would you want to do that?"

"Because, if Wallace can't talk me down from taking over the shuttle, the After-Action Report will," Thomas said.

"Since when?" she said.

"Since I was on the wrong side of the war," he said and swiveled the seat around. He pulled out the rectangle-shaped key and into the slot it went. "Which button?"

"The yellow one will disable the transmitter," she said. "It'll be uploaded in three days."

"Yes, by then, everyone will know," Thomas said and depressed the yellow button. The console came to life and a keyboard ejected itself from the frame. "Once we're through with the report, it's yours to deliver to the nearest House Messenger."

"Like I'll be able to find one," Panya snorted.

"Trust me, you will," Thomas said and tapped away on the keys. "Once I'm through with this, lock yourselves until I say so and call up Wally, Zi, and Vernon. I need witnesses."

"What's wrong with me?" Panya said.

"Because getting into a fistfight with you is the last thing I want to do," Thomas said.

Panya giggled and patted his knee. "Aw, I like it when a man knows when he's beaten."

~

"You want me to what?" Wallace said.

"If I manage to break free of the restraints, you've got less than ten seconds to knock me out," Thomas repeated.

"Why am I knocking you out?" Wallace said.

"Because I switched sides during the war, but I may not remember doing it," Thomas said.

The second-floor cabin was smaller than the one below. The chairs that lined the walls were all up. It made more room for the raised, high-backed, iron chair in the middle of the room. The iron chips in the paint didn't bother anyone except for Panya, but she and her co-pilot had already locked themselves inside the cockpit.

"I always wondered how that happened," Zi said.

"It's a long, boring story. The After-Action Report should cover everything, but sometimes you get a runaway," Thomas said and handed the leather-bound tome to Wallace. "This will fill in the gaps in case the buggers go full-tilt boogey nuts."

"Buggers?" Vernon said. "Why am I here?"

"Trust, mostly," Thomas said.

"You expect me to knock you out?" Wallace said with a laugh.

"Don't worry. If you're unworthy, he has to go through me and we all know how that's going," Zi said.

All three men stared at the old man.

Thomas settled back into the iron seat. Its ankle and wrists locked down automatically. "Lock the door, Zi," Thomas said.

Zi did as ordered. The door sealed itself and the tumblers rolled into place.

"Pan, we in position?" Thomas said.

"Ten thousand feet and no traffic for miles." Pan's voice came through PA speakers.

"Open the vents," Thomas said and the room turned red and his throat closed itself.

The scent of war tickled his nose.

Klaxons wailed of death. Screams of fire.

The jarring ricochet of the rifle butt against his shoulder.

The smoke blinded him, but the sound of those gahforsaken quills twisted his head around.

He shouted out orders and his Dragoons, a fire team made up of six of men and women, armored up from head to toe. They readied themselves for the endless wave of death.

Instead, Thomas Scott's heart pumped its last and the remaining air escaped his lungs in a death rattle.

~

"What happened?" Vernon said. "Is he dead?"

"No, he's not dead," Wallace said. "His buggers aren't working yet."

"Buggers?" Vernon said. "What are you going on about?"

Wallace tapped his plated head. "They didn't teach you anything at that House of yours, did they? Buggers. Augmented blood." He paused and rolled his eyes at the silence he received. "Mister Stuk has Class One Augmented Blood."

"Scott," Vernon said.

"No. The moment those buggers work, Thomas Scott will no longer exist. Thom Stuk, on the other hand, will rise," Wallace said. "It's simple thing, really. In the end, he'll be medically proven to withstand anything." He nudged Thomas with the toe of his boot. "Including whatever they let loose on the Hollow during the war, which was extremely toxic, let me tell you."

"I don't understand. You're telling me his blood is toxic?" Vernon said.

"No. No. No. No. Gahsakes, you took *History One Oh One*. They taught you what we have to sacrifice during the war," Zi said.

"It wasn't mandatory," Vernon said.

Whatever tumbled out of Zi's mouth weren't words and Wallace failed at grimacing.

"Wasn't mandatory? Wasn't mandatory?" Zi said once he regained his calm. "When the war came, the scientists did their best with what little they had, only to find they didn't need much. Someone had done all the work for them. Nanobots in his bloodstream will adapt his body to this atmosphere so he can walk around with a breathing unit."

Vernon sniffed. "Sounds hideous."

"Birth always is," Wallace said and twisted down his tongue. "Death is just a moment. Death will never hold us. We were meant for something better."

"What's the point?" Vernon said.

"It was war. There is no point," Wallace said. "Haven't missed the waiting not one bit. What happened to visiting every six months and building an immunity?"

"They were banished," Zi said.

"I was banished but even I still go home. Even if it is just an empty ocean." Wallace placed two fingers on Thomas' neck. "Still got a pulse. Irregular and hasn't thrown up yet. Good." He eyed Vernon. "If he throws up, you're cleaning it up."

"He won't," Zi said, "He actually obeyed my decree and we're still here."

"What?" Pan said.

"Nothing," Zi said. "Wallace!"

Wallace jerked around, but Thom Stuk already had an arm around his neck and was out of the seat.

~

"Look at this." Thom growled in a tongue Wallace barely understood. "Messenger girl and her master, too. You boy, I don't know you. Open the door."

"Don't open the door," Wallace wheezed to Vernon. "Read the report."

"And he learned the Mother Tongue, too. You're just full of surprises. And what's this?" Thomas wrapped on Wallace's head. "Messenger girl got herself burdened, too. Open the door and I promise it won't hurt."

"Read the report," Wallace said.

"You really think I'm going to listen to you? After what you did? No one changes sides in the middle of the war," Thom said.

"Who be you and who do you serve?" Vernon said.

"Ha," Thomas said in the standard tongue. "It doesn't work like that."

"Deeper," Zi said. "Or he'll tear through you."

"Oh, look at this. Zephyr Crosleigh came out of his little bunker. Yer not in his ear this time, old man. Yer in the shit now with the rest of us peasants." Thomas bounced on the deck. "We're airborne. Can feel the engines reverb through my boots, where are we?"

"Who be you and who do you serve!" Vernon's voice warbled.

"Deeper," Zi growled.

"Read the report or I'm going to beat you with it. You *stukarree*," Wallace growled.

Thom spun Wallace about. His hand gripped his throat with ease. "What did you call me?"

"You and your pathetic Dragoons couldn't hit the broadside of a barn. They left you to die when you changed sides. No loyalty. No Honor. No spines," Wallace hissed. "I have more courage in my pinky than you ever will."

Thomas' grip hesitated, and Wallace took the millisecond of an opening.

A knee to the crotch followed by a right hook to Thom's chin slammed his head into the bulkhead. The sizable dent left would be worth the repair fees and the frowns from Panya.

"Now, you're going to read the report before I knock you out with my bare hands. The old man can't save you." Wallace advanced and punched Thom square between the eyes. "That's the problem with you Dragoons, you can't talk and fight at the time."

Thom pushed himself off the wall and ran his shoulder into Wallace's mid-section. Both slammed into the back of the chair.

"No one talks to me like that!" Thom spat and wrapped his hands around Wallace's neck.

"I said, who be you and who do you serve!" Vernon howled.

"Thom Stuk and I serve at the emperor's behest," Thom said.

"Then as the emperor's messenger, I demand you read the report as it is your duty and honor bound to do so," Vernon said. "Now, drop Lord Stukari and obey your emperor before you bring dishonor and shame to the very House you swore to protect, you backstabbing, little shit."

Wallace chanced a look to Vernon. "Wow."

Vernon held out the report. "Drop the messenger girl and take a seat, Captain."

Thom eased back and released his grip. "You're the emperor's messenger? He chose you to give me his final words?"

"Yes, he said to—" Vernon didn't get the words out of his mouth fast enough.

Thom flung Wallace into the same dented wall. Pivoted and rushed, Thom but collapsed within inches of the boy.

Thom rolled himself over to find his bootlaces tied together.

"A trick I learned from an old friend." Wallace removed himself from the crater in the wall and pulled Thom up by the front. "Let's try this again. Read. The. Report."

"Gahsakes, I am the emperor's messenger. What part do you not understand?" Vernon said.

"He doesn't care. He's got kamikaze orders built in the buggers," Wallace said and pushed Thom back into the seat.

The manacles locked around his limbs and Wallace flipped a switch. "And the chair's wireless transponder wasn't de-activated, hence how he got out so easily. I'll remember that for next time. Rule One: Always escape."

"There won't be a next time. I'm going to destroy you," Thom growled. "I'm going to kill every last stinking, Stukari, bloodless idiot and eat you."

"You're telling me the emperor brainwashed him?" Vernon said.

"No. The emperor didn't brainwash him. He didn't give any of the Dragoons a choice. He re-wrote the codes so they were unwilling servants," Zi said. "We were expendable to them."

Wallace opened the book and within its pages, a faded piece of paper dropped out. "This will reboot the buggers before they self-destruct and take all of us with them."

"That might explain why he's sweating." Vernon stepped back. "Well? Hurry it along!"

"I need to know something before I release you from bondage." Wallace leaned down, nose to nose with Thom. "How does it feel to know your lord and master fled at the end of the war? How does it feel to know instead of being victorious on the field of battle, you go out on your knees with no honor, respect, or love from your peers? Tell me that."

"Wallace," Zi said.

"How does it feel to know you will quench that thirst that burns in your heart to be part of something better than yourself?" Wallace said. "The shutdown code goes like this."

A melodic tune escaped Wallace's plate and Thom slumped unconscious in the chair.

"Are you insane?" Vernon said.

"Yes and no," Wallace said. "Now hush. I need to get this right or he'll blow up and take us with him."

A similar tune brushed through the room and Thom jerked awake. He blinked a few times and looked from face to face. "Hello, Zephyr, Vernon, and Wallace," he said and jiggled his limbs. "Do you guys mind unlocking these?"

"Who be you and who do you serve?" Vernon said tightly.

"Thom Stuk of House Stuk. Seventy-Fifth Armor Division. Captain of First Contact Squad. First Marauding Dragoons Fire Team Alpha and I serve at the Queen Atia Finnegan's behest," Thom said without a second thought. "Excuse me. I just need to update my deep core memories." An eyelid blink later and he winced. "I am missing three minutes since my last back up. What happened?"

Wallace jerked a thumb to the dented wall.

Thom grimaced. "Whoops."

Wallace rubbed his neck. "That's it? A whoops? That's all I get?"

"Sorry?" Thom said with a shrug. "Pan?"

"Still here," Pan's voice said. "You in one piece?"

"Completely." Thom jiggled the restraints. "Guys. Could you undo these please?"

"Not yet. Let's get a refresher: Who. What. When. How. Why?" Wallace said.

"The Weaver," Thom said.

"Say his name," Wallace said.

"Spence MacGregor of the Cross. Missing for the last thirty years, appeared on a shuttle that my sister found in the middle of the New Welles Asteroid belt. The shuttle escaped with Spence and my sister on board who are now on Stuk's Hollow, and we're here to gather a crew to pull them off the planet before Melinda makes it any worse. We were banished ten years ago because we did our jobs and the Houses threw us out. Six months ago, I found an engine mount with evidence that someone is trying to get off the planet without permission, and I believe my aunt is in on it."

"Why is your aunt in on it?" Wallace said.

Thom's mouth opened but nothing came out.

"Someone's been busy," Wallace clucked. "Either a fiction weave or a secure memory."

"No one has access to that type of tech on the planet," Vernon said.

"All things being equal and they're not. Someone does so that narrows it down to three people. Me. Clarence Stuk and *him*," Wallace said.

"Who him?" Vernon said.

"Who do you think?" Wallace, Zi, and Thom said in old tongue unison.

Thom blinked again. "Seriously, lemme out. I'm good."

"You haven't told her?" Wallace said.

"I'll tell her when I have proof of life and not a second sooner. She already knows something is rotten. I don't need her going off the handle and trying to find him by herself. She's the only pilot still in the air I trust with my life," Thom said.

"Told her what?" Vernon said.

"The Weaver is Pan's brother," Wallace said and pointed at Vernon. "And I forbid you to tell her."

"That doesn't actually... work," Vernon wheezed and clutched his neck. "What did you?"

"Sorry. I needed to make sure," Wallace said and with a flip of the wrist, the manacles around Thom's limbs released.

"Sorry and thank you," Thom said and extended a hand.

Wallace smiled and slugged him back into the seat.

"Wallace!" Zi said.

Thom pushed himself out of the seat and came nose to nose with the plated lord. They both cracked a smile and hugged each other.

"I called you a messenger girl, didn't I?" Thom said.

"Several times," Wallace said.

"Pan, prep us for landing," Thom said.

"When're you going to tell her?" Wallace said.

"I'll figure something out," Thom said and the locks rolled back on the door to reveal Pan.

"You're telling me right now," Pan bellowed.

"House business," all the men said.

Pan sighed and batted her eyes at them. "Half of you went through a war and can't even tell the truth."

"Don't look at her, it's how it works," Thom said and brushed by her as quickly as he could without making eye contact.

Wallace handed her a heavy bag of gems.

"What's this for?" she said and gaped at the wall. She shook the bag. "I was going to sell her anyway, but this is a start on the repairs."

"A start?" Wallace choked.

~

Stow's End lay nestled in a cul-de-sac valley. A finger of the Stormer Mountain Range had curved around the valley millennia ago and now made for a natural wall of rock, snow, and Lir trees. Flying over the city now, it throbbed with technology, magic, and power from a dozen different Houses celebrating the New Year. A once small mining town had blossomed into a city through good times and bad, peace and war. Stow's End was always there.

Pan took a slow, leisurely tour of the city with the rear ramp lowered. She explained the House's kids loved it and while it stopped the men from talking, it gave Thom's newly re-activated nanobots an updated map of the city. Everything was recorded and analyzed by the time they landed. The network connection was a rush he had nearly forgotten about, even if half of it was a sea of rumor and stupidity.

"How you feeling?" Wallace said to him.

"Feels like I'm breathing sand through a straw," Thom said. "Lungs're almost ready. The burning sensation behind my eyeballs mean my contacts are going to be useless because the buggers fixed my horrendous eyesight, and the constant ringing in my ears are gone."

"Keep the contacts in. That glowing eye HUD routine doesn't go over well," Wallace said. "We'll be back in a half hour. If we're not back in an hour, you know what to do."

"Take off and forget about you?" Pan said with a wink.

Thom laughed and staggered down the ramp. "At least give me points for not throwing up."

He stopped at the sight of an unmarked APC awaiting with its engine running along with several plain-clothed Stukari Holdings Tier Zero Operators. A brief message from Thom's buggers said they were all on his trust list.

Zi ambled towards the APC. "I made a few calls while we were landing," he said. "I need a secure line to check in. I'll cover her fees for this trip. Have Vernon make sure her ship is prepared. Don't take long."

"Maybe he's not on the outs after all," Wallace said.

"No. According to the scuttlebutt, he's gone. The Houses are in a deadlock over what to do. The good news is no sign of Mindy and no reports of altercations so she's not here," Thom said and turned to Vernon. "Zi says to stay here, guard the ship, and help Pan with anything she needs. Lose the jumpsuit and find some plain clothes that fit. She's got a few trunks in there. Let her dress you. I don't care if she tries anything with you. We aren't here. We're just refueling.

There's five minutes of video from the pad's cameras I want gone. Someone is gonna rat us out, but I want them to work for it."

"If anyone asks, you can blame me and my need for privacy." Pan smiled and ambled deeper into her ship.

Thom pulled Vernon close. "And remember, ignore her. Her eyes are about as deadly as her brother's spell book."

"She's harmless," Vernon said.

"Yes, she is, and she spent years at the Academy to make it look like she's a five-foot six-inch cutie you'd bring home to Mom. Trust me. Do not underestimate her. And before you ask, yes, I have my reasons for not telling her. Now go," Thom said.

He followed Wallace off the pad and towards town.

"I don't trust him," Wallace said once they were clear of the pad.

"Don't worry. She's a good judge of character. If she wasn't, he wouldn't have made it on board along with me and you," Thom said. "I sent out a few invites on our way down."

"Here's hoping someone is still here," Wallace said.

"Next time, please aim for my ankles," Thom said.

"Oh, you'll live," Wallace said.

"You need to stop with the shoelace trick," Thom said.

Wallace looked down in the dark. "Did you actually change your boots before we landed?"

6
SLEEPLESS MAIDEN

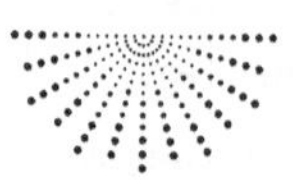

THE WALK INTO TOWN FROM THE LANDING GRID MEANT THOM COULD stretch his legs.

"You still look a little green," Wallace said.

"I'm fine. The little buggers are doing just fine," Thom wheezed and turned the corner, only to find the Sleepless Maiden & Spirits Inn on the outskirts of town was more boisterous than expected. This was due to the New Year's Eve festival going on at the center of town and probably the rest of the bars were overflowing with revelers.

The inn's porch was full of House mages in a sea of black and white robes while on the other end of the spectrum, the Stukari Holdings Tier Zero Operators were decked out in desert camouflage, iron throwing weapons and the less said about the mages' four-legged Totem Animus running around chasing each other around in the dark the better.

Several Avian Animi of different shapes and wingspan hung from the rafters in the roof and ignored the antics of their wingless brothers and sisters. The second and third-floor balconies were preoccupied with Belfry mages, sharply dressed, bald, two legged, humanoid creatures that still had their wings and tails. They were the magical half step between human mages and the old ways.

"This isn't what I meant by quietly slip away," Wallace said.

"They're not with me." Thom ignored the looks and staggered through the bar's doors.

The bar's first floor was standing room only of desert camouflage and mage cloaks.

"Half of them are private contractors to Stukari Holdings. So, half of them are with you," Thom said. "And I don't use House mages in my crew."

"My name may be on the letterhead, banners, business cards, sashes, bullets, weapons and embroidered into the hats, but it doesn't make me their lord and master," Wallace said.

Thom put two fingers into his lips and blew.

The resulting whistle brought everyone around.

"Hi, everybody. Look who's here!" Thom pointed to Wallace.

"Hi, Wally!" everyone shouted back.

"Next round is on him!" Thom said.

The boisterousness raised several decibels much to the dismay of several people who weren't decked out in the yellow and green bandanas of Stukari Holdings.

Thom and Wallace saddled up to the bar where an unfamiliar sandy blonde filled another pitcher of beer. She wasn't Thom's type, the whole busty, bar maiden stuffed into a short-sleeved, white blouse that held back her ample bosom only amplified by it being knotted at her midriff. The quill hair sticks holding up a beehive of hair meant she knew how to use them.

"The prodigal son returns." The bar maiden bowed and held out her hand.

Wallace pulled out his card. "I hate you," he said to Thom and leveled a look at the bar maiden. "And who be you and who do you serve?"

"Grainne O'Hare of the Stow and I serve no one but myself," she replied easily.

"Hello, Gladys," Thom said.

"And he gets points for remembering I hate my first name," the bar maiden said. "And for not being flat on his back. How are you even standing?"

"Oh, a messenger girl smacked me round. Anyone looking for me?" Thom said.

"Some no-good, rotten kids wandered past and went upstairs to the pool table about an hour before you showed up. Ordered the usual and overpaid me handsomely," she said.

"Those would probably be with me," Thom said.

"I seem to remember someone saying we weren't here." Wallace continued.

"It's a good cover. Besides, no one would dare waltz in here looking for either of us now," Thom said and handed Grainne a roll of bills. "If anyone asks, we were never here."

A look of disdain crossed Grainne's face at the money. "You realize your money is no good here. You own this place."

After a moment, she snapped up the money and stuffed it down her full blouse.

"Anyone else I should be looking out for?" she said.

"No one comes to mind," Thom said and raised his hand a foot over his head. "Unless you've seen a certain someone about yay tall got a coat of arms with a penchant for sidearm and sword."

Grainne's dark eyebrows bounced. "Haven't see hide no hair of *him*. Why what've you heard?"

"Keep an eye out and call me if you do," Thom said and moseyed away from the bar.

"Since when?" Wallace said.

"What?" Thom said.

"I didn't know you employed O'Hares," Wallace said.

"It's her place and I don't care what her family did. She's one of the better ones and besides," Thom stopped at the stair's threshold and swept the crowd for anyone out of place. "She's his old lady."

"Her name is on Wailing Seas' Plaque of the Missing," Wallace said.

"So is he and this is the last secure safe house. If he's alive, he'll come here. Besides, she's here. That means so's he," Thom said and crested the stairs. "We'll need all the help we can get."

~

The second floor was reserved for private affairs. The defense wards carved into the walls made Thom's eyes water. Several familiar people, dressed in different-colored House robes, had fathered around a dimly lit pool table. The mood lighting meant someone had blown out the defense candles on purpose.

Thom reached out into the darkened corner behind him and pulled someone a head foot shorter than he was. "Hello, Alita."

Alita Finnegan, his best tracker pulled back her camo cloak's hood. Dark hair braided with Black Arts Tchotchkes. She could've been Mindy's older sister. "Thanks, now I owe someone money," she scoffed.

"That someone has a name." Deidre Yashira, his Hex Wichen staff wielder growled from above their heads and dropped onto the floor. The second fairest skin of them all, the normally long-maned brunette had a short, shoulder bob. "And I told you to hide on the ceiling. They never check the ceiling."

"Can we get back to why the *stukarree* is here?" Alita said.

"Careful," Thom hissed to her.

"I told you he wouldn't leave us in the wind," one of the newbies said. Cherie Leighton, darker than Alita, she was a defense magess to counter Deidre's hex spells.

"I don't care so long as we please stop babysitting," Selene Finnegan pleaded. She was a good foot taller than Thom, fairer and blonder than Deidre ever would be. She and her blessed broadswords meant she was the Shield Maiden of the group.

"Before you ask, I haven't seen *him*," Deidre said.

"Anyone else looking for me?" Thom said.

"We didn't even know you were coming," Cherie said. "Deedee checks a dead drop. She pulls me off detail, letting my journeyman apprentice handle the kids."

"Who's in charge of the kids?" Thom said.

"We met up with Alizerin Leighton six hours ago to hand off the kids," Deidre said.

"Good. Pan is over on pad three. I'm going to need all of you for a mission," Thom said. "Cherie and Deidre, I need a new trunk. Mine got picked and drained. You two got any spares?"

Cherie whistled low. "I got two full go bags but nothing like what was in yours."

"When did this happen?" Deidre said.

"I don't know. We'll figure that out later. Where's Erik?" Thom said.

The group was silent until Deidre spoke. "Erik and Benny split about a year ago. I did the annual six-month check-in and they were fine. That was six months ago."

"Where are they now?" Thom said.

"I went to both their Houses. Lights out and locked up tight," Deidre said.

"You thinking Benny unlocked your trunk and Erik drained the curses?" Cherie said.

"Two people capable of opening my trunk. Me and Dor," Thom said. "But if someone drained them, we've got bigger problems."

"Lichs," Deidre said.

"It's worse than that," Thom said. "Mindy is here."

Everyone smiled ear to ear except Deidre. "She's running Erik," she said.

"I didn't say that," Thom said.

"No. I'm telling you. She's running Erik and I think Benny, too after Narelle disappeared," Deidre said. "I just can't prove it."

"Because?" Wallace said.

"We showed up six months ago and found our houses had been given away," Deidre said.

"Me and Deedee were supposed to take over Erik and Harry's defense slots, but we were told our services were no longer required," Cherie said.

"Houses need defense wards. What're they going to do? Pray?" Wallace said.

"We were first in line with our resumes and were told it was being handled internally and to find another job. Selene grabbed us, and we've been on babysitting detail ever since," Deidre said.

"Deedee has a theory," Cherie said.

"You remember when the Yashira Empire had a little disagreement with itself," Deidre said.

"The was a full-on House war," Wallace said.

"Like I said, a little disagreement with itself. My mother and her House saved the empire but got booted for her troubles by the old guard. I think someone is gobbling up arch mage Houses, but I can't figure out why. It's that same thing that happened before the war erupted. Arch mages went missing and all of sudden, boom."

"That's what was missing, no arch mages on our walk in," Thom said. "That doesn't explain your Houses getting taken away."

"I'm going with user error. I've been waiting for a House liaison to show up, but there's no sign of your wife's House," Deidre said. "That and Cherie isn't front line. She needs another year at least."

"Hey," Cherie said.

"She stays on the ship. I can backstop Alita and her toothpick over there." Deidre jerked a head to Alita.

"You don't make the load outs, rookie," Selene growled.

"He asked. I'm just telling him the truth. Better to learn it now than later when there's a phalanx of Lichs bearing down on your throat and you can't get a spell spun up," Deidre said.

"This is the next freshman class?" Wallace said. "We're doomed."

"I've been in worse," Thom said. "We're missing Benny, Erik, Mindy, Harry, and Narelle."

"I am ready," Cherie said.

"When I say you are," Selene said.

"We don't need them," Wallace said. "I've got enough downstairs."

Grainne cleared her throat and handed a note to Wallace. "This came in for you while you were gone."

Wallace opened the note. "Two of my top mage units took a job a week ago. They haven't checked in since. Damn."

"Going to use them?" Thom said, and Wallace nodded. "All right, freshmen. Get your bags. We're going to find Mindy."

~

The argument was in full bore when Thom and the group crested the hill to the landing pad. Pan and the five were talking to a stuffed shirt.

"I don't care what it looks like now. We're closing the airspace. No one else leaves tonight," the stuffed shirt said.

"Excuse me, on whose authority?" Thom raised his voice.

The stuffed shirt ignored Pan and turned towards him. "Weather," he said. "All the dials are going sideways. That means we're an hour away from a storm, maybe less."

Thom looked around at the star-filled sky. "We can take care of ourselves, right, Pan?"

"Absolutely," Pan said.

"We're closing the blast shields. You'll be locked out," the stuffed shirt said.

"I've got three days of supplies already on board. defense suite is spun up, plenty of fuel and two alternate landing sites," Pan said. "I already told 'em and he tried to lock down the pad when I said no."

Deidre stepped through the argument and lowered her bow to the stuffed shirt's shoulder. "Tell me the truth," she said.

"Truth is if the instruments are going sideways, there's a storm. They've been getting worse and worse for the last week. We opened them for festival, but I don't want a mass panic when they find out they're going to be stuck here," the stuffed shirt said.

"Why are they going to be stuck here?" Deidre said.

"We lock this place down when a storm goes through. The iron in the shields keeps out most of it, but sometimes people don't listen and go out in it. Only they don't come back the same. If you get me."

Deidre lowered her short sword to the other shoulder. "I don't get you. Explain."

"It looks like an electrical storm but even mages say it's not," the shirt said.

"What do they say it is?" Deidre said.

"They say it's an aura storm," the shirt said.

"That's not possible, is it?" Cherie said.

"I've seen things," Deidre said and closed the gap. "You have anti-aura jacking charms?"

The shirt swallowed hard. "Our re-supply is three days late."

"Aura jacking doesn't exist," Wallace said. "It's an old wives' tale."

"I've seen it," Deidre said. "Six months ago. First storm that rolled through town. I saw it. Looks like strobe lighting but it moves wrong. It's attracted to defense wards. It overpowered them and took out an entire section of old town. I had to de-hex thirteen people because someone's aura jacked them."

"And you would know this how again?" Wallace said.

Deidre retracted her weapons from the shirt. "My mother dealt with them before. We were all trained in de-hexing."

"Why haven't we heard about this before?" Wallace said.

"Because the old guard who booted my mother believed aura jacking is their divine right and killed those who stood up to them," Deidre said. "I'm going to stay here. You're going to get Mindy and get back before the storm hits."

"You were rip roaring to go five minutes ago and now you're staying?" Wallace said.

"I'm just an adept. I'm not a full seer. I didn't know until he just told us. If you think I set this up to show off, you're sorely mistaken," Deidre said. "I'll need Wallace, too."

"He was given decree to find Mindy and bring her back," Thom said.

"It can be assigned to you," Deidre said. "I'll need their help in case this storm breaks in. Alita is all you'll need. This is Mindy we're talking about. If it was Cherie than I'd be worried."

"Hey." Cherie stomped her foot. "Wait, why am I still going?"

"You haven't enough ground ops experience," Deidre said. "That and the stars in your eyes are brighter than that lamp over there. Get moving you're losing time the more we talk."

The group boarded the Pan's ship without another word.

"I can see why she's your first choice," Thom said to Selene once they were locked in and headphones firmly across their ears.

"She's my only choice. Who trained her?" Selene said.

"Who do you think?" Thom said.

Selene nodded slowly. "That explains a lot."

~

Pan's running lights disappeared first followed by the stars. The maw of metal and iron that sealed itself above Deidre didn't fill her dread, instead she breathed a sigh of relief.

"These gahforsaken blast shields always terrified me as a child," Wallace said.

"Afraid of confined spaces?" Deidre said.

"No. Afraid of the dark and whatever else is out there," Wallace said.

"Afraid of me?" Deidre said.

"No. It's the other things that go bump in the night I petrified of," Wallace said and nodded to her staff and sword. "One for hexing the other for blessing?"

Deidre nodded.

"Just remember which end goes where," Wallace said with a wink and sauntered off back towards the Inn.

"Where're you going?" she said.

"Once you finish your speech, I'm going to take my men into the festival and warn the Houses personally," Wallace said.

"And introduce yourself so everyone remembers you," Deidre said.

"You have been talking to too many people." Wallace pulled out a weather-beaten wallet and tossed it to her. "Keep this on, just in case."

"What's this do?" She opened the wallet and hissed at the iron badge.

"Heiden Corp Security Badge, just in case," Wallace said and pushed through the Inn's doors.

"I've already written my name on my arms, what's a badge going to do," Deidre said.

"Raise it over your head so they know who you are," Wallace said.

"This isn't going to do nothing with these guys," she said.

"You'd be surprised." Wallace tugged on an occupied chair and the

Stukari Holdings Operator vacated it immediately. He presented the chair to her and she hopped up on it.

Deidre raised the badge over her head and whistled loud enough. "Listen up. We've got a storm coming in. Probably an hour away or less. We're closing the inner and outer blast shields until it's over."

"So?" someone shouted.

"So, our resupply of defense charms didn't come in and is overdue. The same charms I ordered for every single person in town. This doesn't include the people down at the festival. We're going to redouble the defense wards around the festival and the rest of it's on you."

A few grumbles erupted, but Wallace stared them down and silence returned.

"The outer shields are already closed so that means if someone does try something they'll have to walk in some sort of transmitter," Deidre said. "You lock the Festival down quietly. I get a stampede of people up here and it's all over. I'm going to stay out here and make sure nothing else gets through."

"For those of us who aren't fluent in aura storms, what does that mean?" Gladys said.

"It means I've got an hour to spool down the defense genies you have, re-write the spells and spool them back up. That takes a minimum for a week. Down and dirty version takes a half hour. If this turns out to be nothing, then we're fine. But if it does turn out to be an aura storm. That means a simple spark can infect you and then you're autopilot because someone else is driving. I need all of you to keep calm through all this and we'll make it through. All of you have your defense charms on and they're all working. That's the good news. That bad news is someone did their homework and sucked my blessed sword dry," Deidre said. "That puts them in the smart not stupid category. I can re-charge the sword, but it'll take hours. Whatever they want they haven't touched any of you. So, until you hear from me or see Mister Stuk and the rest of his merry little band, you're it. You all know how to spot those Aura Jackers. This shouldn't be that bad but if it is, you call in for back up," Deidre said.

Someone snickered, and Wallace stepped forward only for the snickering to stop.

Deidre sighed. "I shall re-phrase. Do you want people to find out you Tier Zero boys wet your pants during a wittle itty bitty storm that is probably being cause by some mage who couldn't keep it up or do you want to hear about how all of you defended this place until the end with nothing but harsh language and sticks?"

The temperature in the room had dropped. The men and women stared back at her with fire in their eyes she hadn't seen in quite some time.

"That's what I thought. Now, finish up you drinks. Gear up. Lord Stukari will escort you to your detail, personally." She paused. "And, one last thing: If I find out any of you had anything to do with our current situation there is nowhere on this planet that can protect you for me. I don't need the sword or staff. Just remember that."

She stepped off the chair and took an empty seat at the bar.

The operators emptied out quickly and quietly. Deidre didn't make eye contact with them and they didn't make eye contact with her.

"There are two people who made speeches like that," Wallace said, "you're the third to actually make it through all of it without being kicked off the chair."

"It goes double for you," Deidre said.

Wallace leaned on the bar and chortled. A cackle of sorts and clapped. "Now, that is the perfect way to end the speech. You've put the fear of death into them and me. One little problem, what if it's not me?"

"No one smuggles anything around here without you knowing about. No one takes a percentage without going through you first. No one, ever, steals without your permission. He taught me one thing: Who's in charge?" Deidre swiveled around in her seat to stare him down. "And, while you may be the Weaver's friend, the rackets, the clubs, the women, the low Houses all look to you first since you run this place because if it wasn't you, it'd be someone else and they wouldn't last five minutes. So, whatever is going on tonight, keep it away from me."

"Pleasure doing business with you," Wallace said with a bow and exited the inn.

Deidre swiveled back around to face down Gladys. "And that goes double for you."

Gladys snickered. "You're not *him*. Stop acting like *him* and you'll live longer."

"Says the defrocked Priestess of the Hills who nearly brought the universe to an end," Deidre said. "You can admit to spooling down my sword now or we can just admit to the fact someone else is doing this and they didn't get to you first because they too scared or you or him or both of you."

"And how are you going to a prove any of that?" Gladys said.

Deidre pointed behind her. "When you get aura jacked, the mirrors are the first things to reveal your hideous visage." She flipped her hair. "I on the other hand look ravishing while you look like you need a good cleanse because you are nowhere near that weather beaten."

Gladys stood her ground and growled something unintelligible.

"Why yes, I am playing the role of the cursed magess with a chip on her shoulder. Thank you." Deidre finished her drink and grabbed a bottle of water from behind the bar. "Time to close the doors after all the horses are gone."

"Getting everyone pissed isn't the clear sign they aren't already jacked," Gladys said.

Deidre picked up her sword and sheathed it around her waist. "It certainly isn't, but it did get the water away from you because I've been parched all day. I'll be back in hour, don't do anything stupid until then."

~

Gladys closed and locked the second-floor windows. She hand-cranked the iron shutters until the locks thudded into place. She lit each of the defense candles in the hallways and checked the few remaining barrels of heavy water that judging from the dust hadn't been moved in years.

The second-floor pool table hall was already locked down so when she arrived back at the bar to find single cloak at the bar she ignored her instinct to be angry.

"We're closed. No vacancies," she said.

The cloak turned, and her hair stood on end at the passing sight of the Leighton Defense Magi. "Yes, we know." His voice didn't match his lips. The cursed gems somewhere on his body translated for him. "The cargo has been secured and ready for transport."

"I told you to ignore the Witcha, but you just had to drain that gahforsaken sword of hers," Gladys said and went from window to window. The repetition kept her anger in check.

"We didn't," the Magi said. "We obeyed and didn't touch her."

Gladys stopped. "Ha. That little Witcha lied to me. Remember our agreement. Once you're done you leave this place and never return."

"Our master will keep to the terms and thanks you for your service." The Magi placed a small ring box on the bar. "Safe roads and travels, Priestess." He bowed and flowed out the doors before Gladys could throw the ring box at him.

Gladys pulled down the iron security door. The locks slammed into place. The blessed silence was off putting for this time of night but better to be safe than sorry.

Gladys took out the money and dropped it in the tin. "Thank you, Mister Stuk, for your donation to the getting Grainne O'Hare off this rock." She closed the tin and eyed the ring case. "Any and all trinkets are accepted at House Stow."

She popped off the top of the box and her world was filled with nothing but a cackling darkness that knew her name.

7
WELCOME TO STUK'S HOLLOW

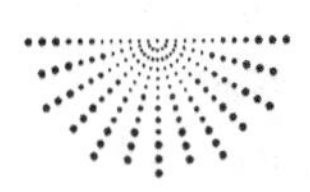

MELINDA LOCKED HER FISHBOWL AND SAT HER SUIT AGAINST THE statue's base. "Not bad. You looked quite alive," she said and tightened the pistol belt around her long johns.

Spence circled the base once more and stopped in front of it. "No marker or plaque." He placed a hand on the nearest stone. "No black arts residue, they actually built you by hand, didn't they?" The remaining outstretched arm pointed east towards the horizon. "So, pointing where? Go back from whence you came? Or go and flourish in the wasteland?"

"Clarence Stuk." Melinda stretched. "On the centennial of the Stuk Empire birth. He commissioned them to be markers to establish his kingdom. They also protected those in need. Judging from the damage *you* did to it, it's been spooled down for years. What?"

"How'd you know that?" Spence said.

"When you're six anything taller than you makes an impression." Melinda pulled off her shoulder torches and tossed him one. "Getting hungry."

Spence pointed to the mountain range to the west that looked impassable. "We need to call your brother, but I don't see any transmission towers. Are you picking up any signals?"

"Not at present, but, the escape pod may be able to boost my signal. Short range scans are coming back." The mask paused. "Inconclusive."

"Inconclusive as in nothing or inconclusive as in blocking you?" Melinda said.

"Unknown," the mask said.

"That's the Stormer Mountain Range and Goslin Grace Spaceport is on the other side." Melinda opened her waist bag. "The spotters should've sent out a Rescue Team by now."

"No one's that quick," Spence said.

"Some lord's kid gets caught on this side of the range after dark, yes, they're *that* quick," she snickered. "Twelve hours out here is a lifetime."

And why are you so eager to leave? Spence thought and nodded to the escape pod. "Let's see what we can see."

The escape pod's impact ditch wasn't that deep. The pod's chrome body tilted upwards, metal feet extended to balance itself properly on the uneven terrain. Except for some minor scoring on the nose, it reminded him of the day he bought it.

"Give me a damage report," Spence said.

"Primary communication stack needs repairs. Seals on the primary casing are damaged. Possible internal damage. Repair toolkit is in the rear cargo compartment," the mask said.

Spence tilted the torch down and crested the lip of an incline. "Any more light and we're going to be walking targets."

"Left pocket," the mask instructed.

Spence patted down the cloak, carefully stuck his hand inside the folds and pulled out a pair of goggles. The glass lenses were big but judging from the amount of inlaid wiring around the frames and the weight of the lenses, someone had gone to the trouble to cram a great deal of surveillance gear into something so simple.

He found the 'on' switch on body of the left lens and pulled them on. Several warm up screens flew by until a slightly pixelated view of the landscape faded into existence. "Outline me in green. I need enhanced night vision." A wireframe outline appeared around his fingers.

He wiped the grit away. A Historical Marker appeared and welcomed him to Stuk Hollow's second tourist spot: The Heiden Ravine. A seven-hundred-foot drop of stalactites, stone walls eroded to perfection by a long dried up river and lovely sandy bottom. For rock climbers, tourists and doting grandparents alike it garnered its five stars rating by being the only place still on the Hollow worth seeing.

"If I had stayed onboard, I would have fallen out," Melinda ventured.

Spence handed the goggles to her. "I'm going to repair the pod. You're on guard duty."

"Sure, I'll repair the pod." Melinda pulled on the goggles. "You can stand watch. You're not using me as bait. My hands are tinier than yours are and I have a Second-Class Engineering Grade waiting for me back on Gunna. So, gimme the emergency tool kit and we can get ourselves out of here."

~

"I wasn't going to use you as bait," Spence huffed.

"Uh huh." Melinda twisted of the screws and the dented hatch labeled COMMUNICATION popped open. A bundle of wires that stared back at her illuminated in green except for two in red. "Looks like a few wires came loose."

"We need extended range. How're the batteries?" Spence said.

"If the solar panels are intact, approximately four hours to recharge," the mask said.

"Shut down non-essential systems. Anything within walking distance?" Spence said.

"Ground repeater stations line Ravine," Melinda said and pointed into the dark.

"I can extend our range to fifty miles. My quills can be used as a portable sensor array and communication grid for long-range missions. I'm shutting down my weapons package to conserve power. I think you two can handle yourselves," the mask said.

The quills and fur retracted into the cloak's body. The hood rolled up and the mask lowered between Spence's shoulder blades. It looked like a standard mage's cloak minus the House sigil piping from waist to cuffs.

Melinda screwed in the last errant wire. "Done. How inconclusive now?"

"Long range sensors are currently off-line. I've detailed instructions on fixing the sensors. Short range scans suggest you shouldn't be a heavy sleeper," the mask said.

"Like a rock." Melinda unscrewed the panel stenciled with faded paint labeled: SENSORS. She carefully parted the bundles of brightly color wires to expose the plethora of circuit boards. "Looks like two of the circuit boards are broken."

"Accessing records for this model." The lenses blinked. "Records match: negative."

"Check under serial number: Bravo, One, Three, Six, Delta," Spence said.

"Bravo is for a Breach Pod." The schematics flashed across the goggle's lenses several of them glowed green. "Correct files found. The files were purposely mislabeled."

"You should've read the instruction booklet." Spence rubbed the tips of his fingers together and pointed a pinky at the circuit boards. "Tell me when."

"There. There and there." Melinda whistled at the circuit board fusing themselves together. "You're more expensive than I am."

"Sometimes things just need a little nudge. Try it now," Spence said.

"Circuit boards now functioning," the mask chimed. "Warning: batteries are at twenty percent. Long Range Sensors will be inoperable until sufficient power is restored."

Melinda closed the hatch. "What did you do?"

"Just a little nudge." Spence ambled around the rear of pod and opened the emergency storage hatch. He pulled out a vacuum-sealed emergency kit and tossed a bag of dry food to her. "There's a blanket, sleeping bag, more rations and a shovel."

"A nudge?" Melinda said and tore open the food bag. "Shovel?"

"Latrine detail," Spence said. "And to answer the first question that's what my techno mage teacher said, too. Spells are catching up with me. Am gonna need to sleep it off." He unrolled the sleeping bag and flopped down. "Exactly, what were you doing on my ship?"

~

Thom buttoned up his tunic to his neck. He didn't miss the weight of the iron lining around his neck, wrists or ankles but mages never played fair. He tightened the gun belt around his waist. His back-up, wooden shotgun was still being tweaked by Cherie. The short sword he borrowed from Selene would have to do until he got back. His boots still fit, and all his shielded electronic gear checked out and got Alita's low whistle seal of approval.

"All of this was banned at the end of the war," she said and stretched so her camo suit was snug.

"My licenses are up to date," Thom said and snapped a weather-beaten badge onto his belt. "And Heiden Corps Badge makes it legal."

"You realize they're gone, right? They're not coming back," Alita said. "They're going to laugh you off the deck."

Thom smiled. "Have a little faith." He motioned her to turn so he could snap bandoliers closed. "You're going to be the first one on the ground. You ready?"

Alita's smile and wink told him enough. "You didn't find me at a charm school, remember." She tapped his borrowed sword with hers. "I've got a few iron daggers if you're into throwing."

"Please," he said and turned to the rest. "All right, time to read you all in a few things. First, thank you for helping me. I'll put in a good word for you once we get back. I don't know how much you've been told about the House changeover, but they're currently at deadlock and have requested additional Houses to settle it. In return, they're going to open a half dozen slots and one of those is going to House Stuk."

"Finally," Selene said.

"You little sneak," Alita snickered. "You turned away Deedee and Cherie."

"I suggested, you'd better be suited with some ground ops experience because Melinda passed her test and hasn't gotten into trouble so the other Houses signed off on her," Thom said.

"Read: They can't get anything done down here and needs a professional," Selene said.

"She'll be getting her titles back in two days. She doesn't know any of this but if she's running Erik, we need to get to her before she does anything else. Once, the ceremonies are over, we'll be heading back to The Roost for training," Thom said.

"Erik and the rest then too?" Cherie said.

"I haven't heard from the rest of the Houses since I landed. Which reminds me, hey, Pan, I need you down here for a moment," Thom said.

"On my way." Her voice cracked through the speaker.

"What I'm about to read you in on is classified House business. A year ago, the standard House rotation gave most of us our titles and land back. It should've sail through, but it didn't. Someone who shall remain nameless got wind of something going out at edge of Wailing Seas Weapons Facility. Someone had dug up an old Daire engine mount between the Facility and Devereux Fueling Station. A ground team was sent in to retrieve all of it, but the engine was unsuccessfully punted into orbit. The ground team was compromised and on House orders was burned."

"Wait, I remember hearing something about this. Didn't Wally get left high and dry?" Cheri said.

"Yes, Mister Stukari was supposed to bring someone in but the Op went south. We didn't know what happened to the Mount until six months ago when she S-Cut her way into the New Welles Asteroid Belt where I found her, *him* and to my surprise, it jumped away before I could exfiltrate," Thom said and let Pan take a seat. "Three hours ago, the mount jumped back into the belt and I had Mindy recon it without letting her in on it. She contacted our guest, only for the shuttle she had found to take off with her attached to it."

"Typical Mindy," everyone said.

"The shuttle was headed to the Hollow and we would've gotten her, but someone drained all my swords and picked my trunk along with sabotaged *Toy*'s defense suite," Thom said. "And, tried to kill Mindy."

"You guys never do anything simple, you know that?" Selene said. "Somebody doesn't want you coming back."

"Can we go back to the person who Wally was supposed to bring in?" Cherie said.

Thom plunked down a video projector onto the prep table and the Necrocloak appeared follow shortly thereafter by a picture of Spence MacGregor. "Spence MacGregor. Picture and live audio from Mindy's camera gear confirm it's him. I need this to exfil to go smooth. We get them on board and we get back to Stow's End before the storm hits. Hunker down and wait it out until our names are called and no one's much the wiser."

"Wishful thinking, Stuk." Alita sighed. "Why'd you bring everyone? I would've done this without all the sneaking around."

"The reason I brought the rest of you is because all of your Houses are on the list to get back in. Your names specifically," Thomas said and ignored the shocked faces. "Yes, I kidnapped you so none of your families decide to change their vote and in return we all get four walls, a roof and meals on this sand trap for the rest of our lives. Questions?"

"When were you going to tell me?" Pan said.

"Your grandmother is on the list to get back in," Thom started. "I need to make sure it's him before you get your hopes up."

"My hopes up? He's been missing for thirty years and you're telling me you need to be sure?" Pan bolted out of the seat and slapped Thom across the face. "If you think I'd turn on him because of my backstabbing grandmother you've got another thing coming." She wiped tears away and kicked him in the shins. "And that's for red teaming me!"

She hugged him and left the cabin.

"I'm going to remind you if you do that red team foolishness on me, I know how to use this." Alita patted her sword affectionately.

~

"— and here we are," Melinda finished her tale. She munched on the dried food bar and pulled the blanket tight. She leaned against the breach pod's landing struts; he dozed on the sleeping bag while the remaining defense candles encircled them in pink and green flames.

Spence growled. "The wrong ship?"

"Was supposed to be this cargo ship set up to spook me." Melinda finished her food bar. "I was the last one on the list."

Spence frowned. "What list?"

"War Orphans get tested between sixteenth and eighteenth birthday so we're not unduly burdened." She pointed a trigger finger out into the night, thumb cocked. "Tommy has been weeding out the ones with augmented genes. Took 'em long enough to take swipe at me."

Spence tilted his head forward. "Stuk? You said Scott."

"House Stuk was black listed ten years ago. Rushford Scott took us in during the investigation, but someone threw some money around and I was banished. They've been after me ever since," she said.

Spence cracked an eyelid. "You're too young to be that paranoid or that important."

Melinda squinted down at him. "I've shot you how many times today?"

"Touché." Spence clasped his hands over his chest and sighed. "Why an engine mount? Completely useless without a dry dock and an engineering crew."

"The wrong ship attached to your flat screen which wasn't." Melinda cocked an eyebrow.

"Some things you don't need to know," Spence snorted. "I'd say this was thin, but Tommy's tests were never this creative if I didn't know better I'd think he is using you as bait."

Melinda snapped her fingers. "How do you know him, again?"

"We went to the Academy together," Spence said. "Why hotwire an engine mount?"

"To go anywhere but here," Melinda muttered. "Navigators handled all the big math."

Spence snickered. "*Now* they do. Back in the good ole bad ole days, the engineers had all the maps and the math. Wait, why do you think they want you dead?"

Melinda sighed. "I stuck my nose where it didn't belong."

Spence's brow furrowed. "Oh, such a bad liar, you are. Melinda, what'd you do?"

Melinda's eyes widened, and she whispered: "Can you hear that?"

Spence leaned forward. "That's not gonna work on me. What did you—"

A gust of wind twisted by and a flame of one of the candles popped.

A soft beep echoed in the night.

Spence stared at Melinda's slack face. "What is it?" he said.

Melinda bound over to her suit. "Somebody just pinged my suit's emergency beacon."

Spence pulled down his goggles and adjusted them.

A pair of red and green running lights zipping low across the horizon. "I can't tell, but I think that might be our ride. Time to use that emergency beacon," he said.

"Once I turn it on I can't turn it off," Melinda said. "Flare gun?"

"In the emergency kit," he said.

A warble from Melinda's suit stopped them.

The warble turned into an annoying, pulsing beep.

"That's the beacon?" he said.

"It's supposed to remind me to stick close," she said. "If I futz with it it'll get worse."

"'Worse?'" Spence said.

"Look, I'm just going to be honest with you. Generally, I would've wander off by now and gotten myself into trouble, so this is the first time I actually stayed put." Melinda knelt next to her suit and furiously clicked away on the chest panel.

The beeping stopped.

The running lights kept their pace, away from them.

"They're not stopping," Spence said.

"Give 'em a few minutes to triangulate us," Melinda said.

Spence pointed to a closer set of running light that had drifted up from the ravine. "Who's that?" he said.

The beeping started, again.

"I don't know," Melinda said. "But I think it's time to..." She stopped and leaned around the suit. She pulled out her stunner. "I think we have company."

Spence jerked around at the sound of quills. "How?"

"Unknown." The mask perked up. "But I am picking up your sister's private network. The dropship on the other side of the ravine is hers."

"Call her. Right now," Spence said and shrugged the cloak back on. "Who else is out there?"

"Short range scan still inconclusive," the mask said. "Multiple possible targets are converging on our position."

"Mindy. Call your brother, right now," Spence said and twisted the cloak's seals. "Tell 'em: Send Everything."

"What does that mean?" she said.

"Just do it!" Spence howled just as the night parted and a phalanx of Necrocloaks descended from the statue's shoulders.

~

The communication panel screaming twisted Thom around and he bound up the stairs.

"That's not for me," Pan said.

"That's Mindy," Thom said and didn't even sit down. A few key strokes and several screens lit up and decoded the message. "Alive. Stop. Unhurt. Stop. Coordinates as follows. Stop. Incoming Quiglies. Stop. Send Everything. Stop." He tapped away. "Sending the coordinates to you now."

"Quiglies?" Pan said.

"Quills. Necros," Thom said. "I'm re-tuning your communication stack."

"— do they look friendly to you?" Melinda's voice squawked over the PA.

"Mindy, can you hear me?" Thom said.

"Perfect timing. Go secure channel six." Melinda's voice cracked, and the communication channel switched over a secure line. "I've got six Necros and their ride. I have the package. Where are you?"

"Tell her to stay where she is. I'm going to double back through the ravine and come up from behind them," Pan said and the ship angled sharply downward. "Mindy, how many of them are there?"

"Six."

"He can deal with six," Pan said.

"No, he certainly cannot," a man's voice said. "Tommy, who else you got?"

Not enough, Thom thought. "A Finnegan and a Whittahare with a Leighton warming up."

"No techno?" the man said.

"Negative," Thom said. "How low are you?"

"Nothing fancy and my cloak is on fumes," the man said.

"Thirty seconds," Pan said. "I'm going to drop the defense package and they can jump right in."

The deck plates shuddered.

"What was that?" Cherie said.

"I dunno, but your defense wards just took a hit. No debris. I think, I think. . . I think it was EMP. We're down to seventy percent across the board," Selene said.

"We didn't hit anyone, did we?" Thom said.

"Negative." Pan leveled out the ship. "I think." She twisted the ship through a curve or two. "I think she's right about that being an EMP blast. Twenty seconds out. I'm cycling the rear hatch. Cherie, stay on board. Selene and Alita, you're up."

"Mindy, we're fifteen seconds out. Get ready," Thom said.

Silence followed.

"Mindy?" Thom said and checked the communication station. "I've got nothing. Everything is out."

"I've still got control of the ship. We're committed. Here we go." Pan reached back and pulled back the levers on the ceiling instrument panel.

~

The Necros landed next to the sarcophagus and Melinda backed away only to bump into Spence.

"It's just me," he said. "Don't shoot them."

"Says the one not in their long underwear. Where are they?" she said.

"Dunno, but I can't hear them anymore and I can't hear the plate either," Spence said and squinted at the Necros. One of them had turned toward them. "I think they're after the chamber."

"How can you tell?" Melinda scoffed.

"Because they're ignoring us," he said.

"Except for that one," she said and pointed to the short quilled Necro with the cursed gem gauntlets.

The Necros focus shifted from them to something above them and Spence chanced a look to find a twin engine, bare metal dropship appeared out of thin air on the edge of the ravine.

"Perfect timing as always—" Melinda squealed in pain. She clutched her head and toppled to the ground.

The Necros followed suit.

Spence rubbed his temples at the splitting headache that blossomed behind his eyeballs when across the horizon, the night parted, and a column of light exploded.

Thunder cracked the sky. Fingers of blue lightning danced across the horizon.

A ground quake threatened to throw Spence off his feet, but the shockwave of energy that barreled across the horizon pitched him towards Mindy. He hoisted her over his shoulder and ran towards the sarcophagus.

Spence hopped over the collapsed Necros and tossed Melinda atop the sarcophagus. Once she was safe, he quickly re-adjusted the candles. "Defense candles will protect us," he said.

"From what?" Melinda yelled and gaped at the shockwave. "We need to get to cover!"

Spence pulled her close. "Trust me. The candles will hold."

"Where'd the ship go?" she said.

"If I know my sister, she'll ride it out in the ravine," Spence said.

"Or land ride on top of us," Melinda said and pointed up.

"She's not that crazy," Spence said and pulled the Necro with the gauntlets across the barrier of candles.

The wind swirled around them. Spence glanced up at the looming belly of a dropship. The double bay doors peeled back. "Then again, maybe she is," he said.

The world of sound, sand and light disappeared only to be replaced by comforts of the dropship's cramped cabin. The eerie glow from someone's blessed broadsword illuminated the confined space along with the other four-armed passengers, Thom Stuk being the only one Spence recognized immediately behind the wooden shotgun.

"Everyone hang tight." Panya's voice echoed over the PA system. "We're ironed up but no promises!"

"If we survive this, we're going to have a nice long talk." Spence pointed at the Necro.

The world outside the ship turned white and filled with a hideous noise before anyone could argue.

8
IN DARKNESS THEY RIDE

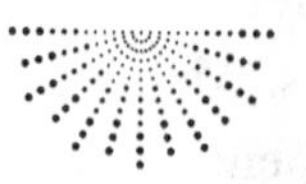

"THIS ISN'T GOING TO WORK," PAN SAID FROM THE COCKPIT. "I CAN'T SEE a thing."

"Trust me. It will," Thom's static voice said of the coms. "The Iron Shielding and the defense suite just saved our lives. I'm getting them secured now then we can get out of here."

"Huh, what did we land on?" Pan's co-pilot, Nat Stukari, Jr. said from his seat.

"On a sarcophagus, what else?" Thom said.

"Sarcophagus as in a resurrection chamber?" Nat said.

"There's a difference?" Vernon said from the engineering station. "There were too many people down there."

"So?" Thom said.

"I'm getting interference from something in the cabin." Nat pointed at several red screens. "And it's growing."

"Wait, what's growing where?" Thom's raised voice said.

"The defense suite doesn't have a hard seal," Pan said. "I can't lift off until we do. Thom stay where you are." She nodded to Nat. "Go."

Nat unstrapped himself from the co-pilot's chair. He popped the iron crash axe out from its cradle above the door and was down the stairs only to stop short at the sight in front of him. Selene and Alita with swords drawn, Thom with his shotgun and Cheri ready with her spell book all pointed at the middle of the cabin where Spence MacGregor, Melinda Scott and an unnamed Necrocloak sat atop a resurrection chamber. The litany languages overlapped until he put his fingers into his mouth and whistled loud enough so everyone in the lower cabin would stop.

"Thank you. Everyone not associated with the trio of idiots sitting on the resurrection chamber needs to take a seat," Nat said. "Selene and Al sheath the weapons. Cherie just keep doing what you're doing. Thom, back it up."

"I am helping!" Cherie said and waved her spell book around.

"Now, as for Mister MacGregor, Miss Stuk and the uninvited guest. Get off the resurrection chamber before you do anything else," Nat said.

"Oh, this is where you've been hiding?" Melinda said.

"Not hiding, Mindy. It's called a paying job. Now, shuffle off the chamber." Nat pointed to the Necro. "Mister Mystery Guest that hasn't introduced himself over there where Al and Selene can see you and keep those gauntlets spun down."

"Alita. Alita," Alita said.

"Al," Nat said. "Now, as for the person who happens to be in the resurrection chamber would you mind spooling down your defense wards, you're interfering with the hard seal."

"There's no one in there," Selene said.

"Why put defense candles around a resurrection chamber if you're not going to use them," Nat said.

"Wha?" Spence squinted at the chamber. "I think he's right."

"And if you can't see him you really do need to sleep it off," Nat said. "May I?"

"No, you cannot touch my sword," Selene said.

"Not talking to you. I'm talking to him," Nat said.

"Who him?" Alita said. "There's nothing there."

"He's right," the Necro's mask chittered.

"Thank you, Mister Mystery Guest." Nat nudged past Thom and stood in front of the chamber. "May I?"

The ship's deck plates shuddered along with the rest of the ship.

The chamber's cover parted much to everyone's surprise. The emptiness that resided within brought a collective sigh to the cabin.

"Told you," Selene said.

"I didn't open it," Nat said.

"Neither did I," Spence said.

"Not it," Melinda said and raised her hands for added effect.

"I asked permission, that's how these resurrection chambers work. Guys, it's not like the dead guy inside opened it himself. That's just creepy." Nat stepped forward and reached into the abyss. He pulled a jeweled scabbard along with its broadsword out of the depths of the chamber. "Here we go," he said. "It wasn't sheathed properly." He did so and there was an audible thud across the deck.

"Solid seal!" Pan said. "Get back up here, we need to get out of here."

"We lost all the external cameras," Vernon said.

"Someone's over compensating," Alita snickered.

"That's a shield maiden's cursed broadsword," Selene said. "It comes in pairs. The blessed twin should be in there, too."

Nat eyed the chamber. "You left it with your body. Well, that makes sense."

"Who are you talking to?" Selene said.

Nat jerked his head back to the chamber. "Him."

"Who him?" Alita squinted at the chamber.

"The Mad Stuk," Nat said. "He says our Mystery Guest is supposed to deliver his body to be resurrected."

"The Mad Stuk is dead," Selene said.

"Yes, which is why one of you is going to resurrect him this night." Nat stopped in front Melinda. "He has requested you to wield this until he is raised at which time he will ask for it back."

Melinda inched away from the scabbard and looked to Spence, but he was staring at the chamber. "What is it? What do you see?" she hissed.

Spence didn't break the staring contest with the chamber. "Do as he says," he whispered.

"What do you see?" Melinda said.

"You know exactly what I look like, Meylandra Stuk," a man's baritone voice whispered from out of the chamber. "Or do I need to remind you?"

"That's not funny," Melinda said and grabbed Nat by the shirtfront. "Stop it, Junior!"

"Not me," Nat said and jabbed a finger at the chamber. "Look for yourself."

The wind picked up outside and electrical systems flickered for the briefest of moments and standing in the chamber was a tall, crooked presence. It ducked the high curved ceiling of the ship and stepped over the lip of the chamber and pair of Death Boots crossed the deck.

Everyone not seated bolted to seats closer to the stairs. The litany of blessings in different languages raised.

"What in gahsakes is going on down there?" Pan's voice warbled over the PA.

The owner of the Death Boots, dressed in blood covered slacks, shattered knee guards, a coat of arms that made Melinda cover her nose. The empty double back scabbard jutted out of his coat. The high collar didn't hide a face, there wasn't one to hide, instead a bone white faceplate with the empty eye sockets turned towards Melinda. Ruby red aura pupils rose out of the dark.

It picked up Melinda out of her seat and brought her nose to nose.

"Do I need to remind you," the presence bellowed.

"Yes. I mean no. I believe you. I said I believe you," Melinda shouted back.

"Good. Now get yer ass moving, they're about to breach your wards." The presence dropped her onto her feet and pointed to the rear ramp.

The lights dimmed, and something twisted about in the confined space.

"Get us in the air!" Melinda howled.

"There's nothing back there," Selene said.

Melinda grabbed Thom's shotgun and unloaded on the closed rear ramp. Sparks flew, the ramp disappeared and a mob of Necros appeared. Quills and plates filled the crumpled door frame. Their gnarled hands reaching out trying to swipe their missing comrade-in-arms.

"Pan, get us in the gahforsaken air!" Nat yelled and pushed past Thom to get to the stairs.

"Have you seen the weather?" Pan said.

"Have you seen what they've done to the rear ramp?" he howled back and strapped himself back in. "Just get us back to Stow's End."

"What did you see?" Pan said.

"Take a look for yourself," Nat said and pointed to screen showing rear ramp's camera feed.

~

The engines' RPM howled, and the deck shuddered. The chamber popped free of the ground. The undercarriage's bay doors closed.

The ship slipped right with the sudden rise in altitude. Melinda grabbed onto the ceiling handholds and a few Necros lost their balance and tumbled away to reveal a lightning filled sky. The horizon from several hundred feet in the air looked amazingly angry.

A mob of Necros orbited the one-armed statue until one by one they turned towards the fleeing ship and followed.

Melinda grabbed the gauntlet Necro and hurtled him to the front of the cabin. "Watch him!" she told Alita and extended an empty hand to Selene. "Gimmie."

Selene tossed the broadsword to her and Melinda stalked down the deck with cursed sword in one hand and the blessed in the other. The magically cursed polar opposite swords snapped tendrils of light and dark magic around Melinda.

"Be gone from this place and never bother us again," she said.

"Louder," the presence said.

The Necros howled a spell at Melinda, but she deflected it away with swords. It dissipated immediately when it didn't connect with its intended target.

"I said be gone from this place and never bother us again," Melinda howled.

The spell rocketed out of the sword tips and the mass of Necros fell away.

Melinda turned the seething swords on the Mystery Guest. "*And you are?*" she said.

The Necros' gauntlets retracted into the furless sleeves. The seals twisted, the hood sagged, and gloved hands pulled it back. The man had a passing resemblance to Spence with lighter skin and light blue eyes, almost white. "I surrender conditionally to your lord and master," he started.

Melinda advanced, the sword tips to his bare neck stopped him. "A name," she twisted down her tongue.

"Mindy, stop," Spence said.

"He can talk for himself, Weaver. Who be you and who you serve?" she said.

"He's my brother," Spence said.

"Horatio Crosleigh and I serve no one but myself," the man said. "I'm here to escort this to Crosleigh's Caves to resurrect the Mad Stuk so he can vote in three days."

"The Mad Stuk doesn't have a House," Melinda growled. "None of us do. They're that desperate to raise you back from the dead to escort him so he can vote?"

Horatio nodded. "You have no idea. I need to talk to him."

"Talk to who?" Melinda said.

"Junior," Horatio said. "Please."

Melinda didn't relax, but Spence placed a hand on her arm. "Old tongue truth," he said.

She stepped back and sheathed the cursed sword. "I'll tell them where we're going," she said and sidestepped the hulking presence. "And you, get back in the chamber. Now."

"As you wish." The presence bowed and floated back into the chamber. The cover closed, and everyone crossed themselves three times and spit on the deck.

"Hey, no spitting on my ship!" Pan crowed from the cockpit.

~

"We're going where?" Pan said.

"Crosleigh's Caves," Melinda said.

"We passed by it on our way from the Stow's End," Pan said. "This explains why we're flying heavy, isn't it?" she looked Melinda up and down. "Where'd you get that sword from?"

"We're going to a resurrection," Melinda said and yawned. "Sorry about your rear quarter. I need to borrow some clothes."

"My trunk is in the upper cabin. Take whatever you need," Pan said.

She leaned down to Nat's ear. "Keep her up here. Horatio Crosleigh is in the back."

"Not funny, Mindy," Nat said.

She tapped one of his screens and zoomed in on the cabin. "You're right, it's not. The dead speaker of MacGregor House wants to talk to you."

~

Melinda closed the hatch and checked the locks on the frame. She popped open the emergency controls and even vacuum sealed the room. She turned and jerked to a stop at the chair in the middle of the room. The iron didn't make her eyes water like most, but it had been used recently. She walked around the chair and depressed the hidden button to lower the chair back into the deck. Once the hatch sealed behind it, she stabbed another button and the wall parted to reveal a lovely array of tops, bottoms, boots, gloves, goggles and air filtering bandanas.

Thank you, Spence for having the sister the same size as me. Melinda thought. Her goggles had analyzed the wardrobe options and matching styles to her measurements.

Melinda looked about, and no RF frequencies emanated from the room. *No cameras. No bugs,* she thought but looked down at the scabbard she held.

The lenses flared up with unknown signals.

You're still in there, aren't you? Melinda thought but the sword said nothing.

"You're still in there, aren't you," she said aloud.

The cursed soul gems in the scabbard hissed but said nothing else.

Melinda found the buttons inlaid in the wall and two taps later, the wall parted halfway to create a privacy wall. It was the sword stand that she found. She lay the scabbard on the stand and immediately went to work on getting three days' worth of clothes together into a duffle bag she found in the back of the wardrobe.

Once she was behind the privacy curtain, she tapped the light switch to find the head and sink was tucked into the corner along with a standing shower.

She pulled off her long underwear and ignored the conserve water sign. It was the longest five-minute shower she'd ever taken, but it felt good to be clean even if there wasn't enough soap.

Melinda got herself into a pair of slacks, boots with ankle iron protectors along with frayed blouse that matched the air filtering bandana. The gloves with the wrist protectors were a bit big, but it was better than nothing.

She came out from behind the privacy curtain and squealed at the stocky man leaning against the wall. A shock of impossibly fiery red hair, shining green eyes and dressed in the same clothes as the Mad Stuk, Roark Knoll looked good for a dead man.

Well, at least his aura looked good.

"Sorry," he said. "For all that down there. Neither of you saw me so, well," he shrugged.

"Even for a dead man you're still apologizing," Melinda scoffed.

"Thank you," he said.

"Don't thank me yet, we haven't even gotten there yet," Melinda said. "How long."

"How long?" he said. "Ten to thirty years this very night. I'm glad they got you out."

"Do you have any idea how long I looked for you?" she said. "No one could find you."

"I know," he said and sighed. "I got myself with the wrong folks. It happens."

"It happens? It happens?" she advanced and stabbed a finger in his chest. "You remember the words you told me. I'm going to check the far side of Wailing Seas and then the gahforsaken coil doors came down and no one has heard from you. I had to call my brother in to pull me out."

"I can only say sorry so many times," he said.

"No. You tell me what happened. I want to know what had to be so bad that you didn't come back to me," she said.

"Horatio, Spence, Lauren and Charles," he said and ticked off their names on one hand.

Melinda snorted. "Don't even. They've been missing for years."

"Yes, and so was I until an hour ago when you smacked into my resurrection chamber. Thank you by the way, there was short circuit and I was running on fumes," he said.

Melinda stood on her tip toes, so she could glare into those eyes of his. "They haven't been seen since the end of the war so what were you—" she slowed. "You went to pick them up, didn't you?"

Roark nodded. "And failed. A year ago, I woke up in a bar with amnesia. Called in for a pick up and we were three days away from Goslin Grace when we came across the engine mount half buried in the sand. I called it in but it was too late. Before I could get out got myself captured with a few others and was interrogated until one night we escaped."

"That doesn't explain why you're dead," Melinda said. "And another thing, why didn't Tommy tell me?"

"You would've rallied the troops," he said. "That was something I didn't need."

"Didn't need? Didn't need?" Melinda restrained herself.

"Mindy, there are people out there that don't care. They cracked me in five seconds and took everything," he said. "If they resurrect me, I'm looking at a court martial for treason against the Crown. Do you know what that means?"

"Immediate life imprisonment in The Depths no chance for parole or mercy," Melinda quoted. "Forfeiture of lands, titles and money."

Roark nodded. "You need to burn me immediately once we get to the Caves. I have no idea what they did to me but if they cracked my access codes, gahknows what else." He rubbed the bridge of his nose and stared down at her. "I missed you."

Melinda crossed her arms across her chest. "Hey, I didn't say yes, yet. Tommy used me as bait and now we're here." She stopped at the scowl that crossed his face. "What?"

"Pan," he said and disappeared, only the sword remained.

"Pan?" Melinda said and gaped. "Oh no." She unsealed the door and impatiently waited for the locks to tumble back.

"Mindy." Roark's voice pulled her around. "Forgetting something?"

Melinda picked up the scabbard and bolted out the door. "What did I tell you?" she shouted over her shoulder to Nat.

"What do you mean, she's right, oh c'mon, she slipped by," Nat groaned.

Melinda landed on the flight deck and Pan had Horatio by the neck and flailing out the end of the ship.

~

"Traitor," Pan growled. "You betrayed us to the Stukari and here you are on my ship?"

"Put 'em down," Spence said.

"Oh, let's not get started on you," Pan hissed.

"Wow," Cherie said.

"What?" Melinda said.

"My brothers, all six of them, couldn't get a drop on anyone and get their hands around their necks and hold them off the plank like that even if they tried," Cherie said. "Now, older sissie Terrie on the other hand, no problem in the world."

"What is that smell?" Melinda said.

Cherie shrugged. "You've got a better nose than me. Too many of us on a confined space. I can barely smell you."

Melinda blanched. "Spool down your aura."

"I just got it spooled up now you want me to spool it down? Make up your mind and don't give me that look you know it's takes me a while to get my aura going," Cherie said.

Melinda put two fingers in her mouth and whistled.

Everyone stopped.

"Selene, Alita, Thom, Spence, Horatio and Pan need to spool down their auras, right now," she said.

"This doesn't concern you, Stuk Witcha," Pan growled in the mother tongue.

"Fine. What does concern me is the smell of petrol in the air. Auras and gasoline don't mix. We're leaking somewhere and it's probably when the Necros were chewing their way in. So, whoever doesn't want to be part of the giant fireball, please continue," Melinda said.

"Pan," Nat's voice came over the PA.

"And, you, the less I hear from you the better!" Pan howled.

"I need you to check the fuel tanks. We've got less than five minutes of fuel left in all the tanks. And sorry for not telling you about Harry. Either fling him over the side and get back up so you can glide the ship in or I'll do it for you. What's it going to be?"

Pan lowered Horatio so they were eye-to-eye. "I'll be back for you in a minute." She dropped him back into his seat and stalked away to the stairs.

~

"Ladies and gentle souls, this is your co-pilot speaking. We will be making a scheduled stop at Crosleigh's Keep where we will be refueling and maintenance to check our poor rear end. We ask aura and non-aura users alike to spool down those auras as we make our descent. If you notice the ship has gotten extremely quiet, it is because we'll be bingo on fuel in roughly four minutes. Our expected on-time arrival is ten minutes. This will be the co-pilot's second time landing this ship dead stick. We appreciate your business and hope you'll fly again with us in the future. So, sit back and enjoy as our captain grits her teeth because she's never actually made a hard landing in her life," the PA calmly squawked.

"Is he always like that?" Alita said.

"Only when he knows what he's doing." Melinda strapped herself in and pulled down the safety crossbar. "Saw him land a refrigerator with wings once."

"Did you raid my sister's wardrobe?" Spence said.

"Yes," Melinda said.

"Least we'll go in smelling like roses," Selene said.

"The co-pilot would also like to recommend no wise cracks from the peanut gallery. Happy thoughts, folks," the PA said.

The noise of the starboard side engine softened followed shortly thereafter by the port.

"Now, that I have your undivided attention. Once we land, any abled body soul is asked to pick up the resurrection chamber in the rear of the aircraft and double time to the Crosleigh's Keep. The Keep's defense wards are still up so our friends are going to be in for a bit of shock when their heads and their assholes meet for the first and last time. For those not carrying the chamber we do ask to remove all belongings from the overheads and dead run to the front doors of the Keep."

"Friends?" Selene said.

The wind whistled on followed by the sound of chimes.

"Oh, how could I forget those." Melinda craned her head back to the mass of Necros rocketing across the sky towards them. "Thanks a lot, Tommy. I actually missed this."

"Don't look me, your dead ex-fiancé came up with the plan, not me," Thom said.

"He's not my ex-fiancé. We never even made it past our first play-date," Melinda growled.

"I said think happy thoughts, Melinda," the PA snapped. "Finally, the co-pilot would like to remind everyone when retelling this story that both engines were on fire and Mindy was going toe to toe with several Necros while everyone else was close to death."

"What was I doing during all this?" Spence said.

"Just a reminder, everyone knows the Weaver always dies first to rally the rest," the PA retorted. "In an effort to conserve power we will be dimming the lights. Please follow the track lighting to the nearest exit unless it's on fire, obviously. Thank you and prepare for crash positions."

The cabin lights dimmed. The eerie light from the horizon sprayed everyone with a ghostly look.

Melinda's belly dropped a bit like the ship. *Must be losing my mind,* she thought. *This feels normal.*

9
BALANCE

"YOU DON'T HAVE TO DO THIS TO IMPRESS ME," PAN SAID.

"I'm not impressing you. We're landing at the caves and walking away from it." Nat tightened his harness. "Problem is we need to burn off some speed because if we don't we're flying off the other side of the cliff and plummeting to our deaths." He tapped the battery gauge. "Batteries are good. Hydraulics are good. Spooling down the defense wards." Three levers later and the ship's deck plates quaked.

"Lowering the flaps." The hydraulics whined, and the ship's speed dropped.

"Landing gear?" she said.

"Negative on that we may need them later if this doesn't work," he said.

"I repeat, you don't need to do this to impress me," she said.

"You've never actually glided one of these in before, have you?" He flipped a switch or two and the fuselage lights flared to life. "Good news is, we've got power and hydraulics. The bad news is no instrument landing system (ILS) or tower so hopefully no one is taxing."

"We can radio them," Vernon said.

"And give ourselves away. No, I don't think so." Nat tapped the radar dome. "Nothing ese out there besides our friends who don't seem to be in a rush." He pointed out the canopy to the darkness. "There it is. Landing field right next to the Keep."

"How can you see that?" Vernon said.

"Whatever exploded passed through the defense grid and hit the rest of the ships. Their defense suites spooled up and make great landing lights," Nat said. "Vernon, do me a favor. Scan the Keep for me."

He angled the ship and circled the mountain top Keep.

"Reading life signs within the Keep and inside the mountain itself. Massive energy signatures at the base," Vernon said. "Aren't we announcing ourselves?"

"To people that are listening, yes we certainly are. Save those scans. We about to land."

Each time the ship orbited, she lost altitude until on the third time Nat had lined up with the runway.

He pulled back on the control sticks and the nose tilted back.

The thump of the rear landing gear kissing the asphalt didn't happen but instead, the friction of the ship's belly.

"Gahsakes," Pan said.

"We're fine. This is fine," Nat said and the hull connected with something and the ship bounced up then came down hard.

Red fire warning lights on the console blinked and beeped.

"We're still fine," he said and stabbed the warning lights to 'off.'

~

Melinda looked out the back to the sight of the ship's rear quarter was on fire. The sparks from the hard landing had lit the remaining fuel drenched frame. One thud and the remains of a fence toppled by. The amount of dirt thrown into the air was almost comical.

The ship tilted up and tried to remain airborne but instead, she came crashing down. Up and down several times and finally, the ride stopped.

Thom unbuckled himself and grabbed the fire extinguisher to put out the ship's fiery behind.

"Ladies and gentle souls we'd like you to welcome you to Crosleigh Keep where the time is exactly midnight. Please be aware that your go bags may have shifted during landing. We ask you to please wait to spool up your auras until you are clear of the aircraft. On behalf of our Captain, we'd like to thank you for flying with us and hope you choose us in the future once the aircraft has been repaired. The Keep's defense wards are up, and our cloaked friends are currently re-thinking their plan of attack. Please keep to secure channel six for updates from the cabin crew. Please follow the track lighting to the nearest exit. Thank you and have a pleasant evening."

"Headcount!" Thom said and everyone including the chamber rattled off "here".

"Alita and Vernon, you're on lookout detail. Mindy, check the overheads and line up everyone's bags," Thom said. "Goggle up. Make sure to tag everyone in green, including Horatio. Nat, where'd you land us?"

"We're behind the Keep. That fence we blew through was for the lookie loos," Nat said. "I got us in the backyard, the rear ramp should be pointed towards the Keep."

"Chamber detail—" Thom said but Selene edged past him without hitting him with her broadsword's handle.

"I've got it," Selene said and Thom didn't argue. "Where's the doors, Mindy?"

"Should be a rear entrance for the servants, but that's not gonna cut it," Melinda said. She whistled to Cherie and tossed her a bag. "Front of the Keep has two doors big enough for all of us just need to close it and barricade it before those cloaks show up."

"How're we getting out of here?" Cherie said.

"The good news is there's a boneyard of ships. People used to come up here and raise their loved ones and leave their ships as collateral. There's an old rail carrier depot at the bottom of the mountainside. Bad news is we just made an entrance and gahknows who heard us land. And if anyone is thinking about it: It's a five-minute air ride out of here. A two-hour rail ride or a six hour walk down the mountain-side plus another hour following the rail line and that's if someone with night vision doesn't grab you first," Melinda said and zipped up her borrowed duffle.

"Lovely happy thoughts, Mindy, thanks," Cherie said.

Melinda shrugged. "We resurrect 'em and wait for our ride to get fixed. Simple."

Everyone's laughter was silenced with Horatio's whistling.

"I need to talk to him." Horatio raised his voice.

Thom pointed at Horatio and Nat landed on the deck without missing beat. "While you guys do that, me, Pan, Alita and Vernon are going to check the ship," Nat said to Thom. "We'll keep you updated if anything changes out here." He eyed Horatio. "What do you want?"

"The network is compromised," Horatio said. "You can't use that damned badge of yours or the messenger bags or any of it. They'll know."

Nat chewed on that lovely piece of intel. "Well, that's good to know," he said and turned to Melinda. "You bring anything in that bag of yours?"

"No. But I can borrow one of Pan's servers. It'll be private, encrypted and running in a minute I just need a tall enough transmission tower," Melinda said.

"Good, Al, you're on boring roof detail. You haven't changed yet?" Nat said.

"Not after that little joyride and not ever," Alita said. "Just point me in the right direction."

Nat knelt in front of Horatio and Spence. "I apologize in advance," he said and multiple camera flashes blinded everyone. "Congratulations, everyone in the cabin is who you say you are."

"I said the network is compromised." Horatio rubbed his eyes.

"My own personally encrypted bugger files. Mister Crosleigh." Nat tapped the side of his brow. "You are the both the real deal. Mister Horatio Crosleigh, you have to check-in with the nearest House to update your death status and have six months decontamination to go through. Mister Spence MacGregor, once I get to House Encrypted Terminal, you'll be deemed alive and kicking. The debriefing for the both of you is going to take years until then," he pointed to Spence. "He's your baggage."

"Gladly," Spence said.

"Roark said to burn him," Melinda said. "They cracked him."

"Bound to happen sooner or later." Nat nodded slowly. "I'll do you one better. You have my permission to burn us all. Just in case anyone gets any bright ideas."

Spence cleared his throat. "Before we start off on this trek. I'd like to thank you for the rescue, all of you. I know you were probably doing more important things, but it means a lot."

"Minding the brats wasn't that important," Selene snickered.

Melinda poked Thom. "Please tell me you brought me something besides my stunner."

"Do you see the righteous mess you made of Pan's rear?" Thom dropped a bandoleer of stun rounds onto her bag. "Nope."

Melinda slugged his arm and shouldered the bandoleer. "All right, the cloaks haven't come through so let's stop wasting time. Follow Selene and watch your backs. Once we get through the front door, we're looking for the chapel and it should lead us to the caves. Last one inside buys the first round once we get back to Stow's End."

"Thanks, Mindy," Nat said.

"And find me a ship while you're at it; nothing fancy, just a pleasure yacht would be nice," she said.

"Don't push your luck," Pan muttered.

Selene picked up the chamber and rested it on her shoulder brought a hush over the cabin. "If someone can make pew pew sounds it'll make this walk a lot more interesting," she said and out the back she went amidst several pew pew sounds from Melinda and Cherie.

"You're grinning like an idiot," Thom said to Spence.

"No, I'm not, you are," Spence said.

~

Once Melinda's party had successfully disappeared into the Keep, Nat and Pan reconvened in the cockpit.

"You should go with them," Pan said.

"Not my fight," Nat said. "Besides, her little party isn't as little as it should be."

"You have any idea how much wanton destruction she's going to cause?" Pan said.

"If they knew any of us were here, we'd have been pulled out of the pool by now," Nat said and twisted the power dials. The cockpit's lightning dimmed. "I'm going to check the junk yard, you get Vernon working on stripping this thing. Once they find out we're here they're going to be looking for the shiniest thing in the yard and that lovely little ditch I just made is going to lead them right to us."

"Wait, you want us to what?" Vernon popped out of the now dimly lit doorway.

"If they're smart and they are. They're going to send a drone over. They're going to scrub every single frame and identify every single ship in the bone yard and when they see this little shining jewel they're going to know we're here," Nat said.

"If someone is already here they know we're here," Vernon countered.

Nat snickered. "Ground Operators don't move without orders. If the orders don't come in guess what they do? They sit back and wait for orders. The communication grid went down when that shockwave went through so guess what they have to do now?"

Vernon scowled. "Wait for orders?"

"Exactly. The good news is. We don't. So, you're going to help while I find us another aircraft to borrow for the time being. Once Mindy's server is up and running, Al can scout about and find the other entrance to this place because I know there are more around here. Once you guys strip her. I'll come get you to change aircraft."

"We can use this one. You didn't even crack the frame. She's flyable," Pan said.

"Yes, she's flyable as a decoy, but we need something with a little more oomph to her and out there." Nat stabbed a finger out at the darkness for extra emphasis. "There's at least three ships out there we can use. But odds are, we're going to need three of them as decoys and one to escape."

"What's the rush?" Vernon said.

"The rush?" Nat beckoned everyone down the stairs and leaned out the remains of the ship's rear ramp.

The star filled sky shone down on them. Crosleigh's Keep cut an angular silhouette across the horizon. There was nothing else in the air. The sound of aero mages' levitation spells was absent along with the constant whine of air carrier's propellers beating the air into submission.

The constant jingle of quills and the eerie light across the horizon.

"Can we talk about the giant explosion before we get to the Necros?" Vernon said.

"Wailing Seas Weapons Test Range is still out there, right?" Pan said.

"Around," Nat said. "Break-In goes wrong and poof or maybe someone cut into the underground mains to syphon off some juice. Find it really interesting it all happened at the exact same time we found them." Nat tossed a rock out into the dark. "The fact is we haven't gotten bum rushed, yet. So, they found another way in. And whoever else is already here hasn't found them or us, yet."

"Who else is here?" Pan said. "Why use Necros?"

"The same reason your brother created them in the first place: scare people out of their wits. We didn't splatter all over the defense wards when we came in so they're friendly, I hope," Nat said. "So, we got the Necros and someone else here, too. That's why Al is going to wander around in the dark until she finds them. Vernon, follow Pan's instructions to the letter and you'll both live through the night."

"Wait, what makes you so sure?" Vernon said.

Nat stepped off the ship and turned. "We have at least six houses or more in the same confined space. There're going to be two or three more by morning, you know what that means? It means they have enough to break the tie and vote. That means one or two Houses don't need to be here and mess with their plans so guess what happens then? Someone is going to point and one of us is going down and it's not going to be any of my friends. So, we're all making it back to Stow's End in one piece whether they like it or not. The good news is the Weaver is alive. The bad news is the Mad Stuk is dead. The good news is I managed to land us with no casualties. The bad news is the Necros came after us. The good news Mindy is here. The bad news is someone's trying to kill her and her entire family. See the balance? Someone went to an awful lot of trouble to balance today and so far, we haven't toppled over. Guess what happens when the Stuk rises up."

"Balance," Vernon said.

Nat tapped his nose. "Head of the class. His opposite number would be raised, too. Now, we all know whose side he's choosing. So, that means whoever else is running around is equal to him. But that also means what?"

"Deadlocked, again," Vernon said.

"Correct. Even odds on whoever successfully raised Horatio Crosleigh from the dead is the tie breaker," Nat said and wandered off into the night. "Now, help Pan because I've been wasting time since we landed."

~

The boneyard was meant to look like any other air carrier graveyard from the air but once you made it past the fence and around defense wards it was a different story. It wasn't a boneyard it was the highest vertical take-off and landing air strip on the Hollow. Most adventure seekers didn't make it past the fence Nat had plowed through and even those trained to avoid the wards didn't make it past the hidden traps some of the pilots had left behind.

The three ships Nat was looking for were in perfect working order. None of them had been touched. *They should be. Those defense wards cost a lot for them to stay out here just in case,* he thought. *We take off, one ship gets hit the other three are decoys while the fourth sits right here.*

The fourth didn't show up on radar or scanners because he had gotten her blessed by a Priestess of the Hills. Those blessings lasted forever so long as the priestess liked you. And the priestess liked him a lot, he was a passive aura wielder that rarely used his aura. Passive meant he didn't show up when a mage presented him, her or itself. It also meant he was a well of unrefined magic that in the right hands was an elixir.

And Gladys Stow had the right hands.

One of the wrecks was a lie. An old Valkyrie transport, double gull winged, two engines per wing. He sidestepped inside and counted to sixty, no sign of a tail he ducked the low ceiling. Through her insides, he hopped over support beams to the nose cone hatch. Both hands on the support bar, he lifted his legs and slid over the frame and into the claustrophobic bombardier station. The hidden biometric scanners did the rest. The station shuddered and descended into the darkness. It stopped, he rolled off and it closed itself behind him.

The hidden hangar was big enough to store four ships. For now, it held just three. It was exactly the way he had left it. Three dropships sat in their respective bays. One of them, a bare metal gull wing, two engine was completely covered in a tarp. She hadn't been used in years. The other one only consisted of a frame. Her hull and innards were strewn about the deck so haphazardly it would've made most people roll their eyes at the mess.

Yep, just the way I left it, he thought and turned to the third.

The heavy assault dropship, *Itty Bitty,* sat in the middle of the hangar. Twice the size of the Pan's ship, she had the extra oomph he was looking for. Iron plating for mage attacks. Tail, waist, top and ball turret along with nose gunnery positions for the dog fights in the air. Cargo bay for transporting APC on lower deck with an upper cabin for crew of twelve. VOTL propeller engines on either side of the gull wings and several surprises that no one else knew about. Her defense wards were standard, but the extra oomph was the blessing Gladys had given, sure it had knocked him out for a week, but *Itty Bitty* came and went like the wind.

He walked around her and listened to every single defense ward hum... except one.

A camo cloak sidestepped in front of Nat and he back pedaled into another one.

The one behind nudged him towards the front of the hangar where a lovely set of legs lounged on the beat-up sofa. The woman that belonged to the legs was clothed in a beat-up cloak, sharp features, dark eyes with dark hair held back by quills that only looked like hair sticks. The Death Boots and stealth suit she gussied herself into meant Kristie Brie was serious.

"Nice landing," she said and pushed herself out of the sofa. "Where is he?"

"Who?" Nat said and looked at the two cloaks. "Since when do you outsource?"

"The Necros aren't with me. Someone else is using them," Kristie said. "Where is he?"

"Who are we talking about?" Nat said.

"You know exactly who I'm talking about." Kristie closed the distance and pointed a finger. "Do not red team me. Not tonight of all nights."

"Can we go back to why you managed to find my secret hideout?" Nat said.

"Oh, it's not that much of a secret, everyone knows you're up here," Kristie spat. "He gave me the password the last time we talked." She glanced at *Itty Bitty*. "Someone's over compensating."

"It's called being prepared," he said. "And, to answer your question: The Mad Stuk's chamber and sword are with Mindy."

A sigh escaped Kristie's lips, but she choked. "Mindy? She's on Gunna."

"She, the MacGregor Brothers along a few others are currently making their way down into the caves to resurrect the Mad Stuk," Nat said.

Kristie gaped. "The MacGregors're dead."

"Nope," Nat said. "Horatio and Spence are alive. You didn't know?"

Kristie cursed. "He pulled her down here, didn't he? I connected him for five minutes and he did this."

"Connected him to what, exactly?" Nat said. "What've you been doing out here, Brie? And why is Roark dead?"

"Wait, what're you even doing here? You're grounded," Kristie said.

"Pan got called in for a private charter by Thom Stuk to pick up Mindy. We got to them before the light show went off," Nat said. "I needed the flight time, she needed a co-pilot and here we are. What did you connect him to, Brie."

"There's a safe house beneath the statue. I had to get him into the chamber before whatever piece of his soul lost itself," Kristie said. "The chamber was already connected to the network."

Nat nodded. "He pulled Mindy down here. That's why Spence didn't land at Goslin Grace as planned. He said something about a short circuit. You were following us?"

"No, I was headed back to buy myself passage back out here with a crew and all of sudden you showed up," Kristie said. "The candles should've kept him stable. Wait, Roark isn't dead."

Nat looked her over. "Tell me something, what do you know about a Daire engine mount S-Cutting off planet and into the New Welles Asteroid Belt about a year or so back."

Kristie frowned. "What engine mount?"

"After the bug out, Roark went missing along with half the other families. I tracked him to a bar, but I missed him by five minutes. I got to the engine mount just as it jumped and when it came back he wasn't on board. Now, all of sudden he's dead and Mindy is sword carrying his soul along with escorting his chamber."

Kristie waved her hand so he'd slow down. "What engine mount?"

"The same one attached to Spence MacGregor's shuttle. The same one Mindy found six months after Thom found it. Someone's trying to get off this rock and they're doing a good job at it," Nat said. "I need to know where you were a year ago, six months ago and tonight because right now you're looking awful guilty."

"Excuse me?" Kristie advanced. "You don't get to talk to me like that."

"I do when I see Brie House has all but disappeared over the range and you haven't checked in for months. I can't get in contact with Barien Brie. I only ask because the network's compromised so who's in your ear?" Nat said and pointed to her earbud.

"Since when is the network compromised?" Kristie said.

"Horatio told me. No badges. No bags. Nobody in your ear until we find out what's going on," Nat said and jerked around. "Uh, oh."

"What?" Kristie said and was blown back into the couch.

The two cloaks whirled around but immediately crumpled to the floor.

A shapely figure in a camo loomed over their squirming bodies. A jerk of the head, the hood pulled back and Alita's head appeared.

"She tells me to look for you and here you are." Alita grabbed Nat by the shirt front. "You're involved with them?"

"She's a friend of the family," Nat wheezed.

"Oh, of course the little pin cushion is a friend. Just like the hidden hangar that I couldn't even see until I dropped in," Alita snapped.

"I'm telling her, you're a friend. Don't do it, Brie." Nat craned his neck around to the couch. "She's a friend and she didn't mean it."

"I certainly did too mean it," Alita said. "Who are you working for!"

"Seriously, she's a friend. She came with me and Pan to get Mindy. Don't do anything stupid," Nat howled.

Alita blinked and leaned around him. "Where'd she go?" She released him and pulled her sword. "Where is she?"

"Just lower that tooth pick of yours and she won't hurt you. She's better at this game of hide and go seek than you are, trust me," Nat said.

Kristie sidestepped out of thin air in front of Alita. "No hard feelings." She pivoted, extended her leg and round house kicked Alita across the bay. "Now, we're square." She turned to Nat. "What's the plan?"

Nat sighed at the mess. "While we wait for the Weaver to raise Roark, we have Al in the bell tower looking to see who else is here. We wait for the ruckus to die down and land back at Stow's End. Hunker down at Sleepless Maiden and rail carrier back into Goslin Grace."

Kristie laughed at that. "And if that doesn't happen?" she said.

"We improvise just like we always do," Nat said. "Somebody doesn't want your ex reporting in. Maybe he's got intel that they're willing to put this much trouble and effort into. That means it's bad. Worst case scenario, Al brings Roark back to Clarence and waves the house warrant that's on file. The debrief room records are just as good as After-Action Reports. Once you start a stir like this, all the Houses must react no matter how slow they are. Instead of stopping them with brute force, we just kill 'em with paperwork."

"Sorry, but none of that works for us," Kristie said and shot Nat.

PART II

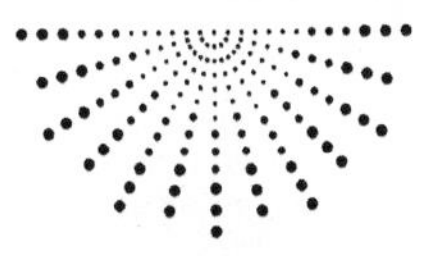

10
CROSLEIGH KEEP

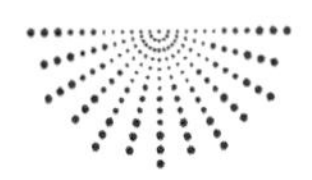

"WHAT WAS THAT?" MELINDA SAID.

"What?" Thom said.

Melinda stuck a pinky in her ear and twisted her earbud about. "Thought I heard something," she said and glanced about the pea green, two-dimension view of the hallway.

The lamps in the walls hadn't been scavenged. The fray carpet was covered in dust but still there and the picture frames along with the walls showing each generation of the Crosleigh family that had stayed at the Keep were still preserved behind the shatter proof glass. The chandelier on the ceiling was still intact.

All in all, the Keep was just as the previous occupants had left it, which left a nagging feeling in Melinda's stomach. Why are the doors unlocked, but the place hasn't been sacked yet?

"Which way we going, Melinda?" Thom said.

Melinda knelt onto the floor and everyone gathered around. She drew one circle then another one surrounding it. She stabbed the center circle. "This is the chapel. It leads down into the caves and the resurrection chambers." She stabbed the outside circle. "We're here. Barracks. Meeting Hall. Kitchen. Dormitories." She pointed a stone outside the circles. "We landed here." She drew a triangle. "We're at the top. We're going down."

"No elevator?" Selene said.

Melinda turned to Spence.

The Weaver chuckled. "Reserved for the Necromancer and the family. Hopefully, we'll get lucky."

Melinda pointed to the far end of the corridor. "That way until we reach an exterior door. Then look for the giant building with all the spikes."

"Spikes?" Selene said.

"Conduits for the souls," Spence said. "The buildings purify the energy before reaching the host."

Selene nodded and hefted the chamber. "Your family and mine have wildly different uses for those spikes."

Horatio shuddered while Spence laughed. "Yes, I remember."

"I'll go first with Selene, Tom takes up the rear. Cherie in the middle with the brothers," Melinda said and she set off down the corridor with Selene at her heels.

~

The doors to the chapel were open much to Melinda's dismay. She tweaked her goggles a bit more and even with the advance electronics the scanners didn't come back with anything moving. The fact the electronic signature of the entire area gave off nothing just didn't sit well with her at all.

"He said there were life signs, but even I would've left someone to guard the entrance," Melinda said. "Nothing."

"I don't smell anything either," Selene said. "Sword would've said something by now."

"I'm not being paranoid, am I?" Melinda said.

"If this was a trap, I'd wait until we were all inside then spring it," Selene said. "No way to escape once I barred the doors from the outside."

"This is why I keep you around for lovely nightmares like that."

Melinda craned her head to the spikes. "Always take the high ground. Nobody."

Selene smiled in the dark. "You did remember all those exercises I gave you."

"Only needed to get caught in a trap once. Once." Melinda turned to the group. "Thom, you're in first, brothers, Cherie, me and Selene."

Thom moved up and tapped the doorframe. He leaned in, shotgun pointed skyward then down and disappeared across the threshold. The brothers went next, Cherie clutched her spell book and followed with Selene next followed by Melinda.

The wooden doors behind her didn't slam shut much to her surprise.

~

The candle lit chapel eased Melinda's nerves, but three-story vaulted ceilings with stained glass windows and uncomfortable wooden pews just meant there were more places to hide. The odd thing that stood out was the folded clothes that littered about the place. Clothes at the front of the sanctuary and cursed/blessed items near the entrance they had just passed through.

At the front of the sanctuary where the pulpit should've been there was instead a giant hole in the floor. Next to the hole was a cloaked figure with a winged Totem Animus perched on its shoulder.

Thom raised a closed fist, and everyone stopped.

The animus head swiveled a hundred eighty degrees, its big purple eyes focused on them. It stretched out it's small wings and shook its white, downy feathers. Its beak clicked together once or twice but did nothing else.

"Lovely trap," Selene hissed and lowered the chamber to the ground. "No house colors on the birdie and that's a mannequin."

Thom tapped his goggles. "I noticed, thanks." He lowered his shotgun and edged closer to the birdie. He extended an arm and the birdie fluffed its wings again only to hop onto his arm. "My name is

Thom Stuk. We're escort detail for the Mad Stuk's resurrection. May we pass?"

The birdie's beak clicked but said nothing.

Melinda tweaked her goggles, but nothing came up with red flags. "Hey, Cherie. Switch places with me, I need your spell book."

"For what?" Cherie said.

"You'll get it back in a moment, trade ya." Melinda dropped the bandolier over Cherie shoulders and accepted the book. "Time to play a game of guess who."

Cherie groaned. "I hate this game. You always win."

"No. You always win. They think you're me and I'm you. So, stop slouching, stand up straight and pulled down those goggles."

"I don't need them," Cherie said. "My vision is fine."

"The less they know about you the better. Now, you may be able to see fine in the dark, but you don't need to announce yourself so suck it up, ram rod straight and go mosey around like you're looking for something. Hand on the stunner at all times." Melinda slouched. "I'll be in the back you in the front."

"Gahsakes, you're really blind, aren't you?" Cherie said and tinkered with settings. She straightened up and moseyed past the group.

Melinda reached the back of the cathedral when the sound of boot footfalls hushed her. Three mages dropped from the second-floor balcony and surrounded the group.

Another group of three rushed across the room from the back of the cathedral. Two men and one woman. Their clothing was a mix mash of military camouflage and cloak. The rushers were armed with iron throwing weapons.

The flapping of wings pulled her attention away to the Totem Animus, an extension of one of mages and had settled atop her head. It smiled down at her only for its small beak to screech to its master.

"Hey, who's back there?" one of the mage's echoed. "Don't move!"

Melinda pointed at the animus. "Hey, I will have you know I'm a founding member of the local Animus adoption shelter! Hush! Shoo!"

~

"The local what?" Spence said.

"Gunna Space Station Animus Adoption Agency," Melinda said and stroked the animus' furry head carefully.

"Since when do mages let their Animi go free?" Spence said.

"When the Houses agreed that it was time to phase out the mages and let the local security forces protect the Houses," Melinda said.

Spence sucked air through his teeth. "That type of thinking never bodes well."

"Stukari Holdings Operators have been doing a pretty good job since they made a deal with the mages to hire them. A certain Mister Stukari has been more than welcoming." Melinda leaned back in the pew they'd been escorted too.

The animus re-adjusted itself, so it was atop her shoulder instead of her arm.

"Which is why I find it slightly hard to believe he's trying to kill us," she said.

"Wait, mages can just pull their Animi back into their aura, why is there an Adoption Agency?" Spence said.

"The Houses phased out the mages as security and tacked on a bill to shutter the local training facility for mage adepts. This little one is probably from one of the old aviary academies and found its way here," she said.

The animus snapped its beak once.

"You're just full of surprises, aren't you?" Spence said and glanced at the gaping hole in the floor. "You going to explain why you want to get out of here?"

The animus snapped its beak at him twice.

"Don't you start, too." Spence pointed at it and it immediately latched onto his fingertip.

Melinda wagged a finger. "Careful. I can command them to do my bidding."

Spence growled, and the animus released his digit. It flapped its wings and settled down.

"You recognize anyone?" Spence said to Thom.

"No, but most of the Tier One Mage Operators didn't run in the same circles," Thom said. "Phineas and Terrie Leighton, I recognize. Harry's uncle and aunt."

The animus snapped its beak once.

"Harry?" Spence said.

"Horatio Leighton," Melinda said. "I couldn't pronounce Horatio when we were growing up, but I could pronounce Harry."

Spence laughed. "Horatio, really. I didn't think we left that much of an impression on Alex."

"Some of us did," Horatio said.

One of the mages, a magess popped out of the hole, layered in cobwebs and dust. She shook herself off and stopped short when she caught sight of them. She stalked over and pointed to Melinda. She was aforementioned Terrie Leighton.

"What did I tell you about staying put," she said. "How're you even here. I left you guarding the kids and now you're here?"

"Sorry." Melinda shrugged and kept her head down.

"Not this time. When we get back I'm talking to whoever is in your House and getting you re-assigned," Terrie scoffed and walked away.

"Same ole Terrible Terrie," Spence said, but Terrie jerked around and pointed a finger at him.

"I don't know who you think you are but..." Terrie blinked and squinted in the low light. "What?!?" she glared at Horatio and kicked his shins. "How long were you going keep me in the dark? We thought you all got blown up and then someone did a deep scan of the complex."

"So, you went to get the sword while she went to get, what, the body?" Spence said.

"Something like that," Horatio said. "Terrie, Spence MacGregor. Selene Finnegan. We've got the chamber as planned."

Terrie reached out and grabbed Melinda's chin and raised it. "Melinda."

Melinda grinned sheepishly. "Hi."

Terrie released her and pointed to Cherie, directly in the pew behind her. "And you shouldn't even be here."

"Blame me. I called them up," Thom said. "Don't blame her. Blame me."

Terrie growled. "I'm not even talking to you. You were banished. How'd you even get down here, you know what, I don't even want to know." She stalked away to Phineas and animated explained what little she knew.

Spence scratched his chin. "Let me guess, Thom used to use pair off with her."

"No, I lost the pool on them." Melinda shrugged off Thom's look. "Big space station. Thin walls."

"Leightons haven't been front line House for years," Spence said.

"There was a void to fill when Daire House decided to get out of the pool," Melinda said.

Spence frowned. "That's not funny, Mindy."

"Whose says I'm being funny. They got out, worst silent coup ever," she said.

Spence leaned closer. "Coup? What coup? No, wait," he turned to Horatio. "Explain to me what's going on before Terrie boots us all."

~

"Wait, Horatio was named after him?" Melinda said.

"Yes," Spence and Horatio said.

Horatio snickered and shrugged off his cloak. "Sorry, it's all just for show. Grave robbers are getting braver these days. No hug for your older brother for all time sake?"

"You were born an hour after me, Lord Crosleigh. How?" Spence seethed.

"Thirty years ago, his lord and master invaded and he got promoted," Melinda said.

"That was my predecessor," Horatio said. "He's the one to blame for your banishment not me."

Oh? Spence turned to Melinda, but she greeted him with nothing but silence.

"Miss Stuk has a House warrant. Immediate banished from the Hollow. You didn't tell him?" Horatio said. "Dear brother, where've you been? Some of us have been looking for you."

"You're the one who hacked my pod," Spence said.

Horatio laughed. "No. All that keyboard jockey work isn't me. However, all the book research is why. Lovely little light show my friends gave us, wasn't it?"

"We are acknowledging the giant explosion, then?" Melinda said.

"Unfortunately, I am but no one else will because I sent them on that merry little chase," Horatio said.

"Who else is here besides us?" Spence said. "Where did you send them?"

"My former employers didn't listen to my warnings and if we're quiet whoever's left of their merry little band won't find us," Horatio said. "I need your help. Both of you."

Melinda bounced to her feet. "After all you've done, why would I help you?" she said.

"Because we both know Thom didn't stage any of this and if my contacts are right, my former lord's merry little band will be here soon. Friends I have no need to cross. I need your help with something and in return I'll ignore that you were ever here."

Spence coughed.

"Help you with what?" Melinda croaked.

"I need to save a man and the only way to do that is to resurrect him," Horatio said.

Spence laughed, chortled and quieted down. "Sure, you are, Harry."

Horatio continued unabated. "My former employers were looking for a resurrection cave. Their lord and master is dying but no one helped so in his weakness turned to someone I didn't trust. They're the ones I sent off on a fool's errand. My contact was supposed to meet me here but as you can see, it's just us. All of these facts don't bode well for our heroes."

"Who am I raising?" Spence said.

"I sent for one via messenger and all I got was reamed out for it by my new friends," Horatio said. "That's how I knew the network was compromised."

Melinda scowled. "When in doubt, wait at the head end and decrypt the messages before they even get to recipients. Smart move."

"Oh, on that point we are all in completely agreement. Funny story, Spence and I started off as messengers. And, since you're in line for an attaché position with your grand uncle, we all know how encrypted those messenger bags are, don't we?" Horatio said. "I've kept my head down and so far, I seem to be keeping five steps ahead of them."

"Ahead of who?" Spence said. "What's so damned important? Wait, why do I even care?"

"I crossed paths with Mister Leighton and I accepted his request to bring the body here. After my dress down, we started gathering mages and Stukari Holdings Operators we could trust. We've been off the grid for three days and were making good time until my maps split in two. One led here and the other to chamber. My previous employers had that little accident then you two just dropped in."

"They'll going to be looking for a body, Harry," Spence said.

Horatio waggled a finger and winked. "Not if I already gave them a body."

Spence eyed Horatio and then Phineas. "Who is it?" he said.

"No names," Horatio said.

"No one is that special," Spence said.

"He's just an acquired taste," Horatio said. "I need you to heal him nothing more."

"Heal him? Anyone can do that," Spence said. "And what do you mean no names?"

"Everyone else aren't you." Horatio tugged at Spence's cloak. "You were a House Weaver for years. Hiding in plain sight with the rest of Necromancers. You have your cloak and book. They chose you because you remember the old ways. You could've had your own House and got entangled in all the backstabbers but instead off to the Academy you went yet the backstabbers followed you. They're all dead and you're still standing. No, I don't need anyone else but you, dear brother. No one else will understand."

"Who is he?" Spence said.

"Kaare Daire," Horatio said.

Spence jerked around, and Melinda's jaw dropped. "The Daire Devil is dead," Spence said.

Horatio smiled. "Oh, quite dead. Mister Leighton found him. We were five minutes ahead of whoever else was looking. We've been following Miss Stuk's maps ever since and here we are."

"And Crosleigh's Caves are the only free resurrection chambers left on the planet," Melinda said. "Mad Stuk's sword was just guarding the chamber. Why didn't I see it?"

Horatio grinned and thumbed to her. "See, kids these days don't even remember details like that. You're worth everything I've gone through to get to this very moment."

"Harry, stop buttering her up," Spence said. "Kaare's dead."

"Yes, presumed dead. Just like you and I. Missing. Overdue. Bound to a cursed carrier never to make port only to be lost at sea until his unending burden is sated. Now, just a myth told when the sea of stars grows dark and those sensor ghosts just seem a wee bit too organized. Reportedly holed up on a barren world so far off the maps even the craziest of carrier drivers wouldn't dare try to find him," Horatio said. "They found him first, only for Mister Leighton and me to scurry away because we remember what he did for us. They've been chasing us ever since until someone put 'em into a wall."

"Not it," Melinda said.

"We didn't say it was you, Mindy," Spence said but the silence from Horatio stopped him.

"Are you sure it wasn't you?" Horatio said.

Melinda jerked her head at Spence. "I was with him and no access to the network. Wait, you just said you did it."

"No, he said he just sent them on a fool's errand. He didn't say anything about blowing them up," Spence said. "Harry, you didn't actually find him, he's dead."

Horatio approached the chamber. He traced a finger across its etchings. "I am sorry about your friend, Mindy, but he believed like I did that Kaare needed to rise. The Mad Stuk sacrificed himself to save this chamber from what happened to the rest."

"The 'rest?'" Spence's voice cracked.

"Someone's been destroying chambers across the Hollow. I think they were looking for something. Something your friend found and felt it needed protecting," Horatio said and paced around the chamber. "Odd, it doesn't have a House seal on it."

And where are they now, exactly? Spence thought idly. "What're they looking for?"

Terrie shrugged. "I don't know, but they've been going to every estate sale across the Hollow."

"Mindy, can you read the inscription?" Horatio said.

"Read it yourself," Spence said.

"I can't read Stuk, but she can." Horatio grabbed torch and shone it down on the stone edifice. "Please, indulge me."

"What's the harm." Melinda shrugged and grabbed the torch out of his hand. She knelt and rubbed off the layers of sand on the side of the chamber but revealed nothing.

Phineas Leighton cleared his throat and handed her a torch that blossomed with a green and pink flame. "Try this," the mage intoned.

Melinda accepted the torch and the wall of the chamber glistened and familiar writing appeared. "There are some old etchings here. Burned into the iron. Whoever built this chamber made sure the etchings illuminate if a certain spell was next to it," Melinda said.

"That's a big leap," Spence's sotto voice said.

Melinda leaned back, and the etchings disappeared only to reappear when she drew near. "Hypothesis confirmed. What spell is this?" she said but Phineas was silent.

"What does it say?" Horatio said.

Melinda opened her mouth, but the chamber dragged itself across the floor, missed Terrie and tumbled into the void.

"Oh, no, we're so not going down for it," Terrie groaned.

~

Spence knelt at the hole. "I think it wants to be down there."

"Whatever's left down there. I've got it all mapped. We just need to find the entrance," Melinda said.

"But something is down there," Spence mused. "Cartography is why you got banished?"

"Not exactly," she said.

"We need a moment alone and a liaison," Spence said.

"You're right one of my liaisons should've been here by now," Horatio said.

"Your liaison?" Spence scoffed.

"Yes, I have a liaison. I did run your House while you off doing whatever," Horatio said.

"Teaching at the Academy. Only to come home to clean up your mess," Spence said but dismissed the oncoming argument with a wave and dragged Melinda towards the piles of clothes.

Spence paced down isle after isle of clothes until he peeled left.

"We're ignoring the chamber then?" Melinda said. "What does it mean? Are you scared?"

"Do I look scared to you?" Spence said and paced down another isle and back.

"Yes, you do. What does it mean?" she said.

Spence stopped in front of her and clutched her shoulders. "Kaare Daire's House was something you should never see in your lifetime. None of you should see what he's capable of. I've been to places he's left in his wake, Mindy. They left him out in the cold for a reason."

"Really?" Melinda crossed her arms. "You haven't seen what they've done to his House."

"He didn't deserve a House not after what he did to my mine," Spence hissed.

"I know he found you on a plague carrier and tried his best to save your family only to fail because there was nothing left. Your family had saved you because they knew you'd survive. That you'd remember them and their ways," Melinda said.

Spence breathed in and his aura cooled. "Do you even know the meaning of the word: Classified?"

"We've been read in, in case one of us finds you," she said. "We know you two don't get along but what you don't know is how bad it's gotten in his absence."

Spence stared her down and extended a hand. "Fine. I'll give him the benefit of the doubt. But the first time he goes off on some blood thirsty crusade, it's on you."

Melinda smiled and shook. "Deal."

Spence handed her two-discarded duffle bags. "Hold this one," he said. "Look for clothes that are blessed but aren't bound to a House," Spence said. He draped tops and bottoms over his shoulders. "Wait, you shouldn't even know what a go bag is."

"Tommy taught me to always pack one in case of the worst," she said.

Spence twisted her around. "Tommy read you in on me? Whose 'we?'"

"Remember the coup with the Daires I mentioned. No one seemed to care except my family. We became public enemy number one," she said.

"What about Charles and Lauren?" Spence said.

"Haven't seen 'em in years. The local Daire House lord is bent," she said and parsed out clothes between their duffle bags. "I think I found some clothes that will fit me."

"Give me the short version," he said.

"On the tenth anniversary of the last House war, I was working on a data reclamation project on the edge of Wailing Seas. Somebody had found an old Keep and needed help translating. While we're out there, a banished Stuk was granted amnesty to bury his father the war hero. Rumor is a misunderstanding between him and a local lord kicked off a forty-eight-hour ground war across the Hollow. In the end, he was granted what remained of his father's House but in the meantime, the project I was on got too much heat and then the Daire coup, I got banished," she said.

"How? There's paperwork to file. War Reparations," Spence rattled off.

"Now, you sound like my sister-in-law," she said. "The paperwork went through clean."

Spence dropped his head into his hands. "Gahsakes. Everyone signed off on it?"

"Not my exact words," she said and turned him around. "How does this look?"

Spence laughed at the two-sizes too big, white Acolyte robe. "Stretch out your arms above your head. The fabric needs to memorize you."

Melinda clasped her hands over her head. "Semi sentient clothing is creepy."

"If it saves from a through and through, it can be creepy all it wants," Spence said. "I'm only angry with who the Mad Empress Daire used to serve. We buried her and her House's burdens. Legends like them are supposed to be just that until they become myths only to then pass into memory."

She poked a finger at his chest. "The problem is you're supposed to be swept under the rug so my generation doesn't go off and do something stupid like hitchhike through a Forbidden Coil and find four missing Houses."

"It was *three*. Your brother exaggerates. A lot," Spence said. "There's more, isn't there?"

"You tell me. I was insulated or at least I thought I was," she said. "The old keep was a fully functional War Keep."

That explains why Terrie is here, recon, Spence thought. "What else are we missing?"

"I've been gone for ten years. Judging from the warm welcome we got along with Emperor Leighton sending his only kids down here for recon," she said. "I'd say a lot."

"I have no idea what you're talking about," he said nonchalantly.

Melinda snickered. "Yeah, that's what Tommy said. Glad to see we're all on the same page. It all goes back to that gahforsaken engine mount."

Spence sighed. "You've gone from being on the hook to being in the mine."

"I passed my tests. No one knows I'm here. No backup. It's just me," she said.

"You just described an Academy Pre-Test for early admission," Spence said.

"I have no idea what you're talking about," Melinda said nonchalantly. "I dunno what's taking Alita so long. If they find us, they'll boot me. I haven't a clue what they'll do to you, but I think the faster we get away from your brother the better."

"The network is down so we're all deaf, dumb and blind. Typical Stukari move," he said and stared down at her. "What else haven't you told me?"

"It's a long, boring story, but it's time to help yer hapless but cute brother," Melinda said.

"He neither that hapless nor cute and don't believe a word he says," he growled.

"Jealousy gets your aura up you know that, always in the eyes," she said and patted his arm. "His cloak is prettier than yours. Every mage goes through cloak envy sooner or later."

"He hides it well, doesn't he?" the mask clicked. "I don't think your brother is alone."

"On that point, we're in complete agreement," Spence said. "And where've you been?"

"Conserving power and monitoring," the mask said. "We may have unexpected guests arriving soon."

"We go down there and there'll be no turning back. Take it from someone who's been digging in the sand. Nothing stays hidden on this planet for long," Melinda said.

"There's an old House saying, enjoy this for you have five minutes to live," he said.

"The Weaver and his Apprentice has arrived." She twisted her tongue down and bowed.

Spence rubbed the bridge of his nose. "You really shouldn't know those words. They banned those propaganda filled books for good reason, Mindy."

She nudged him towards his approaching brother and flipped up her hood. "Stay alive long enough and I'll show you more words I shouldn't," she said.

Horatio cleared his throat. "Are you running or staying?"

"Staying," Spence growled. "Harry, what've you actually gotten yourself into?"

"We found his body. I think you found his aura. He needs to be whole," Horatio said.

"That's it? He can do it his own damned self," Spence said.

"It has to be here and by your book. No one else needs to be involved." Horatio jerked his head back towards the hall's entrance and raised his voice. "Just heal him, mage."

Spence pointed at him but couldn't begin to argue. Instead, the wind changed direction. He winced at the overpowering scent of iron. A squad of six Marauder Operators in cursed leathers passed with armbands of green and yellow effortlessly onto the hall's threshold.

They surrounded the one in charge. She was dressed appropriately for a Lady on holiday, but the more Spence focused on her blessed hand-woven boots, chaps, blouse, jacket, hat and duffle bags made his eyes water. They may have been dust covered and cracked from constant use, but they could stop any of the iron rounds in those drum rifles the Operators carried.

"Bring him," she said without turning or lowering her bags.

Two Necrocloaks carried in a bound body wrapped in a bloody bed sheet.

Spence pulled Horatio away. "What in gahsakes took a bite out of him?"

"There was an accident," the Lady said, and Spence jerked around at her too silent approach. She extended a gloved hand. "Lord Crosleigh's luck is getting better. My name is Lady Lauren Daire and if you don't heal this man everyone on this planet is going to die."

Spence grasped her hand. "Spence MacGregor of the Cross and I'm at your service."

11

DAIRE TELL NO TALES

MELINDA TOSSED ANOTHER PAIR OF NOISE DAMPENING HEADSET INTO the pile. "Ah ha!" she said and pulled out a pair that matched the goggles Spence had given her. "These should work." She pulled the goggles down around her eyes and a pairing icon vanished before she could blink. "Create private channel for myself and user: MacGregor, Spence."

The headset chimed once to note it had successfully done so.

"—discretion is needed." A woman's voice blasted in her ears and Melinda tapped the volume button to a reasonable level.

"I understand completely," Spence said.

"How long will it take to remove the hex?" the woman said.

Why do I know that voice? Melinda frowned and paced around several piles of clothes. The hall was too long. The shadows too deep. The lightning wasn't bright enough for her to get a good eye line on the woman talking to Spence.

"We'll need to find consecrated ground first it'll weaken the spell," Spence said. "Lord Crosleigh may've found something beneath us. We're looking for an entrance now."

The woman chuckled. "The hole in the floor was a nice touch."

"The hole is also getting smaller," the mask clicked. "And Melinda has created a private channel to talk."

Damn, Melinda thought. *Wait, the hole is getting smaller?*

"Tell 'em we're pretty sure the hole isn't the way in and the defense wards are closing the damages someone else made," she said and blanched at the proximity warning that splashed across the lenses. "Switch to passive mode."

The fog of war on the sensor circle closed in to less than five feet in every direction.

"Anything else, Mindy?" Spence hissed.

"The plate was right. We may have company. I'm going to send you a private channel invite. Go to every single person and give it to them," she said.

"Send them an invite, it's faster," Spence said.

"Al still hasn't set up my network yet. If the network is down, then how am I talking to you?" Melinda said and brushed passed an Operator. "We're using someone else's network and it's not mine. I've got the two near the door. You get the rest. We need a headcount." She switched over to the group channel. "Everyone tag a buddy and make sure this channel stays encrypted. I need names and faces from everyone."

The fog of war circle grew back to its original size and several green and blue circles appeared but outside the hall was still dark.

Green for Stukari Holdings. Blue for mage, Melinda thought. "Tag myself and Spence in white. Anyone else not in the group tag as hostile red." She switched over to the private channel. "Tell 'em we'd better hurry it along, your apprentice said so," Melinda said and ducked down an isle of clothes that were most certainly military grade judging from the amount of static that filled her lenses. "Do me a favor and hack user: Crosleigh, Horatio gear."

The headset pinged happily.

Gahsakes, that was too quick. Melinda thought. She grabbed a toppled mannequin and quickly dressed it in robes similar to her own.

"Mindy, we may have found the key to get in," Spence said.

I should be happier, but something doesn't feel right, Melinda thought and tripped over something. She got to her feet and looked down at the empty ground. The empty ground. She knelt and tweaked the settings on the goggles until a box appeared.

Property of Daire House. Camouflage cloak. Melinda read silently. She popped the seals to find a fully functioning military-grade camo cloak. "Anyone within ten feet of me?" she said.

The headset pinged twice.

"And the rafters?" Melinda said.

The headset pinged twice, again.

Key for what? Melinda thought and shrugged into the cloak. She stretched about and as advertised it disappeared against her frame. "Wait, who gave you a key?" she said.

"He did," Spence said. "He's asking for you."

"Whose asking for me?" Melinda threw up her hands at the shoddy work, but the existence of a key was nagging at her. She jogged up the isle until she was at the front of the hall where the group had gathered around someone wrapped in a bed sheet of all things.

The lack of blood wasn't disturbing to her. It was the fact the goggles were throwing a hissy fit the closer she got. She pulled them down in time for Spence and Phineas to part. An iron necklace with a metal keycard the size of her fist was wrapped around his neck kept the bed sheet secure.

"Careful, Mindy," Spence said. "He's been hexed."

"He said you'll need this," Phineas said.

It's an old House key card, Melinda thought and didn't budge but the key had her full attention. "Where did he get that?"

"It will get you into the Crosleigh Caves," a woman's voice said from behind her and Melinda turned around to face down a well-dressed Lady.

"For your services, Lady Daire will be more than happy to provide that for your substantial reward," Horatio droned on, but Melinda raised a hand to stop him.

"I need to talk to the dead Lady before we go anything further," Melinda growled.

"She's right in front of you, Mindy," Spence said.

Melinda extended a hand and twisted her tongue down. "Meylandra Stuk. Who be you and who do you serve?"

~

The Lady was unfazed, much to Melinda's annoyance. "You're taller than I expected."

"And you're surprisingly alive," Melinda retorted, hand still extended. "Whoever you are."

"It took me three months to travel undercover to get down here, and you just show up. Pack it up, Harry, and be prepared to run," the Lady said. "You know who I am, Mindy."

"It's a simple search. No one knows we're down here," Horatio said.

"The problem is word of mouth travels faster even without the network," Melinda said and didn't lower her hand. "Lady Lauren Daire hasn't been seen in years and all of sudden you just pop up. Explain to me where you've been for the past thirty years. Or is fifty or is it hundred? Funny how we both just show up at the same time and no one knew I was coming."

"There isn't some conspiracy, Mindy," the Lady said.

"Says the one who let her sister, nieces, and nephews die," Melinda said.

"Mindy," Thom hissed.

"Your next words best be 'I'm sorry for talking ill of the dead,'" the Lady growled.

"They won't, and I don't care," Melinda said. "Whoever you are."

A fiery aura surged up from the woman's stomach but receded quickly.

Phineas stepped forward, but Melinda wagged a finger.

"Your one and only sister, your brother-in-law and three nephews buried this very night. You disappeared and all of sudden, here you are," Melinda said.

"The same could be said about you," Phineas said.

"My House isn't burning to the ground, Magi." Melinda twisted her tongue close to a Leighton dialect that immediately got his attention. "My family hasn't disappeared off coil and terra. You did a real good job; even I couldn't find you. You've had professional help. And not from one of your sponsors since they're bent idiots burning down the last House of O'Hare. Explain why the next in line for the throne, Narelle, my best friend is missing? Someone thought she was like the rest and gave her a bad day, but they got more than they bargained for. So, don't point that finger at me."

"Mindy," Spence, Thom, Selene and Cherri said.

Phineas said nothing, but the wall of a mage now had a wall of an aura spun up that seethed off his shoulders.

"They went after your stepson instead so if you really must know, I'm here for him. You shouldn't even be here." Melinda thumbed to the body. "That's his body?"

"He's none of your concern," the Lady said evenly.

"Same as -" Melinda didn't finish, the woman's hand gripped her throat.

"You speak their names aloud and I'll forget the fact your grandfather was kind to my grandmother once," the Lady growled in a tongue that made even the Necrocloaks shudder.

"Charles. Louis. Jericho and Rey," Melinda managed. "You're the last one left. You understand that Lauren Ohari? They're framing you for the death of your House. I know they're not dead. I know Narelle isn't dead. I know we can save them."

"They're dead," the Lady spat. "I buried them myself!"

"No. They're not dead. You buried a lie. I know what happened to your family. Now. Let me go or you'll never find them," Melinda wheezed.

"Enough. Both of you." A deep baritone tongue shook the floor. "Release her, Lauren."

Melinda landed into a pile clothes and staggered to her feet to find the body on its own much to everyone's shock.

"If you're toying with me. I've burned people for less, Stuk Witcha," the Lady spat.

"Enough bickering, Lauren Ohari. It's cost us too much time.

Meylandra's right, someone followed you down here. They're doubling back." A gnarled hand detached the key from its neck and flung it at Melinda. "Find the door and open it before it's too late."

~

"Was that really necessary?" Phineas said.

"I needed to make sure." Melinda paced across the hall with the key in hand.

"Make sure of what?" Phineas said.

"Make sure none of you are compromised," Melinda said. "I pushed her buttons on purpose. Raw emotion is its only weakness."

"Compromised." Phineas chewed on that. "Why, what've you seen?"

"I lived on space station for ten years. Some cultures consider it a blessing to compromise the weak. It can be weaponized into a Zomaura Strike. The defense candles protected us, but my blessed long johns aren't going to help. I don't suppose they crossed trained you," she said.

Phineas cocked an eyebrow. "No. No, they didn't. What about the Weaver?"

"He didn't recognize it but whatever we're doing, we're going to need cursed weapons," Melinda said. "There has to be an armory down there."

"He didn't recognize it because I didn't want to scare you." Spence raised his voice from behind them. "Melinda, what's going on, exactly?"

"The only way to help him is Crosleigh's Caves," Melinda said. "It's dangerous. Once the caves are breached everyone will know."

"I understand the danger," Phineas said.

"You actually planned this, didn't you?" Spence needled Melinda.

"Not exactly but yes, Meylandra Stuk plans on taking all the credit," Melinda said with a wink. "Little hellion has been gone for ten years, everyone forgets how much I used to poke my nose where it didn't belong." She nodded to the Lady. "Officially, Lady Lauren Daire died. Once you help him, everyone is going to care about you two and no one is going to care about the Necromancer and his apprentice. You're prepared for what's about to happen next, mage?"

Spence opened his mouth, but Phineas stepped forward. "I am," he boomed.

"Then tell yer sneaky sister get on the coms," Melinda said. "Horatio packing it up?"

"He's done," Horatio huffed over with a backpack over his shoulders.

"Tommy, tell the iron throwers to pack it up and get ready to move," Melinda said.

"I'll go first-" Phineas said but Melinda raised a hand.

"You're his bodyguard. You follow him and protect them. I'm the one with the map and the keys," Melinda said. She rolled up an air-filtering bandana and tied it over the lenses.

"This is why you got banished," Spence said.

"This is why I got banished. Funny how they don't tell you can put bandana across the goggles to filter all sorts of spells out like defense wards, right?" Melinda said.

"Why aren't we getting the goggles and bandana?" Horatio said.

Melinda kicked a bag across the floor. "Have at it. I dunno what traps are down there."

Horatio dropped the goggles in hand and squeaked: "Wait, what traps?"

"I have no idea what we're walking into and you three have probably seen more than I can think of if Tommy's bed time stories are even half true. We're about to open a door that hasn't been cracked in years and guess what the hole is gone." She pointed to solid floor. "Now, for those of us without the augmented genes I suggest a pair of goggles, a bandana and some noise canceling ear muffs because gahknows who else is down there besides us."

Spence looked back at the pile of clothes. "You think whoever else is here found a different entrance?"

"They're not up here with us," Melinda said.

"Why are you helping us? You don't even know who he is," Phineas said.

"Tommy trusts your family that means so do I. Besides, if Lady Daire was a plant we'd be dead by now, instead..." she gaped at the fog of war and the increasing red triangles circling. "And because the body was right we're really surrounded." She poked Phineas. "Now's the time to pull on your sister in here before they figure out we're actually here."

"We're safe," the Lady said.

"No," Spence said. "Melinda's right. The defense wards are fixing the damage. It'll be like we were never here."

Melinda pointed the key at the southwest corner and it gleamed oddly. "I'll be right back. Tell everyone to pack it in before they figure out the front doors aren't locked from the inside."

"They weren't locked when we got here," Horatio said.

"Were they physical or magical?" Spence said.

Horatio paused. "Physical."

"Physical locks are iron and aren't part of defense wards. It means we've got a draft," Spence said and grabbed Horatio. "Forget the doors. Stick with Lauren and Phineas. We need everyone inside now." He double timed it to the Necrocloaks and a hushed command later, they brought the body over to the southwest alcove where Melinda awaited.

"Where is she?" Melinda said.

"I don't know," Phineas said.

"You've got less than two minutes to get to the southwest corner of the hall," Melinda announced over the public channel. She pulled Phineas and the Lady through the alcove. "Sorry, it's faster if I do this."

The marauders double-timed it through the side door with Terrie last. The motley group skidded to a stop when they only saw disembodied hands pulling them through the fake alcove.

"They just came out of nowhere," one of them huffed and glanced at Melinda. "What're you supposed to be?"

Melinda tugged at Terrie's fatigues. "You're short two."

"Leave 'em," Terrie said.

"Not gonna happen. Selene, where are you?" Melinda hissed.

Selene along with the other mage burst through the same side door, bee lined to the now intact floor and leapt over the last of the pews to the alcove.

"We need to go!" Selene huffed.

"Not yet," Melinda said.

"Why not?" Horatio squeaked.

"The alcove is a fake. The defense wards converge here," Melinda said.

The marauders said nothing but shuffled themselves tighter. Iron throwers at the ready.

"Trust me. They won't see us," Melinda said.

"Trust you?" one of the marauders said.

"Because I didn't see it even with the goggles. The key showed me and that means neither will they unless they've got some House rated gear," Melinda said and passed the bag full of goggles, bandanas and noise suppression gear. "If you don't have 'em then neither will they."

The front doors creaked opened and an individual a half-foot taller than she silently passed over the threshold. The camouflage gear wasn't the newest, but the House-Grade goggle and noise suppression headgear worked. The iron throwing drum rifle the scout carried was the newest model. Melinda nearly missed the Totem Animus that soared into rafters.

"Or, I could be very, very, very wrong," Melinda whispered.

~

"Nobody panic," Melinda said. "I just felt the wall move. Somebody push it."

"Push what?" one of the marauders said.

Melinda thumbed to the stonewall. "Push the fake wall."

"And if you're wrong?" Terrie said.

"It beats talking to them." Melinda nodded to the growing crowd in the hall.

Thom shrugged pointed to three junior operators and they pushed the fake wall for a good ten feet. The floor dropped away to reveal a descending stone staircase.

"Huh," Thom said and knelt close only to pull his goggles up. "Can't see."

"Defense wards are up. Terrie, volunteers to go first," Melinda said.

"This is because I didn't go on coms, isn't it?" the magess growled at her.

"What do you think?" Melinda said. "When an inferno spell fries you, you'll thank me."

"I'll get myself out of it," Terrie said.

"When yer lungs are on fire, sure you will," Melinda said and pointed down. "Hop to it."

"Mindy," Spence said and nodded to the hall.

A half dozen people occupied the hall. Two argued over a map. The scout paced through the isle of clothes, stopped briefly at the mannequin and continued searching.

The man bringing up the rear she recognized immediately as Josiah Stuk. Lighter skin than she and a fresh suit meant he had taken the System Admin job that she had gotten fired from years ago. *Of course, they used you to find this place,* Melinda thought. An older man in a sweater, slacks and cane entered last. He was her granduncle, Zi Stuk.

Too little. Too late, you two, Melinda thought and turned back to the stairs. "I'll go first. Terrie and Phineas stay with the Lady, mages and Holding Operators pair up. Once we're through the wall will slide back into place. We'll have an hour before it cycles again. They will find a way through and then we'll have to deal with it but not right now."

"Is that Zi Stuk?" Horatio said.

"Everyone on coms now because I haven't clue what's down there," Melinda said.

"You said that already," the Lady said.

"Repetition helps push through the point that I really haven't a gahforsaken clue what's down there," Melinda said. "You can laugh at me when we're drinking and eating to our quest or when our ankles are being marinated in spit. Time to poke something with a stick."

"This is why you got banished," Spence said.

Melinda hazarded a step and took them two at a time. "No, what we're about to do is harmless. Poking around underground catacombs millions of years old is fun until you find Crosleigh's Cave, and everyone loses it because they buried the old ways of resurrection. They buried 'em so deep, I was actually digging 'em back up because there's nowhere left to bury 'em. The Stuks' Iron Vaults could easily store 'em but no one trusts 'em because they're so aloof to the problems the low Houses are having. No one cared what we said, everyone cared what we did. My family cared only to get blamed and I fucking tired of it." She sighed and glanced up at the group. "Sorry, that little ball of bitterness is going back in the box."

"No, not bitter. Just honesty." Spence descended the stairs and plucked a dust-covered torch off the wall. A flick of his wrist and an emerald hued flame ignited.

The Weaver beckoned the group. "You ladies coming or not? Time to make 'em care."

~

Melinda lit her torch off Spence's and held up the key. "Keep to the walls. One Marauder stays behind and leads our guests through. Don't scream if you get splattered by a spell."

Terrie blanched. "Walls?"

"Ninety percent of the tripwire spells are floor. The rest are wall spells for climbers like Belfrys." Spence pointed his torch up. "The lack of finger holes means floor spells. We haven't been booted by the defense wards, so the key is real. Terrie take a peek with a Marauder."

Terrie scowled at him but a nod from Phineas sent her and a Marauder ahead.

And she's still not on coms, either. Melinda thought. "I don't suppose you can hack hers."

The headset chimed thrice, negative.

Terrie and the Marauder re-appeared. "The area isn't secure, but it certainly goes on for a bit. If there's a door around here, I can't see it. I think she's right, the defense wards closed the hole and it's getting darker down here, I can't see ten feet in front of me," Terrie said.

"Does that mean sooner or later, we're all going to forget about all of this?" Horatio said.

Melinda stepped forward; torch outstretched and pulled up her goggles. "Huh. I can see better without 'em," she said and draped the key around her neck. "Much better, follow me."

The temperature descended as they did. The walls of stone littered with roots of trees long dead and graffiti drifted apart the longer they progressed. They stood shoulder-to-shoulder, lights throwing halogen fingers everywhere. They stopped and drew a collected breath at the cavernous grouping of stalactites and stalagmites that stretched on forever.

"How far does it go?" Horatio said.

"This level or the other hundreds of stories?" Melinda said. "First thing you learn about this place, it's been here longer than any of us and will be after we're all dead. Just put one foot in front of the other and don't lag. We won't be able to find you otherwise."

"How can you tell?" Horatio said.

"Somebody wrote 'this way' in the old tongue on the wall plus there's some man-made stairs."

"Those are scribbles, Mindy," Horatio said.

"Says the one who still can't read the old tongue." Spence's sotto voice was greeted with snickers from the group.

Melinda descended to a plateau and pointed her torch through an opening in an otherwise impassable wall. She turned right and pointed to a crack in the wall.

"No, it's this way, I can hear the Shield Maiden's song," Selene said and point through the hole.

"It's a hole in the wall like all the rest." One of the marauders laughed.

Selene raised her sword and illuminated the wall to be the decapitated stone head of a woman. One eye was intact the other broken. She pointed to one of the walls that were actually the statue's feet.

"Shield Maiden statue means we're on the right track and this hole is probably how the resurrection chamber got through."

"We really are still acknowledging that aren't we?" Spence said.

Melinda nodded and pointed to the marauders. "Now, remember don't shoot anything. The defense wards'll probably just fling it right back at you and I really don't feel like dragging any of you out of here by your tighty-whities while you sob about much those rounds hurt." She breathed in deep and crossed the eye's threshold. "Please watch over your wayward sister, I'm too cute and fuzzy to sacrifice. Please take the rest into your bosom as a payment."

"The blessing doesn't work like that, Mindy!" Spence crowed.

12
WHERE WEAVERS DAIRE, PART I

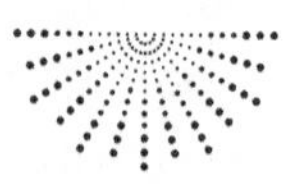

THE DESCENT INTO CROSLEIGH'S CAVES WAS A SILENT ONE. ANY SORT of wisecracks from the marauders had long since abated along with the bodily remains that had all but disappeared only to be replaced by piles of bones and caved in skulls.

Thom and the marauders communicated with the mages through hand signals that Melinda vaguely remembered from one of his old military manuals. There was no sniping between who was in charge. When the Tier Zero Operators got spooked Melinda knew when to shut up and follow instructions to the letter.

Thom took point with Phineas while Terrie with Selene brought up the rear.

Melinda's torch's unnatural light lit the man-made smooth passageway. The fire spell only flickering when it encountered cracks in the ceiling and walls. Beyond the cracks, the light revealed thick, juicy tree roots, the bodies they belonged to long since gone.

"Lir's Forest used to be here," Spence said.

"How can you tell?" Melinda said.

Spence dipped his torch closer to the crack and the flame cooled to embers. He retracted it and the flame popped into existence. "A Lir's aura doesn't produce it sponges off others."

Melinda ignored her flee instinct at the suggestion of movement behind those limbs and kept the group's pace moving.

The widening holes in the floor and the ceiling that led to gahknows where meant the grave robbers were getting bolder or someone else had, once.

"I got nothing and neither do the goggles," Thom said.

"I don't sense anything. If we're late then where's the party?" Phineas concurred.

"Maybe they didn't make it out," Horatio said.

"Or there's an exit we don't know about it. Either, way, hush," Melinda said and wandered down a narrow outcropping.

She extended her torch and Spence did the same.

Twin seven-foot-tall, stone Shield Maidens flanked a darkened arch that was layered in hand carved protection spells appeared out of the darkness.

"Thom," Spence called out.

Melinda reached out and touched the arch only to jerk her hand back. "Mother—" she swallowed the rest of the curse. "Still works. After millions of years it still works."

"Back then we scryed things to last, Mindy." Spence winked, and the rest of the group appeared.

"What is it with you and having to touch things that you know are going to hurt you?" Selene said.

"Thank you, I get it enough when he's around," Melinda muttered.

"She touched the defense ward, didn't she?" Thom said. "This is it. All the other paths are blocked."

Melinda hazarded a step forward only for one of the Maidens to block her path.

"I can barely read the old tongue on the door's wards," she blinked away the grit.

"We're ignoring the chamber size hole in the wall?" Spence pointed to the hole in the wall.

The shield maiden spoke. An odd jumble of sounds that sounded lyrical.

"Announce yourself," Melinda said and spun down her tongue. "I think. Announce and you shall pass? Melinda Scott of House Scott."

The shield maidens stood firm.

Melinda lowered her tongue deeper. "Meylandra Stuk of House Stuk and I'm here to resurrect the Mad Stuk. Now let me pass."

The shield maidens retreated, and the arch's hollowness brightened.

~

The resurrection cave's roof was held aloft by eleven shield maidens. Each represented a House and protected a resurrection chamber. Those chambers formed a circle in the middle of the room. All made of the same material as the Stuk Resurrection chamber Spence and Melinda encountered, those belonging to the house could only read the inscriptions on each chamber.

Melinda sneezed at the well-lit chamber. "Gahforsaken defense candles. Why?"

The marauders cracked light sticks and spread them out across the dirt-covered ground.

"Daire, Leighton, MacGregor, Ohari, Finnegan, Kiledere, Knoll, Brie, Wilde, Lir, Whittahare," Spence said and pointed to the twelfth in the middle of the circle. "Stuk."

"I thought there'd be more," Melinda said.

"Houses left behind after the last war don't have a say or a chamber in here," Spence said.

"The Maidens explain why no one's ever breached the door," Melinda said. "And whatever was out there explains why no one survived to breathe a word about where it was."

"How long do we have then?" Phineas said.

"Depends on how well my grand-uncle can read the breadcrumbs I left when we came in." Melinda shrugged off the looks. "He's my life-line. I'm going to get reeled back in soon."

"Whoever built their House right on top of a resurrection cave was smart," Spence said. "Probably a Cross or O'Hare since their chambers aren't here."

"More like suicide," Horatio said. "What happens when you turn people away?"

Spence sighed. "You don't."

Melinda paced about and stopped at a shiny plaque drilled into the wall. "This officially denotes these resurrection chambers are meant to be used by all. Safe roads. Safe travels unto you. This hallowed place is guarded by the Mad Stuk. Play fair and be welcome. Play dirty and its ankles or wrists."

What? Melinda thought and poked the plaque. *Nope. It's quite real.*

"He guarded this place since the end of the war instead of just coming home?" she said.

"He's been dead for years, Melinda," Horatio said. "The dead don't come back."

"The Necromancer in the highly guarded resurrection cave kindly disagrees with you," Spence said and pulled Horatio aside. "Grave robbing is a new low, even for you. You can't fool me I know what defense ward wounds look like."

"It's not what you think," Horatio said.

Melinda ignored the conversation and bumped into the Stuk Resurrection Chamber. She walked around it and the person sitting atop it. "Get off the chamber, it's not play thing," she said and read off the inscription in the mother tongue:

"For in darkness I ride.

Never seeing home.

Never knowing peace.

Unending is my vengeance.

Sated only by the drums of war.

All others will fall.

I shall rise.

Unyielding.

Unending.

For I am the darkness.

Now and forever," Melinda recited. "I know those verses. Where did I see those before?" she back pedaled. "Oh no. It can't be him."

"Mindy, who're you talking to?" Phineas said.

She pointed at the man in the slacks and boots. He sat atop the chamber, was interested in the brothers arguing, and caught her staring. He waved hello.

Melinda rubbed her eyes, but the afterimage remained. "Anyone else see the grinning idiot sitting on the chamber or am I overtired?"

"You're overtired," Phineas said.

The grinning idiot shrugged at Melinda, raised a finger to his lips and winked.

The Mad Stuk doesn't have a House. He doesn't get a vote. He is commoner cursed to wield the Mad Stuk's mantle. Horatio said he was going to use the chamber to resurrect Kaare Daire but Daires don't use resurrection chambers. He lied to us, she thought and wandered over to the Daire Chamber. *Daire Chamber looks real. Lauren led them down here and they came up stairs to find us. He put the sword in the Stuk Chamber to protect whoever is in there and the chamber because we can resurrect anyone. Only two types of people get plated and death boots. Not Kaare Daire and pilots of the Mechanized Armored Air Calvary.*

The grinning idiot tapped his nose and nodded.

Pilots are all gone. Except one, Melinda thought and looked down at the Daire Chamber. She kicked it, hard.

The chamber's side crumbled. She smashed it to pieces. The commotion broke up the argument the brothers were having.

"Mindy, what're you doing?" Spence said.

"When the was the last time you went to a Daire Resurrection and they used a chamber," she said.

Spence's jaw tightened. "Never."

Melinda stopped her desecration when something heavier stubbed her boot. The dust cleared. A sword sheath with gleaming blessed gems and an ornate wooden box lay in the middle of the remains of the chamber.

"Your brother is right about some of it. Someone's been going around, destroying chambers because they didn't want him to rise. So,

Roark, let them know full well he didn't need one because he carries it with him all the time. The only thing he needed to do was to get the chamber out. Your brother was supposed to pick it up and probably destroy it because whoever's got control of the Necros knows what's going to happen next." Melinda picked up the ornate wooden box. The metal inscription plate still held its shine. "For services rendered. For discharging duties above and beyond. From a grateful Queen and Coil." She lowered the box and the twin sheaths onto the Stuk Chamber.

The chamber's lid opened, and the items dropped inside.

"Mindy," Thom said. "Who is it?"

"Property the Seventy-Fifth Mechanized Armored Air Calvary Division," she said.

"There wasn't a Seventy-Fifth Calvary," Thom said.

Melinda nodded. "Against all odds and back against a wall. The remaining Armor Divisions of every single House along with several war mage divisions, a few support groups, three Queens, two Empresses and one mother to us all were supposed to die on Crosleigh's World by decree of the dead emperor but instead, they survived and fled onboard *Last Hope*. It's considered to be the defining moment of the last House war."

"Still with the reading of the banned books." Spence sighed.

"The books, the movies, the comics and the After-Action Reports, the only reason I actually liked ancient History Class because it was stupid things like hiding a ship inside a planet makes no sense whatsoever but, in the end, in actually threw up several red flags because how do actually hide a ship inside a planet." Melinda chuckled. "It doesn't matter. What matters is your brother did something right and brought the Mad Stuk home."

"That's not funny, Mindy," Thom said.

Melinda pointed to the chamber. "For in darkness, I ride... "

Everyone spit on the floor and crossed themselves.

"Whatever burden is in that chamber is going back onto that body." Melinda pointed to the sheeted body. "The Daires were down here before we got here. The Ohari Chamber is full. I still haven't heard anyone on the coms. So, it's time to decide. How far are you willing to go?"

~

"They required proof before we raise him. It's a simple resurrection," Horatio said.

"It was simple resurrection when I thought it was going to be. But if the chamber is Stuk, the burden is Stuk, that means so is the body and the House key that Melinda needs to give back, sooner or later," Spence hissed. "I am not about to raise some unnamed Stuk."

"What's the problem?" Melinda said and continued to stare down the ghost.

"The problem, Mindy, there're some Stuk that have been dead for years and will never be resurrected, ever and for good reason. I know you want him back, but it may not be whatever is left of Roark. All of a sudden, we just drop in and get whisked away down here. I knew something was wrong I just couldn't place it. I'm calling it, no," Spence said.

"He saved our lives," the Lady said. "I promised him I'd return him."

"And you did. You did," Spence said. "You just didn't promise to raise him. But even better, he doesn't need to be raised, he can do it himself."

"He can?" Phineas said.

"He's forgotten more spells than I ever will. He's a war mage for gahsakes," Spence said.

"Why haven't you said his name?" Melinda said.

"I don't feel like summoning him that's why," Spence said.

"He's right there." Melinda thumbed to the bed sheeted body. "And there. Wait, you're saying he could do it all by himself?"

"He doesn't need the books or support structure to resurrect himself, he's been a show off ever since I met him. He split himself apart just like I do in times of need. His wounds from whoever caught you stealing?" Spence said to Horatio. "Or did you attack someone? What did you do to even curse him?"

"They were trying to save me." The baritone voice stopped everyone.

The bed sheeted body and the afterimage stood in the middle of the room. For the briefest of moments, the nameless Stuk was whole.

~

The closest marauders backed away with their hands raised and weapons lowered. One glanced at the Lady and she shook her head.

Melinda stared down the silhouette of a man; a pair of coal eyes the only thing that made sense. She twisted down her tongue. "Who be you and who do you serve."

The man laughed, his eyes grinned. "Only you, Meylandra. Only you."

Melinda raised her stunner in line with his head. "Yes, only me." She lowered her tongue. "Now, one of you didn't answer me, that's fine but not two of you."

"Mindy, put down the gun," Horatio said.

"No," Melinda said. "I've had it with people not introducing themselves. It's impolite. Now, drop the glamor spell."

The Lady cleared her throat. "You really don't want to see him."

"Roark Knoll, burden carrier of the Mad Stuk's plate was guiding war survivors out of this coil when he came upon a struggling House and offered to help. While he repaired their house, he figured out they were Liches, but he didn't care. They fed off his body. He'd bound his unneeded aura to a sword years ago and gifted it to a needy house. In time, they returned her, and they fed off her too," the man said.

"Unending, unyielding and unstoppable," Spence rattled off and the man nodded.

"When your brother discovered this, their House was too big. They were still living off him until he got word to Terrie. They rescued his body. Terrie stole his sword back. He put himself back together in time to escape but it was too late. The wounds from their cursed weapons never heal. In the end he had a Plan C for my aura," the man said.

"Plan C is simple: mail yourself. We found the chamber exactly where it was supposed to be just in time for you rendezvous with it," Spence said and advanced on the man. "What happened to Rule One: Get yourself out of it?"

"Even he had limits and their feeding cycle was too ironclad," the voice wheezed.

"When we confronted the House heads they didn't deny it. By that time, the House mages were in charge and wanted the Liches gone," Phineas said.

"If it helps, you two were in the same House for a time. We couldn't get you both out," Horatio said. "So, we waited for the leadership hand off."

Spence chortled. "You started a coup. Why am I not surprised?"

"No. We didn't," the Lady said. "The House agreed to a change in leadership in return they'd give both of you back. During dinner they all turned."

"Zomaura outbreak," Melinda whispered and off the startled looks. "What? I live on a space station with hundreds of different religions. At least one thinks it's fine to aura jack a body to get in touch with their gods. Don't look at me, I didn't make up the rules."

Spence turned back to the man. "All of this because of you?" he said. "My brother does something actually righteous for a change and all of sudden they stick all of us together on the same planet, underground with one way out."

"You haven't asked the two questions that's been bugging you since you figured out who I am," the man said.

"What questions," Spence snapped.

"First, what were you doing in your own House with a bunch of Liches and two: How bad can it be the nigh unstoppable killing machine that came out of the last war managed to get hexed to the point of death," the man said.

Spence pointed at him, but his jaw snapped shut. "An attack on one is an attack on us all."

The man nodded. "Someone's been very busy and if it worked on me. Guess how bad it needs to be to resurrect your brother, yourself and me. You know what that means?"

"We've all got five minutes to live," Spence said.

"Less in some cases," the man said.

"Mindy, lower the gun. I need you to do something for me." Spence raised his book. "I need you to resurrect him. I need to you resurrect the Mad Stuk."

~

"What?" Melinda said. "And why is he talking in the third person?"

"I need you to translate this verbatim in the old tongue," Spence said.

"I'm not a mage." Melinda squinted at the page. "I can't cast a resurrection spell."

"You don't need to be to cast a spell. Just speak it out loud, before his body dies," Spence said.

"And just what are you going to be doing when I do all this?" she said.

"Channeling the energy so it doesn't burn either of you out," he said.

"Wait, why does it need to channel through me?" she needled.

"Mindy!" the baritone voice jolted everyone around. "Hurry it along."

Melinda sighed. "If this goes wrong I know where all of you live."

"Everyone get behind me," Phineas said. "And don't shoot him."

"Or me," Melinda added. "What happens if I mess up?"

"You won't," Spence said. "Besides I can't read it."

Melinda laughed and squinted at the pages. The writing shifted about until the Mother Tongue filled the page. "I can read this. I can actually read this. Wait, how does it know?"

"Like I said," Spence said. "Verbatim or you'll bring down the ceiling on us."

Melinda cleared her throat. "Protect me and mine in the time darkness. Help those wandering souls in time of peril. Be a beacon for those lost souls on their trip home to their rightful homes. Guide the forgotten and the forbidden down the righteous path towards your holy house and protect them in their time of need. Do unto them as you were do unto yourself. Bless this union of heart, body and soul until the end of his days."

The ceiling cracked open.

A beacon of light shined down.

A circle of loud, hot, screaming, energy encompassed the chambers.

A bolt of energy ripped down from the heavens, slammed through Spence's body through Melinda's and raced across the eleven chambers until it crashed into twelfth.

A clap of thunder deafened Melinda briefly.

A wave of energy exploded outward from the circle of chambers.

The air filled with aura fireflies.

The noise of their wings smothered Melinda's beating heart.

Their mass swirled around the body.

The air crackled with light and sound.

The inlaid gems and old tongue writing seethed with unspeakable power.

The remaining fireflies swirled around the chamber, fingers of aura lightning leapt from their tiny bodies and the hum from the chamber's hidden genies roared.

The bed sheeted body staggered to his feet and shambled through the fireflies. An arm reached out to the chamber. The linen burned away in time for the body, the twelfth chamber and the burden to occupy the same space at the same time.

The world exploded and kicked everyone off their feet.

~

Melinda coughed and rolled onto her knees. She batted away an errant aura firefly and grabbed Spence's book.

"Headcount!" she managed and sneezed the firefly off her nose. "Headcount!"

The voices popped out of the darkness one at a time.

Melinda ignited one of her torches so she could see, and the Marauders followed suit.

Melinda aimed it in the only direction that mattered: the twelfth chamber.

Its walls had crumbled. Its precious iron rusted away. Gems cracked.

The aura fireflies flitted away, and an erect human figure cut through Melinda's torch beam. The twin swords back in his hands arced tentacles of magic everywhere.

A hand gripped her shoulder and Phineas came into view. "You did it," he breathed.

"I did?" Melinda croaked.

Spence wheezed and helped the Lady to her feet. "Simple old school resurrection. One percent to the recipient. Ninety-nine percent to anyone within a fifty-foot radius. He blessed the rest of us, I think he healed my bad shoulder."

"I did all that?" Melinda said.

"You cast a resurrection spell that did all that. And, correctly, I might add," Spence said.

Melinda's grin vanished. "Wait, what would've happened if I hadn't?"

"Generally, it loops back on the caster," Spence said.

"And does what, exactly?" Melinda said.

"Burns you from the inside out." Spence coughed. "He used all the energy to bless us."

"You can do that?" Melinda said.

"No, he's just a show off." Spence, Phineas and the Lady cursed in unison.

The floor beneath Melinda quivered and she twisted about to witness the wall behind her collapsed.

The shield maiden toppled down and smashed through the floor with all too relative ease.

A cacophony of voices echoed over the cracking of stone.

"Mages: buddy up! I want a door in thirty seconds!" Thom ordered.

"Mindy! No don't!"

Melinda dashed forward and skidded on her knees to the hole where a lone hand gripped the edge of an upturned slab of rock. The cursed sword wedged into the rock. The fingers slipped away, and she reached out and the vice grip made her cry out.

"Hang onto me," Melinda said and reached down with her other hand. "Forget the stupid sword! You have to grab my other hand I can't hold you like this."

"The door is right here!" Selene shouted.

The shadows parted for the briefest of moments and those coal-like eyes froze her soul. "Promise me you'll save him. Promise me," he told her.

"I promise now take my other hand!" she said.

The eyes smiled. "Take the sword and watch your back."

His hand released hers and tumbled away.

"Find me an exit and somebody get Mindy away from that hole, now!" Thom roared.

Melinda picked up the cursed sword and the floor beneath her followed suit.

The world tilted, but Spence grabbed her free hand and pulled her up out of the widening hole.

The ground beneath their feet rippled.

Spence pointed to the far side of the chamber. "We're gonna jump. Follow me."

Melinda dropped the sword into her bag and they retreated into the farthest corner that hadn't disintegrated.

They leapt across the gulf to the hidden passage way.

Two marauders caught them just as the cave disappeared.

The wobble in the steps made their ascension even faster.

Melinda swallowed any complaints of them stepping on her heels just like the steps behind them.

The walls and ceiling crumpled.

The dust choked out the light.

The last two steps they jumped and never landed.

13
FALLEN

GRAVITY WAS WRONG.

The lighted doorway to the cathedral disappeared from Melinda's sight.

The marauders and mages vanished into the darkness.

Spence slipped from her fingers and was gone.

She ricocheted off something rock hard and then crashed against someone who cried out.

The descent was the worst feeling. The goggles didn't help.

The wild ride came to an end when her body slammed into sturdy object that refused to budge. Sturdy enough her right shoulder dislocated and a rib or two cracked.

Ow. Ow. Ow. Melinda thought and rolled onto her left side only to suck in her breathe.

The goggles fed her an image of a never-ending crevasse. Debris from the resurrection cave rained down, never to be seen again.

She rolled right and patted the rocky terrain underneath her only to bite back a scream. Ribs, shoulder along with probably her hips and leg were hurting.

You can do this. Just shuffle away from the falling debris and you'll be fine, she thought.

One of the chambers landed vertically, inches from her head and toppled into the crevasse.

A warmth filled her bones and before she could take a breath her blood was on fire. The fire surged out from her heart and spread to broken areas of her body.

Buggers. Oh, I didn't miss this feeling at all. Melinda hissed and tried to ignore the military-grade nanobots raging through the bloodstream to fix her damaged body. *Just sit still and they'll stich you back together again.*

The buggers could've done more than just stitch her limbs back together. They'd been the biggest skeleton in her family's closet and per several House decrees, they'd been coded to be dormant until a need so drastic arrived that a valve inside her heart released a swarm of them throughout her body.

Her hips and legs were first on the list and snapped back into place. This instant healing sounded good in theory but pushing the bones back into position was just as bad as breaking them in the first place.

Melinda covered her mouth to smother the scream. Standard Buggers would've shunted the pain. Military Buggers, like the ones her and Tommy had thanks to dear ole grandmother didn't believe in anesthetic. She reached out with her good hand and grabbed Spence's book. Her ribs came next and felt like a kick to the stomach. Her right shoulder pulsated with pain, but the warmth of the buggers disappeared, and she laughed.

"Seriously? You're not going to fix my shoulder?" she crowed and instantly covered her mouth.

She shuffled to her feet. One doorway in the stone wall was highlighted in the goggles while another highlighted behind her. She let the goggles do their work and found herself on a stone bridge. She immediately got off it and pushed the closest wall to know it was sturdy.

Military industrial grade nanobots. The biggest scientific discovery in millions of years and they can't fix a dislocated shoulder. She growled, counted to five and slammed her shoulder into the wall.

The bone popped back into her socket. Mindy pulled up her goggles and wiped tears away. "Need to rendezvous with everyone else," she said and tapped the goggles. "Passive radar only. Tell me if anyone else pings me. And tell me how far we fell."

The goggles pinged twice.

"Let's follow this until we get somewhere." Melinda rolled her shoulders. "Going to check those bugger's settings once I get back I shouldn't have to do that myself."

She stuffed Spence's book into the hidden pocket built into her apprentice robes and ran an inventory on her bag.

Five hundred feet below last known location appeared on her lenses.

"Good, three hundred more and I'd be in trouble. That's where the House-Guarded resurrection chambers." She stopped at the archway. Man-made stairs descended into the darkness. "Two rendezvous points: the ground floor or the Keep's lobby. I'm closer to the ground floor."

A man's voice grumbled, and Melinda dug around in her bag. She produced Roark's sword. "What was that, you cursed sword."

"I was just saying it'd be a good idea." The sword's gems gleamed. "Where is he?"

"Gahknows, but he's sturdier than I am and sneakier." Melinda tweaked the goggles so they'd stop futzing up errors around the magical weapon.

She descended into the catacombs gripping the sword in one hand and the stunner in the other. "This still isn't the stupidest thing I've done in my life."

"That much we can agree on," the sword said.

"Oh, hush you or back in the bag you go."

~

"Doesn't make sense. Why bring Kaare down here?" Melinda turned a corner, but the level was like the rest of the catacombs. Sloped walls, all carved out by hand or mages using their fingers. It was just as empty and unmarked as the rest. "Unless they're looking for something they can't find anywhere else."

"What would he be looking for?" the sword said.

"Oh, now you're talkative?" Melinda growled and turned around to check behind her. "Anything?"

The goggles pinged once.

"We aren't being followed. I would've sensed other auras," the sword said.

"All things being equal and they're not," Melinda said and moved on. "The lower we go the closer we get to the ground floor. Either no one knows about these upper catacombs or they're following me and waiting to pounce." She stopped at the stair's threshold. "I'm not that lucky."

Nothing jumped out at her or pulled her up into the ceiling to feast on her, so she continued her descent.

~

The campfire on the ground level was cold. The hastily lined up canteens were empty and the un-opened Stukari Holdings MRE bars meant someone had cooked or they weren't that hungry.

Melinda scarfed down the bars and didn't drop dead even if her stomach recoiled at the bars and the extra protein they contained.

"Thank you, Wally," she said between bites and pointed the sword in either direction every so often. The gems neither hissed, howled or cried out. "There's only one thing beneath the ground floor and that's the weapons vaults."

"Why would he need weapons?" the sword said.

"Same thing anyone else need weapons for: he with the biggest stick wins. If I were him, I'd find tech to stop his House from burning down because some idiots didn't listen and install Narelle like they should've," she said and tweaked the goggles settings to brighten the pea green surroundings. "Either they're following us or I'm really that lost."

"It's okay to be scared. The shock and stress of the last few hours can be unsettling you can wait here," the sword said.

"I'm not scared. I've never been this lucky before and generally." She slowly looked about and the scanners came back with no movement. "Smart odds is they would've left guards behind, so they could leave the same way they came in. The only other way out is the underground rail carrier station and I haven't heard back from Nat or Alita so down is the only option."

Melinda wandered around the ground floor until she recognized unmarked, armored-sealed doors. She turned a corner and was home. The lobby had been the showroom floor for Crosleigh House before the war had broken out across the Hollow. The stone archways that led out into the desert had remained. The cold metal deck plates that lined the floors were untouched. The carpets had seen better days. The chandeliers were too high in the vaulted stone ceiling for anyone to steal.

The reception desk and the chairs in the waiting area been retracted into the floor. Armored door irises had sealed the shut the elevators and the stairs. But not for lack of trying, someone had tried to open the private elevator door with a crow bar.

Crosleigh Keep had been made to house millions of people. Instead of a traditional spacefaring House, the Keep was ground based and never moved. To Melinda this never made sense because it just meant the Keep was a constant target. But the defense wards did its jobs and kept the scavengers out.

Now, The Keep was just an empty shell of her former self.

The war helped with that, Melinda thought and stopped in front of the armored doors that kept the Museum safe. It was the door she had been drawn to the most.

The armored door pealed back without her touching a thing.

She drew Roark's sword and her stunner. "Anything?" she said.

The goggles pinged a no.

The sword's silence kept her rooted to the spot. "No," it finally said. "Wait, didn't you used to work here?"

"Hush," she said and edged across threshold. "What is that?"

The goggles pinged back: Inconclusive.

"That doesn't help me," Melinda growled and inched forward.

The Museum was paid for by the Stuk's Hollow Historical Foundation. It was the closest thing Melinda had ever gotten to the war besides reading the instruction manual of her space suit. Even if most of the extraneous blow 'em to smithereens items had been removed, her aunt's spacesuit was the first thing that greeted her at the door. It had never been used since Aunt Freda and her Necrocloak had been outed by some backstabbing stukarrees. The height requirement sign was laughable then as it was now except for the fact she was now well over the size requirement.

Yeah, the bubble helmet looks better than that helmet condom. Melinda snickered.

The inner lobby's walls were lined with framed propaganda posters. Each of the twelve Houses represented.

There was a thirteenth house, a house that was no more and would never rise again: Crosleigh. The identical sets of Cross mechanized, jet black, body armor flanked the museum's inner curved doorway was remembrance enough of a time that not even Tommy talked about.

Each of them was eight feet tall and could withstand anything thrown at them. Even the arch mages told nightmare stories about going up against The Cross and barely making it out alive. No weapons graced their backs or hips. They didn't need them. The cursed armor plating had been forged by an unnamed Priestess of the Hills after the death of her fallen lover. They were just as shiny as they had marched out of her now since burned House.

Melinda jerked herself out of the speech she had prepared to scare the kids into wetting their beds and pointed the sword back from once she'd come.

"Nothing," the sword said. "But the goggles are right. Something isn't right."

Melinda reached for the door's handle, but the goggles pinged thrice due to proximity and she stumbled backwards.

The doors flung open and the world slowed down while Melinda's heart was in her ears.

One the Cross suits, an old maintenance model strode through the open doors. At six feet five, it paled in comparison to its comrades-in-arms, but those pair of red electronic eyes zeroed in on her. Its bone-white, lipless faceplate swiveled next and the rest of the body pivoted to follow her.

Melinda pulled down her goggles so she could see. The cursed armor did just as it was supposed, playing merry hock with the electronica in her goggles. "Melinda Scott. Shut down sequence: Romeo Kilo Bravo, Eleven-Fifty-Three," she shouted.

The armor ignored the command and continued.

Melinda repeated herself, but the armor hastened its pace.

I know I coded that shutdown command into you, you tin can. Melinda dropped the sword and quick drew her stunner.

Five rounds landed dead center in the armor's chest.

The electric rounds shorted out its central chest panel and it keeled over onto its back.

Melinda breathed a sigh of relief and reloaded. She reached down to pick up the discarded sword when her goggles pinged thrice with a proximity alert.

A pair of fingertips graced the back of her head.

"Now, tell me something," a man's hoarse voice said from behind her. "What was the first thing you did wrong?"

~

Melinda growled. "Took my eyes off the target."

"Close," the voice said. "It's okay to run."

"I beat it," she said, but the armor rolled itself over and pushed itself back onto its feet.

Its plate snapped around and resumed its advancement.

"Unit, recognize, user: Roark Knoll. Authorization: Romeo Kilo Bravo. Eleven Fifty-Three," the man said in a tongue Melinda could understand.

The armor slowed to a stop and stood at attention.

Yes, that would be the Mad Stuk you just resurrected. Melinda winced at the thought.

"Where's Tommy?" he said.

"I don't know," Melinda said. "Wait, you dropped down here before I did. How'd you get here last?"

"I doubled back to find them. Which reminds me, what are you doing here?" he said.

"I was trying to find anyone. Either they landed somewhere else or they went a different route," she said and chanced a look over her shoulder, but his fingers poked the back of her head.

"Let's get inside and I can freshen up before we go off and find the rest of your party," he said. "Lights would be nice."

"That's half the reason I came. The backups are in the back of the museum," Melinda said. "This place is run off a geothermal. The lights shouldn't be off unless someone triggered an EMP. Not me. By the way."

"Good thinking and I know it wasn't you. It was them. I'll follow you," he said. "Romeo Kilo, escort duty, recognize, Scott, Melinda."

The short armor's eyes flashed. It took two steps forward and dropped the rounds into Melinda's palm.

"And you two." The two guarding the door stiffened. "Anyone else comes across this level, you tell me. Do not engage or provoke. Recon only."

The two eight-foot-tall walking walls of death stepped down off their pedestals, marched past, and stood at attention at the hallway.

"Damn," Melinda said. "I worked here for ten years. How long have they been able to do that?"

He chuckled. "It's my House, Melinda. My burdens. My armor. And to answer your question, their batteries last forever plus five hundred years. Now, let's go and keep those goggles away from me."

"Why?"

"Because you have them slaved to the camera gear in your bag, that's why," he said and nudged. "Start walking."

"I just resurrected you, and I get treated like this?" she scoffed.

"Which is why I didn't have Junior knock you out. Now, quit stalling and get inside before someone else comes back and finish off those MRE rations you didn't touch."

~

Welcome home, Melinda thought. *Ten years gone, and the place hasn't changed.*

She walked past the hermetically sealed glass cases full of ancient armor and stopped at the information desk. The brochure holder with the listing of items was splayed out across the table. Her keys dangled on a hook behind the counter. Nothing had changed with the minor exception that someone had added a bell. She laughed at this tragic set of circumstances. "I've been replaced by a bell."

"Keep an eye on the door," he said and disappeared into the stacks before she turned around.

She eyed Junior. "He always like this to the people who just saved his life?"

"I heard that." The lights inside the museum flicked to life and Melinda growled at the goggle feedback from the lights. She pulled them off and sighed at the sight of all her hard work.

"And you're right about EMP. It only goes off if someone tried to breach one of the vaults," he said from the backroom.

Melinda grimaced at the word 'breach.' "Even I'm smart enough not to do that."

"Mindy, how long have you been down here?" he said.

"I just got here," she said. "Before Junior and I got better acquainted."

"You didn't hot wire the back-up generators to the lower levels then?" he said.

Melinda scowled. "Even I know that's a bad idea. Someone would need access to the museum's biometrics to get in to do all that. Who would be desperate enough to cause a feedback and blow the place up?" She stopped. "Unless it's to cover their tracks and bury us along with evidence."

"Not it," the sword said.

Melinda pulled out the sword. "Start talking or back in the bag you go permanently, you little toothpick."

"Mindy, who are you talking to?" he said.

"You left your sword behind in your chamber. Remember? Now spill it. Who else is here besides us?" Melinda said.

"About that," the sword said. "You needed a nudge."

"A nudge? A nudge?" Melinda hissed. "Wait, who do you belong to, really?"

"Faking what?" His voice jerked her around.

Out of the shadows, a pair of unnatural green eyes appeared, followed by a narrow peach face, sharp nose, and a red head of hair that looked like it had been combed in a wind tunnel. "I don't have a sword," he said.

"You did. He does," the sword said. "I was raised to the rank of lord. He backed up his aura into this sword and made sure to hide me in plain sight. Someone is going around and crushing all the resurrection chambers on the Hollow and the chamber you were in was the only option left. It was my job to get Melinda and you back on track before anything else happened."

He picked up the sword and squinted at the pommel along with the hilt. "Looks like mine. I don't remember making you and I don't have the know how to forge you."

Melinda cleared her throat and quietly said, "It was a birthday present from me."

He smiled. "I do remember you pushing me to get my foot in the door. That means there are pieces of me still missing. Lovely."

"You also said to burn yourself," Melinda said. "Immediately."

"That sounds like me," he said and handed her back the sword. "You'll need this more than I do. It's the right thing to do."

"The right thing to do?" Melinda scoffed. "The network is down. I'm back where I started before I got pulled into this House mess. Right now, there's a good possibility there's a horde of Necros waiting for us in the basement vaults. You still haven't introduced yourself. How am I doing so far?"

"You forgot the part about being armed with me and stunner with no backup. But, yes, that pretty much covers it," the sword said. "Also, your ride is still incommunicado, but he's resourceful and will get himself out of it."

"No," Melinda said. "I'm calling it. No. This isn't my fight. You don't need me."

"You have to choose a side sooner or later," he said.

Melinda whirled around and stabbed a finger in his chest. "I did. Mine. I kept my ego out of it. I didn't show off. I followed your 'rules.' I didn't let the power go to my head and look where it got me. Look where it got everyone else. The Houses turned on all of us and what do I get for doing my gahforsaken job? Banished. Indefinitely. I'll be lucky to explain it to them when I get back."

"You're not dead, yet," he and the sword said.

"Oh, don't feed me that. Either of you," she seethed.

"Who cares what they say?" he said. "Melinda Scott isn't beholden to anyone. In fact, you've kept your fake identity so clean you could use it to your advantage."

"Because they're the ones who're still in charge," Melinda said. "And the only thing they need to do is pull my file and find out who I used to be. How am I going to explain this?"

"Easy. Blame me," he said.

"Oh, who's going to believe that?" she said.

"I hacked Spence's shuttle to bring you two down next to the chamber. I've been pulling your strings since you 'found' Spence's shuttle," he said. "They're manufacturing Goodnight rounds, Mindy. It's that bad."

"Oh, you don't get it. It's always that bad. Everyone just turned a blind eye to it," she said. "And you can't manufacture them, my family is the only one who has the formula and that died with my grandmother so whatever they tried to hex you with is something else."

"And what happens when they come for you what're you going to do, surrender unconditionally or fight?" he said. "I already did and look what happened to me. Close to death and even your resurrection spell didn't. What happens when they come for you and Tommy?"

"I'll deal with it," she spat.

"I dealt with it too." He leaned down and the briefest of moments the eyes glazed over to coal red and back to green. "You really want to see what they did to me?"

"No. I don't need to see it." She glared at him. "You're walking and talking."

"Am I or is it Junior?" he said.

"Enough with the mind games," she said. "And don't pull the reverse psych bullshit on me. I haven't gotten involved because I don't care. Let me show you how much I don't care."

She pulled off the key from around her neck and held it out. "This is yours. I'm leaving."

Junior accepted it and looped it around its neck.

"You can leave whenever you wish. There's an express elevator in the back room that'll take you up to the landing pad," he said. "Just remember, do you really want to do this?"

"If I don't leave now, I never will. I don't like being under glass." Melinda walked past him without looking back.

"I wasn't wrong about you when I hired you," he said. "You still care about this place."

"Don't even think about following me, Junior," she said and dropped the sword back into her bag. "If you don't want it, I'll put it to some good use. I hope you enjoy yourself in here with all the rest of the relics."

"Seasoned, Mindy. We're season," he said.

"My brother said it best: Leave before become part of the scenery. I know what he's talking about now," Melinda said and pushed through the door labeled Employees Only.

A bundle wires snaked across the floor just as he had said which made the small room seem even smaller. The break desk and chair sat in the opposite corner next to the time clock. The faded calendar was woefully out of date. The concealed weapon shelf in the desk hadn't been touched.

I don't care. Melinda thought and stabbed the elevator button. *I'm done. Get topside and I'm gone. I'm never coming back and that's final. Find Tommy and get off this rock. No more of this.*

The lift's doors whisked open and Nat's body tumbled out followed by Alita's. The force of their bodies kicked Melinda back into the wall and they all crashed onto the floor.

Wha— Melinda's train of thought derailed. The bodies trapped her on the floor, but she pushed Alita off easier than Nat only for the elevator's light to be blocked by silhouette.

The silhouette reached out and a gaping hole of a pistol's barrel stared down at her.

~

Melinda restrained herself from grabbing the gun, spinning it around and double tapping it between the silhouette's eyes. *Don't do it,* she thought and winced at the pain from her shoulder. She pressed fingers to Nat's and Alita's necks. She breathed a sigh of relief when she found a pulse.

Melinda refocused on the gun and reigned in every single ounce of her being that said, Take it. Take it. Take it. Take it. Whip it. Nobody holds a weapon in one hand. Grab it. Take it. Take the gahforsaken shot! You're on your knees, it's a perfect attack position. Jump her and wrestle it out of her hands and pistol whip her!

Instead, she raised her hands over her head and said in a neutral tongue: "I surrender unconditionally to your lord and master so our Houses won't be tarnished by this heinous act. I request a Liaison of my choosing to defend my rights and well-being until I am returned to my House unharmed."

"You speak and read the old tongue?" the silhouette said.

"No, I just memorized that speech in case I get caught past curfew of course I can," Melinda said without thinking and instantly regretted it.

The gun was holstered, and she was pulled inside the lift.

"Good, because I need your help." The silhouette stabbed the button for the vault levels. "You lie to me and so help me I will use this."

I don't doubt it, Melinda thought and said, "Where're we going?"

"The Vaults." The silhouette twisted about and the camo cloak filled out into three dimensions. The hood folded back, and a scared woman appeared. Darker skin then Melinda, bald and her one good eye was blue, the other was an expensive cyber replacement. Judging from the jig jag scar that ran from her right temple to the back of her head, she had survived a head shot. "What're you looking at cousin?" she said. "Oh, your friends will live. They're just knocked out. If we don't hurry your other friends may not be so lucky."

Melinda squinted. "Who?"

"Anji Scott." The woman smiled. "Thank you for not wrassling the gun out of my hand. It would've ended poorly for you."

Great, the psycho assassin Tommy told me to never talk to has you trapped in an elevator going down to the Vaults this can't get any worse. Melinda thought.

"Wait, what other friends?" she said.

The doors hissed opened and Anji nudged out into a well-lit, wide, stone hallway where the rest of the marauders, Dragoons sat on the floor, weaponless. Tommy was there too, but the manacles around his wrists meant someone had done something stupid or someone was very smart. There was no sign of Phineas, Cherie, Selene or the other mages.

The fact Spence wasn't with them set off warning bells along with a stench that never should've existed in nature, but it did. A trio of men dressed in rags turned and Melinda caught sight of Horatio. The men's long finger nails, hair and body odor said Liches.

Liches were just mages without their auras. No more glamour spells to hide their true forms, they trailed behind mages for the contact high. Where one was, more followed.

Anji nudged her around the corner and Melinda had forgotten how big the vaults were.

The twin iron doors were several stories tall and hadn't been opened in years. A scar ran down the twin halves said someone had tried to unsuccessfully burn through. A rat's nest of wires running from the wall lock said someone had failed to re-wire them properly.

And this is why the EMP went off, she thought and spotted Spence on the floor. Sweat covered his face and Melinda immediately skidded to his side.

"Finally," the Weaver managed in a vague tongue. "Please don't shoot. The Liches." He reached out and grabbed her wrist. "If those aura suckers come any closer to me, shoot them. Just don't shoot him."

Who him? Melinda thought.

She placed Roark's sword in his hands and said, "Who?"

"He's probably talking about me," a familiar man's voice said from behind her and she pivoted around to see the leader of the group surrounded by Anji, Horatio and the Liches. The entourage parted, and Melinda blinked at the sight that stalked towards her in a three-piece suit. The cufflinks and tie clip meant nothing to her, but his face did. "So, can you open the door or not?"

It was Spence MacGregor.

14
A BURNT CROSS

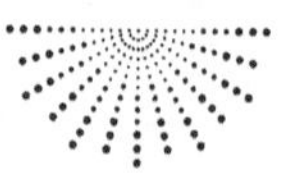

"WILL HE SURVIVE?" AN ELECTRONICALLY FILTERED VOICE JERKED NAT Stukari, Jr. awake.

A pair of gloved hands gripped his shoulders so he wouldn't thrash about. A still aura calmed his racing heart.

"He's alive." The concerned voice belonged to a woman and her still aura. "Thankfully, she's a shittier shot than I am."

Nat squinted at the woman, one of the camos that Kristie had brought with her. Dark skin in an even darker room meant no way to know who she was. Green aura eyes flickered hello at him. Probably a Leighton magess since no aura around the shoulders and no ones or zeroes.

Not Kristie. She doesn't use guns. A lie. Nat's brain managed through the pain that was radiating outward from his palm.

"You weren't supposed to shoot him. My time here is precious enough, and now you've gone and shot him." The filtered voice came from a fourth cloak, House Grade no less than twisted facial features. A man. Generic cufflinks and tie clip meant a newly minted House lord. "I said I needed to talk to him."

Nat curled away from the person and the hands receded into the dark. It gave him a moment to look at his palm.

The pain radiated out from there since that's where the bullet resided.

It didn't feel right. Nothing felt right. No precious blood over the deck. No de-activated buggers in his blood to steal.

Nat blinked away the tears and swore he saw the all too familiar HUD appear across his eyes, but it vanished before he could be sure.

Focus, he thought. *Need to focus. Calm down the buggers before they go ballistic and think you've been shot at.*

It had taken all the focus he had to catch the gahforsaken thing in the first place. Something that no one could've done without Academy Training. And here he was on the deck, surrounded by four strangers in his House. It was just like guests to trample in all the dirt.

"You said this was a simple milk run. What's the hold up?" the concerned one said.

"We've got plenty of time." Kristie's voice came from across the hangar. "Ignore him and let the poison do its job."

"I'm sorry. I didn't quite catch that? I said I wanted him alive," the fourth voice said.

Poison. Swell. Nat thought and clutched his head in his hands. The crushed bullet looked like any other until something blue dripped down his hand.

The liquid immediately disappeared.

A tranquillizer bullet. Really? Nat failed to focus. The liquid had been in the cavity of the tranquillizer bullet.

The fact it disappeared quickly didn't make the news go down any easier.

You've been poisoned. Now what? Where's Al? He thought.

"What are you looking for? This isn't what I signed up for," the concerned one said.

"Don't you move," the second camo's voice butted in and Nat chanced a look and saw Alita on the deck still. Sword not on her hip but across the floor.

She looked relieved to see him moving.

"Are you even listening to me? Why did you shoot him?" the fourth voice said.

Kristie growled and nearly drew her weapon, but the concerned one got between them.

"What are you doing? He's our client, you stupid—" the concerned one growled.

The House-Grade camo cloak knelt over Nat and grabbed his injured hand with ease. "Nice catch. Once you survive." A rectangle slab of wood the size of his palm was dropped into his other hand. An old House encrypted phone. "We need to talk. Later."

"It's not here." Kristie pushed the House camo cloak out of the way and the bugger's HUD re-appeared this time and wireframed her entire face. "Where is it!"

Nat blinked away the HUD, but it remained and through the static of ones and zeros, the words: TRAITOR appeared.

Kristie gripped his shirt front and glared at him. "Where's the database, Junior! You brought it back with you before the bug out and it's listed on the inventory, so where is it?" Her sneer melted when she saw his hands weren't covered in blood.

"Surprise," Nat growled and did the only thing that came to mind. He grabbed her jacket and head butted her hard enough that they both saw stars.

She staggered backwards and one of the camos chuckled at this.

Kristie regained her stance and pulled out the gun. "Outta the way, gonna shoot 'em again and this time, it's gonna take!"

Nat laughed and the glint of his sidearm came into sight. *You didn't frisk me? I don't care,* he thought but every inch of his hands burned.

His vision remained focused and Kristie's limbs wireframed in red. Critical points targeted.

Everything was red.

The klaxons in the hangar bay wailed twice.

Proximity alarm. Nat flung his other hand around the handgrip. "Just have to ask yourself one question: You really want this?"

"We need to go, now. They're early!" The second one passed by him and grabbed Kristie. "He's dead already, move!"

The concerned one grabbed Kristie, too and they hurtled out the nearest exit.

Alita scrambled over to him. "What was that about? And what's with all the alarms?" she grimaced at him. "Are you all right?"

No, he thought and holstered the weapon. He ambled over to one of the walls and pulled open a hidden hatch to reveal several screens, all of which displayed a green circle in the center and a red circle advancing. "Someone's entered our airspace. We need to get Mindy out of here, now." He leaned against the wall. *Before I collapse,* he neglected to add and stabbed one of the screens. "We've got an hour and half or less before they're on our front door."

"We're ignoring the three of them?" Alita said.

"They were looking for something." He opened another hatch and pulled down a lever. "Outer doors are sealed. The only way they can get back in is via the lift. Which they won't be able to do."

Nat breathed in deep and let it out. "I need to get to a med kit before it gets worse." He stopped. "You mean four."

"I meant three of them," Alita said.

Nat whirled around, his sidearm at the ready and pointed out into the darkened hangar. "You wanted to talk to me?" he said.

"There's no one there," Alita said.

"Yes, there is," Nat hissed.

The darkness was still for a moment, but a flick of movement and Alita had her hands gripped at her sword handle.

"Where did they go?" the voice demanded.

"Outside. I left them alive," Nat said. "What do you want?"

"We need to talk. Outside. Alone. Call me on this number and I'll send you the coordinates." The suit moved across the deck with frightening ease. "I'm sorry she shot you. That wasn't part of my plan." It walked up to the exit door. The door swished open by itself and the doors were closed before Nat could say anything.

"We should be going after them," Alita said. "There should be a first aid kit over there."

Nat holstered his sidearm and rubbed his temples. "Brain feels like I'm in an oven."

The lift pinged.

"First aid kit isn't here." Alita waved about an empty box. "Downstairs?"

"Museum will have them. You'd be surprised how many people leave them when half the people on this planet are immortal." Nat staggered over to the doors and watched the lift numbers tick closer and closer. "Wait. Did you press the button?"

Alita's eyes widened. The doors popped open and someone knocked them to the floor.

~

"What happened?" a familiar voice dragged Nat back to consciousness.

Nat rolled himself over and blinked at the small space he currently resided. "Museum breakroom?" he managed.

A blurry face popped into view. Roark Knoll. Very much alive.

The HUD appeared and wired framed his face.

KNOLL, ROARK— 100% flashed across Nat's eyes and he blinked away HUD. "Gahforsaken buggers," he growled.

Roark scowled at him. "You got what?"

"Shot but I caught it. They poisoned me. My buggers may've been compromised." Nat rolled onto his feet and squinted at Junior. "How long has he been here?"

Roark looked at Junior and back at Nat. "Why?"

Nat waved it off. "Forget it. I need medical. Where's Mindy?"

"You just missed her, I think," Roark said. "What's going on?"

"We have ninety minutes or less to get out of here before someone rolls in," Alita said. "You got any spare swords around here?"

Roark jerked a head to her hip. "And just what's that?"

"That's a toothpick. I need something sharper," Alita said and bounced out through the Employee's Only door.

"What do you even see in her? Sword Maiden's kid sister routine gets old," Roark said.

"Oh, please, have you seen her in that stealth suit." Nat clamped his hand over his mouth and sagged against the wall. "We need to get to

House ID card station and burn the rest of me. I think someone's trying to hack me. Where's Mindy?"

Roark pointed to the Lift indicator. "The Vault's it looks like."

"Good, she can't do much damage down there." Nat wandered out into the Museum and grabbed the First Aid kit from behind the information desk.

He popped it open and ripped open the packaging for a fresh needle. He pricked his thumb and waited.

"Why poison you?" Roark said.

"Because I sleep with too many people and sometimes angry boyfriends take it one step too far." Nat looked about. "Al, check the Cursed and Blessed wings."

"I am. They're all dry." Her voice echoed.

"What?" Roark said. "Since when?"

"Swell, we're dead running it to the Forges and they're gonna be empty." Nat pulled the blood tab out of the needle and stuck it in the palm sized reader. "Just gimme all greens and I'll be happy."

Four green lights blazed on the palm sized reader. The fifth light pulsed red.

The reader beeped, and the ratio dropped from 4:1 to 3:2 then 2:3 then 1:4.

"Seek immediate medical attention," the palm sized reader's tiny electronic voice said.

"Damn," Nat said.

"Those things never work," Roark said.

"I'm barely standing. My hearing is going, and my eyesight is shot. And my buggers are throwing hissy fits," Nat said and pocked the reader. He closed the First Aid Kit and clipped it onto the back of his pants belt loops. "Sooner or later, it's going to hit my brain and I'm dead."

Alita waltzed back in and announced: "We're bone dry."

"Bullshit," Roark said.

"Utterly. Bone. Dry," Alita said. "Only thing I found was the daggers and the only reason I found those was because someone hid them in the ventilation duck. We gotten an even dozen which work."

Nat grabbed two and clipped them onto his belt. "Roark, check-in with Mindy. Make sure she's okay then we're gone."

"That bad?" Alita said.

"1:4," he said.

Alita sucked in her breath. "Gahsakes, who did you piss off?"

"I dunno but if they meant it it'd be 0:5 and I'd be breathing through a straw right now. Call down to Mindy and send Junior in for back up. We're going to the Tech Deck to burn our Houses down," he said.

"Why? Your House is fine," Roark said.

"No, I've been compromised, and I've got guests acting like they own the place. First House rule: If House head gets poisoned: Burn and wait. Now, hop to it before she's carrying me over the threshold. Junior, get the Granger to Mindy, now."

"I'm not giving Melinda a rifle," Roark scoffed.

"It's under the desk in the other room. Better to be safe than sorry." Nat turned to Al. "I need you to go outside and do what you do best and finish that wireless install so we can communicate with Mindy."

"I'm coming with you," Alita said.

"Someone's trying to kill you," Roark said. "We need all the help we can get."

"We can take care of ourselves while Junior backstops Mindy. But, gahknows what else happens when we poke our head up to help Pan," Nat said and waved the House phone around. "And yes, I'm painfully aware someone is trying to get my attention. They have it. Now, both of you hop to it before we lose them."

Alita opened her mouth to argue, but Nat shook a finger. "I need you listen to me. They don't know who you are or what you can do. To them yer another trust fund brat trussed up in your mom's clothes playing war. We both know where you trained and why. They won't be expecting you and that's what I'm counting on until they figure it out now go. Please."

Alita hugged him and slapped him.

"That was for the camo suit remark, wasn't it?" he said.

"You know that was for," she said. She flipped up the hood and disappeared, much to Nat's relief the Employee Only Door didn't budge.

"I take it back, she does know what she's doing. Now, who are we trying not to lose?" Roark said exasperatedly.

"The people who are down at the Tech Deck right now," Nat said and closed his eyes. "And now I can't see shit. Yeah, you've got my undivided attention now. Gather up those swords. I'll carry 'em."

~

"It's ten decks below us and we're walking?" Roark said. "And how are you leading the way blind?"

"Somebody tagged all the hallways, doors and corners with Black Arts Scry." Nat shuffled around and saw a flutter of blue ones and zeroes behind him. "You've been trying to get your aura up on the step since you woke up. I can see from here."

The flutter stopped, and the blue ones and zeroes turned red. "Excuse me?" the flutter filled in and looked like a person.

"There we go, now I can see you keep it up when the time comes. And the reason why we're walking is because the last time I got into a lift I got knocked out for my troubles." Nat stopped at ninth landing of the stairs and leaned over the railing. "They're here. I can see 'em."

"You got poisoned and now you can see auras?" Roark laughed. "Right."

"Got my mother's vision and my dad's buggers. I always had the sight, but my buggers muted my aura. I can't do both, so I went with the buggers. My aura sight was never hundred percent. I think the poison is dampening them, so my raging aura is picking up the slack." Nat continued slowly down the steps to the next level. "The problem is, they're going to see me coming."

"I can't even see you," Roark said.

"Because I don't want to scare you," Nat said and stopped at the tenth landing. He reached out and touched the pressure door that blocked their path. "House ID card machines are on the left and Weapon Forges on the right, right?"

"Yeah."

"There's a queue," Nat said.

"Seriously! I can't even see them," Roark hissed.

"Maybe that's the problem. You can't see them. By the way," Nat looked back and down at two short swords that were dangling from his waist. "Where's Mira?"

"Nearby," Roark muttered.

Nat cocked an eyebrow. "Where?"

"I'm perfectly fine," Roark said.

Nat turned and stared him down. "Where is your sword, Techno Lord."

"Mindy has it. Happy now?" Roark hissed. "I was trying to get her to commit and she called my bluff and took it before I could swap it for a fake one."

Nat sighed. "I sent the six-foot suit of armor to back her up, so she's got your sword and Junior. This is why you can't get your aura up on the step, the rest of your aura is still in Mira. Swell."

"But we got your mouth," Roark said. "So, we should be fine."

Nat twisted the pressure door wheel and the seal broke. "Infamous last words."

~

Level Twenty in any House or Keep was considered the Tech Deck. If a techno mage was better with their head, they were sent to the Tech Deck to play with ones and zeroes as a Number Cruncher. If a techno mages was better with their fingers they were sent to the mechine shops to be a gear head. And if for some bizarre reason they were better flying five feet off the deck without the use of a jet pack and sleeping upside down they were sent to the Hanger to become a Flyer. Each position said theirs was the best even if the Gear Heads and Number Crunchers took one look at the Flyers and crossed themselves at the insane aerial acrobatics they did.

The Tech Deck was where a great many things were stored that weren't ready for public consumption. This included the House ID card (HICM) and the blessed/cursed weapon forges.

Nat and Roark pulled open the metal door.

The empty corridor lay before them. The animated neon sign in the ceiling pointed left for HICM and right for the Forges.

"You said there was a queue," Roark said.

"I did." Nat stepped through the door frame and spun the wheel closed behind Roark. He lowered the three duffle bags full of weapons onto the floor in front of the Forge's door. "HICM first then the forges."

"Someone is going to steal those," Roark said.

"Nope. It says Property of Lord Knoll all over them," Nat said. "Anyone tries to steal them the words get bigger and louder." He stopped. "What? Tactile spells, my friend. Tactile spells used by scrying."

"Is a myth started by old grannies who didn't want you to steal candy," Roark said.

They passed through the door frame for HICM and a queue of robed people snaked down the stairs and through the narrow corridor. At the top of the stairs, the queue snaked left. On the wall sat a neon sign that pointed left for HICM.

"Excuse me." Nat raised his voice and Roark groaned. "This is the line to burn down your House, right?"

The queue of robes all nodded.

"Great. Are we all part of the same House or different ones?" he said.

"Different," one of them said.

"It takes less than ten seconds to do this so what's the hold up?" Nat said, and everyone turned to glare at him.

"What're you doing?" Roark hissed.

"Swipe. Sign. Burn. Issue new cards. New House metrics created, and we're gone. So, why're we all queued up?" Nat said.

"Why are you blindfolded?" One of the cloaks said.

"I was poisoned ten minutes ago. I think they're trying to track me through my buggers." Nat leaned around the line. "No. Seriously. Why are we still queued up? Let's get a move on I've got guests to throttle and my House to retake." He clapped his hands. "Did someone forget how their card goes into the machine or you trying to hotwire HICM?"

One of the robes clambered down the hallway and stopped in front of him. She was a foot shorter than he was and unruly hair like a moppet. "Do you mind. She's trying to work," she said.

"Are you trying to hack HICM, yes or no?" Nat raised his voice.

"No," the robed moppet said.

"Swipe. Sign. Burn. Issue. Name. Bang done. Get a move on some of us want to get out of here in," he looked at his naked wrist. "Forty-five minutes before death from above arrives. Are you sure you're not trying to hack HICM, because it doesn't like to be hacked."

The corridor filled with a blazing light and a swear.

Roark dropped his head into his hands. "They're trying to hack HICM."

Nat sighed and nudged past the robed moppet. "Excuse me. Allow me." He cut past the line, up the stairs, turned left and walked over the smoking cloaked body on the floor.

The innocent looking wall mounted machine sparked.

"First things, first. Reset connection to the network." Nat stabbed two buttons and counted to ten. "Sign in with your old keycard." He pulled out his keycard from around his neck and swiped. "Confirm, Crosleigh, Junior, Nathaniel." He stabbed the confirm button. "Third option down. Burn All. Confirmed. Confirmed. Confirmed." His keycard sparked. "Re-issue card for primary user. Check. Confirm. Confirm. Confirm." He stabbed the button three times and a new card was issued. He broke off the old one from the lanyard, dropped it onto the floor and smashed it underfoot. He clipped the new card around his neck. "House Crosleigh. Population: One."

"Are you insane?" Roark said. "You just burned everyone."

"Who said I had anyone in my House?" Nat wagged a finger. "My guests, if I have any left will be informed of the current situation and will be told to shelter in place until I return. Anyone else in my upper echelons knows exactly what to do . . . if I had any upper echelons."

"Wait, you said House Crosleigh," Roark said. "No one names their House that."

"I did," Nat said with a shrug. "It's my name. It's my house. Not some poser. Not some wannabe. I'm the real deal accept no substitutes. Now." He stepped back and pointed at HICM. "Time to burn, Lord Knoll."

Roark mimicked the entire procedure and less than ten seconds later he was done.

"Welcome back to the living, Lord Knoll." Nat extended a hand and grasped the techno mages hand. "You're currently on a six-month decontamination routine due to your recent resurrection. You will be contacted by a certified house health care professional to make sure you're not a Lich. Once you're cleared you'll be safe to rejoin the rest of magic fearing society." Nat clasped his hands together and turned towards the robed figures. "Now, who's next?"

The crowd parted, and the moppet stepped up with a small metal cage. The cage held a water bottle, a running wheel and a lot of shredded paper. She saddled up in front of HICM, burned her House in record time, draped the key around her neck and deposited the cage into Nat's hands. She produced a clipboard from her cloak and a leadcil. "Nathaniel Crosleigh, Junior, I need you to sign here, here, here, initial there and thumb print there," she said.

"Aren't you a little young for a messenger girl?" he said.

"And you're running three hours behind but who's complaining," she said.

Nat handed the cage to Roark, turned him around and put the clipboard against his back. He signed, initialed, and thumbprinted on the intellipaper. The sentient stands that made up the paper did the rest. He handed the clipboard back to her. "Now, what did I just sign for?"

"I don't know but whatever it is, it's been hiding under that paper since I picked it up at the Wailing Seas Data Center." The moppet checked the paperwork. "You've got worse handwriting than my father."

"Wait, I don't have any pets." Nat grabbed the cage out of Roark's hands. "Wait, who sent that to me?"

"I don't know but I think it's diversion," Roark said and pointed to the cloak on the floor that was empty.

Nat sighed. "See, I knew it. HICM doesn't incapacitate." He swiveled about at the sight of Kristie Brie at the end of the hall. "Just the person I wanted to see," he said and before he could drop the cage, Kristie leapt forward. Her finger tips pressed into his neck.

"Yessiree bob, that's the real Master-At-Arms Kristie Brie disarm and neck pinch maneuver I remember," Nat wheezed and immediately collapsed onto his back.

The cage along with its occupant landed on his chest.

15
IN HIS SHADOW

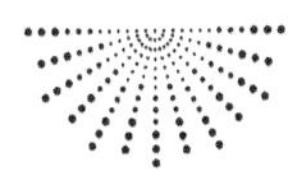

"YOU DIDN'T NEED TO DO THAT, KRIS," ROARK SAID.

Kristie Brie, the real one, stalked over to Roark and flung her arms around him.

Roark returned the sentiment. "I missed you, too, wife."

Kristie released him and smacked his shoulder. "You couldn't wait for me to come back. You called in for back-up? Back-up? You?"

"There was a short circuit in the chamber. I had too," he said and nudged Nat with his boot. "He really has been poisoned."

"Oh, please, he'll live," Kristie said. "What're you two doing down here, anyway? You're supposed to be airlifted out with Pan."

"And the Weaver and Mindy aren't even supposed to be here but here they are," Roark said.

Kristie frowned. "Weaver? He's dead."

"And so was I an hour ago until Melinda resurrected me," Roark said.

Kristie squinted in the corridor's low light. "Did she take some years off you?" she smacked his shoulder again. "Wait. Melinda is on Gunna."

"No, she's not," Roark said. "She's here along with the Weaver and gahknows who else. All that still doesn't explain them." He pointed to the cloaks. "By the way, you have a doppelgänger running around that shot him."

Kristie laughed. "Shot. Him?" She knelt and examined Nat's bruised palm. "You're not joking."

Nat's hand jerked away. "Nope," he wheezed. "Now, can someone please tell me why there's a bushwhacker kneading my chest."

"We need to know," the moppet said.

"Just who in gahsakes are you?" Roark demanded.

"K. D. Stukari, Duchess of the Wailing Sea." The moppet bowed. "Dinah to my friends."

"You're a Duchess. My ass yer a—" Roark advanced and a sword point touched his chin.

The sword that was in the Dinah's hand. "I am and a glorified messenger girl," she said. "Everyone else is gone. I'm the only left ever since someone's guests rolled in and took over."

"This can wait," Kristie said.

"No. Not anymore it can," Dinah said. "He needs to understand how bad it is. But first, I need to make sure."

"Of what?" Roark said, and the moppet pointed to the cage.

The shredded paper mount shook itself and the top of the cage popped open. The jingle of quills rose and a small, armored, four-legged animal popped out of the cage. The quills that covered its already armed body should've been cute but instead, the jingles reminded Roark of Necrocloaks. And for good reason, the quills of the Brie Short Haired Bushwhacker were just as reality bending as the creature itself.

The same creature that now sat atop Nat's chest.

"Benny is going to make sure he's not compromised like the rest," Dinah said.

Benny, the pigmy bushwhacker rolled onto her back and her quills sunk into Nat's chest.

The harmonics that filled the corridor for those who couldn't hear the ultra-high frequencies was just a dull ache in their ears.

Roark doubled over onto his knees along with Kristie while the scream that escaped Nat's lips was nothing a human could hear.

Benny rolled off Nat's chest. Her quills chimed happily, and Dinah dragged a duffel bag across the deck. In an explosion of little aura fireflies, Benny, the bushwhacker's body quaked and trembled. The small stubby limbed creature soon disappeared, and a sweat covered, naked woman appeared.

She pulled on a pair of pink sweatpants, combat boots and halter top. She shook her head and a bob of black cornrows that stopped at her shoulders.

"You okay, Benny?" Dinah said.

"I'm fine and he's completely clean," Bernadette "Benny" Bedriskah Brie said and shrugged into an identical robe like the rest. "Except for the poison. But he's fighting that, really well."

"Thank you all for the concern," Nat groaned.

The sea of cloaks parted, and the sound of quills jerked Nat halfway into a sitting position.

A half dozen people in flowing white robes had silently filled the corridor with frighteningly ease.

Nat's dagger wailed at this new development.

One of them stepped forward. Shorter than the rest.

"We've been looking for you, Lord Crosleigh," a woman's voice said from the hood's abyss.

~

Nat staggered to his feet. "Could you come back in five minutes? I'm still trying to figure out why she shot me," he said and turned to Kristie. "Excuse me, I'll be right back. Don't go anywhere." He stepped in front of the hooded woman and the dagger screamed. "I'm sorry. This thing just doesn't know when to shut up. I don't recognize the cloaks. Who be you and who do you serve?"

"What're you doing?" Roark hissed through clenched teeth.

"I'm introducing myself. Nathaniel Stukari, Jr. and you are?" Nat extended a hand.

The robed minion pulled back her hood and a woman with passing resemblance to Kristie appeared. The sharpness of her cheek bones and nose made her look more hawkish than she really was. Black quills blossomed from her skull and ended in white at her shoulders. A black art defense tchotchke dangled at the end each quill. A pair of cursed earrings graced her pointed ears. She donned a pair of bifocals and accepted his hand. "Hollie Brie. Nice to meet you, finally." She twisted his hand over and gazed at his bruised palm. "Where is it?"

"Right, here." Nat dropped the bullet casing into her palm.

"Be careful it may still be full of—" Roark started but Hollie had licked the casing dry and chewed the rest. "Why do I even bother?"

Hollie's body shook, quills whined, and she coughed up dust. She immediately deposited it into an evidence bag that one of her minions produced. "Not my poison," she announced happily and poked Nat in the eye. "He's not dead."

"Ow," Nat said.

"No, he's not," Kristie said. "Happy now, mother?"

"No." Hollie opened his mouth and pulled out his tongue. She released his extremity.

Nat pulled out a chair from the wall and settled in.

"What are you doing?" Hollie said.

"I've been shot at and knocked out all in one day. I just don't feel like getting hurt more," Nat said. "I'd be kissing the floor but shooting spells out of your toes is a lost art and I don't feel like getting shot at by someone's pinkie toe. What do you want from me?"

Hollie spit out the bullet casing. "You caught this?"

"Yes," Nat said.

Hollie tossed it at him. It just bounced off his forehead and rolled back to her.

"You're not very quick," Hollie said. "Tell me something, what do you want?"

Nat stared at Roark then to Kristie then back to Hollie. "What do I want? I want to know why she shot me. I want to know what's going on with that engine mount. I want to know why the network is down. I want to know why Mindy is here. I want to know whose side I'm on because I can't tell anymore. Hers or his. Yours? And I want to know who's in charge because there's some weird stuff going on and no one seems to care. Because sooner or later, I'm going to start caring."

"You're not caring now?" Dinah scoffed. "Unbelievable."

"You think I have answers for you?" Hollie said.

"No grandma. I think you know what's going on and no one is going to trust you after what you and grandpa Kirkus did," Nat said. "I think you think it's going to get worse and you'd rather douse the flames now instead of watching whatever survived the war burn."

"You sound exactly like your father. Too bad he's not here," Hollie said.

"Aren't you under House arrest?" Roark said. "Please tell me you didn't eat your guards."

"And you're supposed to be dead," Hollie chittered. "I'm not here to kill him. He passed. And no, I didn't, they simply left in the middle of the night."

"Of course he did. He's my son... our son," Kristie said. "Wait, they did what?"

Hollie eyed Dinah "Is there anything else?" she said.

"If Lord Crosleigh would do the honors of burning the other Houses. Please." The moppet's request dripped with ice.

"I'm not a lord or a Crosleigh," Nat said and glanced at the cloaks filling the growing ever so smaller corridor. "But, since you asked so nicely."

~

"Done and done," Nat said.

"You've done this before," Roark said.

"I didn't take the messenger position because I'm not a glorified mail man. I set up a chair next to HICM and you'd be surprised how many Houses didn't get read in how to use this thing properly," Nat said. "Like all these fine folks." He turned to the queue of cloaks and ignored the moppet. "Stupid question, what're you all doing here? There's a HICM for the Range Houses."

"It wasn't safe," one of them said.

"'Safe?'" Nat said. "There's a HICM in every single Range House bunker."

"It wasn't safe," another repeated.

Nat's eyebrows popped up. "Sorry, the eyebrows only go this high. Wasn't safe? From who? Wait a minute. There's a HICM at the Wailing Seas Data Facility. You guys didn't come in from the Range just to do this."

"They did," Dinah said.

"And just what did you do again?" Nat snickered.

"Escort detail since one Lord Crosleigh was busy," she snapped.

Nat seethed. "Still not a lord or a Crosleigh."

"Don't get angry at me. Last time I checked flyboy once you get a lordship title that means you're grounded. Remember that next time before you leave the Range House unprotected," Dinah said.

Nat growled, and Dinah laughed.

"Whachya gonna do. Draw down on me for besmirching your honor? Where were you when everyone else picked up your slack."

"I was busy," Nat said and pushed past her.

"Too busy for what?" she needled.

"You want to know?" he cursed.

"Yes. I really do. I want to know why when I called you to protect these people I got nothing but dead air. I want to know why I had to step up and defend the Range while you just disappeared into the ether and I want to know why you haven't come back to explain yourself," Dinah said.

"It's none of your concern," Nat said.

"Tell that to them, Lord Crosleigh." Dinah jerked her head to the sea of cloaks.

Nat stared down the crowd and walked around them. "Excuse me, I need to check on the forges next door and stop calling me lord. No paperwork. No title."

~

"She doesn't mean any of it," Roark said once they were out in the corridor.

"No, she's right," Nat said and picked up the bags at the forge's door. "She's right about all of it."

"I don't think you should be walking," Roark said.

Nat placed his newly minted House ID badge to the door frame. Built-In sensors did the rest and the twin doors pealed back. "Hopefully those locks did their jobs," he said.

The forge bay was one of two places in any House or Keep that had never evolved. It should've been the nosiest room. The constant shaping of metal along with the bonding of either cursed or blessed runes was always a hardhat and ear suppression area. The clang of the metal workers and exhaust of the hot steel wasn't the most glamorous job for an apprentice. The screaming of the runes being imprisoned in the weapon's hilt or handle either attracted members touched by a divine being or those who had understood they could live with themselves when they were told the runes were captured souls of living creatures. Souls so powerful, they needed to be harnessed until they burned out.

The second place that had never changed was the Resurrection Wing.

Nat often joked about not being to tell the two apart. Techno mages and Necromancer laughed at the joke. The rest just rolled their eyes and crossed themselves for the gallows humor.

So, when the inner doors opened before Nat or Roark could get their sound suppression headsets on and nothing greeted them, no sound nor light or even wind meant only one thing.

The circular shaped room had forged every ten feet and descended some twenty or so levels. Each level continued to get older while the forges expanded. After twenty levels that's when the defense candles stopped flickering and Nat's imagination, such as it was, took over and the abyss stared back at him. The occasional aura firefly fluttered into and out of the light, it's behind leaving zig zag lines in the dust filled air.

"Wha?" Roark covered his mouth and his echo drifted down several levels.

Nat pulled his gaze away from the depths and refocused his mind's eye on the forges closest to them. Even the scry in the old tongue was gone from the stone frames.

"These are bone dry." Nat passed by two of the apprentice forges. The same two that had been kept in perfect condition. The ones everyone saw before being shown the forges that had been transferred stone by stone, cursed fire log by cursed fire log from the old Houses. The Houses no one ever talked about because they were gone.

"Stay here, I'll check the rest. I don't want you climbing down these stairs," Roark said and wandered out of his line of sight.

Nat kept the bags over his shoulders and squinted at the curved walls. The same walls where the plans for weapons should've been stuck too. "This is all my fault isn't it?" he said. "And they're paying for it."

"Why would this be your fault?" Kristie said.

"They took the generators, too. Never seen anything like it, they must've been at it for months." Roark's weak aura popped out of the darkness and settled onto one of the forges. "Reminds me of the bad ole days when they took all the instructions, stones and the forgers. Only thing left of the Kincaid's were empty Houses. Like a plague just swept through and took 'em all."

"Are they fixable?" Nat said.

"They're gone, Crosleigh. They ripped 'em out and took 'em with them," Roark huffed. "You two don't look so surprised."

Nat refocused and found Kristie's and Hollie's form in the doorway.

"This place was cracked months ago," Kristie said. "What were you expecting, to re-charge and re-arm?"

"Yes," Roark and Nat said.

Kristie laughed. "Right."

"What's she doing here?" Nat said with a nod to Hollie.

"You have bigger problems," Hollie said. "The resurrection chambers are compromised."

Nat sighed. "That's what it was. The light."

"If it was that we'd all be dead by now," Roark said.

"Not unless they hadn't gotten to Pan's defense wards in time. Those Necros were awfully happy to chew their way through the ship when we were still mobile," Nat said. "Which reminds me, there's a second ship out there and probably a squad of Necros in here."

"My grandson is right, at first we thought you had tried to resurrect yourself, but then we saw you take off," Hollie said. "We need to check the other chambers before anyone else tries to use them."

"Melinda already resurrected me. What's the difference if we find them now?" Roark said.

"Which reminds me, did you have to do it so soon? I had people coming in to help," Hollie said Roark.

"Try it when you're split up into three or four different pieces being pulled apart every which way. It's not a pleasant experience to say the least," Roark said.

"By the way, where is Mira?" Kristie said.

"Melinda has her," Roark said. "And the rest of my memories."

"If one piece of those chambers is off you've got a bomb. Anyone tries to use it or open it the wrong way and ka-boom," Nat said and looked about at the concerned auras. "What? I listened in Resurrection One Oh One Class when they got to the part about touching things under the hood. You don't even crack open one of these things they were put together on a wing and prayer the first time. Technically they shouldn't even work but they do."

"We didn't have Resurrection One Oh One class at the Academy," Hollie said.

"He transferred that year. I remember, I signed the permission slip," Kristie said. "We've got other swords we can use."

"These are the ones from the Museum," Nat said. "Somebody brought a few Liches in here and we're down to a dozen knives."

"We need to warn Mindy about the chambers," Roark said.

"We have Necros running around, Mindy and the Weaver are still in play while we got someone else who poisoned me." Nat patted the House phone. "And Dinah out there with half the Range Houses because it wasn't safe. Lovely kill box they got us in. I think someone's on orders not to engage. If that's the case, they've got a private network and someone's backstopping them maybe running a war table."

"That's a lot of ifs," Kristie said.

"This Keep isn't that big, we would've run into some of them by now," Nat said. "I played Hide and Go Seek in here with five different Houses, this is longest I've got without actually seeing someone else. Unless they're waiting it out down at the underground rail stop which gives them the advantage even if they're hundred floors under us." Nat turned towards the open door. "You're coming with us."

Dinah laughed much like her anxious spinning aura. "Says who?"

"Sez me. I'm assuming you're bringing them to the House vote at Stow's End. We got two ways out of this place and on foot isn't one of them. I'm assuming you made a deal to get them out."

Dinah's silence was enough.

"I'm assuming there's an armored rail carrier in the basement waiting for you since you're escorting them, so they can chew off Clarence's ear at the problems yer all having." Nat turned to Hollie. "I'm assuming your cloaks are family or body guards."

Hollie nodded. "Bodyguards. What are you thinking of?"

"I need to ask a favor, I'm obviously not a hundred percent and without Mira, Roark isn't either, no offense," Nat said.

"None taken," Roark said.

"If you escort her and the House's representatives to the rail carrier, Roark and I will meet up with Mindy but first, I need throw up the rest of whatever they tried to poison me with. Somebody grab a bowl over there. I can't feel anything past my waist."

~

The poison was gone, and his sight returned first followed by his feeling in his toes and legs.

"Better," he said and hobbled to his feet. "I forgot take Benny with you. She can run point."

"Do you ever stop talking?" Dinah said.

"I keep thinking and talking. It keeps the buggers moving," Nat said. "They haven't been poisoned in a while. They're revising code as fast as they can. If they aren't in tip-top condition, I'm not worth my name."

"You're expecting them to ambush us and kill five Houses?" Dinah said.

"I would," Roark, Nat, Kristie and Hollie said.

"You all sound like my dad," Dinah said. "I gladly accept your escort invitation. It's a simple House vote."

"Nothing is simple when you come to a House vote. Maps have changed. Wars ended just as fast as they began. They don't want you making it to Stow's End. Whatever was so bad you had to escort them off the Range in the first place," Nat said and paced. "The After-Action Report on this isn't even going to be read it's just going to filed and no one is gonna care."

"Which reminds me." Hollie poked the slime in the dish that had one been inside Nat's body. "You haven't filed in six to twelve months."

"I will when the operation is over," Nat said. "And so will Lord Knoll because the last time I checked, you were alive and not split up into a million pieces."

Roark pointed at him but the techno mage's jaw worked. "He's right, I don't remember except I explained it to everyone before the resurrection. Phineas and his Totem Animus got us out, but the rest is a blur."

"Once we get back, you and Phineas are going to find a Priestess of the Hills to get you two straight and file. I think you and Horatio found something that no one else wants found and all of it is linked together with the Range House."

"A lot of 'ifs,'" Kristie said.

"No, he may be right," Dinah said. "About all of it."

"Swell, now we really do have to make it out of here alive," Nat said and stretched. "Benny!"

Benny leaned her head in. "'sup boss?"

"Don't call me that, please. I need you to run point for the group down to the rail carrier station while we go get Mindy and the rest of the stragglers she found," he said.

Benny nodded and walked away only to return. "Mindy? As in our Mindy?"

"Yeh, she's here along with the Weaver, Tommy, Selene, Cherie and a few others."

Benny nodded and walked away only to return. "She's where?"

"Here. We got separated when she resurrected Roark and the floor dropped out from under us," he said.

Benny nodded and walked away only to return. "She's where here, it's a big place. Wait, she can't resurrect a plant."

"It's a simple spell even I can could do," Dinah scoffed and shrugged off the looks. "What? I can. Just read the instructions."

"The Vaults," Roark said. "With our guests who we're going to be kicking out once they're done. Which reminds me. We need to check-in with her. The place isn't on fire yet, so she has to be alive."

Nat pulled out the House phone. "Funny you should mention that."

"What else has been going on since I've been in my cage. Anyone else come back from the dead I should know about?" Benny said and looked down at her clothes. "And I need to change."

"If you see anyone with Kristie's face and two camo cloaks, you have my permission to wound them. Wound. Not gravely injure. Not sucking chest wounds. Just wound them. I want to know who the serve because I'm pretty sure I know who suggested I get poisoned," Nat said and glanced at Hollie.

"I have no idea what my grandson is talking about," Hollie said, nonchalantly.

"Yep, sounds like conversation only my dad would have." Dinah tugged on Benny's sleeve. "Follow me, there's a spare armory on this level."

16

DEVILS DAIRE, PART I

SPENCE MACGREGOR STARED AT MELINDA SCOTT. "WELL?"

"Well," Melinda said and extended a hand. "Meylandra Stuk, attaché to Zi Stuk. Who be you and who do you serve?"

Spence MacGregor cracked a smile. "Mister Spence MacGregor and I serve no one but myself. Baroness Meylandra Stuk of the Wailing Seas was banished."

"And, yet, here I stand. My brother, Thom is over there. What do you want, Mister MacGregor? My psycho cousin didn't explain anything to me on the way down," Melinda said.

Spence MacGregor pointed to the doors behind her. "We need to get into the vaults."

"Absolutely, your House key will get you in and access your vault," Melinda said.

The smile didn't twitch. "I don't have my keys."

"And neither does your cute but annoying brother who is supposed to be dead, I assume," Melinda said.

"Correct," Spence MacGregor said. "Did I do something to you or your family I should know about because you sound a little pissed."

Melinda paced around him. "You. Charles Whittahare. Lauren

Daire and Layla Yashira in a room, ten years ago. Do you remember because I do."

"I'm sorry but I don't," he said.

"No, I guess you wouldn't. There seems to be so many of you walking around these days." Melinda stopped in front of him. "You keep those lovely men away from the Weaver and we won't have any problems. Deal?"

Spence MacGregor blinked at the simplistic deal. "That's it?"

"Allow me to rephrase." Melinda stepped closer. "The lord of the Keep is about thirty floors above us. Someone tried to incapacitate my ride and judging from the lack of reincarnation chambers not sitting around here I'm the least of your concerns." She extended her hand. "Deal?"

Spence MacGregor grasped her hand. "Deal." He released her hand. "The lord of the Keep is dead, you're not Meylandra Stuk and he's not a Weaver."

A buzzing stopped him.

Melinda sidestepped closer to the Weaver's prone form, pushed in a hidden wall panel and a wired headset in the cradle popped out. "Excuse me," she said and donned the headset. "Door Seventy-Five, how may I direct your call?"

"Mindy." Roark's voice caused her to smile. "You still have my sword."

"I certainly do," she said.

"Put Mister Spence MacGregor on," Roark said.

"Absolutely," Melinda said and handed the headset over. "He'd like to talk to you."

"Who?" Mister MacGregor said.

"The Mad Stuk," Melinda said.

She pulled the Weaver's spell book out and dropped it. "And this belongs to you."

"Closer to my chest next time, Mindy," the Weaver hissed.

~

Mister MacGregor deposited the headset back into the cradle. "He says he's willing to ignore the fact we tried to break in and once we're complete our business, we're free to go."

The Weaver staggered to his feet. "Sounds like him. Please tell me he didn't activate Junior."

"And two eight footers, too," Melinda said.

"He's fortifying himself. If you thought you were going to take over this Keep, best reconsider," the Weaver said to Spence MacGregor and deposited the book back into his cloak.

Mister Spence MacGregor ignored the Weaver and rejoined the group of Liches.

"Thank you for keeping an eye on this," the Weaver said to Mindy.

"No problem." She eyed his doppelganger. "Who's that?"

"Someone needed my help but without the aura, I split myself up," the Weaver said.

"Just like Roark did with his sword," Melinda said.

"The fewer we become the more powerful our legend grows. People seek us out, ones who truly need our help and so we break a piece of ourselves off," the Weaver said. "Done properly and Mister Spence MacGregor and I can co-exist without affecting each other."

"What happens if you two need to merge," Melinda said.

"Either it'll feel like a subtle breeze passing or this entire place is going to vaporized," the Weaver said and stretched. "I don't recommend the second."

Melinda snickered. "Like you'd survive?"

The Weaver leveled a glance and she stopped her snickering. "You have no idea."

"He doesn't remember the war," Melinda said.

"And neither do I, I might add," he said and winced. "There's another one then."

Melinda nodded absently. "I think there's one more of you walking around pulling the strings he can't. Oh, and if you're keeping score, we should've landed at Goslin Grace but someone who shall remain nameless rerouted us because his chamber had a short circuit."

The Weaver sighed. "Of course he did. He really is up there?"

"Does it look like I am lying?" She eyed her cousin. "So, this what's left of your brother's previous troupe?"

"No. I think these guys split off before the main group got themselves blown up. What're you going to do?" he said.

Melinda shrugged. "Time to get rid of the wrench."

Spence nodded. "So long as they want to leave."

"There's only one way out of here and that's the rail carrier station on this level," Melinda said.

"There's the lift." The Weaver jerked his head back to the corridor and someone screamed.

The crowd of marauders and holding operators scurried down the corridor at the sound of boot footfalls across the floor. It was the only time Melinda had ever seen her brother flee from anything even the Weaver had the sword at the ready.

"Gahforsaken, cursed ironed up jack boot..." the Weaver growled in a tongue Melinda barely made out.

Junior's entrance was exactly what anyone would've wanted. It may have been walking suit of armor, but it was a walking suit of armor that had survived so many Houses rising and falling over the years it lived up to the rumors. A once proud House, taken down in its prime by suspicion and greed of others.

The Crosleigh Model Seventy-Five aka Jack of All Trades Mobile Encounter Suit may have been standard in space born Houses but on a backwater planet like Stuk's Hollow, it was rare as finding the Weaver. It was also the only thing left of Crosleigh House and as Melinda has already discovered immune to her stunner. The crowd had ignored the rifle case it carried over its shoulder. It was taller than he was.

Junior stopped in front of Melinda and placed the case at her feet.

The Weaver lowered the sword back into his cloak. "What is that?"

"It's the Granger Rifle I kept in the office in case anyone felt their House was being besmirched," Melinda said and accepted the carrying case.

Junior stepped back. Its lower waist twisted left, its upper body followed, and it moseyed over to the wall plate. It plucked the wires off one-by-one. The plate swiveled about and kept its eyes on Mister Spence MacGregor.

The wall plate snapped shut and a key pad popped out of the wall. The suit stabbed one key at a time.

"Besmirched?" the Weaver said.

Melinda pressed her thumbs to the locks and they popped instantly. She removed the Granger One Oh Nine assault rifle from its cushioned confines. She didn't have to check the battery pack it was humming along quiet peacefully on its own. "The museum has a few sensitive articles like diaries and gun camera footage that doesn't show some people in the best light. Some people really take offense when their family gets labeled as a *stukarree*. I've never had to use this."

"Your brother lets you use that?" the Weaver said.

"It's a giant stunner," she said and collapsed the eight-foot-tall rifle in on itself until it was only two feet long.

"Let me guess, it uses the same iron stun round from your stunner," the Weaver said.

Melinda took out her stunner and placed it in the middle of the rifle's body with an audible click. She closed two panels and several green lights shined. "Close. Just an add-on. In case I have to deal with a runaway," she said.

"No more shooting me," the Weaver said.

"I didn't say you—" Melinda's sentence was cut off by several chimes coming from the key pad that Junior had been typing away on.

The iron doors screamed. Layers of rust rained down. Inch-by-inch they parted. The flicker of defense candles illuminated the darkened corridor beyond. The ceiling lightning illuminated a boring gray colored walls, ceiling and decking.

The walls of the corridor were lined with iron doors. Each had their own keypad and had been painted with a number. The defense candles tugged at Melinda's nose while the lack security raised her heart rate.

And no one here to greet us so that means no one knows we're coming. She thought and wandered across the threshold then turned to the crowd forming behind her. "A few rules before we go running willy nilly into the dark. People still live down here. Families. They are free to come and go as they please. If they get attacked or otherwise accosted they pick up a phone like that one," she pointed to the one she had just used, "and there will be no where you can hide because the Mad Stuk will find you." She pointed at Junior and for added effect the armor swiveled about at the waist, plate re-centered, its waist followed and crossed its arms across its chest. "Whatever you're here for, you're getting it and then getting out. The less time spent in here the better. If you notice the doors are closing behind you it's not your imagination it is because you are leaving via the underground rail carrier stop."

"How many times have you practiced that speech?" Horatio said.

"Enough to know that no one ever listens," Melinda said. "Now, where're we going and what do you need translated?"

"What makes you think we're going to let you?" one of the Liches finally spoke.

Melinda sighed. "Do you have any idea the diplomatic incident I would cause if I left any of you down there to fend for yourselves? I don't need that. You don't need that. Unless you have keys around your necks that say you live here then you're here for as long as he says you are and not a moment sooner. He's a lord. That means if you get out of line and Junior or I need to exercise force on you, our After-Action Report will cover us. We come out smelling clean while you get to scrape the floor for six months for not controlling yourselves. Are we clear?"

"The network connection is down. So, it doesn't matter," the second Lich said.

"First thing you have to understand about this planet: Nothing stays dead and buried forever. Someone always digs it up and claims they found something irreplaceable," Melinda said. "Now, are we bringing the marauders and holding operators with us or are we leaving them here?"

"They stay here," Mister Spence MacGregor said. "Along with the Weaver."

"He's coming with me to make sure I don't shoot any of you by accident," Melinda said. "Now, why are you here?"

"That's none of your concern," Mister Spence MacGregor said.

"Until I'm dragging you out by your hair after you open the wrong door," Melinda said and shrugged. "Anji and Tommy, wait for Zi. I'll be right back."

"Why am I waiting for him?" Thom said.

"Because, you're my lifeline in case they do something stupid and I need to save them, that's why. Also, you need to tell him, I've got this handled," Melinda said and wrapped one arm around the crook of the Weaver's elbow and the other around Junior's. "Shall we?"

"We're actually trusting her?" the third Lich croaked.

Melinda tossed a glance over her shoulder. "Just a reminder, none of you are actually worth my time. Now, forward march boys."

~

Through the corridors they passed. The motion sensing lights pushed back the shadows. The curved corridors all looked the same after a while. The four-way junctions were all numbered and the level markers illuminated at every T-Junction said they were moving down. But the silence that crept around them made Melinda jumpy.

"Where are they?" Melinda said. "Where're all the people?"

"They may be on a different level," the Weaver said.

"Three levels and no one either means plague or security all took a coffee break at the exact same time." Melinda turned to Mister Spence MacGregor's group. "Where are they?"

"We sent them into town. We need some privacy," Mister Spence MacGregor said.

"Unarmed?" Melinda blanched.

"What've you done?" the Weaver said to Spence.

"The same thing you always do. Move all the collateral damage to a safe distance and let the adults play with their toys. They're perfectly safe. Alizerin Leighton escorted them to Stow's End where they are enjoying the New Year's festival," Mister Spence MacGregor said. "We're going to the Daire Vault."

No word from Roark. So much for my backup actually helping, Melinda thought and stopped at the closest lift doors. "The vault is four levels down," she said.

~

The lift opened, and the scented defense candles drove Melinda to pull up her air filtering bandana. There were only seven doors on this level. The silence was one thing, the sight of three resurrection chambers on dollies was worse. They were the same chambers that'd had fallen through the floor. The dust was an easy giveaway. The energy that was surging through each of them meant they had just gone through the ritual. Each of them waited outside their respective door.

"Someone's been busy," the Weaver said. "Each of them will be welcomed back into their House once the New Year arrives."

This explains why I beat him to the museum. He was taking them home. I hope, Melinda thought.

"And none of our concern. Our concern is the last door," Mister Spence MacGregor said.

The Weaver stopped at the resurrection chamber sitting in front of the second to last door on the right. A cloak had been draped over the end of it. He peeled it back and dropped it. "I'm assuming you have a key?" he said.

"We do." One of the Lichs passed by him.

The other two Lichs pushed the resurrection chamber out of the way and pulled lanyards from around their necks.

The double iron doors parted on the darkened vault for there were no defense candles. Simply several dozen crates that had been stored here.

The Lichs grabbed several crow bars and bashed open the cases.

~

Melinda's earbud ringed with a new wireless connection. She casually brushed her ear and accepted it. "Took you guys long enough," she quietly said.

"I've got no eyes on your location, Mindy," Roark said. "Everyone still together?"

"Hmm hmm," Melinda said.

"I need either you or the Weaver to check the chambers and confirm which ones are working," Roark said. "Copy?"

"Hmm hmm," Melinda said and turned towards the Ohari Chamber. "I don't get it."

"The rampant pillaging?" the Weaver said.

"No, that's just idiots being idiots. I mean." Melinda paced around the chamber that Liches had pushed out of the way. "When do Daires need a resurrection chamber?"

"They don't use them. The swords hold all their auras until they're ready to constitute themselves back into reality," the Weaver said. "It's simple if you know what you're doing."

Melinda knelt and read the inscription on the chamber. "Property of the Daire Devil. Return to family when found," she said and placed a hand on the frame. "Kaare Daire and the rest of the family were banished at the end of the war for supporting the wrong side. They gladly accepted their fates, packed up and left. So much so the hole they left has never been fully healed."

"It wasn't nearly that clean, Mindy," the Weaver said.

"No, it was. That's just the point. The Daire got up, took all their toys and disappeared in twenty-four hours or less. They also don't have a photograph of Kaare Daire because the House database got hit during the beginning of the war. Single most loss of information anyone had ever witnessed," she said and jerked her head to get the Weaver's attention. "Check each of them. Real or not?"

"What's the point besides you hacking the network for all of that?" the Weaver continued without missing a beat. He nodded and thumbs up on the Ohari Chamber.

"All Museum guides are given full access when they join. The rigorous verbal test alone goes on for a week. The easy part of reading, writing and cataloguing an entire vault comes later." Melinda stepped back from the chamber and wandered over to the Leighton Chamber. "When does a Daire not need a chamber?"

"I'm starting not to care, and I do this for a living," the Weaver said and joined her.

"When they aren't, and the three idiots are ransacking the house before burning the vault down to cover their tracks," Melinda said. "The Daire Devil isn't a man."

"The few remaining records say otherwise but let's hear it," the Weaver said and blinked at the writing on the chamber. He waggled his hand. "I can't tell. I don't read Leighton but the migraine I just got sure thinks it's good."

"After a blood-filled night of debauchery it was found all the males of Daire House were susceptible to aura jacking. It was thought someone had sabotaged their Keep's defense wards. It was the beginning days of the war, so nobody had time to check so they were all shipped out of range of the signal broadcasters. Kaare Daire, left to fend for herself and immune to the signals rallied the women of Daire House. She kicked off a house war between Daire House and Yashira. She gets the nickname because she was devilishly cunning and didn't kill anyone." Melinda turned towards the MacGregor chamber, but Horatio blocked their path.

"Unsupported hearsay. The Daire Devil has always been a man," Horatio said and lowered his voice. "What are you two doing?"

"After-Action Reports back up everything. The history books are always re-written by the winners. Once the war was over, the men came home and thanked the women by kicking them back to the kitchens. Unfortunately, it turns out the bloodlust curse didn't just stop with the Yashira Cursed Hexen Witcha and their weapons being destroyed," Melinda said and sidestepped him. "Kaare bides her time and confirms that someone wanted Yashira House to fall along with their cursed weapons. Kaare is laughed out of the meeting with her House head so she pulls up stakes, grants amnesty to Yashira House because she didn't kill any of them during the war and disappeared across the sea of stars to the next coil. She rebuilds Daire House with the help of Knoll's techno mages, Leighton's magi and the Yashira's hexen witcha to create a defense grid to keep out the signal. Effectively pulling up the welcome mat."

"This rigorous verbal test with or without help because I remember that welcome mat line from somewhere," Horatio said and looked from chamber to chamber. "What is it?"

"Those banned books helped a lot, too." The Weaver sighed and lifted the cloak on the MacGregor chamber. He placed an ear to it. "That sounds like home."

"Without help. The problem I'm having with this is someone tried to burn down Yashira House and didn't even cover their tracks. Daires come in triplets. Sword, Shield and Crown holders." She glanced at the three Liches. "All boys because, someone needed to inherit the throne to listen to their lord and master's voice, right?"

The Weaver stepped back. "Mindy."

"Yes, I know. If they're the children, why was Lauren so hot-to-trot to get in here."

"You mentioned a dead sister," the Weaver said.

Melinda nodded. "Kaare Ohari is in the chamber. Neither of them was Daires. They were both from Ohari House, a support House that split off from O'Hare House when they found out they had auras. They rise through the ranks because the men were tired and stupid. The men had to keep the bloodline going but learned from their mistakes with the Daire Devil which is why Neale and Narelle side of the family got kicked out. The women can't hear the signal." She turned to Mister Spence MacGregor. "How am I doing so far?"

The glow of the cursed broadsword that filled the Daire vault stopped the conversation.

"I may have problem," Melinda said to Roark.

~

"Take 'em all," the head Lich said.

"All three are good," Melinda said to Roark.

"That wasn't part of the deal," Horatio said.

The head Lich pointed at Melinda. "Yer smart. Yer gonna show us how this place works. It's ours now."

"Someone cracked all the forges. We've got no blessed weapons, you need to get out of there, now," Roark said.

"Why does nobody ever listen to me?" Melinda said.

"You've got what you came for," Mister Spence MacGregor said. "There's a rail carrier waiting for us. I kept my end of the deal."

"Doesn't mean we have to," the head Lich said and patted the broadsword. "This will run out and we want more."

"That will never run out, you fools. It's an unending aura. It never will. Take it and go. Be thankful I don't do anything else to you." Melinda twisted her tongue down.

"Not helping," Horatio said.

The head Lich jabbed a finger at the chamber that had been in front of the Daire Vault. "Open it."

Melinda stepped back and his two brothers tilted the chamber onto the floor, and nothing but sand spilled across the floor.

"Find her. She couldn't have gotten far," the head Lich said, and his two brothers pushed past Melinda to the other two chambers.

"Melinda, do you need back-up?" Roark said.

"Yer gonna show me everything about this place," the head Lich said to her.

"No," Melinda said.

"Excuse me?" The Lich got in her face. "What do you mean, no?"

"You heard me. I said, no. I'll follow it up with a don't," Melinda said. "And if you ever as so much as breathe on me again, I don't care who you used to be. You will never get up again. So, if you don't mind, take yer shit and get the fuck out. I've had it up to here with you and I barely know any of you. If you think yer gonna run this place, yer sorely mistaken. The only person who runs this place is in my ear, and he answers to someone else. That someone is the boogeyman himself. Now, you know what's gonna happen when the boogeyman comes down here to talk to you. He's gonna take the meeting and then wipe you clean off the face of this planet because the one he serves, the fire-breathing witch, Atia Finnegan doesn't negotiate. Does not care one tick about any of you. This is me trying to save your insignificant little lives. Now, be a good little Lich, take yer brothers and yer fucking glowing sword and get, the, fuck out of my face."

The speech did exactly as it was supposed to do. The Liches laughed in her face and ignored two important things.

"Mindy," the Weaver said.

"Trust me. Don't," Melinda said.

"Don't what?" the Lich said.

"Don't shoot them," Melinda said.

"Who's going to shoot me? I've got hostages," the Lich said.

"No. We aren't tied up and secondly, he doesn't care," Melinda said.

"Who doesn't care?" the Lich roared.

"Who do you think?" Melinda jerked her head to the corner of the corridor where the shadows had pooled a bit too much for their own good. Down here, in the older sections, the maintenance crews hadn't gotten around to installing overhead lights, so candles were the only things that provided light.

Junior had picked the spot for only one reason: he had every entry point covered and since the Lich's poor eyesight meant the only thing he needed to do was simply stand there while the situation melted like urinal cake.

It's not Junior I'm worried about, Melinda thought.

Kaare Ohari had set the trap extremely well. The chamber was the bait. The rope, metaphysical as it was, was tightening around the Lich's ankles the longer they kept their back to the open vault since she had opened the doors for them and simply sidestepped out of the way like Terrie had.

For someone who had been quite dead, a presence drifted about just over the threshold, unarmed, but her hands and feet were enough since the Ohari didn't use crude weapons. They were the weapons.

Talking about sidestepping, which reminds me, is the Leighton vault behind me? Melinda absently thought and chanced a look over shoulder and yes, the doors were ajar.

A flick of light.

Probably from Selene's blessed broadsword. Melinda thought and refocused on the wretch in front of her.

He had upped his intimidation to stabbing her in the chest with his long nails. His mouth kept moving, but her heartbeat filled her ears. Her personal space had been violated. Her bad shoulder twitched, the buggers knew full well she could respond to such an affront with one of three ways: gun, mouth, or magic.

No. Ignoring you is what I'm going to do, she thought and the heat from the buggers retreated.

"Mindy, repeat your last?" Roark's voice sounded so far away.

"Hey, these doors are open," the second one said and pushed open the doors to the Leighton's vault.

Melinda sighed, an un-ladylike swear whispered past her lips and looked over her shoulder to in time for the Lich to get skewed right in the gut by Selene's blessed broadsword.

He collapsed onto the floor with Selene atop him and a crowd of people rushed out of the vault.

17
DEVILS DAIRE, PART II

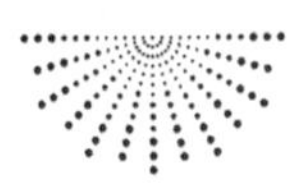

PHINEAS AND LADY DAIRE JOGGED TO THE OPEN LIFT.

The Leighton magi kept the Lady blocked at all times and they were inside before the second brother could register what was happening.

The second brother was more focused on Terrie covering their escape. Or rather, focused on her dual wielding iron throwing pistols. It was overkill, but Melinda remembered vaguely she always overpacked.

Cherie's shield spell surrounded all of them and did as advertised. She had had the necessary time to spool up her aura, something she didn't like to announce because all Leightons magess were supposed to be hot the moment their boots hit the ground.

The head Lich wrapped his arm around Melinda's neck. The stench was worse than his touch.

The second brother was in motion. He pushed past Mister Spence MacGregor and the Weaver, but all three tumbled backwards into one of the chambers.

The chamber landed on the decking and the lid cracked ajar.

A frothy wave of water spilled out across the three men.

The tide swallowed all in its path and dragged the unsuspecting back into the chamber.

A lone hand reached out of the angry sea only for it too to succumb.

The chamber's lid slammed shut.

Selene extricated her sword from the first brother. One look towards the lift and she lined up with Cherie and Terrie abreast in a corridor meant to have two breasts easy.

The calls for surrender in the old tongue just washed over Melinda.

Yes, this replaces my worst dreams by far, Melinda thought.

She leaned back. "I warned you."

Melinda clenched up her fists and stomped on the Lich's ankle. She twisted out of his grasp and followed it up with a punch to the face.

The broadsword clattered to the floor. She kicked it away but failed to escape his grasp.

"You think that's enough to stop me," he howled in her ear. "You can't stop—"

"It's handled," Melinda said and ignored the rest.

She reached down and grabbed his crotch.

Unlike most burden carriers, his genitals were still completely intact and judging from his lack of cup, his wheezing and screaming wasn't the worst she had heard today. He released her, again.

She twisted about and kicked him back into the Daire vault.

The trap was sprung.

The doors closed, and blessed silence followed.

~

"Mindy?" Roark's voice was muffled over Selene's call out for a headcount.

The howl that came from behind those doors was something Melinda never wished to subject anyone to in her lifetime.

The doors re-opened and the Lich screeched past Melinda, his body engulfed in a fireball spell.

"See, if you were her kin, she wouldn't have been able to do that to you but here we are, aren't we?" Melinda allowed herself a chuckle.

Terrie tripped him up and he landed face first on the floor.

"Whoever you are in the corner, identify yourself!" Selene said.

"It's Junior." Melinda coughed.

"I didn't ask you, Melinda. Identify yourself, now!" Selene said.

The shadows pulled back. Several running lights gleamed in the darkness and Junior raised his arms over his head.

"You know what, I'm good," Terrie said.

"Head count!" Horatio said through the smoke and a gentle breeze passed by and the fiery Lich was doused.

"What happened?" Cherie said.

Melinda staggered over to the chamber and righted it. "Property of Lord Spence MacGregor of the Cross." She lowered an ear to the cover. "I think I hear water."

"I meant why did the Lich just get doused?" Cherie said. "It wasn't me."

"My stepson needed to relearn some manners," a horse woman's voice drifted out of the vault. "Now, somebody tell me who the jacked boot armor belongs to or do I need to light someone else up, too?"

Spence's chamber sat up, much to Melinda's surprise, and a drenched body flopped onto the floor.

The second brother appeared by candlelight. His long hair and nails gone. He was whole again, judging from the aura that sputtered around his shoulders. The sputtering stopped. He breathed in deep and let it out only for his fiery aura to ignite.

"Alive." He giggled and waggled his fingertips. "No more burdens."

"Yes, you're free," a familiar voice said from the depths of the vertical chamber.

Spence MacGregor pulled himself out and the lid closed behind him. "We're even." He eyed the Daire Vault and twisted down his tongue. "And the other two?"

"Please," the voice said.

"Gladly," Spence said and the cursed Daire broadsword skittered off the floor into his hand. "Selene watch him. Mindy, you okay?"

"I'm fine, nothing a hot bath won't cure. Where'd he go?" she said.

"Where'd *who* go?" Spence said and stopped at the twitching burned body. "Prepare yourself to receive what is rightfully yours. Passed down from father to son. Until the day you can no longer wield its strength. This is yours." He slammed the sword into the Lich's gut.

The fire that encompassed them wasn't real.

Melinda lowered her goggles to witness what was scientifically impossible.

A piece of the aura attached itself to the Lich's body and it burned off whatever had taken over him. The goggles fritzed about and Melinda gaped at the remaining burden. It flailed about as if it were alive and was gone before she could blink.

"Unbelievable." She breathed.

"No. He used to do this for kicks to tourists at bars after they came back spelunking in the forbidden ruins. They'd come back half-cursed and we'd have to bless it out of them," Horatio said and shrugged off the looks from Selene. "Backwater burg with ancient ruins means spelunking tourists and old dotty professors looking for some ancient relics. When your brother is a Necromancer, this cursed, slash-hexed, slash-blessing cycle just becomes mind numbingly normal."

"Nothing about this is normal." Spence pulled the sword out and the first brother was free. "Someone did this on purpose to slow us down." He pointed the sword at the head Lich and he too burst into flames. "This is yours." He held out the sword, but it toppled to the floor as did he.

"Get him back in the chamber. He's not whole. Not by a long shot." Horatio got on one side of the Weaver and Melinda on the other. "He shouldn't stay in there but does he listen? No, he does not."

"You need to find the rest," Spence said to Melinda. "Chamber can't recycle what's already lost. You're worthy of this burden. Do you accept?"

"Yes," Melinda said.

"Good. Do not wake me until you've found the rest," he said and fumbled for Roark's sword. He placed it in her hands. "Keep it. He needs it more than I do. I can handle myself."

They deposited him back into the chamber and the lid slammed shut.

The lift doors opened, and Phineas leaned his head out. "Terrie?" his voice boomed.

"We're fine. The boys have been cured," Terrie said.

A cloaked figure exited the Daire Vault. A faceplate adorned the face. The paint was faded, but the gems that represented the eyes and mouth gleamed in the dimly lit corridor. The way the figure moved said she was a woman. The doors closed behind her and she deftly picked up the sword. "Magi Leighton. Good to see you again. My sister?" the plate clicked.

"Right here, hiding in the lift." Lady Daire smacked Phineas' shoulder. "Oh, dear. What happened to my nephews?"

"They'll live," the figure said. "The Weaver saw to that. We need to get out of here before they figure out what happened." She jerked around, her sword ready at Junior's silent approach. It picked up MacGregor's chamber with ease. "And you, you walking tinker toy need a bell."

Melinda turned over the dolly and Junior rested the chamber on it.

"Mindy?" Roark's voice echoed.

"We're fine. All chambers accounted for and all of them look like they're working. I think," Melinda said.

"There's rail carrier above us. We take that and get out of here," Lady Daire said.

"Melinda may have resurrected us, but I'm still too weak." The figure turned to the Phineas, Terrie and Cherie clustered around the chamber in front of the Leighton's vault. "I don't know who's in there, but I didn't see anything during my resurrection. I am sorry."

"Melinda." Cherie thumbed to the chamber and Melinda ignited one of her torches and walked around the chamber.

"No name. Just Leighton. The chamber is working fine, too. Maybe whoever's in there needs more time," Melinda said. "Once the Weaver is on his feet we can ask him."

"You're ignoring the fact he was two people and now he's one?" Selene said.

"I'll keep an eye on him. We need to worry about how we're going to handle the others. Harry... Horatio, I'm assuming you've got a passcode for my cousin. We get Kaare back in her chamber, we walk all three out with the brothers, get on the train, and have my ride provide escort back to town."

"That's the plan," Roark said. "We need the rest of the chambers before we go. I'll get back to you."

"And the Necros?" Selene said.

Melinda looked around. "I know. I know. I haven't seen 'em since we got in here. We keep an eye for them and keep moving. First, we get to the nearest phone and call Anji to tell her where to meet us."

"That may not be wise," Kaare said.

"Nobody knows what happened down here. We tell them the truth. The Weaver saved you, blessed them and now he's resting it off," Melinda said.

"No one is going to believe that," Kaare said.

Horatio cleared his throat. "Yes, they will. Trust me. Their eyes will glaze over after you get to..."

~

"I could care less about who is resting it off," Anji said once they had regrouped at Vault Seventy-Five's door. "We can't just take the Pan's ship back to town?"

"I can recite the rules on air carriers transporting resurrection chambers, if you want," Horatio said. "I'll call ahead and tell them to expect us."

"The short version is the defense wards conflict with each other. There's no way we're flying back into town defenseless just to get blown up," Melinda said. "We'll take the rail carrier back. Tommy and the rest can cover us from the air. We'll meet outside of town at Sleepless Maiden."

"We're packing up now. Tell Harry he was right. Someone cut into the network," Roark said.

"You think someone is going to care about you this much to try anything?" Anji said.

You've no idea the day I've had. Melinda glanced at the rag tag group surrounding the three resurrection chambers. "I'm counting on it."

"Melinda." Horatio's voice brought everyone around. His face was just as white as his eyes. He pulled off the headset and held it out to her. "We're taking Pan's ship."

"Necros got the rail carrier, didn't they?" Thom cursed.

"We're taking Pan's ship and are free to go once you hand yourself and the Weaver over to them," Horatio said. "They say Roark already agreed to it."

~

"Anji, Cherie and Phineas stick with the chambers," Melinda said. "Tommy and Terrie, that lift is an express to the rail stop. Roark is going to meet you down there, so we can finish this."

"Roark?" Thom said. "Mindy, who've you been talking to?"

"He'll give you the network password once you see him," she said. "Any of them you trust with your life you add them."

"Wand everyone down, Mindy and keep the sword close, I'll need all of it," Roark said.

And we are so talking I see you because this idea stinks. Mindy thought and pulled out Roark's sword. She wanded everyone down. "We're clean."

"Hand out any blessed or cursed daggers. The defense genies aren't secure," he said. "Check in once you've got all the chambers, we'll rendezvous with you from there and I'll explain it all, trust me."

"Where're you going, Mindy?" Thom said.

"First, I'm finding the other chambers and confirm they're real and not duds then I'm going to take the Weaver down to the rail carrier and meet our new friends. Selene is coming with me to make sure I don't do anything stupid."

"That's a horrible plan, Mindy," Thom said.

"You're just using me to carry things, aren't you?" Selene said.

"Hey, it's my plan. Besides, they haven't sent anyone up here to get us. That means either they want to talk, or he scares them that much. I'd rather be in his shadow than in front of him," Melinda said and turned to Selene. "No, I am bringing you as muscle and to carry things. Besides, Shield Maiden escort means I know what I'm doing."

"I'm not a Shield Maiden, Mindy," Selene said. "I was cast out."

"For doing your job and quite well at it, too. They don't know you've been cast out unless you sisters have branched out and gone freelance," Melinda said.

Selene cackled. "Like they'd be caught dead down here in a place like this with any of you." She winced at the looks she received. "No offense."

"No, she's right, they don't schlep," Anji said and everyone went back to work.

~

"This isn't the best idea. We don't know where the chambers fell, exactly," Selene said. "Why bring me?"

"Because that blessed broadsword of yours will make them think twice about doing something stupid," Melinda said. "Roark didn't tell me anything about this plan so either he vetted it or doesn't want me to do something stupid. And using Junior helps."

The catacombs the trio traipsed through didn't look even remotely familiar but the farther they traveled to the other side of the Keep, the more things looked vaguely the same.

The armor had stopped every so often. It wasn't grating on Melinda's nerves. If someone tried anything stupid they'd blast the armor first, wait for the smoke to clear and come after either of them. The fact Junior had two of Selene's blessed short swords at the ready meant if anyone had laid traps, the gems would sense it first.

So far, the swords had been deafening silent.

"Why this level?" Selene said.

"It's the lowest level on either side if anything fell it'd be here," Melinda said. "You okay?"

"Rather be on the ceiling right now," Selene said and ducked under a fallen archway. "I'm sorry I didn't come after you. Phineas said it was best to protect her."

"Hiding in the Vault was a good idea." Melinda angled her goggles up but nothing on the high ceiling was tagged. "I'm guessing Roark has some back up I could actually hear his voice."

"I most certainly did," Roark's voice said from in front of them.

The rifle was in the crook of Melinda's shoulder and aiming down the sight out of instinct, but Roark Knoll's form melted out of the shadows, three meters in front of Junior.

The techno mage smiled at her and thumbed to Junior. "Good idea." He stepped closer, but Selene raised her broadsword and wanded him down.

"He's clean," Selene said. "I'm going to take Junior ahead and scout."

Melinda nodded, and the duo left her alone. "I leave for five minutes and you get trussed up for a war," she said and pulled the sword out of her bag. "I believe this is yours."

Roark accepted the sword and the darkness around him from the cursed sword lifted. The tentacles returned, and his body sagged against the wall.

A string of words that even Melinda couldn't understand spewed forth.

The briefest moments, Melinda re-considered letting her friend go on, but Roark sheathed his blessed sword and for the first time he looked whole. "Thank you," he said. "I'm sorry I pushed you."

"I needed it. Now, what in gahsakes is going on. The chambers we found were clean," she said.

"We didn't check all of them before you did your little spell," Roark said.

"Wait. If I did the spell, shouldn't they be in-op?" Melinda said.

"No, the energy released by the spell is held until it's needed," Roark said.

Melinda gaped. "You're telling me I spooled up nine possible bombs?"

Roark nodded. "Sorry. I wanted to tell you in person. We've also been requested for an audience by a friend of the family."

Melinda cocked an eyebrow. "Friend of the family? Oh, no, escort detail? To where?"

"The New Year Festival," Roark said and pointed down the corridor. "The rest of them are down here."

"Somebody finds them and boom. Gahsakes." Melinda followed him.

"Don't worry about it. It takes a special kind of someone to wire these things in the first place. Turning them into a bomb just goes to show you who we're dealing with," Roark said.

Melinda's earbud pinged and the wireless connection to network appeared. "Finally. What have you two been doing?" she cursed.

"Tell Roark the network is secure. We'll meet you at the rail stop," Nat said. "Hey, everything okay?"

"I'm fine. Weaver is sleeping it off and we're almost at the rest of the chambers. Anything else you want to fill me in on?"

"Well, Crosleigh Aviation and Mail does have an opening for a sys admin," Nat said.

Melinda laughed. "Wait, mail? As in messenger boy? That's great. Wait, you want to fly the mail?"

"Little steps, Mindy. Little steps," Nat said.

The corridor opened and six chambers littered the ground. Selene and Junior had separate them. Three on one side, three on the other.

"Hot over here." Selene pointed to the ones on the left. "Not over there and I checked. No one is inside."

"The spell should've super charged them all," Roark said.

"Which brings us to our next point." Selene lowered her broadsword to the three cold chambers. The sword wailed.

Selene pointed up. "Fresh claw marks on the walls. Figure they came down sucked out the energy and went back the way they came to cover their tracks."

"Quick little buggers, aren't they?" Melinda said. "We took care of the Daires so who else is in here besides us?"

"Daires?" Roark said.

"Kaare's stepsons. They were part of Horatio's little party. Lichs all. Weaver put their auras back in and they're clean," Melinda said.

Roark whistled. "And he calls me a show off?"

"The problem is, we're pretty sure there are more of him walking around. I saw three people get sucked into his chamber and two came out," Melinda said. "So, we're looking for Liches and possibly a few more Mister MacGregors."

Selene lifted one chamber onto her shoulder than the other. "And you missed this?"

Melinda laughed, echoing back through catacombs. It caused all of them to look about even Junior growled at something unseen.

The armor unwound a grappling hook from its waist pouch and attached it to the third chamber. It pointed to Selene and then the chamber behind it.

"Good idea." She lowered the chambers and connect them so Junior could drag them behind it. She unsheathed her broadsword. "I think it's time to go."

~

The underground rail station was under lit. The painted scene of mages, machines and mortals on its ceramic tiled wall was a nice reminder of what come before. It shouldn't have been that crowded but by the time Melinda, Selene, Junior and Roark exited the lift with the chambers in tow, there were too many groups of people clustered about on the platform.

A low mutter between the Stukari Holdings operators and the marauders was silenced when the group arrived.

"And you were worried," Horatio said to Thom.

"We're also all in the same place," Thom said and gaped at Roark. "Alive and well."

Roark smiled, walked up to Thom, and punched him. "Alive and well. That's for leaving me and the rest of us behind."

The marauders picked Thom up and the well-armed humans formed ranks behind their former boss.

"They rescinded my orders to come and get you," Thom said.

"I hope so because I shouldn't have to split myself up, roll someone's animus in a jailbreak only to have to mail the rest of me and lastly, hijack your sister's pod to come and get me," Roark spat and turned to the marauders. "At least they tried a rescue op. Rescinded orders. Since when?"

"Since your boy got himself cracked. He gave them everything. They've got the kids and his House. We had to burn you all once we found out you'd made a deal with them. All of this was before we could even get boots on the ground. That's why," Thom said. "If it was Mindy, I would've done the same thing, but we thought you'd turned."

"That's a big if, I might add," Melinda said and alleviated the tension. "We've got three chambers. Total of seven. The other three we found were in-op. Someone sucked their batteries dry before we could reach 'em. The forges are dry too, so Selene and Roark are going to wand everyone down before we even step inside that rail carrier. Once everyone is clean, Thom is going to arrange fire teams, try to split up the remaining mages evening. Sound good?"

"Mindy. Nat," a familiar woman's voice rang out and Melinda grinned at the sight of Benny. She stood at the door of the rail carrier and beckoned them inside.

"You heard her," Phineas and Horatio said. "Fall out into squads."

"Do I even want to know who the friend is?" Melinda said with a jerk of her head to the carrier.

"I haven't a clue," Nat said.

"Taking charge," Benny said and nodded to her attire. "That's why I smell Pan and not Erik's blessed long undies."

Melinda stepped on board and followed Benny a few cars forward. "Which reminds me, my suit is still out there somewhere."

Two Shield Maidens guarded the next car they came to. The two winged Maidens wanded each of them down and they were allowed through the doors to the next car.

The stained, wood, hand-buffed chrome and clean carpet was like stepping back in time. The curtains covered up the fact the iron shielding around the windows were sealed tight. The connection to her personal network was severed. The smell of fresh food wasn't lost on her.

The grouping of people in the car looked vaguely familiar to Melinda until she realized the person smiling and introducing himself was Kirkus Wilde. Hollie Brie remained seated on a couch.

Yeah, this explains the Liches, the network and all of us being here, Melinda thought and accepted Kirkus' outstretched hand. "Meylandra Stuk, it's a pleasure to meet you, sir."

Kirkus Ulysses was an unassuming man. A head foot taller than she was. Dark hair peppered with gray at the temples, tan skin, a pair of blue eyes that shimmered like Roark's. Dressed for comfort not for climbing through catacombs. According to everything she had read, he was a doting widow to his three daughters. They'd been banished before the Houses were formed and never attempted to return until one day, his creations had brought the newly formed Houses to the brink of war. Cooler heads prevailed when each of the Houses newly formed intel bureaus found the instructions Kirkus had left that led them to his front door, so he could point them in the right direction.

This direction was the opposite of what the House heads wanted, but that's why he explained it must be done because the House heads didn't care.

He saved them all and asked for nothing in return. Except a deathbed confession ratted him out then his family, his House, along with Hollie went into hiding because the House heads wanted him dead and they had very long memories. He'd kept his first name but married into the Wildes. So Kirkus Ulysses, his family and House fell in one coil and in the next, Kirkus Wilde rose for all the wrong reasons.

Kirkus smiled and clapped. "And she can speak the old tongue, too.

How I missed hearing it. Please, take a seat. I have a request to make of you and your party. I don't know how much they explained to you all, but the Houses are voting in three days, and I need to reach Stow's End. I've heard wonderful things and would like to offer my services in any way I can."

Even if you don't have a House and nearly everyone in this car are the most wanted war criminals in the Universe, Melinda thought.

"It would be an honor," she said.

18
AS PLANNED

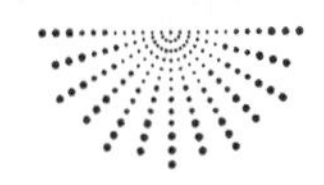

"It's simple. We burn down your House," Melinda said.

"Again with burning down Houses. That's not the answer to everything, Mindy," Hollie said.

"Not physically burning. Just deleting your biometric file in the network and replacing it with a new one. See, someone else is here and they've been avoiding us but good. I need to light a fire under their asses so they do something stupid like oh, I don't know, blow up the three dropships that will be escorting us back to Stow's End," Melinda said.

"Wait, how many ships do we have?" Kirkus said.

Nat pointed up. "I have them fueled and ready to fly. They can't focus on two of us at the same time. So, we use the three decoys, they get blown up, and the rail carrier hightails it back to Stow's End with the remaining chambers."

"Why not split the group?" Kirkus said.

"That means we're ready to start a fight which we aren't. Once they blow up the ships, they'll be ordered to stand down and let the rail carrier go," Melinda said.

"You seem awfully sure of yourself this will work," Kirkus said.

"Would you believe me if I told you this was all just a test and right now, there are some freshmen Houses camping out atop the Keep, waiting for us to make a move so they can take a pot shot at us?" Melinda said.

"A pot shot? You said three ships are going to get blown up," Hollie said.

"Right, once they overreact," Nat said.

"Overreact to what?" Hollie said.

"An After-Action Report that shows all of us together having completed our task and rescued the Mad Stuk and brought you all safely back to Stow's End," Nat said.

"The network connection is down," Hollie said.

"Yes, but the messenger system isn't. One of the mid-Houses is playing babysitter to the freshmen and one of them has a messenger bag," Nat said.

Kirkus frowned. "Wait. This is a test?"

"It's a playdate slash test slash let's bring in people from the cold. We do this every six months," Nat said.

Kirkus glanced at Hollie. "I see."

"After the war, a lot of Houses were stuck on the other side of the range," Nat said. "Miss Stuk and I were tasked to bring them in."

"You've been banished for ten years." Kirkus nodded to Melinda.

"And our predecessors weren't as interested," Melinda said. "A year ago, my banishment ended but the current House heads didn't care until six months ago when they were given a choice, get out or play ball. They grabbed their tickets and bolted before their Houses knew what happened."

"This explains why we can't contact them," Kirkus said.

"I can tell you we do know what we're doing. We have enough marauders, Holding operators and mages to bring you all in," Melinda said. "If you have House phone, we can call ahead so they're prepared for our arrival."

"Tell me what happened last time you did this," Kirkus said.

"The Houses involved were brought in. They were debriefed. Their original House's files were burned. They were given new names and files. They boarded the star carrier and jumped as planned," Nat said.

"I've heard different story," Kirkus said. "I heard one of you was comprised and something about launching the Weaver's chamber out the back of the carrier before it jumped into S-Cut. The Weaver had to be split up because Mister Crosleigh was compromised only to lead them back to his House, the children under Lady Brie's care disappeared in the middle of the night and right now the two of you are attempting to fix the problem by getting you merry band back together because whoever is out there has been hunting for you and with the both of you being here has brought this heinous calamity to my front door. Is that how to you describe as planned, Mister Crosleigh?"

"Actually, he launched it out of the torpedo tube because I was inches from taking the door off with a crash axe, but yes, I'd say it went as planned," Nat said. "And it's Stukari, by the way."

~

"In his defense, whoever took him over knew what they were doing, sir," Melinda said.

"And how do you know they won't try it again?" Kirkus said.

"As far as we can tell it's a one-shot deal and whoever did it can't control him along with the rest," Benny said.

"Well that's... 'the rest?'" Kirkus choked. "'The rest?'"

"I wasn't assigned to the previous operation. I was too entrenched on a separate operation when my ground crew was comprised, and I was forced to retreat to the nearest safehouse. I awaited extraction and they walked through the front door like it was nothing," Nat said. "It can't control that many of us at the same time. I was a tipping point and have been on medical ever since. Benny checked me and besides the hex someone put on me, I'm clean."

Kirkus turned to Hollie. "This isn't you?"

Hollie shook her head. "The antidote I gave him worked. He's clean."

"Gave me? Gave me?" Nat chuckled and flexed his palm.

Melinda leaned over and gaped. "How many times have I told you, stop catching bullets. Wait, how're you even still here? That should've taken your arm off."

"What separate operation?" Kirkus cleared his throat.

"A techno mage House on the Range found an engine mount on the edge of Wailing Seas. I was sent out to confirm proof and found the Weaver in his shuttle. I called in for back up and by the time my back up arrived they'd turned. They blew up my ride before I knew it and I ran to the nearest safehouse," Nat said.

"How many in this ground crew of yours?" Kirkus said. "I'm just thinking it through so indulge me, please."

"Six to seven. Three Priestess of the Hills and five seniors," Nat said.

"Gahsakes," Hollie said. "You didn't tell me that."

"I burned them and myself before I was captured. They can't get back in until they surrender unconditionally," Nat said. "The system that myself and Miss Stuk devised is a simple one and has enough fail safes where if we lose people they're burned automatically with five seconds of not checking in. Which is why I'm currently Mister Stukari and not Crosleigh. It worked for Miss Scott and so far, it's worked for me. But to answer your original question, I believe they used me to warn the Weaver to get off the star carrier before it jumped."

"Wait, who this 'they' that tried to help you?" Kirkus said.

"An interested third-party," Nat said. "Once I burned myself I was burdened with one of their own to help."

"Burdened with what?" Kirkus said. "You're still walking and talking so it can't be that bad."

"I accepted the burden willingly," Nat said. "With their help, I managed to break free of their control. I got on board and warned the Weaver to get off before the ship jumped. The scuttlebutt I've been hearing is the ship hasn't been heard from and a few people are getting nervous."

"You said you accepted it willingly. From who?" Kirkus said.

"As I said an interested third-party," Nat said. "It's my belief that they're warned us because something bigger is going on and if we're not careful we're next."

"I can concur with that belief," Benny said.

"Evidence? After-Action Reports?" Kirkus said.

"Horatio is correct the network has been hacked. No bags. No badges. No reports," Nat said. "Whoever is out there in Wailing Seas Data Center doesn't want us to know what's going on. I'm fine with that until we get the rest of our crew back together because we're missing a few. Once we get you back to town, we can re-organize and get a recon group together to check."

"I think we have more than enough evidence," Kirkus said. "One of the Wailing Houses requested my protection and judging from what you've and the Duchess have told me I believe they may have escaped just in time." He nodded to one of the Maidens and the exited the car. "They said they were approached to help dig something up but when they refused, they were isolated from the rest until we showed up and asked for amnesty. We've wanded them down so there's no problem there but they're scared for their lives."

"Range Houses? Which one?" Melinda said. "Which Duchess?"

"The Kincaids," Hollie said. "Dinah has proven herself during our trek across the sea to get here."

"Dinah Stukari?" Melinda said and raised her hand up to indicate the moppet's height. "She's here?"

"Erik's cousins," Nat said. "They're harmless. If you don't mind, can I bring Junior in on this I like document their report."

Kirkus nodded and picked up one of the wired headsets.

"Techno mages?" Melinda said. "Why would a support House decline to help another that's the first basic support rule. It can't be that bad." She touched his hand. "You sure you're okay?"

"Fine," he said.

Melinda looked back at Benny and smacked his shoulder. "You two."

"What?" he said. "She wanded me down. So what?"

She smacked him again. "That's for phrasing. Erik is going to kill you."

The door to the car opened and Junior, minus whatever blessings, curses or hexes on its armor, clomped in with the Shield Maidens in lock step, weapons at the ready.

"Oh my." Kirkus stepped back at the six-footer. "Look at you. I've never seen one alive before."

Hollie rolled her eyes. "And off he goes to tip toe through the tulips."

"And still in perfect condition too." Kirkus waved off the guards. "May I?"

Nat nodded. "It's okay," he said to the armor. "You can come out now."

Junior stopped in front of Kirkus at parade rest. The hands reached to the plate, released the seals and pulled the plate off.

The empty headspace was empty. At least until a red, hard-shell arthropod popped into view. Its hidden legs balanced on the armor's neckline. A pair of tiny, purple gems had been inset on the front of its carapace where it's compound eyes should've been. It leaned forward at Kirkus' approach.

"Unbelievable," Kirkus said. "They burdened you with this?"

"You mean burdened me with him." The arthropod chittered and jerked its spiked tail in Nat's direction. "The old man finds me an aquarium and brings me to the hottest, driest, sandiest planet, ever. You can understand why I stay in there."

"It talks," Kirkus said.

The eyes gleamed. "Of course, I talk. What did you expect me to do, sign language? Do you see how short my legs are?" it twisted itself around to get a lay of the room. "There's a ten-foot aquarium in a car behind us. May I?"

Kirkus nodded and the two guards were gone. "I'm sorry to stare. But I haven't seen any of you since I was at the Academy and even then, the only thing the old one did was sleep."

The arthropod nodded. "I was wondering where she'd gotten too. No wonder she stopped answering my calls. Now, before the other shoe drops you aren't here to eat me or ask me to end world hunger, are you?"

"No. Nothing like that," Kirkus said.

"Ask me to save a love one?" the arthropod continued.

"No," Kirkus said.

The arthropod closed its eyes. "Ask me to go off and do something stupid with Junior over there."

"Probably," Kirkus said and the Shield Maidens re-appeared with the aforementioned fish tank.

"Yeah, I figured." The arthropod scurried down Junior's arm and after tasting the water, it slid itself in without spilling a drop. "Bring them in and just ignore me. I'm just part of the scenery. They'll be focused on Junior more than me."

Junior deposited its fake head back onto its neck and twisted the plate closed.

"Someone write this down, he's speechless," Hollie snickered.

~

The family of four accepted the hot tea and ignored the tank. The young twin girls stared at Junior in awe even if their older brother glared at it the most. The patriarch of the family was the mother of the twins or at least Melinda assumed she was. Same red hair, freckles across peach colored skin. Junior was the odd man out, dark hair, skin and light eyes. Probably part of the House foster program and wouldn't be cherry picked until his aura emerged. They were all techno mages even if he didn't have an aura like Roark, sooner or later his fingers would start sparking and then they'd have to iron up his hands with gloves until he could successfully control it.

"...thank you again for accepting our request," the mother finished.

"I'm duty and honor bound as I said before," Kirkus said. "I was hoping you could explain to my friends what you told me about why you had to leave in such a rush."

"Like I told Mister Wilde, about a year ago, we were staying at my mum's place when it happened. Big explosion and all these pieces dropped through the roof. Didn't hit any of us. We weren't even home, but we tried to figure out where it all came from. They showed up an hour later. Magi cloaks. They didn't talk much until one of them came up and said he was sorry for the ruckus and offered to take the pieces out.

"At first, I thought Junior had been playing around in the barn but turns out they were testing something, and it got away from them. So, they fixed the house and offered to take us in since the House wasn't like it used to be. But we said no. All of the Range House know each other so when Magi shows up out of the blue, we know they're on their pilgrimage out to the other side of Wailing Seas, but so many of them some of us thought we were being invaded and locked ourselves in the ole bunker. But they left once all the pieces were gone.

"About a day later, someone else shows up, just one with a coat of arms all official with a badge and asked which way they had gone. I told 'em they just up and vanished. Then nothing until one by one, each of us started getting offers on our Houses. We turned them down flat. Our Houses aren't for sale. About five months after that, the other Houses decided they were done on the Range and took the deal that'd been offered them, but we stayed. We were born here, we're gonna live here. The new owners start fixing up the old Houses. They dug out the rail stop and the air carrier station. Everything was left to rot once the war ended ten years ago and none of us were young enough to put our backs into anymore.

"When the rail carrier showed up one day with arch mages, we were delighted to see them. Hadn't seen them in years, but they weren't right. Too quiet. Too organized. They walked out into the desert like it was the sanest thing to do, and we never saw them again. Then quakes started happening and the House wasn't too sturdy to begin with. We stayed in the ole House Bunker for the rest of the time until the quakes stopped and then we saw it one night." The mother stopped and chugged down the entire contents of glass. "I've never seen something so big. My cousins used to work on the carrier dry docks, so I've seen air carriers before. Whatever it, she, was, she wasn't an air carrier. She was bigger than that. Junior knows about them more than I do."

Junior, the soon-to-be techno mage, stopped scowling at Junior the walking suit of armor and refocused Melinda. "She looked like a chariot-class space carrier except someone had decided to weld this hideous bridge blitz onto her nose. She was there three days and nights. On the fourth day, she was gone."

Melinda grabbed a pad and slid it across the table. "Show me."

Junior swiped through several images and stopped at one. "This class. Exactly like this one."

Nat leaned over and grimaced. "Well, that narrows it down, lovely."

"And she just vanished?" Melinda said.

"No. She waited until they got the second one up onto the drydocks and they both disappeared."

"Two of them?" Melinda said.

"They come in pairs. One carries the life support, the other carries the defense and offense," Nat said. "And they tried to recruit you to repair them?"

Junior locked eyes with him. "No. I couldn't do what they wanted. At least not yet."

"Repair? Arch mages aren't part of damage control like refit and repairs on carriers. They're part of fire control. Offense and defense. Big spells not... repairs," Melinda said.

"I tried to tell them that, but they didn't care. The rest of my family turned them down flat. Told them the carriers didn't belong to them and shouldn't mess with them," Junior said. "Then one day they moved down the tracks. Dug out the next stop and moved away from us."

"Mission creep. Nobody around to raise a fuss so instead of killing you they just moved on. Smart move," Nat said.

Junior nodded. "By the time I figured it out they had almost gotten to another group of families then Mister Wilde showed up and we bolted in the middle of the night with as many people as the rail carrier could carry."

~

After the family had been dismissed, Melinda stretched across the sofa. "You got all of that?" she said.

Junior nodded and scooped the arthropod out of the tank. "They're telling the truth."

"Awfully rehearsed but also very creepy. I have to ask then," she said.

"Hmm?" Kirkus said.

"You believe them?" she said.

"The mother or all of them?" Kirkus said. "And yes, I believe them. You weren't there."

"Anyone get a photo of these carriers?" Melinda said.

"Mindy," Nat muttered.

"I'm asking because when I file the After-Action Report that not one but two war carriers are just flitting about without a care in the world, someone is gonna ask for photos. I'm not being bitchy. I'm ruling out the possibility that the would-be techno mage got a good look at the entire operation and managed to be the sole survivor of whatever is happening out there. If it's the truth, fine. If he's lying and happens to be the brains behind the operation and only wants to get out before the rest of this hits the fan, I need to know now before someone bags me and questions me in a debrief room that doesn't exist to demand to know why I let the brains get away," Melinda said, rubbing her temples. "And none of them were properly introduced. We're really off our game."

"No, I didn't see any of it. But, I did see the empty houses but never saw the bunker," Kirkus said. "All the right questions, though. I heard you were sharp."

Melinda smiled. "You're not exactly catching me at my best." She glanced at Nat. "Tag, you're it because I've had enough of a day."

"I didn't want to say anything in front of them, but the Keep's radar did pick up a ping. It may be nothing, but we do need to get out of here," Nat said. "The rest of you go to Stow's End. We'll meet you there."

"I thought you said splitting up the group was bad," Kirkus said.

"I didn't say I was going to split up the group. What I said was, once we take the picture and upload the report, you're taking the train back. Melinda brings you in and debriefs all of you. While everyone is focused on you, I sneak away and check things out, only to re-appear as planned at Sleepless Maiden, and no one is much the wiser," Nat said.

"If they're all dead in the bunker, you are hightailing it back here. Because you have no back-up," Melinda said and picked up the slate with the profile of the carriers. "I've seen the gun camera footage of what these war carriers can do. It's the stuff of nightmares."

"Wait, how do you know how to find this bunker?" Kirkus said. "It's a chariot class, not a war carrier."

"No, it's a war carrier. They re-classified all the carriers after the last House war because anything with war in the title, well, you get the point," Melinda said.

"We've all been cross-trained and read in," Nat said. "The aw-shucks mom with her three kids just reeks, but it's also our first real clue. We are missing several arch mage Houses and someone is trying to kill Mindy. Time to get our photo op and file. If the Keep isn't on fire by time the rail carrier leaves the station, I'll be very unimpressed."

"And, to keep the den mother happy, I'm going with him," Benny said.

"Three people search team and someone to stays on board the ship to monitor or did you actually forget how many people you need for a ground operation?" Melinda said. "This isn't gonna end well, is all I'm saying."

"I'll bring Vernon, too. Happy?" he said. "I can't bring Alita. She's the only defense Pan has."

"Vernon?" Melinda's head jerked up. "Vernon's where?"

"Guarding the ship with Pan. Remember?" he said. "How long have you been up?"

Melinda rubbed her eyes and admitted: "Too long."

"You need to get some sleep while we're gone. I promise I'll be careful."

"Which means, I'll be keeping him out of trouble," Junior said and twisted its plate back on. "And she's right, it cannot be that big. Nothing that big survived the war."

Melinda pulled Nat aside. "Once I get into town I'll track down everyone else. We're still missing a few people. Watch your back."

"I know," Nat said.

"Seriously. This is all been too easy since we got here. I've got this close, I'm not letting up and remember neither should you," Melinda said.

Nat gripped her shoulders. "I am prescribing bedrest after the photo. Because you need some rest."

"I heard you the first time. We haven't gotten this close before and splitting us up now isn't good idea, but I think they're telling the truth even if they're creepy," Melinda said and hugged him. "Good luck."

"It's bad luck to do that, Mindy." Nat hugged her back. "And don't try siphoning my aura off to keep yourself awake, I think Benny took enough to last her for a week."

"No more cuddling with the trans-dimensional weapons master." Melinda released him. "Do me a favor when you're out there. Get my suit and his pod while you're out there."

"You really expect it all to be there?" he said.

"It hasn't moved," she said and motioned outside. "Let's get this over with before I collapse. Everyone, if you'll follow me, we need a group photo to celebrate."

~

The chambers were lined up first in the half circle formation. Melinda had pushed Spence's chamber into the center where she stood and directed people much to everyone's chagrin. The Marauders spread themselves behind her. The Holding Operators out on the edges. The mages stood behind their House chamber while Phineas didn't stand behind the Leighton Chamber, Terrie and Cherie did. Benny, Selene and Alita flanked the Weaver's Chamber on one side, Nat, Dinah, Roark and Junior on the other. Kirkus and his cadre sprinkled themselves throughout the group. Melinda stayed atop the Weaver's chamber much to Thom's annoyance.

In the end, the black and white photos was the most redacted since after the war.

The flash bulb extinguished, and a thud reverberated through the flooring.

"Wow. They're serious," Kirkus said.

"We shouldn't be able to feel that," Nat said and the next quake sent everyone onto the floor. "I think our friends just showed up."

"'As planned?'" Kirkus chortled.

"Sure, that's it, just rub it in." Nat pushed himself up and pointed his crew to the stairs. "Forget the lifts, we're taking the stairs. When we get back, first round at Sleepless Maiden is on me."

No one cheered, and the platform listed.

"All right, listen up," Thom roared over the quaking. "Chambers get loaded first, I need parameter of three Tier Ones and three mages! Keep an eye out if anyone tries to bum rush us on the way out. I want a headcount of name and faces before we're Oscar Mike. Somebody get that engine started. We're going to Stow's End!"

PART III

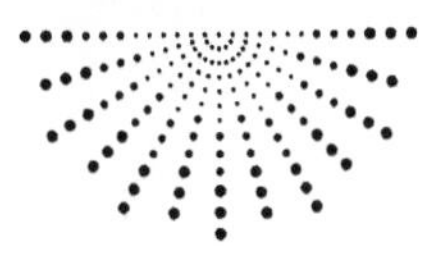

19
CHARIOTS OF THE GODS

ROARK "ROYER" KNOLL, JR. WAS KNOWN FOR TWO THINGS, THE FIRST was he was one of the "Juniors" and second he should've been off the Hollow six months ago but alas, things didn't go as planned and now he was babysitting a pair of Freshmen Houses in the middle of the night atop Crosleigh's Keep highest bell tower while they impatiently waited for arrival of their significant others, a pair of Houses from the other side of Wailing Seas. Sooner or later, the four would be recognized to take over their respected Wailing Houses.

As planned.

'As planned,' my ass. Royer thought and pulled out his fog watch out of his vest pocket. He popped it open and the glowing arms ticked away. *They're three hours behind schedule.*

The night had been going too well, so much so Royer had made the mistake of dressing up for a celebratory "I'm leaving this gahforsaken sandbox" dinner before they had inserted into the Keep. They'd set up their position and then the world exploded much to everyone's amazement the defense genies had held and across the now glowing night sky a lone dropship had appeared.

Only a fool or some idiot trying to impress a woman would be out in this, Royer thought.

The ship had landed spectacularly across the front lawn without pinwheeling out of control was jaw dropping enough until Royer saw who was leading and kept any smart remarks to himself about Melinda Scott and her rather large party made their way inside unaccosted.

When the Freshmen's significant other didn't identify themselves when Melinda's group passed under them they waited. Royer didn't blame them for the cold feet when Selene Finnegan carried the chamber by herself passed into view while carrying her blessed broadsword, too.

Yeah, that's a motivational poster I didn't need to see, Royer thought and suggested it may time to check in with the other two Houses that were now significantly late.

But, the two sucked it up, much to his dismay and said the significant others had been late before.

Royer nodded at that and reminded himself to re-read the rules of this playdate because Melinda didn't mess around and why in gahsakes would you need that much firepower?

Lay off thinking like that, the war is over. You keep seeing things that aren't there, he thought.

The arrival of Zi Stuk's group came an hour later and by that time Royer had really stopped caring.

The bean pole of a husband didn't ignore his instinct and bluntly asked exactly how busy was this place supposed to be in the middle of the night, really?

The couple and their playdate had looked simple on paper. Royer had been offered it three days ago over dinner at Sleepless Maiden by one of his friends and in return, he'd get a ticket on the star carrier that was getting off this rock, which was three days away. It was his for the taking. The golden ticket had made him forget about the couple, why they'd been married to stop a vague war when they were just babies and now they'd grown up. Neither were novices since they had come from an old House that was a three-day rail carrier ride past the far-flung Range Houses. Far enough into Wailing Seas that even the crustiest of loners at Maiden had done a split take and said, Fuck 'em. The ticket ain't worth it.

Neither of them or their hand-me-down desert fatigues were worth writing home about, the woman with a flowery name like Begonia or Calluna or Camellia or maybe Zinnia. She was your standard Whittahare sword carrier going for the brass ring: Finnegan House. The faintest of auras occupied her sword now while her husband was a dull bean pole of a man with brown hair except for the creepy bone white full faceplate because the air was toxic. He had even shown Royer that has wasn't cheating, but Royer couldn't have cared less. These kids were House trained and could've done this without him. This should've been a playdate but instead, the two lovers were actually enjoying this because out here in the dark there was no one else but them.

Royer almost told them to shoot Nathaniel Crosleigh, er, Stukari, Jr. traipsing through the graveyard like he owned the place. *And that's how you landed it, you had a Junior. No one will ever know,* he thought, but the show off had ducked inside a Valkyrie hulk before the Freshmen could see him clearly.

There were too many Juniors running around but that's what happens when certain Houses needed a Knoll, R, Crosleigh, N or Leighton, A in the database. No matching names and the House mainframe would shut down. Too many juniors. *Could be worse,* Royer thought. *Least I'm not a Finnegan. They have to look like Grandma.*

Now, it was going into hour four and beyond Pan stripping her ride down, all three of them were getting itchy. They'd run out of wrecks to ID and the wondrous glowing horizon only lasted for so long until they figured out it was ruining their night vision.

It was into hour five when someone in a stealth suit scaled the tower, by hand. All three gaped at the upper body strength and all of sudden, a familiar and secure wireless network ID popped up across Royer's tablet: MADMINDYS WIRELESS NOT YOURS.

The stealth suit didn't come down from the top of the bell tower. Instead, whoever it was repositioned several times until the boards stopped creaking and the world was silent.

Mindy, what are you doing? Royer glanced at the ceiling. *And who's above us and why set up a private network when...* He stopped and tapped away on his tablet until he found several other not-so-subtle wireless networks so weak they barely showed up. *Wait, who else is in there besides her?*

Twenty minutes passed, and the wind changed.

Something brushed past Royer.

It wasn't the wind, either.

It was a nudge.

Royer, like all good techno mages, had a certain thing he did with his aura so everyone knew who and what he was. Either the aura eye routine or tweak out his dull, black hair so it was red as his father's or shifted around by itself like how the Finnegans would do to make themselves look bigger by giving themselves a mohawk. But, in times like this, Royer liked to hide in plain sight and make his aura disappear.

Sidestepping was one thing. This was just Royer being an Magehole. This pissed off the other mages because after a while, the radiation from their auras caused blindness. Plated mages meant two things: someone had a massive ego that couldn't stand to let everyone else know they were blind or two, a massive, sucking head wound. Using their auras to see was fine until one of them waltzed around like an aura-less human. It wasn't looked upon too kindly.

Royer jerked around at the presence that passed by. The tablet dropped from his hand and her husband caught it immediately, missing the aura's half gainer off the tower and landed on the ground. It dotted through the graveyard and disappeared.

What. The. Fuck. Royer thought and glanced up at the ceiling. One of the boards shifted. *Okay, so I'm not the only one who saw that?*

The flowery bride with the semi-blessed broadsword jerked around too and sheathed her moaning sword.

Sorry, she mouthed but he pointed to it and mimed opening it.

She did so, and the sword moaned.

Royer pointed up, but the sword was silent. He pointed out to the graveyard, it was silent. He pointed to the Keep, it screamed.

Her husband swiped his finger across his throat and growled at her, but Royer didn't chastise her.

Damned Liches and those cursed gems of theirs. Royer thought smacked his forehead. *That's it, I'm calling it. Who in gahsakes else is out here besides us?*

The stealth suit climbed down through the arch and cleared her throat. "I think we have a problem." The augmented voice sounded like Alita Finnegan and a moment later, her disembodied head popped into view. "Sorry for ruining the fun but did you—"

Royer nodded and spoke for the first time in hours: "The aura that just jogged by?"

"No, I meant the targeting spell that's across the top of the Keep," she said.

"What targeting—" The bride got off before the world turned white and screaming pierced the night.

~

Royer blinked away the suns that burned into his eyeballs. "Gahsakes, what was that?"

"Concussion spell. Impacted on the defense grid before it went off," the wife said and wiped her eyes.

"I think she's right." Alita hopped down into the bell tower and pointed to specks that crossed the horizon. "Three airborne mages. Two are targeting the Keep and that one is firing for them. Targeting spell is back, too."

"Just the Keep or us?" Royer said and squinted about. "I can't see anything."

Against the still, ever-glowing horizon, two specks buzzed the tower and another explosion on the other side of the Keep.

"What're they shooting at?" Royer said.

"Defense genies," the bride said. "They're taking out the generators. Uh oh." She pointed. "Second attack run coming in."

An inhuman scream pierced the air. Explosions followed.

The rock and debris rained down smacked against the tower from below.

"Get Zi!" Royer yelled to the couple over the howling of spells. "Rendezvous at Pan's ship. Stay off the coms."

"And our ride?" the bride howled back.

"Don't worry. I'll work on that," Alita said.

"Before they figure out—" Royer whipped around as the shrill noise was too close. "They've got a target lock! Abandon tower!" he yelled.

They leapt, and the tower exploded above them.

Much to Royer's delight, they tumbled to the ground, rolled across the uneven terrain and came up standing. His mistake was allowing to take the moment and smile. If it had been anyone else, they'd be on the deck with broken legs but instead, they did a headcount and split up.

Unfortunately, the ground erupted in front of them and they landed on their asses.

Royer dusted himself off and rose to his feet only to find a magess now blocked his path.

The other two had landed in front of the couple's and Alita's paths.

The night brightened for a moment and Royer swore he recognized one of the magess, but it wasn't a mage, it was a Priestess of the Hills.

Well, this is a nice way to go out, he thought.

"Yield," the one said in front of him.

I know you. Where do I know you? Royer thought and laughed.

"Yield," she said.

Amara? Royer thought and squinted. *Wait. What? Amara Whittahare?*

"You were burned," Royer said. "I remember... I voted. We burned you." He turned to the other priestesses. "All of you."

"That's what we'd like to talk about," an unfamiliar man's voice said from behind the priestesses. "Where's Mister Crosleigh?"

"Right here." A familiar man's voice jerked them all around and Nat Stukari, Jr. stepped out from behind one of the hulks with Junior and Benny Brie two steps behind.

"How?" Royer said.

"Those In Case of Aerial Bombardment signs come in handy. You learn fast where the stairs are since the lifts stop working," Nat said and eyed Royer. "You okay?"

"Just peachy, who in gahsakes is this?" Royer said and jerked his head.

"I have no idea. Looks like he wants to have sit down before we get blasted into vapors," Nat said. "I'll be right back, don't do anything stupid while I'm gone."

~

"Mister Crosleigh. I'm happy to see you survived." The dark-haired man stepped up to Nat and extended his hand. "Count Victor Stukari of the Wailing Seas and I have a proposition for you." He motioned and one of the priestesses brought out two folding chairs. "Please, before my colleagues do something rash."

"Nathaniel Stukari, II." Nat released his brother's hand and almost didn't recognize, Victory Crosleigh at first. He'd taken after his mother's side of the family with the dark hair and blue eyes. His gray suit had no cufflinks or tie clip so either he was a newly minted lord, or someone had thrown a suit at him that looked like it fit. *A good tailor and you'll fit right in.*

"You never liked that name, that much I do remember," Victor said.

"It's Stukari," Nat said and the dark-haired stranger began to look vaguely familiar. "Always has been, Victor."

"You do remember me," Victor said.

And either you don't know what happened to my house or you're playing really dumb for your new bosses, Nat thought.

"Every bit of you," Nat said. "This is a bit much for you, isn't it?"

"Oh, them?" Victor nodded to the three priestesses. "They're not with me. They led me to you though. I asked for five minutes before they blow this place sky high. They wanted to see what they could do, and they don't disappoint. But I don't think they know what they have. You weren't planning on doing anything stupid, were you?"

"Why would I do that?" Nat said. "Go take a look for yourself."

"No. We have trust, don't we?" Victor said. "I have a favor to ask of you."

"A 'favor?'" Nat said. "A 'proposition?' Which is it, Victor?"

"Yes, a personal favor. My family and I are leaving on the next ship. I'd like you to watch after my House for me," Victor said.

Several thoughts blazed through Nat's brain, but he kept his emotions like his face, slack. "I'm sorry to hear that you said you had plans."

"Oh, I still do just not here. Tell me something, how did you and, Junior, is it? How did you two get paired up?" Victor said.

"I read the instructions," Nat said and allowed himself a laugh which Victor shared.

"Read the instructions." Victor clapped his hands. "Really? That's it?"

Yes, that's how all burdens work. You read the directions and accept it willingly and you're unstoppable. They wrapped a blind contract around your neck, didn't they? You can pull it off, why the dog and pony show? You hate that. Or is that the point. To show me you're in control and not them? Nat thought and stared him down whatever was going on behind Victor's eyes. There was something behind those baby blues that caught Nat's curiosity and his trigger finger. "I decided it was time for change and accepted it willingly. All told it took ten seconds," he said.

"And like that you go from a Stukari to a Crosleigh?" Victor snapped his fingers.

"It was ten seconds of the most painful experience of my life," Nat said. "Those lovely buggers of mine did the rest but I survived. Why?"

"I wanted to know how you survived when so many hadn't," Victor said and allowed a glance at the armor. "That thing. That plate. Is it worth all the pain and suffering?"

Exactly what happened to you? You can't stand it just like everyone else. Nat's brain threatened to jump the tracks, but the hill it was racing down didn't have a bottom. *And why are you leaving because you were going to run this place. Unless, unless, they're at your House and are never going to leave. Ever. Wait, if they took my House over, why'd they take yours, that's too much for so few. Are you running? You never run. Unless, that stupid attack computer said so. Gahsakes, that's it, isn't it. That stupid attack computer of yours said you're going to fail. You can't stand that. You always have to win.*

"It already saved my life so, yes, it was worth the ten seconds to re-activate my buggers and change Houses. Even if I lost my aura doing it," Nat said. "You bring the paperwork?"

One of the priestesses appeared out of the dark with the thick leather-bound tome. She moved too quick for him to focus on her.

"Feel free to read through," Victor said. "You can't free them not now."

"I wasn't planning on it." Nat flipped to specific pages, pages he knew of, pages he had marked off as weak spots and found the just as they should be, covered. It was the same House Contract they had presented at the Academy to plug the holes that had never been plugged. It meant Victor was serious. It meant his "family" was really leaving.

The problem was Victor Stukari had no family. He was lie hiding in plain sight. He had started off a war orphan like the rest of them until Nat had found him and through no fault of anyone found Victory Crosleigh had survived the bugger purges.

He had been burdened recently. The fact he was dressed from neck to toe in a suit meant the contract was either around his neck, arms or legs. The scarred skin would still be visible. Whether the contract was one way or two ways was the next thing to answer, but Nat needed to read the entire contract first.

While he did that, his brain churned. It also meant Victor's new "family" was the wrench, Mindy had bemoaned about since the beginning of this mess. A group of Houseless people that had been for a lack of better word couch surfing from House to House since the end of the war thirty years ago. The same ones that had taken over Nat's House six months ago.

And now they were leaving.

Are we going to live through the next five minutes? Nat thought and closed the contract. "Reads fine to me. Benny, can you read through this one more time to make sure I didn't miss anything." He refocused on Victor and saw nothing wrong, at least not yet. He hadn't signed the contract yet. *This was the final stage before you took over a dead House, I sign off on it and you kill me only to take over both our Houses.*

Benny handed it back to him. "Reads fine to me."

"Thank you." Nat opened to a page, signed it, pressed down in thumb in two places. The fabric in the paper bit into his skin. Nathaniel Stukari fell and officially Lord Nathaniel Crosleigh II of Wailing Seas rose. Once the network connection was fixed there'd be a lot of piss off people to find Count Victor Stukari had ceded his House to a Crosleigh.

But, I don't care. Nat stuffed the House Contract under his arm and it immediately slid into a hidden hold of his clothes where it would stay until his death or he surrendered it. Neither of which would be happening any time soon.

"I have one final request," Victor said and Nat failed at flinching. This was where most young Lords died.

"What can I do for you?" Nat said.

"I have need of Mister Knoll's ticket."

~

"No," Royer said.

"Just hear me out," Nat said.

"No. I am getting of this rock," Royer said.

"I know. And you are, just not the ticket you have in pocket. It's a blank, isn't it?" Nat said.

"What difference does it make?" Royer said.

"There's a big different between a blank business class ticket and stamped House First Class ticket," Nat said.

"No, there's not," Royer said.

"Yes, there is," Nat said.

"Says who?" Royer spat.

"Says the pilot's first mate that spent years growing up on the long-haul carriers and hating every single minute of it until I got a carrier of my own. I'm the only one who aced the pilot's, engineer, and crew exam. I had to re-write the exams because they were so outdated. Wanna know why they me kicked down here? I never had one stowaway ever during my long hauls. I made those carrier contracts iron clad so even if someone did stowaway, it wasn't my fault when I kicked them off at the next port. So, do you trust me or the guy that dropped this in your lap?"

Royer stared him down. "Seriously?"

Nat nodded. "I made sure lords of the Hollow get one first-class roundtrip pass per six months so their journeyman apprentices can gain experience before coming home to start their own House."

"I'm not coming back." Royer laughed.

"I didn't say you were. It's an open-ended roundtrip pass. If you get my drift," Nat said.

Royer blinked. "I give him my ticket and you give me this first-class pass, and then what?"

Nat shrugged. "No strings attached. You are on your own, my friend. Understand one thing, you do this and you're not coming back. Ever."

Royer stared at him. "Says you?"

"Once you accept this, Roark Knoll, II is dead in this coil. Whatever coil you land in, you're on your own. Understand?" Nat said.

Royer nodded and extended a hand. "Completely. Ticket?"

Nat opened his newly minted contract and pulled out an envelope. "Ticket."

Royer nearly dropped it. "Gahsakes, Cross, what's in this?"

"It contains everything you need to start on a new world, no questions asked. Good news your arm is still attached to your body," Nat said and closed the contract. "Now, ticket?"

Royer pulled the ticket out of his jacket pocket. "Ticket. Is this going to come back on me?"

"No. You are under my House's Flags and Colors until you see fit to start your own. Now, let's go see what happens with Victor and don't shoot him," Nat said.

"Why would I shoot him?" Royer said.

"I'm not talking to you, I'm talking to Alita, she repositioned herself while I was signing the contract."

~

"Wonderful." Victor clapped his hands together. "We thank you for returning this to us and wish you a pleasant evening," he said and folded up the chairs. "Oh, one last thing. We found Zi Stuk and his party. Could you return them to their Houses for us."

"Absolutely," Nat said.

"I wish you safe roads and pleasant travels," Victor said and he walked away with the priestess behind him.

"Hey, Victory." Nat twisted his tongue down and caused Victor to stop. "Watch your back."

Victor nodded and disappeared with the priestess as quickly as he'd arrived.

"He's a dead man," Royer growled. "You're not going after the priestesses?"

"No. The first stupid thing they did was they burdened him. The second thing is they let him out of their sight. The third thing is I'm going to be a very, very, very, patient lord," Nat said and jerked his head over the next hill. "You three go help Pan with her belongings before they change their minds. Keep Zi with you, he doesn't need to walk through any more tonight."

Zi's group turned the corner and Royer waved them over. "Right on time, if you'll all please follow me we can get on our way." He turned to the couple. "Escort him, if anything so much as touches him, you'll never hear the end of it."

~

Royer staggered over the next hill and stopped at the dropship's rear ramp or lack thereof. The lack of people inside caused his heart to skip a beat. "Anyone here?" he said and knocked on the frame.

"Right here." Pan's disembodied arm pulled himself inside and through whatever defense genies still worked. "We turned on genies once concussion spell went off." She answered his confused look. "What're you even doing here?"

"Stupid answer later, we need to get out of here before they come back," Royer said.

Pan hefted her go bag over her shoulders. She picked up two more and dumped them at Royer's feet. "Carry these. We need to get out of here, right now."

"Wait, you're seriously burning your ride?" Royer gaped at the go bags over Vernon's shoulders. "Oh, don't you look so happy to be here."

"At least I'm helping," Vernon's icy tone said he was ready to go home.

"If anyone asks, he makes a lovely pack mule." Pan grinned and gaped at the shape rising up over the Keep. "What did they dig up?"

Royer turned around at the shape that filled the horizon. It blocked the afterglow.

It blocked everything.

"Slow down, do I look as young as I feel?" Zi's voice cursed.

"Um, Zi." Royer pointed to the chariot-class carrier that now filled the sky. The solid metal body had a rounded nose and engine mount. The turrets that lined the middle of the ship were the sizes of three story houses. There was no flag or House colors being waved but sooner or later, there would be. For now, the three bare metal drop-ships that zipped across the sky in front of the carrier was just the scale that no one actually asked for or needed.

"That's impossible. How?" Zi whispered.

"Beautiful," the still un-named husband said and jolted everyone around.

"He speaks?" Royer said.

"For all the wrong reasons." The bride smacked his shoulder.

Pan looked about and said, "Where is he?"

On cue, a spotlight from the heavens basked her ship and everyone craned their heads skywards. *Itty Bitty*'s silent descent was marred only by her VTOL engines kicking up sand. She hovered next to Pan's ship. Her extended Belly ramp lowered with Junior's armor at the edge. "Well, what're you all waiting for an open invitation?" the plate clicked. "Move yer asses. Pan." It tossed her a bag. She caught it with ease, pulled a pin and chucked it inside her ship.

The combined group scurried up the ramp.

Junior counted heads. "We're missing one." The plate clicked to Royer. "Zi."

Royer jogged back up to the man. He had stayed his ground, staring at the carrier.

"Sir, we need to go before they decide to do anything else," Royer said.

"They already have," Zi said. "They promised me. They promised me." He stepped forward and waved his cane. "You promised!"

Royer didn't touch him knowing full well something had triggered within. The old man wasn't old, and he wasn't a man. He was Zephyr Crosleigh during the war even if he had taken the name Zi Stuk in peace time. But, whatever had triggered him, Royer didn't move, didn't touch him and just let him be.

"Not to be that guy." Nat's voice in Royer's ear pulled him back to reality. "We need to go. They're starting to scan the junk yard. I think they figured out what we're doing here."

Royer edged as close as he dared. "Zephyr, please," he said.

Zi lowered his cane and leaned on it, every year of his life exposed. And a moment later he was back. "Yes, I know. I know." He extended his elbow and Royer looped his arm around it. "You're a credit to your family. But if you ever speak my name like that outside of mixed company, they will never find your body."

"I apologize for my slip and would never, sir," Royer said.

Zephyr patted Royer's arm and they boarded the ship. "Credit to your family. You may have some use to me yet."

The ramp closed behind them. The deck plates shuddered.

They were well in the air when the explosive charges turned Pan's ship to slag.

20

CROSSED OFF AND FORGOTTEN

MELINDA WAITED FOR THE REST TO BOARD THE RAIL CAR AND PUSHED the Weaver's chamber down the narrow aisle. She thanked the two holding operators for clearing her a path and pulled open the last free birth.

The medium sized compartment was the same as all the rest. Two convertible bunks and a washroom so tiny she'd probably have to leave to change her mind. The oval window revealed nothing due to the iron blast covers were lowered. The unlit defense candles were a happy sight.

She pulled in the chamber and locked the cart's wheels so it wouldn't move.

Melinda pushed up the two bunks. She grabbed a pillow from the overhead compartment.

She reached across and tripled locked the door. She opened up her bag and pulled out her tablet. She swiped through the hello screens, tapped through the connect screens to open her virtual private network and tapped 'YES' to connect to the birth's wireless.

She plopped the pillow down atop the chamber and was happily snoring away in less than five minutes.

While she snored away, her buggers lined her mind to protect her private mind server.

~

Melinda's private mind server was a half inch by half inch by half inch iron-lined House hard drive that resided at the base of her neck. It looked like a mole to the uninitiated. But to the techno mages and augmented humans, she was the next generation of Rig Runner or House head. A certified human that could connect to any house network. A messenger girl or bodyguard if the needs called for it.

Across the forgotten land of wireless networks, her mind server was the lighthouse with a fiery beacon that never stopped. She was the last hope for the cross off and forgotten houses or operators that wanted to come in from the cold.

Attached to her lighthouse was a two-story, wooden barn.

The first floor had four stables and was full of hay for when she needed to cross networks to deliver messages. Sure, it was all ones and zeroes but who said she couldn't have fun with the ones and zeroes?

The second floor had been converted and contained a living space with a couch. The kitchen was fully stocked with a round kitchen table with a flowery tablecloth. A curtain separated the kitchen from her bedroom which was an exact replica of her bedroom on Gunna. She even had indoor plumbing, even if it was utterly inaccurate.

Melinda rolled out of her virtual bed and flipped on the lights. The sweep of the lighthouse's eye across the first floor made her jump. She flipped on the lights for the lower level and paused at the sight of Spence's Chamber sitting there covered in a tablecloth. "Don't do that," she cursed. "Hey, you're supposed to be asleep."

The Weaver occupied a wooden chair and stared at his flat screen that had been mounted to a support beam. "When I can't sleep, I file reports," he said. "Nice virtual private network, I can actually small the hay."

Melinda sighed. "Since when do you have a VPN?"

"I wasn't always a Weaver," he said. "If you want to upgrade your coding, I think my walled garden is a bit more walled than yours."

Melinda clomped down the stairs. "I'm sure it is," she muttered and opened the barn's doors. The cold air nipped her nose. She flipped on the last light switch and ceiling lights illuminated an empty rectangle table with four chairs around it.

"Mindy, what's that?" The Weaver thumbed to the empty table.

"I was tasked with the dubious honor of bringing operators and or houses back in from the cold. It just means I'm on call when I'm sleeping," Melinda said.

"They think someone is just going to knock and wander in?" he said.

"Happens more than you'd think," she said and nodded to the open door. "They'll circle for a bit to make sure it's not a trap and then send one in to make sure. After that, the queue will go on forever until someone rats me out."

A flicker of movement passing by the door caused her to squeak. "Forgot, Barn, recognize user, MacGregor, Spence. Make sure the barn's firewalls are updated."

Several virtual cows appeared and happily ate their fake hay.

"Bovines as your firewalls. Cute," the Weaver said.

"I used to use pigs but getting eaten by something that small wigged some people. Someone is sniffing around. Probably someone who shouldn't be here," she said and settled down at the makeshift table the chamber made. "Once they figure out I'm not to be messed with, they'll go bother someone else."

The Weaver glanced at the door then back to his screen. "Why would they do that?"

"Some people like to make a name for themselves and my servers have never been hacked. I need to make sure they're real before I let them in or else I get brute force attacked and swarmed."

The Weaver nodded at the logic. "Why is my flat screen here?" he said.

"Because someone connected it to the Stow's End network. I helped Erik and he ignored the fact I installed a backdoor program, so

I can come and go as I please," she said. "If they access it, we'll know. Which reminds me, I need to check my mail. Haven't been here in years."

"I think I can hear the ocean," the Weaver said. "Where are we, out there?"

Melinda looked about then craned her head up. "We're on the rail carrier with the others. First time I've had to rest in a while."

The flat screen in the barn fizzled to life. A close circuit camera view of the exterior of Stow's End dome appeared, followed by an interior camera view of the New Year's festivities.

"What are you doing?" The Weaver stood and got closer to the flat screen.

"Its connected to someone else's secure network. Probably from another war table. The same table they were using to keep themselves out of my way because they knew I needed to raise Roark," Melinda said. "The flat screen onboard your shuttle. It's your war table, isn't it?"

The Weaver tapped the screen and several icons appeared. "What have you done?"

"I don't think they can see us or the cows would start exploding," she said.

The Weaver edged his chair closer to the flat screen and away from the cows. "Smart move. If the network goes down, create your own. House Certified according to the certificates," he said. "You can't access this type of feed without a rig."

"They're making portable rigs smaller and smaller. Smaller than the one in our necks. Sooner or later, it'll be the size of a nanobot," Melinda said.

"They already are as small as a nanobot," the Weaver grumbled.

"Yeh, but those are buggers. Buggers need to be harnessed and controlled to work this fast. These smaller rigs farms are fire and forget," Melinda said.

The camera view changed to a closeup of the crowds of people. A constant sea of colors and shapes was overwhelming.

"Do you—" The Weaver pointed.

"See him?" she said. "I didn't know what I was looking for at first but even he can't hide forever."

The Weaver tapped the screen and in rapid order, several head-shots with House affiliation appeared.

The wave after wave of people made it humanly impossible to catalogue. But the flat screen did as it was built to, do all the heavily lifting and in mere minutes, everyone in the crowd had been identified until something passed through the crowd.

"Wow," Melinda managed.

"Names and faces, that's all it is. Facial recognition is a simple process that is supposed to be behind the curtain," the Weaver said.

A silhouette flashed through the sea. NO FACE. NO NAME. A red and yellow striped sub screen flashed.

"There he is," she said. "He's still alive and moving... showoff."

"Who?" the Weaver said.

"Who do you think?" Melinda twisted her tongue down. "They tried to banish him thirty years ago and tonight he's back. The network is down so private security is using their own rig farms to parse the flow of data. He's probably not even showing up."

The silhouette stopped and turned towards the camera for a brief instant, only to keep moving. The blurry picture showed a bearded man in a suit coat.

"Can he see us?" the Weaver said.

"I don't know. He doesn't have his plate. So, who knows. Knowing him, yes," Melinda said. "He's the one who read us in on you."

The Weaver sighed. "Of course, he was. Wait. Why'd you get read in on me?"

"You disappeared. He was worried about you. Well, Pan was worried about you and she suggested putting out lures to try to find you," Melinda said. "Besides, what're you going to do with several House Rig Runners that aren't Rig Running."

"Serves him right for getting banished by trying to find me," the Weaver said.

"I was the one who banished him," Melinda said.

~

The Weaver sputtered at that. "You what?"

"We banished him because that's what the House Attack Computers (HAC) said to do. They said if we banished him, the enemy should've stopped but they didn't. Instead, I was replaced and later re-assigned because I didn't kiss up to my new bosses. So, I did what you're not supposed to do: I air gapped my server and crunched the numbers myself. I burned my House. I went off the grid. Re-built my servers from scratch and followed the paper trail. They didn't cover their tracks well. They'd spread the money around to find out where our server farms were. They corrupted the information in the farms and thought they could get away with it. I knew I couldn't do it by myself, so I recruited allies. Some of them tried to turn me in but I was prepared. I got my little misanthropes and ne'er-do-wells together and we went on the offensive. We started a silent war that hasn't ended in thirty years," Melinda said.

"And that's why you got banished," the Weaver said.

Melinda nodded. "My brother had his own problems. So, while he and his Dragoons were away, they quietly tried to take over only to be stopped be a burned-out Rig Runner and her friends. So, I got banished to Gunna Space Station and here we are."

"Why are you telling me this?" the Weaver said.

"Because you, Charles Whittahare, and Lauren Daire let them in," she said.

"If Mister Spence MacGregor said he didn't remember, I won't either, Mindy," the Weaver said.

Melinda sighed. "I had to try. Just another piece of you I have to find."

"You need to stop, Mindy," the Weaver said. "You don't know who you're playing with."

"I thought I was playing against you. Table running is what you did during peacetime. I'm guessing the other piece of you made sure to cover your tracks because sooner or later, the Houses are going to tasked to bring you in. Except, no one knows about those two war carriers."

"What war carriers?" the Weaver said.

The flat screen flickered, and several black and white aerial photos of carrier hulks littered the ground like forgotten toys. All covered in sand with what appeared to be ants crawling across their hulls.

"Those are workers," the Weaver said. "Gahsakes, that looks like a Chariot Class war carrier."

"It's what the arch mages have been doing because the techno mages turned them down flat," Melinda said. "The war footing I put us on years ago can't hold out much longer. It needs to stop so we can rebuild. Somebody didn't like that idea of going back to the way things were and has been derailing our efforts ever since. Instead of coming in from the cold, the Range Houses hunkered down on the other side of Wailing Seas and waited. Six months ago, we proved this would work when I brought your House back in from the cold. Do understand what I'm trying to tell you? I am not trying to take over the Hollow, it's on automatic. There's no need to take over something that's on the merry go round. Right now, I've got someone trying to jump the line and I can't stop them without you."

"Without the both of us," the Weaver said.

"Right. The problem is I think there's more than one of you. I don't think he's going to be a problem. As for the rest, I dunno about the rest of them."

"Who?" the Weaver said.

"Your brother was stationed at Wailing Seas Data Center when they rolled in ten years ago and requested asylum. We declined their request, and everything went pear shaped after that," she said.

"Wait, you asked me if I remembered that," the Weaver said.

"Right, I needed to make sure and throw them off his scent because sooner or later, they're going to figure out why Horatio Crosleigh didn't die that day," Melinda said.

The Weaver stopped. "I was at the Data Center."

"Yes," she said.

"I was there when everything went fubar," he said.

"Yes," she said.

"Layla Yashira, Charles Whittahare, and Lauren Daire were compromised," he said. "All of them?"

"Right, until you stopped them, but it took everything you had to do it. Your brother is carrying your memories and final words. The problem is, his House crashed and burned getting the survivors out. No one has seen him, Lauren or anyone else, until tonight."

The Weaver rubbed the bridge of his nose. "My brother. Saving people."

"He's braver than you think," she said. "A lot sturdy than the rest. I'm the one who burned their Houses. I want you to understand, I had to. If not, whoever found him and his House would be in charge instead of him."

The Weaver turned away from the screen and settled down across from her. "You couldn't have told me this sooner?"

"I haven't had time to get you to alone since we landed," Melinda said. "Do you understand what I need to do?"

"You need to find the gaps in my memory before you merge me back together or else it's going to get very messy," he said. "And file an After-Action Report so everyone knows because Harry wasn't the sole survivor to warn everyone else. No one knows until one of us files. Otherwise we just keep spinning on the merry go round."

Melinda sighed happily. "Thank you. I had to use diagrams and puppets with Tommy."

"It also means once my brother does this, whatever blind contract is around his neck is going to re-assert itself," the Weaver said. "Along with Layla, Lauren and Charles."

"I have it on good authority your brother can take care of himself," Melinda said.

"Whose authority?" the Weaver spat.

"My authority." A man's baritone voice jerked them around to the open door.

~

A silhouette stood on the barn's threshold.

"Mindy," the Weaver growled.

"Sorry, the door's sensors said it's him."

"Who him?" the Weaver said.

"Who do you think?" she replied and raised her voice. "I don't suppose you want to drop the cloak."

The silhouette's ambiguous head swiveled, and a pair of red pupils popped into existence. "I don't suppose you want your mail," a baritone voice said and underhanded a mail bag onto the table. "It was hanging on your door with this." A sword belt with a full sheath was deposited gently onto the table.

The Weaver picked up the sword. "Daire Blade and from the Royal Court."

Melinda opened the messenger bag carefully and pulled out a leather-bound tome. "*Where Weavers Daire*. It's an After-Action Report that can't be opened." She turned the bag over and shook it until something dropped onto the table. A data stick the size of her pinky finger.

"May I?" She nodded to the flat screen.

"Be my guest. This is Neale Daire's blade, where'd you get it from?" the Weaver said.

The silhouette thumbed to the door. "It was on your door."

"Told you I needed to check my mail," Melinda scoffed.

A howl stopped the conversation.

"That's not me," the silhouette said and raised his hands over his head.

A presence flicked around the barn's exterior. Fists banged on the walls with wails to be let in.

"Who the—" The Weaver said.

"Don't. Someone's just pinging me see if anyone is in here," Melinda said.

"They know you're here. They know you're here!" the voice screamed, and something arced through the open door and landed on the table between the them.

It was a sword.

"They know! They know!" the presence howled but was dragged out into the night by forces unseen.

The Weaver pulled the sword out of the table. "MacGregor's Crest. This isn't mine. This is Harry's."

"Harry?" the silhouette said. "Horatio MacGregor is dead. Toss it. It's a bait."

The Weaver shoved the sword under the nose. "Read the inscription," he growled. "And take off that gahforsaken cloak off."

"Horatio MacGregor is dead. You know what, I'm gonna come back later when you two are less busy," the silhouette said and stepped back. "Because I think you guys got bigger problems then me." He pointed to the flat screen.

The flat screen flickered to an internal close circuit camera view of the hallway outside Melinda's birth.

"Damn." Melinda stepped closer and gaped at the ever-growing crowd outside her door. Benny Brie and Horatio Crosleigh were at the front of the group.

Horatio did *not* look happy.

~

The birth's door chimed.

Melinda rolled off the chamber immediately checked the locks on the door. *Still locked,* she thought.

She stretched out the kink in her back. "Gahsakes, that's uncomfortable."

"No one's complained about it before." The Weaver's voice jerked her around.

Spence MacGregor rose vertically out of the horizontal chamber in a fresh blouse, slacks, boots and his cloak such as it was folded across his arm. "This is House business. You don't need to be here for it."

"And you need a witness in case they don't do something stupid like wrap a blind contract around your neck," she countered and squinted at him. "And Horatio's right, you should be back in there. I can barely see your aura."

He pointed to the defense charm around her neck and she disappeared it under her clothes.

The birth's chime pinged again. Melinda twisted the locks back and opened the door.

Benny stood there with a dull expression across her face. Her cornrows were gone, and her hair was held back by two quill sticks. If Melinda didn't know her as well as she did, the black and blue power suit would've looked stylish, but house contracts was the bane of Benny's existence. The quill sticks were ornamental for most Brie, but for an Arms Master, it only meant one thing: Benny didn't see this ending well for anyone.

"Miss Stuk, it's pleasure to meet you I have several clients who would like to talk to you and Mister MacGregor in private," Benny said.

Melinda's watch went off and everyone stiffened.

"May I?" Melinda said.

Benny nodded.

Melinda silenced the alarm. "Congratulations, that's the fastest anyone has back traced me without a network." She turned to the Weaver. "Shall we?"

"You're not necessary, Mindy," Benny said.

"I insist. You won't even know I'm there," Melinda said.

21

HOUSE KEEPING

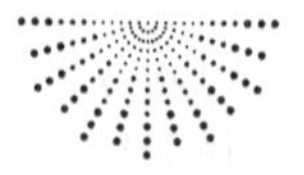

THE RAIL CARRIER'S PRIVATE DINING CAR WAS THE ONLY CAR NOT occupied and so the group pushed two tables together.

"My clients realize that your brother's worth and would like to change his contract," Benny said. "They also understand your worth and would like to re-iterate that they had nothing to do with your death at the Data Center and wish their heartfelt apologies this may have caused at this time. They also wish to say, that if Melinda tries to shoot her way out of this it won't end well for her since they are planning on voting for her House's re-instatement by end of week. The previous House head that had control over your House has been retired and we will be releasing your House back to her. But first, they would like to go over some ground rules for the next two days. The rules are simple: Don't."

Spence coughed. "I'm sorry?"

"Esther." Melinda sighed and raised her eyes skyward. "Thank you."

"Esther who?" Spence said.

"Esther Whittahare, Charles' daughter. I was wondering where she was. She's runs tables."

"The only way to do that is to build one yourself, Mindy," Spence said.

"At the age of five and has been working for the Historical Society ever since to find the rest of them," Melinda said. "She's in your ear, isn't she?"

"All the tables were crushed after the last war, Mindy," Spence said.

"Supposedly," she over-emphasized.

"Also, once this week is over, Melinda will go in and take out the backdoor program she installed," Benny glowered. "Some of us enjoy our privacy, Mindy."

"Not it." Melinda raised her hands.

"Excuse me?" Benny winced and pointed to the earbud in her ear. "Seriously, yer gonna take it out."

"Not it," Melinda said. "Sorry, I enjoy reading the book until the end. It's not me." She turned around. "Oh, Dina! Get your moppet butt up here."

Dinah Stukari tromped up and dropped herself into the chair across the aisle. "Wot?" she said due to the earbuds in her ears. "Yes. I installed a backdoor program. It's cute, fuzzy and adorable and not hurting anyone."

"Seriously?" Benny and Spence said.

Dinah pulled her earbuds out and snickered. "Oh, that. Sorry. I've got alerts out for him."

"For who?" Spence said.

"Who do you think?" Dinah said effortlessly. "He's my father. I need to make sure I get home before he realizes I out past curfew. Tell, Easy, the backdoor program was my idea and it will be discontinued once our House is raised up at week's end. The keylogging program on the other hand won't be, sorry."

"He's your what?" Benny gaped. "And don't call me, her, that."

"What?" Dinah grinned. "He had kids, big deal. Everyone has kids after you do that much for Queen and Coil. The old bats said it was time to ankle him, so they waved their wands and poof. Impotency goes bye-bye. Besides, for some of us to move from this coil to the next, he's going to be leading the space bound Houses."

"Explain to me why you couldn't have told me in the first place?" Benny said.

"Do you have any idea how much trust issues he has with all of you?" Dinah said. "If you're not on his network then you've got problems."

"You just told us," Melinda said.

"He knows where we live." Spence's head sagged into his hands.

"Exactly. See, you ride with him long enough you just fill in the blanks. Now, if you will excuse me, judging from the looks I need to get home before he figures out I'm here." She pulled her House key out and in poof of aura fireflies was gone.

"Wait, she can summon herself home? Why can't I do that?" Benny said.

"Summoning yourself home looks cute but the aura fireflies never leave and just nest in the eaves then you have to call an exterminator or have an arch mage to fumigate," Melinda said.

"Arch mage?" Spence laughed. "Wait, they came back?"

"And how," Melinda snickered.

Benny cleared her throat. "To get to the task at hand. Mister MacGregor, we'd like you to remove whatever curse or hex you've put on your brother, please."

"I didn't curse or hex, Harry." Spence sighed and squinted at Horatio. "It's your contract that's having a problem with him. Re-write the contract and he'll be fine."

"They demand . . . request obedience and whatever is in him is interfering with that," Benny said. "Their contract is non-negotiable."

"Little boys playing with toys that don't belong to you. It's going to burn you one day, and no one is going to care," Spence snickered in a tongue Melinda barely understood. "Just remember where your exits are, Esther."

Benny's brow knit together.

"Nothing." Spence turned his gaze to Horatio. "Thank you."

"Just get it over with." Horatio sighed.

"No. I mean it. Thank you," Spence said and extended a hand. "Dad would be proud of you and so am I."

The brothers shook and if Melinda's goggles hadn't been on they would've missed the dramatic body temperature drop and the shine in Horatio's already white pupils dulled.

"It's done," Spence said.

"That's it?" Melinda said.

Horatio stiffened up and the sizzling noise emanated from his neck, wrists and ankles. The same dull look Benny had crossed his face. He pushed himself out of the chair and ambled down the stairs to the first floor escorted by two holding operators.

"At week's end, he'll be free," Benny said.

"And, oddly enough, I don't believe a single thing you just said," Spence growled.

"Mister MacGregor, Miss Stuk has gone to great lengths to bring you back from the dead. The amount of guess work she's done without a table and burning all the evidence in her wake is some of the biggest feats I've ever seen. The fact she left everyone alive and didn't go on a mass murder spree that last time tells us one thing. She's willingly to ignore certain missteps in favor of the bigger picture. What happened to you, your brother and several people at Wailing Seas Data Center was a tragedy and hasn't been properly documented, yet. We hope someone files a report on it soon because a great many of us wish to go back to the way things were," Benny finished and took a deep breath. "In closing, thank you for understanding. We hope to deal with you in the future."

The dull look on Benny's face disappeared.

She pulled the earbud out and dropped it in a glass of water. "Gahsakes, I hate her. She made me get gussied up, too. Sorry, I'm going to change and put this suit back in the closet where it belongs."

She shook her hair back down and jingled away leaving the two in silence.

"He's not coming back," Spence said. "The only thing keeping that contract off him was me and that's it."

"We'll get him back," Melinda said. "Esther is good to her word."

"If we roll into my House and he's not there. You forgive if I tell that you're far too trusting." Spence sighed. "I'm sorry. You were right,

I shouldn't have even gotten out of the chamber for this." He staggered, and she support him immediately.

"Ladies and Gentlemen," the PA squawked. "The rail carrier will be leaving the station momentarily. We ask everyone take their seats. We will be arriving at Stow's Landing in two hours."

"I like Junior's announcements better," Spence muttered.

They ambled back to the chamber and he got back in without a word.

The cover closed, and Melinda deposited herself on the bed next to the chamber.

The engine roared and the rail carrier moved out of the station.

The movement lulled Melinda to sleep and back to the barn.

The chamber table was gone but the flat screen remained.

Melinda pulled up a chair in front of the screen. She plugged the data stick in and the flat screen flashed. A picture of herself appeared with her name beneath it.

A red and yellow striped message box appeared. "Unable to open data stick. GPS locked. Who triple locks a data stick? Gahsakes, someone is paranoid. Where's it locked to?" Melinda said.

A series of coordinates flashed across the screen.

"New Welles Asteroid Belt. Of course, it is." She pulled the stick out of the screen.

"Mindy." The silhouette's voice beckoned her from the door. "How's our boy?"

"I got a lot of him but there are still gaps," she said. "You'd better be at the station when I come in two hours."

"You'll see me when you see me," the voice said.

"Seriously?" Melinda said. "I'm doing all the work here."

"Remember Rule One: Use what you got. You've got too much back up coming in with you. Once they leave that train, follow Tommy's instructions. You're doing good work. You're bringing in a lot people than anyone else has."

"I just lost Harry," she said.

The silhouette shrugged. "He's sturdy and he'll survive that's a good thing."

"I'd rather bring in one than ones we don't need," she said.

"All the Houses have to be there for the vote, Mindy. They're votes go a long way with people you don't know," he said.

"Hey, how'd you get back in?" she said.

"How do you think I got back in, Mindy?" he said.

"Half of me thinks you never left and the other half thinks you were in that Foo Fighter I tagged."

"Get some real sleep, Mindy. You're going to need it." His voice grew faint.

Melinda waited at the table. A timer binged after thirty minutes and the doors closed.

The screen stared back at her. The word COMMAND pulsed.

"Compile all the information on present targets. Add Crosleigh, Horatio to the list. Run Victory-For-All program. Show me every single simulation, wipe all my filters including Everyone Wins Nobody Loses. Execute. Execute. Execute."

Melinda picked up the two swords. "Activate piggy of death virus protection."

A pen of virtual pigs oinked their way into existence. In the middle of the pen resided a shielded trophy case. She deposited the swords inside. The case locked, and several lights chimed green. *No curses or hexes. But that doesn't mean much,* she thought.

Whatever information they had would be protected. The shielded case would keep any dormant hexes and curses at bay. She pocketed the thumb stick. Its contents saved to a duplicate stick that resided permanently in the hidden folds of her bag.

A ping said no viruses or hidden programs.

She ambled back to the second-floor bed and slept to the sound of the waves of the ocean.

~

"All passengers, we'll be jumping into S-Cut in one hour. Please return to your births. Officers and Crew, please report to your Supervisors for final checks and pre-jump assignments," a voice announced in Meylandra Stuk's earbud.

Meylandra turned over in bed and poked the naked scaly back across from her. "That's our cue," she said and tumbled onto the floor to find the rest of her uniform. "Time to be the face of your House."

"You said this crew posting was boring," a voice muttered from beneath the sheets. "I haven't taken that stupid uniform off since I got on board." A head of dark hair popped up. A pair of aura pupils glowered at her. "How can you rise and shine that quick."

"Benefits of not sleeping," Meylandra said and buttoned her slacks. "You look good dark."

The aura eyes disappeared, and the dark hair of bed head changed to blonde. "Nope."

Meylandra sighed. "You realize doing that is going eradiate your head and all your hair is going to drop off, Narelle." She shrugged into her long sleeve top. "Let's go."

Narelle Daire growled and tossed back the sheets. She sat up and her prehensile tail shook itself awake. She rolled her shoulders and the wings attached to her shoulder blades disappeared. The only thing that remained of her lineage was the elongated ears and the serpentine yellow eyes. "Gravity still doesn't feel right."

"Shakedown cruise means shaking off the bugs." Meylandra pulled on her boots. "I already told them, and they know." She looked up at the ceiling where the iron bar had been installed so Narelle could sleep properly, inverted, like the rest of Belfries. "Shouldn't that be higher?"

"If it was higher I couldn't eat the rats," Narelle said.

"Do not leave me presents like that. We're past leaving dead presents on my pillow," Meylandra said.

"Captain Daire and Master Sergeant Stuk, report to the bridge," Spence MacGregor's voice popped into Meylandra's ear.

"On our way," Meylandra said and gazed out the window of their quarters.

The stars never looked so good.

Narelle pulled on her slacks and made sure her tail fit properly through the hole this time. "What is it with the pants. Why couldn't he've embraced the kilts I suggested for gahsakes?"

"You can't fool me you just want to see the boy's legs," Meylandra chortled.

Narelle stopped, and her tail swayed happily. "Yes, legs are nice." She pushed off the bed and pulled her top off the lamp shade. Buttoned herself up and shook her head back into some semblance of order. "More escorting people to pods. More reports. Six months of this?"

"It beats anything on planet," Meylandra said. "Now, forward march."

Meylandra exited the room and Narelle finished checking her hair.

Melinda Scott stopped at the dimmed chrono clock on the wall. The dates didn't make sense. "This is six months ago," she said. "What is this?"

Narelle turned to her and said, "This is Narelle Daire's last After-Action Report. You are to bear witness to these events because no one else knows."

"The data stick," Melinda said.

Narelle nodded. "The report is designed to compile itself the next you log in. You are to deliver it to Clarence Stuk upon seeing him. I forbid you to involve the rest of the Houses. I forbid you to tell anyone else. Do you understand me?"

"Absolutely," Melinda said.

Narelle smiled. "Good. Now, I need to go play grown up."

"If this is yours then where in gahsakes is mine and why don't I remember any of this?" Melinda said.

"You'll see." Narelle smiled, and her canines retracted. An eye blink later and her baby blues were back. "I'm keeping the ears and the tail. If they don't like they can bite me."

"Who're you talking to?" Meylandra's voice said from the hallway.

"Myself," Narelle said with a wink and sashayed out the door, tail held high.

~

Melinda stepped out into the hallway and the amount of technology was welcome relief from Gunna Space Station. There was a hum through the deck she couldn't place but once she passed a T-junction, she realized the amount of tech was meant for only one thing: A star carrier.

She was never assigned to a star carrier and neither was I, Melinda thought. "Where in gahsakes are we?" she finally said.

"If anyone will follow me please, we'll get you to your births and bedded down before the jump." Meylandra's voice pulled her closer to the gaggle of parents and kids.

Kids, Melinda thought. *Where'd all these kids come from?*

"Welcome on aboard *Crosleigh's Hope*. I'm Master Sergeant Meylandra Stuk, and I'll be your guide during our six-month voyage to the edge of this Coil. At which time, you will dis-embark and continue your journey to *Hyde's Bluff*."

"I'm showing you this so you understand what happened. Whatever the Houses say, this is what happened," Narelle said to Melinda. "The pre-flight was going perfectly until this happened."

The corridor changed to a split-level bridge. Captain's Chair in the middle with the Navigator Well, or The Pitt as some had nicknamed it. Helm and Fire Control at the front of the bridge. Communications and Damage Control behind the Navigation Well. The blast shields was lowered so no view of where they were but it didn't matter since all space looked the same.

"What type of signal is it?" Meylandra was bent over Communication with a headset to her ear.

"I don't, Captain, but whatever it is, it's getting stronger. It's all around us," the Communication Officer, Ollie Brie said.

"What's it sounds like?" Meylandra said.

"I don't know the anti-psychotics filters are doing their jobs and keeping all of it out," Ollie said and jerked around at movement. "Get down!"

Meylandra whipped around and dove for cover.

Ollie disappeared in a cloud of aura fireflies and the crash axe sparked of the console. The pygmy bushwhacker bounced out of her chair and rolled across the deck plates. The angry windchime alert her quills announced got the attention of everyone on the bridge.

Narelle whipped around from the captain's seat. "What're you doing!" she howled.

The navigator, a Leighton Magi, brought down the crash axe onto the communication station with little effect.

Narelle triple tapped her earbud. "Bridge to Security, I need full containment team up here now. Someone check those defense genies, now!"

"Internal Coms is down," the fire control officer said and grabbed the axe out of the navigator's hands. "Someone find the manacles and restrain him, now."

"What?" The navigator staggered about. "What happened?"

The fire control officer pivoted about and swung the axe into the navigator's console with the same results.

The officer scowled at the axe then the station.

"Yes, you bit off more than you could chew." Narelle pulled her sword from her sheath. "Where're my coms?"

The fire control officer turned towards Narelle, a twisted smile plastered across his face Two seconds later, two stun needles embedded themselves in his forehead.

The screams erupted from his lips and something twisted away into the dark.

The officer crumpled, and the axe clattered to the ground.

"Either a cursed weapon or an aura jacker," Meylandra said. "Nobody touch the weapon. Get internal coms restored. Do not break out the weapons until someone ironed up checks them!"

"Aura jacker," Narelle said. "I saw him die but there're probably more."

"Lock down the bridge, and vacuum seal the compartments," Melinda said and the bridge doors hissed open.

"Finally, Crosleigh, where have you been?" Narelle said.

Melinda opened her mouth, but it was too late.

The axe hurtled into Nathaniel Crosleigh, Jr.'s hand and with one leisurely toss, it was embedded in Narelle's shoulder.

Narelle toppled to the deck. "Someone shoot him! Shoot him, May!"

"Crosleigh, what in gahsakes are you doing!" Meylandra screamed.

"Shoot him!" Narelle howled. "Shoot the fucker, now!" She staggered to her feet and pulled the axe out of her shoulder. "You want it, come and get it."

Crosleigh reached forth his hand but the axe remained in Narelle's hand.

"Yeah, cursed weapons don't work on me, you jack-booted ass. I can hear it. I'm just ignoring it." Narelle backed away, tail at the ready while Crosleigh slipped forward. "May, do me a favor and shoot this asshole, please."

"Kill the Witch," a tiny voice dribbled out of Crosleigh's mouth.

The axe twisted out of Narelle's hand. She landed face first on the deck and the axe was back into Crosleigh's hands.

"Shoot. Him!" Narelle cursed and pushed herself up to see the stunner pointed at her. "May, what're you doing?"

Meylandra's hand quaked. "I can't... control. It knows my name. I can't—"

"Leave them be," a familiar voice said, and Spence MacGregor appeared. "I don't know what you want, but I'm sure we can work something out."

"Like shooting both of them!" Narelle seethed. "I shouldn't be able to hear that cursed thing in the first place. Charms." She placed a hand to her. "Blessed necklace was around my neck last night. Where is it?"

"I think we both know where it is. Which is why Meylandra is holding up better than you are," Spence said and sidestepped in front of Crosleigh. "Now, what do you want?"

"Kill the Witch," Crosleigh said.

"If this is because I didn't include you in all this, you know why. Now, either stop or I'm going to spin the defense wards back up and you'll leave the Hollow ever again. We had a deal."

"Kill the Weaver," Crosleigh hissed.

"No. Not today. We had a deal. This little misstep is going to get worse if you don't listen to me carefully. Drop the axe, tell me where you are, and I'll make sure personally you get a fair hearing. None of this is going to end well if you keep this up," Spence said.

"Kill the Witch. Kill the Weaver. Kill the Rider." Crosleigh swung through.

~

The carrier's whistle pulled Mindy out of her sleep.

"Ladies and Gentlemen, we'll arrive at Stow's End in approximately ten minutes," the PA speaker in the corner of the wall announced. "Please make sure to return to your births for debarkation."

Melinda rolled upright. Something dropped onto the floor with a thud.

She bent down to get whatever it was and found herself gripping her stunner.

The chamber was exactly where it should've been.

Melinda's blood raced. Her heart throbbed in her ears. Her mind was on fire. The fire traveled from her head to heart. The fire either meant upgrades or someone had tried to brute force their way into her mind server.

What was that? she thought and looked down at what had dropped onto the floor.

An After-Action Report. Where Weavers Daire. The same one from her mind server.

A knock at the door and Melinda raised her stunner. She dropped the report into her bag and she thumbed the intercom. "Yes?" she managed.

"Mindy, we're ten minutes out, you ready?" Thom's voice said.

Melinda touched the charm necklace around her neck and found it right where it should be. Its gem shined properly.

"We'll be right out," she said and breathed in deep. Her heart no longer in her ears.

I was never on board a star carrier. I broke up the group a year ago. Narelle and Erik got headhunted immediately and the rest I haven't seen until tonight. We don't talk anymore. My name is Meylandra Stuk, I'm named after my grandmother. She died so I could live. I was banished, and my family was taken in by Rushford Scott and given fake names ten years ago. I was never on board Crosleigh's Hope, she thought. *That was my grandmother in the report, right? Right?*

The rail carrier's whistle was the only answer she received.

22
STOW'S END

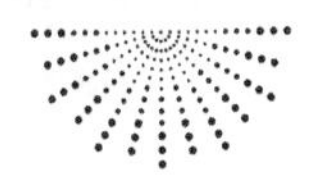

Itty Bitty's TREK TO STOW'S END HAD BEEN A SILENT ONE.

The lights from the town were gone and all that remained was a curved silhouette of metal rising out of the sea of stars that was spread across the horizon.

Should be enjoying the view, Nat thought from the pilot's seat.

Instead, he was more focused on the view from *Itty*'s external cameras cycled through his center console monitors. Alita knew how to narrow down possible targets, so the sweep of the area was a clean transition from port to starboard, bow to stern, and ended with views from the belly and roof turrets. The House-Grade surveillance suite may have been ten years out of date but on Stuk's Hollow, it along with whatever he'd squeezed into the ship's frame was the most expensive piece of hardware on the planet. Besides, the light behind them showed nothing else was in the air.

Nat had leveled *Itty Bitty* off at fifty feet and besides the occasional boulder or left debris from the last war, nothing else jutted out of the flat landscape to strangle them into the sand below.

The dome creeped closer. It had seen its fair share of attempts to break in, but the combination of blessed metals and defenses had kept out aerial bombardments even orbital strikes. There was a reason why the town had been dubbed Stow's End. House Stow had retreated to the domed in valley and waited until their enemies had either run out of ammunition or simply given up and accepted terms. The town had come later once General Stow and his daughter decided to put down roots.

In the early days of the Houses, when the war mages and their carriers were plentiful, the city would've been lanced from orbit without a second thought. Now, it was different. No more war mages or their carriers and certainly no more ways to get glassed at the whim of some snot nosed House.

But all things being equal, the sight of the chariot carrier over the Keep had knocked Nat's gung-ho attitude down a few notches. He took no chances once he was out of the carrier's firing solution and spooled up *Itty Bitty*'s defense suite.

Three red buttons on the overhead control panel pulsed. SBD. Silent but Deadly or in this case, Silent Battle Deadly. It meant the iron kegs situated around the dropship's innards kept her off the radar, her heavy use of the defense suite was silent to anyone listening for the spells the kegs were churning and she was still able to use her offense suite without alerting anyone.

The only downside was she was a slow moving, silent target for anyone who could see the black arts exhaust the spells produced that kept her hidden. Once the defense suite was compromised the blessing from Grainne Stow would stop anything until Nat could get himself out of it. She was also the only thing in the air and that had kept Nat from reporting in until now.

"November Fifty-Five Romeo Romeo to tower requesting landing clearance," Nat said and released the communication toggle on the control stick.

The frequency replied with nothing but dead air.

"There's an opening in the top of the dome," Alita said from the Radar Intercept Office Station behind Nat.

"That should be closed, too," Nat said. "Either Deedee forgot to plug the dome, or someone's already come through. Any other contacts?"

"No other contacts besides unnamed Carrier Charlie. No flags or House colors. I can raise ours, Lord Crosleigh," Alita said.

"No, we're not here. And, please don't start with the lord stuff. Keep an eye out for where that rail carrier pops out of. Mindy is gonna have to get to Stow's End to open the blast shields." Nat pulled back on *Itty Bitty*'s yoke and changed altitude. Nothing but a metal horizon filled the two-tiered cockpit.

"And no supposed aura storm front either," Alita said. "Weather is clear for miles."

Where are you, Mindy? Nat thought and clucked his tongue. "Could already be inside."

"Why aren't they chasing us?" Junior said from the bombardier station in Itty's nose. "Why attack the Keep only?"

"My family isn't well liked in this Coil," Nat said. "Besides, it's survived worst."

"You really might want to check the rear cameras," Alita said.

Nat tapped one of his center console screens and a view from a rear camera appeared.

White flames appeared only to disappear due to rapid explosions that whited out the camera feed.

Swell, there goes my hidden hangar, Nat thought and toggled the intercom. "Ladies and gentle souls, your captain from the flight deck would like to welcome you to the inaugural flight of Crosleigh Messenger Services with direct service to Stow's End. Our flight time is brisk thirty minutes and we ask for everyone to stay in their seats until we've landed. The secure House phones under your seats will let you call out to arrange a pick-up curbside. If anyone has the urge to explode or blow up, we ask you to look at our lovely loadmaster who will accepting applications to our time-honored Mile High Clubs which includes kicking your compromised self out the back before we land. In the meantime, sit back and ignore the fact Crosleigh Keep is burning itself to the ground." Nat cut the PA and stared at the rear camera feed. "Gahsakes, it's a giant inanimate structure. Al, do me a favor, check the strong box behind you. The crash axe still locked inside?"

Alita twisted around. "Yep."

"Okay, do me a favor, go help Royer and wand everyone down," he said.

"Why me?" she said.

"Because I haven't heard from Mindy and the rail carrier is nowhere in sight," he said. "While you do that, Junior is going to change seats with you so he can monitor for Mindy's signal. We ain't landing anywhere until the blast dome opens." He toggled the internal com. "Vernon? Al is coming back to wand everyone down, send Pan up here."

Alita pulled herself out of the chair and Junior replaced her.

Pan had crawled into the nose without making a sound.

"Getting crowded down there?" he said to her.

"Nope." Pan strapped herself in and adjusted her rearview mirror to see him. "I think they're clean."

"Probably are but I'm not going to be the one who cracks open Stow's End to a full-on outbreak," he said. "I'm not getting stuck in a decontamination room for six months."

"You'd have some cute company," Pan said.

"And you need to get back into someone's good graces to keep your flight status," Junior said.

Nat glanced in the rear-view mirror at the plate. "Yes and no. I'm not an adrenaline junkie. They didn't take us out, but I didn't use the decoys either."

"I would've," Pan said.

"There're may be two chariot class carriers in the area. The decoy ploy got put on the back burner once I heard about that. The problem I have is if there's anything else up here as fast as *Itty Bitty* is," Nat said. "Which may explain why we're the only ones in the air right now."

Junior thought this through. "Why would we be the only things in the air?" The console beeped. "New contact," it said. "Rail carrier with Melinda's secure wireless signal."

"Thank you, Mindy." Nat tapped a screen and a heat bloom cut across the horizon. "Just ahead of us. Now let's see if they can that dome open. And to answer your question, air superiority always wins."

"No one has used aerial mages since the war," Junior said.

"Right, their auras run down after constantly using thrust spells. Someone on that carrier was using three priestesses as Air Cav to target and then blow stuff up without worrying about draining their auras. Add in the carrier as a floating base of operations and it puts them in them in the: 'I know how to use my toys properly' category."

"I'd be running too," Pan said.

"I'm not running. I'm dropping off my passengers and reconsidering my business model because if they think they're going to own the skies then I can impatiently bide my time on the ground and wait for them to get bored," Nat said. "And, yes, I know, I owe you a new ship."

"I didn't say a thing," Pan said. "I like it down here. It's a great view and I just sit back and let you drive for a change."

"Uh huh. I know a lovely junk yard off the beaten path. We'll find you a nice ship." Nat chuckled.

He stared at the rear camera feed one more time and flicked it off.

Next time, Nat thought. *Next time.*

~

"We're locked out." Melinda's sketchy voice came through Nat's headset. "Contamination Protocols kicked in an hour you left and sealed the dome."

"Explains why we can't get radio contact. Anti-psychotics filters are blocking everything," Nat said off Junior's puzzled look and pressed the com button. "Let me guess, House keys or badges?"

A short pause and Melinda responded with an affirmative.

"Once we open it up, they'll know we're here and come ah runnin'," Nat said.

"Unless they're already inside," Pan said. "Doesn't feel right. Even Deedee would be standing watching. There's a ladder coming out of the hole. We could land someone there and meet at the control tower."

"No sign of Wally, either," Nat clucked. "Two teams, Al and Junior go down the ladder." He depressed the com button. "Melinda, meet at the control tower and we'll—"

The dome shuddered. A line formed down the middle and the two pieces pealed back.

"I didn't touch a thing." Melinda's voice was barely heard over the roar.

"Maybe Deedee saw us," Pan said.

"No, no, we've been SBD since we left." Nat angled *Itty* into a slow orbit around retracting dome.

The outskirts of Stow's End weren't much to write home about besides Sleepless Maiden, the combination air and rail carrier station. The foundations of several houses jutted out of the sand. They were a prime example of over extending ones reach instead of concentrating on the existing infrastructure. The remaining foundation skeletons made for lovely cover if someone had some mages wanted to launch ground-to-air spells.

Itty's HUD targeted the two-story buildings belonging to the air and rail stop along with Sleepless Maiden.

The Inner Dome that covered Stow's End itself was still closed.

Nat reached up and depressed the defense grid buttons. The soothing hum of the defense genies disappeared and was replaced by the roar of *Itty*'s engines. "Defense grid is on stand-by. Light 'em up."

A few clicks later and the *Itty*'s scanners targeted the town. "Short range scans showing no signs of life," Junior said. "Long range, still no contacts. Carrier is barely in range but still not moving. Switching over to thermals for genies."

The view changed on Nat's screens and Sleepless Maiden silhouette pulsed with rainbow waves. "Sleepless Maiden's defense genies are working," Junior said. "Can't tell what's inside but she's locked up tight. I'm sweeping the rest of the area now."

The camera's view zoomed out and the only two rainbow buildings was Sleepless Maiden and the rail stop.

"No sign of Deedee or Grainne's life signs," Junior said.

"Landing grid looks clear," Pan said. "The defense genies were working when we left."

"They're bone dry now," Junior said.

"Oh, I don't think so," Nat growled. "No more coms. Type this out on the keypad: No sign of life. Stop. LZ too hot. Stop. Secure parameter at Rail, LZ and Maiden. Stop. Tommy and Selene sweep. Stop. Stick with the Weaver, Phineas and Roark. Stop. Watch your back. Stop. Al will meet you at Maiden. Stop. Confirm receipt."

Junior tapped out the messages and one of the spotlights on Itty's underbelly relayed the message.

"Receipt confirmed. They're rolling into the rail stop now," Junior said.

"Time to see how much sway Zi still has," Nat said. "Pan, get up here. I need to borrow Zi and his House phone. Time to get an APC out here cuz there's no way we're marching in without an escort."

"New ground contact," Junior reported. "APC with House Stuk flag and colors rolling up the landing pad. They're sending encrypted message now."

"Wow, someone listened to my announcement. I'm shocked," Nat said.

"A few someone's, more APCs rolling in. House Daire and Leighton. All of them sending House flags and colors. All encrypted and confirmed," Junior said.

The landing grid lit up with hazy rainbow then solidified.

"Thank you, Cherie, I take back all the bad things I said about you," Nat said.

"I can still hear you," Cherie's voice cracked over the coms.

Several operators hustled out of the protection of the rail carrier station and formed a parameter around the station. Once there was a perfect half circle was formed another steam of Tier Zero Holding Operatives formed two squares around the landing pad.

A single green and yellow flare sparked to life in the middle of the pad.

"Daire and Leighton have picked up their passengers and waiting on your signal," Junior said. "No ground movement. No auras."

"Thank you, Mister Stuk." Nat eased *Itty* into a hover directly over the flare. "Landing sequence initiated." He flipped on the intercom. "Ladies and gentle souls, we do ask you stay in your seats as we are about to touch down. We do ask anyone needing extra time to press your call button now and our loadmaster will help you out of your seat and into the awaiting APC that will be meeting us on the tarmac. Please remember, it may be a secure tarmac, but anything can and will happen. All auras wielders are asked to spool yourselves down until the captain has turned off the non-smoking lamp. We thank you for flying Air Crosleigh and hope to do business with you in the future. Crew, prepare for landing."

"Still need to get a better name," Pan snickered.

"Oh, hush, I'm working on it." Nat flipped down the landing gear levers in the center panel. He twisted a wheel on the right console panel and *Itty*'s engines rotated from horizontal to vertical propulsion. Once the deck plates stopped shuddering, Nat exhaled. "Signal them, on my mark. Rush the Maiden, in three, two, one. Execute."

Nat pulled back on the throttles and *Itty* swiftly landed on the tarmac. Her parameter was promptly surrounded by crouching operators and mages alike. Targeting Spells and green lasers bounced out into the dark.

Selene bound across the tarmac with the resurrection chamber over her shoulder made him laugh. Melinda, Thom, Roark and Cherie followed. The brief glimpse of them together was sight for sore eyes even if they weren't all bundle up. Terrie's squad of operators came next along with a stream of Operators and the few mages they had left led by Phineas.

The Stuk APC rolled onto the tarmac. She chugged around *Itty* and backed up so her rear door would have a hard seal with the *Itty*'s rear ramp. A seal was formed between the two vehicles. The telltales blinked from red to green on the overhead panel and the airlock's doors popped open.

Across the screens, he watched Zi, Josiah and the rest of his entourage make the transition with Alita.

The APC decoupled, and it roared across the tarmac and out of sight.

Alita's face appeared across the cameras and her form vanished.

Nat keyed the intercom. "Time to decide, folks. We sit here like a giant target or we bounce out to the Sea only to come back in time to pull Mindy's rear out of the fire."

"I think she can take of herself," Pan said.

"That's what worries me. Because it's been a cake walk until now. We're about to stick our noses where they don't belong. And that means someone is gonna notice and they're gonna take a swipe at either one or both of us. So, whoever wants out, now's the time. They'll secure Maiden and Al can track down Grainne and Deedee," Nat said. "But, I need to see what's happened and I'm not taking the rest of you along if you don't want to. Two carriers in the air under gahknows whose flag is gonna turn this planet on its head because they haven't seen what those things can do. I used to fly 'em before, during and after the war. This is no word of a lie they show up and people just surrender because their parents or gahforbid grandparents remember. Nobody on this planet wants to go back to how it used to be, six houses on one side, six houses on the other and it only took one match to throw us back into the bunkers waiting for one side to call it quits. So, time to decide. How far are you willing to go?"

All the call buttons went green.

"All or nothing," Pan said.

"All right, everyone strap in," Nat said and switched over to a secure com channel. "November Fifty-Fifty Romeo Romeo to all points, thank you for the cover. We're going full burn in thirty. Take cover and we'll see ya all soon."

The operators and mages immediately doubled timed it into the dark.

Nat flipped a few switches and tightened his eight-point harness. "Ladies and gentle souls please lock yourselves down. We're going to pop up and punch it. High Gs will be in effect for a good thirty seconds or more. Defense wards are staying down so if anything breaks through I fully expect one of you down there to shred 'em before they get to cockpit." He flipped another switch and the doors on the primary and secondary flight decks swished closed. Locks tumbled into place.

"Fuel?" Pan said.

"Three primaries are completely full. We'll burn one tank out, one tank back in," he said.

"You expect it to be that bad?" she said.

"I expected us to be dead by now. I think that carrier is supposed to persuade us not to do what we're about to do," he said. "Those priestess got one job to do, blow stuff up and keep the lookie loos like us away."

"They aren't catching us," Pan said.

"Nope, they certainly aren't." Nat flipped a switch. A thud later the landing gear retracted. "Junior, how we doing?"

"Decoys Alpha, Bravo and Charlie are in the air and lapping the Keep. No signs of hostiles contacts," Junior reported. "This isn't a wise idea."

"Noted," Nat said.

"What idea is that?" Pan's voice peaked.

"We're going to give Count Stukari a proper send off and I wanna know what the fuck is going on," Nat said. "That high-speed camera suite still rolling?"

"Since we left," Junior said.

"Perfect," Nat said and keyed the intercom. "Prepare for Gs in three, two, one."

He pushed the throttles to the firewalls.

The engines howled, and the G-Forces pushed everyone down into their seats while the ground vanished at a violent rate.

At two hundred feet, he pulled back on the throttles, twisted the wheel and the engines slammed down into horizontal propulsion. He pushed the throttles back up and clutched the control sticks with both hands all the while the G-forces pushed him back into his seat.

Itty shook herself every which way.

"Have the decoys form up on me," Nat said.

Pan arched eyebrows in the rear-view mirror silently repeated her question. She looked left and yelped at how close Alpha then right to Bravo then up to Charlie.

"All right, let's see what's so damned important about the Keep because you are so going in my After-Action Report," Nat wheezed.

"I can spool up our weapons," Junior said.

"No need, we're just giving Count Stukari a proper send off. Just the three of us," Nat said and banked *Itty* around so she was lined up behind the carrier. "All hands, prepare for high speed maneuver. Do no leave your seats and wait for the all clear for me. On my mark, three, two, one and execute."

Alpha, Beta and Charlie pulled in closer than Pan was expecting. She would've yelped but the throttles pushed to the firewalls and Itty's turbine engines howled to full afterburner. The sudden change in g-force pushed everyone back into their seats.

The three dropships roared across the carrier from stern to bow. As planned, the three decoys fired off fireworks. They exploded well over the carrier and in different time, kids would've been clapping at this.

Instead, in a blink of an eye, Alpha and Beta were destroyed by anti-aircraft deck guns.

Charlie survived the assault until after they well past the range of the AA Guns.

A flash of light sliced off her wings. She pinwheeled out of control and pancaked across the desert floor.

Nat eased off the throttles and the Gs stopped sitting on his chest. "You got all of that?"

"All of it," Junior said. "You happy now? You pissed them off."

"They chasing us?" Nat said, and Junior's silence was enough.

~

"Yer ego is going to get us all killed, flyboy," Royer growled over the intercom.

"That is the plan," Nat said. "They know we recorded them and now they need to decide who's more important, me or Mindy. Didn't you used to fly two feet off the ground without a helmet?"

"That was before I learned to stop showing off. You think we can handle all that firepower?" Royer said.

"Three priestesses against all of us? No," Nat said. "But, it splits them up."

"And if it doesn't?" Royer said.

"Then why let me back into my own House when you went to all the trouble to kick me out of it a year ago. You take a house and you keep it. You don't just take what you want and leave," Nat said. "So, we go re-take my house and see what in gahsakes can be that bad you need several Houses worth of arch mages and two chariot class carriers."

"Arch mages are defense," Royer said. "They're too big to repair anything. That's what techno mages do."

"I know that. You know that. I don't think they do," Nat said.

"Wait, you don't have a house," Pan said.

"That is correct. I'm renting the old Brie place while my House was being built," Nat said.

"Wait. What would they want at the old Brie place?" Royer said. "Hold it. Why're you renting?"

"Whatever they wanted was in the house," Pan said.

"What's in the old Brie House?" Royer said.

"Got me but whatever it is. They had three priestesses bust down the safe House I was in to get to it. We've got an hour to think about it," Nat said and closed the intercom channel.

"You know what they were after," Junior said.

"No, I haven't clue they were after you. Remember, we were bonded after they stopped us from getting the Weaver off that engine mount, compromised my ground crew, blew up my ride and we get burdened only to kick the Weaver off the ship before it jumped for gahknows where then it's blank," Nat said. "We didn't accomplish a thing except move pieces around the board. They're after Mindy and the Weaver just like they always have been. I think whatever's in the House was something left over after the war. I think it's whatever is causing the aura storms. I think someone found a way to amplify getting aura jacked."

"If that's the case, they're already in Stow's End," Junior said. "Along with Mindy and the others. You led them into a trap."

"No, this is all hypothetical until we find evidence. If it was my fight, we'd have been sweeping Sleepless Maiden right now. But, it's theirs, not ours. They're the scalpel. We're the sledgehammer," Nat said. "I can sleep easily tonight if I just walked her into a trap. She needs to get her head in the game because sooner or later, she's gonna have to start caring."

"Have you lost all sense of reality? Life isn't a game," Junior said.

"This isn't reality. This is fantasy. You're a highly intelligent crustacean inside a mechanized suit of armor. Pan used to breathe underwater. Royer used to be in the air more than on the ground and the less said about my ability to wield three burdens at the same time without breaking my back the better. And we're traveling at speeds so fast that *Itty* should be a melted piece of slag. Make no mistake, ever since Mindy crashed this has all certainly been a game. We're lagging while someone has been enjoying the fruits of their victory. I think it's time to play catch up."

Nat inched the throttles up and *Itty* roared across the skies towards the unknown.

23
CHERIE PICKED

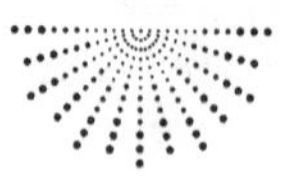

"GAHSAKES, IS HE ALWAYS THAT LOUD?" THOM CURSED.

Melinda turned about, and her goggle lenses adjusted to follow *Itty Bitty*'s twin blue fiery afterburner trail until they disappeared only to be replaced by several sonic booms. She tapped her earbud. "You still with us?"

"See ya all soon." Nat's voice rose above the static and was gone.

"He actually popped up this time." Selene sniffed. "Usually he's five feet off the deck."

"This time?" Thom said.

Selene hefted the chamber to her other shoulder. "I thought he was trying to impress me, but he actually enjoys doing that."

"I already told you I wasn't interested in him," Melinda said. "I thought you two had called it quits."

"We did." Selene reached out and grabbed thin air. "I told you to stay with him."

Alita's head popped into view. "Don't look at me in the tone of voice, you've seen one flyboy you've seen 'em all. Besides he told me to."

Thom snapped his fingers, and everyone stopped. "I don't care who's going to sleep with him once he comes back and saves the day. Alita, sweep ahead and get back to me, clear."

Selene released Alita and she disappeared.

Thom beckoned one of the holding operators closer. "Reform a security detail around the landing grid along with the rail carrier. And keep off the coms, runners only."

The operator nodded and disappeared back up the hill.

"We get to Sleepless Maiden and hunker down for the rest of the night, right?" Cherie said.

"That's one plan," Melinda said and leaned around the corner of the ruins they had squeezed against.

The goggles did the rest and wireframed the two-story building. Every inch of it throwing up errors across her lenses.

The front doors the only thing not throwing up errors and wide open.

"Swell. No welcoming committee or sign of Deedee," Melinda said.

All of Alita popped back into view. "Front doors are wide open. The rear exit is barred from the inside. The stairs leading to the second-floor rooms are open. Me, Cherie and Melinda can clean it out. Half of you cover the chamber and the other half cover the stairs."

Selene lowered the chamber. "I'll cover the roof with Phineas. Swords?"

Melinda raised a hand and Selene passed out the remaining of her blessed short swords. "Now, if you'll excuse me, I'll be right back," she said and double timed to Sleepless Maiden's front door before Thom could stop her.

~

Sleepless Maiden was empty.

Melinda waited at the threshold and knocked loudly on the door-frame. "Melinda Scott, looking to talk to Grainne Stow. Hello?"

Cherie and Phineas descended the second-floor stairs. Neither looked very happy.

Melinda crossed over the threshold and the goggles mapped every inch of the building.

"I've got nothing. Where is she?" she said.

"I don't know but the manager's office is locked up tight," Phineas said. "No signs of a struggle, nothings broken."

"And HICM?" Melinda said.

Cherie pointed to the innocent looking dispenser resided between the sexless bathrooms. "Intact and working." She held up an empty ring box. "I found this on the bar."

Thom with Roark and a half dozen holding operators crossed over the threshold. He pointed two operators to the back of the first floor, three to the pool table level and another four to the roof.

Melinda waved the sword over the box. It moaned. "A trap for us if we made it back or a snatch and grab gone wrong?" she said.

"Looks the same as we left it a few hours ago. If it was a snatch and grab there'd be evidence. This is more like she just walked away," Thom said. "If we did make it back, yeah, I'd set a trap, too."

"Why just her?" Cherie said. "She's a bartender."

"She was a Priestess of the Hills during the war," Thom said. "Before that she was high priestess to the O'Hares before she burned down the last temple. She also his wife which puts her in the don't fuck with me category. So, whoever sent her the present knows what they're doing."

"Yashira or Leightons," Roark said and eyed Phineas. "No offense."

"No offense for what? And no sign of Deedee, either," Cherie said.

"During the war, some of the Houses used cursed items to take over another House from the inside." Phineas waved the ring box around. "Innocent looking jewels and once you put it on, you don't remember a thing because there's a cursed gem magi puppeting you."

"And Brie House, too," Roark coughed.

Thom leveled a look and sighed. "And the Brie, too."

"Wait, you're blaming us?" Cherie said.

"No," Phineas said. "Not us. Just your grandfather's House."

"Mom or Dad's side?" Cherie said.

"Mother's side," Phineas said.

Cherie blanched. "Yeah, that makes much more sense now."

"What does?" Phineas said.

"Scrying on the door frame of the manager's office is in Leighton." Cherie pointed to the back room.

"Deedee was supposed to get shipment of blessings in but it never showed up," Thom said and looked over Roark's bag of bladed weapons. "How many of those are bone dry?"

"All of them. They drained the forges at the Keep but there are forges in there." Roark jerked a head towards the inner dome. "We swipe in and bee line it to the forges before they do."

"You also said to burn yourself," Melinda said.

Roark raised a House ID card. "While you were getting the Daires sorted, Nat and I visited HICM got new ID cards issued. That just leaves you, Mindy."

"We do that, Mindy and they'll know we're coming," Thom said.

Melinda grinned. "Not if we go private it is. The network is still down. That means any of the house security details will be working off their private networks. They'll have to ping us to request our house profiles. I'm not ready to announce ourselves."

"Which reminds me, I can fix that problem with the network with enough people," Roark said.

"In due time and you were right, Melinda Scott is clean. Any third-party house can get a tent at the New Year's Celebration so long as they pass all the tests. Which, I can with ease and since Rushford isn't coming this year because he can't stand the celebrations. So, we burn everyone, and House Scott rises," Melinda said. "This will give us a clear path to find out what's going on and lets Roark and Phineas get to the nearest priestess to get a check-up."

Thom snorted. "Mindy."

"I have to agree, they'll have look outs," Phineas said. "A 'check-up' would help. We may have a bigger problem."

"Lord Knoll and Mister Leighton have been through a lot and need to make sure their auras are tuned up before going back out and fixing the network because everyone needs to know," Melinda said.

"While you do that, I can figure out why the engine mount is here with Mister MacGregor."

"No, it's not," Thom said.

"Unfortunately, it is." Melinda pulled a slate out of her bag. She swiped through handshake screens and a pulsing red dot appeared. Several blue dots appeared away from the red dot. "We're the blue dots."

"And the mount is the red," Thom finished. "It jumped down here?"

Melinda shrugged. "Don't look at me. I failed fourth and fifth dimensional math."

"If you do the math right, you can." Roark sighed. "Erik."

Melinda nodded. "Erik."

"This explains why we couldn't find him," Cherie said. "If he got in tight with them on someone else's orders."

"I have no idea what you're talking about," Melinda said nonchalantly.

"Mindy, they're gonna know," Thom said.

"Third Party Houses are private until someone requests our ID cards, or we introduce ourselves," she said. "Until then, everyone can be my guests while we snoop around and escort certain people back to their houses or to Clarence."

"They're really gonna know, now, Mindy," Roark said.

Melinda looked around at the silent as tomb Sleepless Maiden. "Really? Cuz, this screams trap, and no one is here for us. So, either someone slacked off or someone's in the uprights waiting to swoop down and trap us."

Selene dropped down from the uprights and Tommy squeaked.

She dusted the cobwebs off herself. "Nope. All clean. No rats. No mice. Nothing," she said.

"That just leaves the Manager's Office," Phineas said.

Melinda pulled out her stunner. Selene drew her sword and Cherie's aura popped up instantly much to Melinda's surprise.

"After you," Melinda said to the two aura wielders. "Don't touch anything until we get back there's at least two sub-basements that aren't on the blue prints of this place."

Thom looked down at his feet. "We should've come down from the roof, shouldn't we have?"

"Now, you're thinking like me," Selene said. "And that's a good thing."

Thom snapped his fingers and all the operators quick timed it out the front door along with Roark.

~

The manager's office door didn't budge.

"What happens if I unspool the spell," Cherie said.

"Then it could blow up in your face," Phineas said. "You can't unspool it."

"They were in a hurry. They didn't finish," Cherie said. "The wood is too weak. It's not meant to hold the spell."

"It's a trip wire spell," Selene said.

"They expect us to kick down the door, it completes the circuit and ka-boom," Cherie said. "The problem is it goes ka-boom while we're inside the Maiden, the defense wards will contain it all and we've got an oven."

"We don't need to go in there then," Phineas said.

"Yes, we do. If the evidence is in there, then we need it. So, we need to move the spell from the wood to another inanimate object and get it outside so it can go ka-boom without flash frying us," Cherie said and turned to Melinda. "I need an empty keg from behind the bar."

"Since when?" Phineas said.

"Six months of removing spells from dead Houses. The scrying isn't as good as most, so we just convince to move somewhere else," Cherie said and Melinda returned with an empty keg. "The spell feeds off the molecules in the wood. The healthier the wood. The longer the spell takes to go ka-boom."

"How many times have you done this?" Phineas said.

"Enough to know they're still in the building and are impatiently waiting for me to get on with it," Cherie said. "Selene, let our friends pass. They aren't here for us."

Selene swiveled around and growled at the cloaked Magi at the bar. "They're what?"

"I said let them pass," Cherie raised her voice. "Tell Tommy not to shoot them, Melinda."

"Mindy, the Leighton APC just rolled up." Thom's voice echoed in Melinda's ear.

"I know," Melinda said. "We're almost through. The Leightons will be leaving in a moment."

Cherie pulled the scrying off the wood and dropped it into the keg.

The keg danced around. It hummed while the writing stretched out across the keg and the familiar glow of a spell radiated outwards.

"Tripwire spell contained," Cherie said.

The keg bounced about.

"Or not," Melinda said.

She picked it up and bolted for the front door. Got it outside and heaved it away. "Fire in the hole!" she shouted and dove back inside.

The keg corkscrewed around and around. It jolted fifty feet in the air and exploded in cloud of green aura fireflies.

Melinda picked herself up from the floor and every fiber in her being kept herself from picking up her stunner.

The Leighton Magi loomed in front of her. Selene's blessed sword wailed.

Melinda extended a hand. "Melinda Scott. Who be you and who do you serve?"

The Magi stillness wasn't right. None of it was right. The figure shouldn't have been but was. The cursed gems fused to his limbs was worse than those gahforsaken defense candles.

"Mindy, what in gahsakes was that?" Thom's voice squawked in her ear.

"Manager's office has been de-hexed," Melinda said. "Tell, whoever is in the Leighton's APC to come collect their guests. Alita, escort our guests to the APC, please."

The Magi turned, and Alita popped back into existence. Her sword on her hip and not in her hand. "If you'll follow me," she said in most polite voice Melinda had ever heard meaning full well how pissed she was.

Cherie joined the Magi. "Thank you, for all the fun," she said and tossed a keycard on the nearest table. "I'll see you later."

"Not if I see you first," Melinda said.

Terrie stepped inside and flanked the Magi. She didn't even look at Cherie or Melinda. She instead focused a look at Phineas. "Not you," she simply said.

Phineas didn't budge. "Good work," he said.

"Thank you," Cherie said and joined Terrie.

"I think you forgot something." A raspy woman's voice jerked everyone around and gem hurtled through the air and the Magi caught it with ease.

Grainne Stow staggered past Phineas. "The next time you try to hex me you dolt, I'm burning you and yer House down."

The Leighton group boarded their APC and roared off into the night.

Thom and the rest bound inside and barred the doors behind them.

Grainne toppled into a bar stool and her head sagged onto the bar. "So, how's everyone else's night been?" she lifted her head up and squinted at Roark. "You look just like I feel."

~

"Balance," Melinda said once the subbasements had been cleared, twice.

"Yeah, that's the only thing that makes sense," Selene said.

"Balance?" Roark said. "Explain this to me, slowly?"

"You fell asleep during Nat's Balance One oh One class, too?" Selene chuckled.

"The short version kiddies goes like this," Grainne poured herself a drink. "One House rises and its equal yet opposite number does, too. Cherie just got popped and someone needed to see if she could drop that spell into that keg without char broiling you."

"Exactly what did he try to do to you?" Melinda said.

"Mindy," Thom said.

Grainne waved it off. "No, no. It's fine. They wanted me out of the way, so they tried to curse me. Instead, I managed to lock myself in my office and wait it out until the cavalry showed up."

"You can do that?" Melinda said.

"Yes," Grainne, Thom, Roark and Phineas said.

Grainne hopped off the bar stool and wandered over to the MacGregor chamber. "Mister MacGregor, nice to see you again. Which one of got tasked to find the rest of him?"

Melinda raised her hand.

"Yeah, figures it'd be you." Grainne wandered behind the bar, fished out an empty keg, hopped it over her shoulder and dropped it on the top of the chamber.

The keg disappeared, and sound of rushing water flowed around the room.

The keg reappeared and Grainne picked it up and dropped it behind the bar. "Thank you for the re-fill. You're welcome here any time."

"I will never understand that," Selene said.

"You're carrying around a six-foot broadsword that was coupled with the aura of a dead empress and you're saying you don't understand how MacGregor just refilled one of my defense kegs with heavy water? Really?" Grainne chortled.

Selene blinked. "Are we related because I can do that whole lift the heavy rock, too, trick."

"Where's Deedee," Melinda said.

Grainne shrugged. "Haven't seen her since she took off. Right after they went looking for you." She counted off the people in the bar. "You're short a few people, Mindy."

"They're off checking into something," Thom said.

"That's what I heard," Grainne said. "How bad is it?"

"There's a possibility there are pair of chariot-class carriers in the air and no one knows where they are or who's piloting them. We've already de-hexed the Ohari Brothers and I'm pretty sure there are a few more MacGregors walking around that I need to find and make 'em whole," Melinda said.

Grainne nodded slowly. "That explains why we lost all of our arch mages. They paid so well, too." She rubbed her temples. "Time to burn yourselves then get Mister Knoll and Leighton to one of my sisters because sooner or later it's not going to matter." She eyed Roark. "Please, tell me she didn't resurrect you."

"She did," Roark said.

"Uh huh. Don't let that go to your head, Mindy," Grainne said.

"Can we go back to the fact if I did it wrong it would've looped back on me and just vaporized me?" Melinda said.

"Vaporized? Nah, it would've looped back and given you nice tan, ya know, after it tried to immolate your insides," Grainne said. "No one said this job wasn't without it's down sides."

Melinda wandered over to the House card machine. "Let's see if I can get this right the first time." She failed to pull out the ancient keyboard from its cradle and instead pecked away.

"Mindy, there are other ways," Thom said.

"Like surrendering unconditionally and be someone's guests until Clarence decides to see us in a few months? Or couch surf while the Houses decide. No. Baroness of the Wailing Seas is bringing in Crosleigh's Weaver as she promised along with whatever other shenanigans have been going on out there while I've been gone. No. I know what I'm doing," Melinda said.

"Just remember. You are burning everyone else, too," Grainne said.

"I know," Melinda said and typed away on the keypad.

"Do they know? Because once you do that there's no going back," Grainne said.

"Yes, I notified my members once I landed. One hundred percent agreed," Melinda said and stabbed the execute button three times. "Break out the good booze, we're going to be expecting some company."

~

The Stuk APC disgorged it's contingent at Sleeping Maiden's front door ten minutes after Melinda keyed in the final sequence. She pulled over one of the circular tables and tossed her keycard atop it. Selene followed suit along with Thom and a few of the operators.

"This isn't a great idea, Mindy," Thom said.

"Of course, it's not, but it's my idea," Melinda said and Zi entered with his entourage. "That's new record, most people would've ignored the fact their keys didn't work for a week before back tracking the kill codes," she said cheerfully.

"Mindy," Zi said. "What did you do?"

"I burned my House down and I'm starting from scratch," she said. "Time to re-issue keycards so Josiah can take over where I left off."

"What's that supposed to mean," Zi said.

"Simple question: Who's in charge?" Melinda said. "Answer it right and you can walk out of here as free as when you walked in."

"Not funny," Josiah Stuk, her cousin said.

"It's not meant to be funny. It's the truth. Who's in charge? The job I had since I landed on this rock is going to you, cousin and I just need to hear it from you. Who's in charge?" Melinda said and paced around him. "See, I ran the cleanest operation ever. Above board. Clean books means a clean house. Somebody thought I was doing a shit job, so I got canned and you got the job without explanation. So, I must ask, who's in charge?"

"You are," Josiah said.

"Incorrect. The Wailing Seas Data Center has been running on automatic since it was installed. We're just the janitors," Melinda said and handed him a new House ID badge. "Never let anyone tell you anything different. Live and be well."

"What kind of sick head trip are you on?" Thom said.

"Hmm? Oh, I'm not. The System Admin position at Wailing Seas is just a janitorial position. It's automated. Whoever got me fired gained nothing. I'm guessing they wanted something else at the center that I didn't have access to," Melinda said and tossed Thom his key card. "Would you be a dear and sit at that table. We're going to expecting more shortly."

"You've got 'em on a short leash," Roark said.

"Wait, how many of them are under your Wailing Seas Flag?" Grainne said.

"Enough to be counted as a player but not enough to be considered a threat," Melinda said. "Rushford doesn't care what I do so long as his House dues are paid on time and the toilets work. Personally, I don't care what happens to ya. No one looks at the house names anymore. Sooner or later everyone forgets until someone decides to switch sides and suddenly, I've got leaks. So, I just burn us all, start from scratch and wait for someone to keep trying to log in until I track 'em down and politely ask them why. Minus the stunner to the back of their heads, obviously."

"Obviously," Thom said.

"What do you want, Mindy," Zi said.

Melinda picked up a fresh key card and extended it to Zi. "My attaché position and Baroness Title that goes with it. My lands on Wailing Seas and my house back, no questions asked. And if whoever threatened you has a problem with that they can come talk to the Baroness of the Wailing Seas. Otherwise, nothing. Except for a ride into town as your guest, I've got a rogue engine mount to find and these two fine mages need to get sorted before their misaligned auras blow us all to kingdom come."

Grainne cleared her throat.

"Oh, right, also the Weaver tasked me to find the rest of him," Melinda said. "Little things like that."

"How could we forget that," Thom said.

Zi eyed the key card. "That's it?"

Melinda nodded, and he accepted the card. "I think we can all agree that I'm more than capable of getting myself into deeper trouble without anyone else's help, right?" She turned to the remaining regulars. "Selene stick around here then head back to guarding the kiddies. Alita, you're not with me but thank you for coming after me."

Alita pouted. "Next time I'm staying on the ship." She tapped her ear. "Alita Finnegan. Why yes, I am available." She turned to Melinda. "Can I get a lift into town?"

"Me too. Grainne can handle herself," Selene said. "Why am I going back to the kids? I can cover you."

"Because Finnegan Security is going to need all the word of mouth it can get once the house vote happens. If we really go third party we're going to be started from scratch and you disappearing for a few hours is okay, it's not okay for a few days," Melinda said and turned to Grainne. "You good?"

Grainne gave her a thumb's up, and Melinda's party left the bar.

~

The Stuk APC roared off and Grainne closed the front doors of Sleepless Maiden.

The Tier Zero Operators had left with them without so much as an argument.

Grainne stalked back to the Manager's Office. She closed the door and glared at the two cloaked Leighton Magi that hovered over the body of Grainne Stow.

She pulled off the blessed wig and the blond barkeep disappeared to be replaced by a polar opposite, baldheaded, dark mahogany skinned, robed Leighton magess. "Gone. Finally." Her clipped standard tongue sounded worse in her ears than ever before. She sighed and concentrated on her words. "She's still holding her own?"

One of the cloaks nodded. "No change. No movement. How is this possible?"

"Priestess of the Hills has more tricks up their sleeves," the magess growled at the act of defiance. "They warned me about this, but I didn't believe. A priestess deflecting a zomaura gem attack." She shook her head and wandered over to the vanity drawer. She dropped the wig back onto the mannequin head. "And this blessed mop is suffocating my brain." She turned at the silent phone. "Romeo hasn't called?"

"No. Control doesn't think he's coming. We've been given new orders," one of the cloaks said. "We are to execute her and you're to take her place."

She wagged a finger. "Never underestimate him and you'll survive the night. No. Take her to the truck, she'll be valuable asset when the time comes. I'll wait here and join you later."

"Those aren't the orders," the other cloaked Magi said.

"I know. Now go. I'll meet you later," the magess said and dismissed them. Once they were gone, she breathed a sigh of relief. "Thank you for taking the brain dead clone and not checking for pulse you idiots, Grainne Stow of the O'Hare lives to fight another day."

24
BEST LAID PLANS OF MAGES AND MELINDA

THE APC WASN'T ONE THAT MELINDA RECOGNIZED AT FIRST. ALL THE squat, iron armored rectangles on four wheels had the same interior. The color insignias painted on their exteriors had worn over the years but this one must've been in moth balls because the interior wiring was all original and the bucket seats hadn't been replaced with something soft for the fat asses to sit on. All the interiors were the same unless the motor pool had paid a techno mage to re-design with the latest and greatest.

The bucket seats lined each wall so the occupants could face each other, and if one was lucky enough, his seatmate was shorter so their knees wouldn't knock together.

Roark, Melinda and Phineas on the portside with Selene and Alita while Zi and Thom occupied the starboard. Each of them had a headset since the roar of the engine made communication next to impossible.

"You're calling mom once we get in," Thom said.

"How'd you get the short straw, anyway?" Melinda said and wiggled about. "I am missing that suit."

Thom leaned close. "What?"

"I said, I am missing my suit," she said.

"No, Melinda, we aren't stopping off to get you new clothes. You've got two bags worth to go through," Thom said.

Melinda frowned. "Is she angry at me?"

"If you must know, Freda did show up," Thom said.

"That would be a 'yes'," Roark said.

"And you." Thomas pointed a finger. "I did as I was told so don't give me any more lip."

"How long are we staying at The Roost for?" Roark said to Thom.

"Long enough for everyone run through decontamination," Thom said and turned to Roark. "How long will it take to get the network fixed?"

"Wouldn't mind seeing some of the New Year festivities before we leave for Gunna," Melinda said.

"I'm sorry to say you won't be going back to Gunna any time soon," Zi said.

"What?" Thomas said and the shock across his face was genuine.

"The messaging services have been on the fritz and with you leaving we couldn't contact you. Melinda's banishment has gone on for long enough," Zi said. "Don't you agree?"

"We need to talk about this. Alone," Thomas said.

"You can talk to me later about it. But for now, consider her exile rescinded and her House attaché position re-instated," Zi said. "It went through after you left, Gunna."

Thom glowered at the snoring coming from the last row of seating where Phineas, Selene and Alita had somehow lolled off to sleep against the wall of the APC's cabin.

"We'll drop you off at the edge of town. I wouldn't worry about the network problems, I think they'll be fixed soon. The accommodations are on the House." Zi pulled a messenger bag off the seat next to him. "And this belongs to Mindy. The only thing I ask is you use it wisely."

Melinda accepted the bag but didn't open it. "I'll do my best," she said.

"You said—" Thomas started but a daggered look from Zi pushed him back into his seat.

"I was wrong." Zi's twisted tongue drowned out the engine and even Phineas cracked an eye. "Your After-Action Report will be detailed enough to explain the Necrocloak you saw?"

"I have no idea what you're talking about," Melinda said nonchalantly.

Zi smiled. "I thought as much." He tapped the wall with his cane and the APC's engine downshifted. The machine came to a halt and idled. "Mister Leighton, Miss Finnegan, if you see your parents before I do, please give them my well wishes. We shall be seeing more of each other soon and want to extend to them my compliments. They are welcome at my table at any time."

Phineas nodded. "Thank you. Safe roads and travels to you and your family," he said.

The rear hatch seals popped. Phineas, Selene, and Alita were outside before Melinda could blink.

"You are bringing your lovely wife to the ceremony. If I hear you weaseled your way out of me meeting her again." Zi growled at Roark.

"I promise this time you will meet her. Honest, Dad." Roark edged away, and Phineas dragged him out into the night.

"If you wouldn't mind waiting outside, I'd like to talk to Meylandra alone for a moment," Zi said. Thom exited the cabin without a word.

Zi pulled off his headset and twisted down his tongue close enough to the mother tongue without prompting. It meant there were no lies only truth along with the encouraging fact the APC was probably bugged. "You had three days. Now it's down to one. Your amnesty is going to end when the Houses bring you back in. I have no expectations of you. Whoever you're dealing with doesn't care. That doesn't mean you have to think like them. They should've killed us ten years ago but instead they let us go to lick our wounds. If they wanted us dead, we'd be dead by now. Revenge is always for the weak. Whatever happens, remember: you're the face of your own House. Don't let that go to your head. Do you understand me?"

"Yes," Melinda easily replied.

"The young Houses have gotten used to ignoring problems like this. They'll let it fester until it knocks on their door and they just let it in because they know they can survive what happens next. Eventually, they won't survive and there'll be no survivors to warn anyone else. They must understand a problem like this affects us all. That doesn't mean you have to blow it out of proportion to get their attention, you just need to make them understand one thing: We bow in front of no one. Do you understand?"

"Completely and utterly," Melinda said.

"Whatever happens, everyone is proud of what you're about to do even if they're going to bury you at every turn because change is good and worth the trouble you're about to cause. This little 'problem' is how house wars start. Not because of your actions but because someone thinks they can nudge us around only to sit back and watch us destroy each other. They haven't learned a gahforsaken thing that there are consequences to their actions. You are that consequence. There's a reason why Zephyr Crosleigh died and Zi Stuk rose in his place. The same reason why Meylandra Stuk will rise again and Melinda Scott can be forgotten about," he said.

"Actually, Melinda is going to do for now until they figure it out," she said.

Zi sighed. "Meylandra."

"What?" she said.

"I had this speech planned for thirty years stop derailing me, please," he said. "If you're not going to take this seriously I'm switch back to standard."

"Fine by me," she said.

Zi stopped. "Really? Why keep your alias?"

"Why throw away a perfectly good Weaver?" she said. "Or, for that matter, a perfectly good Empress."

Zi stared her down. "You need to let Narelle Daire choose her own path."

"No, I lost Narelle I'm not losing anyone else and I'm not going to have to fire a shot. I'm just going to let them fall over each other until they learn who's in charge," she said with a shrug.

"You don't need to tell me, you know," he said.

"Yes, I do. By the time they scrub the audio of this conversation I fully expect you to have already been kidnapped and I'll have to come and rescue you, Clarence and everyone else when they figure out what's really going on," she said and shook the messenger bag. "By the way, this isn't the unicorn I've been asking for."

"You and your unicorns. Do you have any idea how much money they cost? They smell and have the foulest of mouths you ever heard," he said. "And their wings make no sense."

"No, that's a Pegasus. So, they do exist, too. Good! I want one. " she laughed.

"I'm trying to finish my speech please stop," he chortled. "I guess I can forgo the no back-up and no cavalry part and just tell you: good luck. Oh, there is one last thing I should tell you: just because you conjured a spell that raised Mister Knoll don't let that go to your head."

"I have no idea what you're talking about," she said nonchalantly and hugged him tightly good-bye. "Give them a warning for me," she whispered in his ear. "Tell them I'm coming for everything that's mine and if they any of them stand in my way, they'll get what's coming to them." She patted him on the back. "Have a good trip."

"I will," he said, and she hopped outside.

The door closed, and the APC without any House insignia plastered across its iron hide roared off into the night. Thom, Phineas, Roark and Selene remained. Alita was gone.

Thom grimaced down at her. "What did you do?"

"Can't someone have a pleasant conversation without all these horrible accusations," she said and opened the messenger bag to find a small wooden box. "Still not my unicorn."

"Mindy, you—" Thom started but the APC's reverse lights popped on and came to a halt next to them.

The hatch re-opened, and the avian animus flew out only to land on Melinda's shoulder.

"And you want a unicorn?" Zi howled from inside and the APC roared off.

"I keep saying that, but she doesn't listen," Thom said and poked the box. "If that isn't an ivory handled stunner I'm going to have a nice long talk with him."

The animus snapped its beak twice much to his annoyance.

~

"The town of Heiden Valley is the oldest town of mortal beings on the Hollow," Melinda said while the group now minus Selene, walked down the wide dirt road that curved whenever a tree stump blocked its path. "One night it's said that the ground quaked and the mortals lit their torches only to find night had become day. The arrival of the first star carrier they'd ever seen. The town folk, knowing full well that stars did fall out of the sky knew how to handle space beings and readied their iron throwers. But, they didn't need them because the crew was already dying. Victims of a plague that the town's people were immune to. Each of the survivors gave the town's people their last words and died together just as they had lived."

She pointed to a hill lined with a wrought iron fence on their left. She stepped off the road and pushed open the fence. "They were finally buried over there." She jerked a thumb to a second hill where the crowds were five to six people deep. "I say finally buried because the very night the towns people buried them here in consecrated ground, a rogue arm of House Lir desecrated this holy place the town's people had done so well forging and took the bodies back to their underground Vaults to meddle with things they couldn't possibly understand. The plague that turned out to be burdening intelligence of nanobots seeing fresh bodies jumped species but didn't seek revenge on the Lir for they had simply lost their footing on the path they done so well staying on." She dusted off the grave markers. "Once the Lir were sorted, they left the Hollow for which they had named after themselves and left in care to the lone survivor. He in return, left it to the town's people and they reburied the shells over there. He was never seen again and most think he is a creation of the town's people since they hadn't a clue, but they knew about the defense wards so obviously they used to be someone just that time forgot. Like the survivor who set off the beacon that led a group of wandering Knoll techno mages who disappeared the ship at his request and in turn settled in town. They offered their services and re-christened Knoll's Valley into what you see today only for the Stow to show up and brought the war with them."

"Depressing uplifting piece of whitewashed history," Roark said. "You reported the truth."

"And how, teacher gave me a F and told me if I ever deep dived the network for show and tell again, they'd send me to normal school," Melinda said. "You dig deep enough and find things that aren't supposed to be, but they just keep redacting what they don't understand."

Phineas knelt and read the plaques aloud, "Zephyr Crosleigh. Meylandra Crosleigh. Horatio Crosleigh. Spencer and Femi Crosleigh. Thomas Crosleigh."

"Plague of the Cross," Roark said. "I didn't think anyone survived. Especially my father."

"Emperor Hilal Spencer Crosleigh followed quarantine laws and sealed the Coil Doors. It kept the Crosleighs in but the Houses out. He launched the last ship carrying his family along with his new wife," Melinda said. "I figure she de-orbited years later and soft landed here."

"Still can't find the her, can you?" Roark said.

"Erik gives me a clue every year and I still can't find the gahdamn thing," Melinda said and motioned back to the road. "Next stop on the tour is the Sleepless Maiden & Spirits."

~

"Mindy, this is the wrong Sleepless Maiden & Spirits," Thom said.

The one room schoolhouse was closed. It said CLOSED on the doors, the windows and even the fake grass had posted their hours of operation.

"The is the location of the first Sleepless Maiden & Spirits," Melinda said and jiggled the box. "They moved to the edge of town once this was declared a historical site."

She ran her fingertips around the box's edges and found the hidden switch.

A click later and a key dropped into her hand.

"Zephyr is on the board of the Historical Society, isn't he," Roark said.

"Along with all the founding members of every single House because least we forget what we lost to get here," Melinda said and turned the key.

She opened the door and found no motion-activated lights to illuminate the simple medium sized room. Framed pictures on the walls of severe looking town folks with smiling techno mages. The old black and white photos had a severe effect on their auras. Several desks clustered around the blackboard. A few, wooden toy soldiers lay in a display case.

Phineas leaned left then right at a photo. "Their auras are following me."

"Wait, didn't this burn to the ground thirty years ago when the Stukari showed up?" Roark rubbed his temples. "It was the first thing they did once they got here."

"Along with the town's people descendants who save these." Melinda tapped the frames and stopped at one of them. "Here we go." She stood on her tiptoes and the picture of the scowling town folk shimmered and a flash popped off.

"Identity accepted. Stuk, Meylandra," a disembodied woman's voice said and the wall parted to reveal a shiny elevator door. In turn, it slid back, and a lovely glass walled car awaited.

"Well, I think if they were going to kill us they'd do already," Melinda said and entered the car. The door swished shut and the car descended.

"Leighton, Phineas. Knoll, Roark. Stuk, Thom. Welcome to Stuk's Hollow Observation Outpost Number Zero. Your rooms have been prepared. You do have a freight package waiting. We do ask any animus or animi be registered and any personal coms be put through to our local wireless network for security sake. Any questions please ask. We hope you enjoy your stay."

The elevator door opened to a maroon carpeted corridor. The wallpaper matched carpets. The lights on the wall and ceiling didn't make Melinda's nose water. Potted plants flanked numbered doors. A soft jazz number filled the temperature controlled cool air.

"This looks like Sleepless Maiden & Spirits," Roark said. "Even down to the music."

"I remember these. It's a House Observation Outpost, isn't it?" Phineas said.

"Left over after one of the wars, I forget which. Something about the old Stuk Generals waged their war down here while it happened up there," Melinda said and pointed up for effect. "Every house has one, judging from your sister, she probably has one floating around."

"My father disapproved of much of my mother's and sister's desires," Phineas said.

Melinda walked down the corridor. Each door had their name. The corridor ended at a medium sized common room complete with couches. "Someone went with Plan C," she said.

Spence MacGregor's chamber lay there on a rather large pushcart.

"Mindy, we need to talk about this, now," Thom said to her quietly.

"Change of clothes first then you can try to talk me down," she said and stopped at her door. It had a wooden caricature of her in a space suit riding a rocket ship. Her shit-eating grin made her laugh. Someone had gone to the extra step of animating wooden sparklers popping out of the engine.

Melinda opened the door and found her room had been perfectly preserved. The two-bed room, one bath, and one living room was almost too much space compared to her room on Gunna.

The bedroom had photos plastered across the walls. A bare wall tugged at her memories and the double doors of a walk-in closet full of clothes, shoes, boots, hats, gloves. Everything she had left behind those years ago. The medium-sized iron box on the bedside table was new.

The animus snapped its beak and Melinda carefully held out a hand. It clamped onto her finger and she deposited it in an iron box. "Tell me when it's safe to be removed from quarantine," she said, and the computer pinged affirmative.

She opened up Zi's box. Nestled within the red velvet was a set of ivory handled wooden revolvers. The wood shimmer in the light and once she gripped the handle she knew what it was, someone had crafted a revolver out of a wood from Lir's Forest. Property of Meylandra "May" Crosleigh was engraved in the ivory.

A price tag tied on the trigger guard by a string. The tag read: Compliments of the establishment. Visit Brie's Weapon Smith and Emporium for complimentary gun belt and sword sheath. Good luck, Meylandra.

Melinda flopped onto the bed and enjoyed the comfort. *Five minutes to live,* she thought and rolled off the bed and shed layers of borrowed clothes.

The bathroom with its wrought-iron tub and clawed feet wasn't as big as she expected but she didn't care. The warm water was the purest form of joy she'd felt, ever. "Enjoy this now, because Tommy is going to pitch a fit," she said and just let the water beat down.

~

Melinda exited her room to find everyone lounging in the common room sofas. The stench of the coat of arms wasn't lost on her. "You and that coat," she groaned. Even the animus now stationed on her head chittered at Roark's attire. His matched her own, a pair of tan slacks, button down shirt, iron-toed boots. The gun and sword belt gone but a brief glimpse of shoulder holsters meant he wasn't completely unarmed.

"Explain this to me again, you're going to do what?" Thom said.

"There wasn't time to check and see if our auras are right," Roark said. "Phineas can back me up. The resurrection wasn't that bad."

"That's your answer for everything. You called my third wedding that," Thom said.

"I've been to worse. The last Ohari Resurrection was a blood bath," Phineas said.

"Only because they did it wrong, Weaver did it right and everyone wins nobody loses," Melinda said and squinted at Roark. "Yeah, I took some years off, didn't I?"

"I will have you know, I've always looked like this." Roark smacked his cheeks.

"Liar," Melinda and Thom said.

"You two are taking this extremely well," Melinda said. "No more fist fights."

"I'm not liking this plan of sending you without an escort," Thom said. "I've already sent operators to set up your tent."

"You worry too much." Melinda straightened up her messenger bag so it wasn't strangling her chest. She checked her rose colored abaya and matching jilbab. "Remind me, I need some defense tchotchkes."

Thom growled. "I'm going to strangle him when he rises up. Wait, I don't even remember stowing him in the APC."

"I'm bringing him to the techno mages," Melinda said. "The graves out front haven't been touched, I get him sorted and I can check to see if anyone has seen him walking around."

"We can sweep for clues all before the morning rail carrier leaves," Roark said.

"I need to find Erik first. I'll drop Spence and Roark off at the Knolls and look around from the safety of their bunker," she said.

"I can't backstop you on this," Thom said.

"Since when did you piss off the Knolls?" Melinda said.

"He means you're on your own, Mindy." Phineas cleared his throat. "Point of no return."

"I will check-in from the tent. I will check-in once I get to the Knolls and I will check-in once we leave," Melinda said.

"No. No, you don't have to I want you to understand if you do this I won't be there to pull your butt out of the fire. You don't have to check-in, but I want you to understand, once you do this, you're on your own," Thom said.

"Good, that means we plan B it once we're sorted," Roark said.

"You aren't taking her to Hairpin to celebrate," Thom said.

"I'm just happy not to wear that gahforsaken plate all the time. I can breathe for a change," Roark said.

"Are you still wearing it or not, I can't tell," she said. "Tell me something, Mad Stuk?"

"Mindy," Thom said.

"No, it's okay." Roark reached back and pulled the plate from between his shoulder blades. "This is the Mad Stuk, or what's left of him. Just a plate but put it together with a coat of arms, a few swords, boots and you get a seven-foot-tall walking undead protector of Wailing Seas. Just old family heirloom that was passed down until it got to me and it worked."

"So, which came first, the Mad Stuk or *him*?" Melinda said.

"Oh, he was first and the rest of us came afterwards," Roark said. "Which reminds me, thank you, Mindy."

"I'm just sorry you got into this mess in the first place," she said.

Thom sighed and pushed off the couch. "Just waltz in the front door and knock. Isn't the best plan but live and learn," he said. "I'm going to check-in and find out why Dor isn't answering up the phone." Thom wandered back into the elevator and it whooshed him away.

"He's very proud of you but also very worried," Phineas said.

"Alita will probably be ghosting us all the way into town." Melinda snapped her room key onto lanyard of her new House key. "But, he's right. Check-in from the tent and then track down a priestess that Grainne suggested."

"He could've come with us," Roark said and stood. "More the merrier."

"Same reason why people get out of the shallows when a predator just swims in circles out past the warning buoys. Unless he has house approval, there's no need for him to be here. Thing is, he'll attract others and the shallows suddenly become less shallow and very deep." Melinda pushed the cart with relative ease. "The Families show up with their kids to get trained because they know the shallows are tame but not that tame. The boogeyman and his ilk belong in the deep end with everything else that's too old and faded into legend."

"This explains why my father can't stand *him*," Phineas said.

"It's not that." Melinda coughed into her hand. "How's your standing with House Knoll?"

"Impeccable," he said. "What exactly did he do? No one will tell me."

"It's what he didn't do and it's not my place," she said. "Once we surrender unconditionally the Knoll it'll give me time to figure out what's going on."

Phineas tapped the elevator button. "What's the plan after that?"

"Get you three sorted then find Erik because I can't poke around without his keycard. Remind me to check my defense charm when we get there. Lock down the engine mount if it's here. Find any evidence of who's trying to kill me," she said and pushed the resurrection chamber into the lift. "We keep this party small and not use Terrie, no offense."

"None taken," Phineas said and the doors closed. "She's complicated."

Melinda and Roark said nothing, and Phineas smiled at the silence. "Thank you," he said.

The door swished open into the cool night.

A cacophony of light and sound beckoned.

"Let's go play," Melinda said and pushed on.

25
ADVENTURES IN WEAVERSITTING

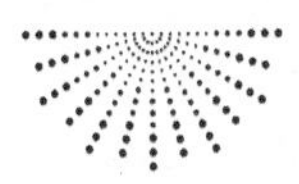

This was a bad idea, Melinda thought and pushed the chamber through the crowds. The flutter of wings tugged her gaze skyward where winged belfries flitted across the air above followed shortly thereafter by aero mages. The yearly game of tag was in full swing.

On the ground, techno mages with their illuminated, cursed weapons lined one side of the street along with their mechines of wonder while on the other resided the nature bound mages. Several Lir trees had stretched their branches above the elemental Houses. A mote of water similar to what was sloshing through the MacGregor resurrection chamber she was pushing lined the trees' parameter. The cacophony of spells and alien languages was delight.

Private security teams flanked the entrances of the House tents. Goggles or blast glasses scanned the crowd. Iron throwing rifles across their chests. They didn't bother looking twice at her. They were more concerned with the queue of people wishing to talk with the local House lord. All the while, mortals, demi-mortals and immortals bought and sold items in their ten-by-ten tents.

"Is it always like this?" Phineas said.

"Always. Every single House should be here. Three days of celebrating followed by the lower Houses sorting their freshmen before the academy's entrance exams," Melinda said. "Clarence used to have it at his House but it stretched on for months. This is simpler and usually with wider roads than this."

"This plan may actually work to our advantage," Roark said. "I can't even focus."

"Faster we find the tent the better before the ones holding the private security's leashes start scrubbing the feeds looking for someone to bring in," Melinda growled and stopped at one of the signposts in the middle of the road.

The signpost had several wooden characters traipsing about in mock fights much to the delight of a group of children. One of the techno mages had animated the wooden toy soldiers to gather children's attention and sell his services judging from the tent number on their wooden backs. Three of them were having a battle across the top post while a fourth was climbing back up from an obvious defeat.

"I need some directory information," she said to the forth.

The forth stopped and focused on her. It hit the post and several hidden signs popped out. "Our house tent is a few ones down and Rushford stayed home because his replacement is an ass. Leightons and Daires didn't show. Crosleigh Aviation is on the other side of the town at Hairpin. Freshman are with Phineas' brother, Alizerin. No sign of the Finnegans or even the Bries, wait, here we go, the Knolls are running the cloak tent."

The character waved and pointed away.

"Other side of the city?" Melinda said. "Where, past Hairpin?"

The character nodded and went back to enticing children by scaling the post with ease.

"Cloak tent sounds small," Phineas said.

"It's bigger than you'd think. Techno mages and the houseless belfries run it," Melinda said and prodded the post. Her wooden helper stopped. "Pass it on, check the D-Genies. Spells are wrong. Cook 'em and restart 'em. Aura jacker may be on the loose. Tell 'em all to lock it down."

Her helper nodded and whistled to his or her comrades. The companions picked up the whistle and it echoed out across the city.

"That's not a low profile, Mindy," Roark muttered.

"Oh, hush. Half of these iron throwers don't even know what that whistle means." Melinda grabbed the handles and pushed on.

"The cloak tent may squeal on us too," Roark said. "Sorcha doesn't like me much."

"They owe me a favor and if the prep guys are bent they'll know it was me who warned them," she said and swerved around two drunk mages in the middle of the street.

A stun round dropped her first. It took several to bow Phineas. Roark didn't have time to spin up the spell and toppled to the ground.

The last thing Melinda remembered seeing was someone dragging their bodies inside a tent along with the chamber.

~

The light blinded Melinda before the body odor did. Her eyes adjusted to a world full of falling feathers of all things. Details of a large tent emerged. A fluffy rug covered the ground. A table with three chairs occupied a far corner while a dresser and vanity in the opposite. A cast iron tub with clawed feet sat behind a privacy curtain. It was the only thing old enough to steal.

She gaped at the queen-sized bed. The source of the feathers was too big to steal. Judging by its ornate frame it was the most expensive thing and would be the first thing to be used as firewood. It frilly lace canopy was a total write off. Lastly, a half-hidden trunk sat under a drape that divided the rest of the tent.

"Lookit this, fellahs. We got a surprise in ours. Finally." A man's voice drawled.

The resurrection chamber tilted, and Spence tumbled onto the fluffy rug covered in sand.

"No water in this one," another voice whined. "Go help the boss with the other two."

Because he absorbed it, Melinda thought absently and batted away the feathers from view.

"Where are we?" Spence crawled over to her and checked her neck for vitals.

"Location check: unknown. Medical check: all vitals within norms." The mask's voice popped back in Melinda's ear. "My apologies, your heart beat is within norms. They're fine. Take a deep breath and breathe. The chamber cycle was done when these heathens showed up."

Spence batted away the cloud of feathers. "Where in gahsakes are we?"

"We got pulled inside a tent. We gotta go. Now. Get Roark." Melinda grabbed Phineas' limp arm when the tent's flat burst apart and two men dressed in dirty robes came in with two hooded hostages in tow. "Where dah ya think yer goin'!" one of them said and grabbed her.

"Excuse us, but..." Spence managed when a subtle wind passed through the tent and he unceremoniously collapsed.

"Get him over here," the lanky leader said. "Looking for some alone time, were we?"

"Wouldn't believe me if I told you," Melinda managed.

"I'll search her. Take the chamber in with the others," the leader said.

"Do we get to keep her?" the short one said.

The others? Excuse me? Melinda thought and ignored her gut to shoot everyone. *Sooner or later they're going to find the stunner and then what?*

Spence jerked to his feet without help and second robber stepped back from the Weaver.

Melinda's gut twitched. It wasn't due to the men's horrendous body odor. Something else.

A shimmer danced around Spence's head and shoulders. Not his aura. His aura was pleasant this was something . . . else. His body movements weren't right.

"What's wrong with him?" the third one quietly said from behind her.

"Don't shoot him, everyone will hear it," the leader said and de-hooded the couple. "They friends of yours, your majesty?"

The couple was briefly sketched in; the man was older than Jainey by three to four decades and had a good tan. The gray beard was charming without being scruffy. The woman was robed from head-to-toe; the only thing that sent out alarm bells was the black arts defense braids tchotchkes around her abaya, wrists and ankles. She had lovely serpentine eyes.

Wha? Melinda thought and narrowed in on the 'woman.' *If she's a 'woman' I'm the next Empress but he's human. You've been mugged and they're getting robbed. If Spence is out, then it's up to me.*

Spence had shuffled himself to the exit. Shoulders and head slumped. The electric fingers danced around his head and jerked him upright.

Just like the lightning or just like getting aura jacked. Melinda thought and focused on the men's dirty cloaks and found what she was looking for: defense necklaces around their necks or sewed in. *They jacked him because the rest of us are protected,* she turned back to the third man still in the shadows or at least keeping himself out of the light. *And why can't I see you or your aura?*

"Yer gonna tell me where it is or um gonna kill 'er." The leader's remark dragged her back to the barrel of a pistol he aimed down at her. It didn't stop her runway train of thought.

"Who be you..." Melinda's voice cracked, her tongue still numb from being stunned.

"Lookit this, she thinks she can talk like her majesty," the second one said.

"I said," Melinda focused and howled: "Who be you and who do you serve!"

All three men covered their mouths and mumbled.

Spence jerked back. His fingers clenched up. Jaw clamped down. Unwilling.

"He's been jacked," Melinda said and pointed to the exit. "Get out!"

"She right," the 'woman' said.

"We aren't going anywhere until -" Phineas and Roark grabbed

Spence's arms and hurtled backward through air. The amount of noise outside meant they connected with someone or something.

Yep, he figured out how use the cloak, too, Melinda thought as Spence's face twisted into a grin. "I know something you don't know." She bolted to her feet and Spence pointed a finger.

Everyone winced waiting for the oncoming spell, but nothing happened.

Melinda breathed a sigh of relief. *Thank you.*

Spence recoiled and flicked both hands, now. Nothing.

"Yeah, once you aura-jack a mage, you can't use his aura," Melinda said and raised her stunner. "Wanna see what happens when you over-clock your stun rounds?"

Spence lunged only to have all five rounds landed in his chest. Tentacles of electricity radiated out. An inhuman howling spewed forth from his contorted lips. The electricity shouldn't have been as flashy, but the signs were there now. Someone was trying to control him.

The Weaver collapsed, smoke rolled off as the last of the electricity danced off his teeth.

An after image leapt through the smoke but Melinda's defense charm did its job and deflected it into the vanity only for additional three out of the five rounds to connect.

The electric rounds and the magical aura didn't mix. The aura jacker's form lashed about in the boiling air only to explode in a cloud of aura fireflies.

Melinda pointed again to the exit. "Leave now and I'll forget your faces," she said.

The leader bolted and grabbed the second one off the ground. The third one still a vague impression was the only one to look back and smile?

Melinda nudged Spence and received the groan she was looking for. She loaded her last clip and extended a hand to the couple. "Mey-landra Stuk, Baroness of the Wailing Seas. My apologies for interrupting your evening. My friend and I were traveling when they tried to mug us. Could one of you watch the door? I need to fix their defense genies before they come back."

~

Melinda parted the drapes and found a medium sized room where footlockers lined one wall and squat, iron kegs on the other. The kegs hummed with defense spells. "Here we are."

She waltzed over to the kegs and a defense spell kicked her back into a wall of footlockers. Something dropped into her lap. She picked it up ready to hum it across the room but found it to be a bone white faceplate. "Sorry, nerves," she said and placed it aside.

"What do you think you're doing?" the woman stormed in.

"Trying to fix our problem before they come back." Melinda pointed to the kegs. "Their defense genies aren't stopping whatever just tried to aura jack him. We need to fix 'em."

The woman laughed. "You think they're coming back?"

Melinda dusted herself off. "This is their tent. They mugged me, kidnapped you while someone else tried to aura jack Spence all at the same time. Once they figure out Phineas or Roark isn't chasing them they're coming back for their stuff. I don't know what they've got in this tent, but somebody's been doing good job from robbing people from the looks of it."

"Then it's none of your business. Is it?" the woman said.

Melinda reloaded her stunner. "It is now," she said. She pushed past and into the main room where the old man stood over Spence. "Who be you and who do you serve?"

The old man didn't budge. "He a friend of yours?"

"I asked you who be you and who do you serve," Melinda raised her voice.

The old man chuckled. "Your parents brought you up right, those House tutors trained you well. No aura. No ego. No burdens, eh? It doesn't work on all of us, kiddo."

Melinda nudged the tip of her stunner into the back of his neck. "I don't care about you or whatever else is in this tent. I care about him, the Leighton Magi and the techno mage. Now, can either of you hack the defense spell on those defense genies or not?"

"Mindy. Don't shoot him. He's a friend." Spence struggled to stand but collapsed.

The old man picked up the Weaver and deposited him on the bed. "Alita, help our friend with disarming the spell. She's right, they're coming back," he said.

Alita growled something unintelligible and retreated. "It's disarmed," she said.

Melinda holstered the stunner and joined her. She twisted the dials on the generator. Several of the outputs changed from red to green. "First rule for defense is you let the spells warm up first before you stick 'em in the generator," she said. "No one gets back in besides us."

Alita's glare didn't soften but her hand behind her back did. "You think it's safe now?"

Because I trust Spence, he trusts the old man and obviously trusts you, Melinda thought. "Guard the door with that toothpick of yours while I figure out a way out of here that doesn't include blasting my way out and then I need to check on the mages."

"You're not even going to ask why I'm here?" Alita said.

"Since Tommy threw a fit about not following me I'm assuming he told you and Selene the same thing." Melinda tweaked the dials. *Remember what Harry told you. Let it breath and fill the air. It'll grow only as far as the generator will allow.* She swiveled about at movement.

Something skittered across the floor on little itty-bitty legs and disappeared into the pile of footlockers in the corner.

Melinda rubbed her eyes. *And, I'm hallucinating,* she thought, and the old man entered.

"He'll live but he needs some rest," the old man said. "What you doing with a resurrection chamber? It's pretty much done for."

"If it's still here it's not 'done for'," she said evenly. "You know him?"

The old man smirked. "Once."

"Is he a good man?" she said.

The old man nodded. "One of the best."

I knew you were going to say something like that, Melinda thought. "I need to fix his chamber. I'm going to get him out of here before they come back. You have a wheel barrow."

The old man laughed and stroked his chin beard. "You're just gonna wheel him out of here without anyone noticing? How in gahsakes you think I know anything about that coffin?"

"The planetary network is down. The personal security teams can't use it that means it'll be messy out there running down fugitives so personal facial recognition services—" she said.

"Shoot first never ask questions, I know how dirty the world is, missy," the old man spat.

"Good, you're not an idiot, either." Melinda smiled. "I need to borrow a hat and button up his cloak. I'll wheel him out of here before they come looking for us."

"What makes you so sure they're coming for you?" he said.

Melinda pointed to her earbud. "Because the locals are screaming about a Leighton Magi and techno mage flying without the use of a spell and there's a squad of Stukari Holdings operators on their way."

Alita cleared her throat at the drapes. "We've got company," she said.

Damn, they can't be that fast, Melinda thought. "Our old escort buddies?"

"No, worse," Alita said.

Melinda pulled up her air filtering bandana. "Get the wheelbarrow. Get him in here. Alita, stall them while I get out of here."

~

"This isn't the best idea," the mask said over Spence's lazy snores in the wheelbarrow.

"No one is going to care." Melinda grabbed a robe out of one of the trunks. "Just need to make it to the cloak car and I can figure out what in gahsakes is going on."

"Who're you talking to before? Describe the old man," the mask said.

"He hasn't tried shooting me so that's a good thing." Melinda tightened up the robe. She looked in an open locker and found a hat. She deposited it atop his face. "Yep, that works."

A footlocker pushed itself out from the pile. It was older than the rest if the real wood had anything to say about it. The others were just hard plastic with metal corners.

The same bone white plate she'd tossed aside had crawled up the locker's side, deposited itself onto the lock and an audible click later the locker lid popped open.

The faceplate crawled to the edge but skittered around and spied Melinda.

"I'd appreciate some discretion when you explain this," an unfiltered man's voice said.

"After the night I've had, I'm hallucinating," Melinda replied.

The plate bowed. "Thank you. There's a hole in the wall, if you wouldn't mind. I'll tell your brother you're fine, Meylandra." It hopped inside, and the lid closed.

Melinda opened the hole in the tent wall and the trunk hopped out into the night.

Melinda shrugged. "People talk to themselves, I talk to inanimate faceplates." She pulled up her robe's hood and pushed the wheelbarrow out into the night.

~

"I'm okay." Phineas struggled to stand inside one of the Knoll's Tents.

"Rest it off. I'm not doing that again." Roark sighed from a fold out chair.

"They face planted into my mechine animus. You both need to rest it off, mates," said the dreadlocked techno magess. Her mechine animus was a four armed and legged aquine. She snapped her fingertips to spin up an illumination spell. She held the lit tips in front of Phineas' eyes. "Yeh, yer still concussed for at least another hour." The magess blinked at Spence in the wheelbarrow and laughed. "I'm sorry, that was rude."

"I need you to do me a favor. Can you let him rest it off here? That tent." Melinda pointed to the tent across from hers. "Someone's been hustling people. Lot o'footlockers. I fixed the D-Genies. You need to check yours, now."

The magess straightened up. "I will have you know—"

Melinda raised a hand. "Did you set up the tent yourself or was it prepped for you?"

The magess opened her mouth, and it snapped shut. "Prepped," she said and pointed her fingers at Melinda, but she looked away. "Wait, were you the one shooting off those sparklers?"

"Tell everyone to check their D-Genies we wouldn't want any of you run amok, would we?" Melinda said and squeezed Phineas' arm. "Don't get up. Rest it off. It wasn't your fault. Hey." She lifted his chin. "It wasn't his fault and it wasn't yours, either. It was mine. You know where I'm going, I'll see you soon."

"We ain't going anywhere for a while," Roark said. "We can handle ourselves."

Melinda turned to the magess. "Where's Erik?"

"Why would I know where he is?" the magess snorted.

"Because, Talia, after I left, you two were supposed to pair up. I'm guessing that didn't?" Melinda said.

Talia, the magess and her mechine animus stiffened. "Just who in gahsakes do you think you are? No one talks to me in my shop you little -" she reached out and the tip of stunner graced the underside of her chin. A casual spark lit Talia's surprised face. "Mindy?"

Melinda smiled. "If I find out you were tagging rubes, there's nowhere on this planet that will hide you. Tell 'em the Baroness of the Wailing Seas said so. Now, be a good little messenger girl and pass on the word. I really would hate those aura jackers to come back and do to you what they did to my friend. Me and my sparkler gun may not be here the next time."

Melinda pulled the stunner away and retreated from the gaze of Talia's curiosity filled customers inside her tent now completely aware of what just transpired.

"There she is!" a voice broke the silence and Melinda swiveled left to vaguely familiar mob of smelly people. "She's the one that assaulted us."

"You're complaining I assaulted you? What about that assault on my nose," Melinda raised her voice and got the proper laughter she was looking for. "I'm so happy to see you," she said to the group of vaguely familiar Stukari Holdings operators. "There's evidence in that tent that should be of some interest to the authorities. These men were just leaving to get help when I showed up with my friend." She patted Spence's leg and on cue he snored louder than the laughter from the techno mages. "I'm sure there are some rewards for the missing items. It can be split equally amongst them. If you'll excuse me, I have a date the cloak car."

She gripped the wheelbarrow's handlebars and pushed on.

"Smooth," Spence uttered.

"What'd you expect?" Melinda said and ambled back into the crowd. "To shoot them?"

"Yes," Spence and the plate said.

~

Melinda navigated herself and the wheelbarrow through several twists and turns to arrive at the Hairpin Curve Bar. The crowd was enjoying food and spirits. She ignored the catcalls until one of the catcallers gave her behind a squeeze.

He was on his ass with a bloody nose before she knew she had pistol-whipped him.

She holstered the stunner and restrained herself. *Ignore the leaches,* she cursed inwardly. *Focus on the goal, you're almost there.*

The leach staggered to his feet, red with anger filled his fat face while blood rushed out of his nose. He tried to give chase, but his comrades pulled him back.

The goal was past Hairpin Bar. It was the ninety-degree turn where the bar received her name. The road dipped at a forty-five-degree angle. It was empty of stragglers. The hastily erected tents gave way to the stone skeletal remains of the town of Stow's End. It was here where the cloak tent had set down roots at the end of the dead-end street.

The four to five story remains of the town gave the winged belfries what they wanted: the high ground. The winged humanoids were buttoned up tight in their aviation, blessed leathers, goggles and head-gear. The amount of them clustered about meant their house had decamped where no one else wanted and made it the last place anyone would come looking for her.

Yeah, I came to the right place. My digital footprint just vanished, Melinda thought.

"Multiple airborne targets above us," the mask said. "None of them targeting us."

The amount of belfry security whispered across the sky above didn't surprise. *It's the fact they aren't stopping me,* she thought and spotted the two women guarding the door.

"I don't care what ya heard. The defense wards are fine," the younger of the two, Sorcha Knoll said. She was Jainey's drinking buddy from the "good ole bad ole days" and her blessed clothes weren't nearly as defensive as her mother's, Murdina "Dina" Knoll.

"It's been whistling across the city for the past half hour," Dina said. Her cloak spoke volumes so Melinda breathed through her mouth. "Sorry dearie, the hotels are back up the road."

"I need asylum." Melinda twisted her tongue down. "And he needs a medical check-up."

"Does this look like a hospital to you?" Sorcha snorted.

Melinda pulled back her hood. "I need asylum and a digital bath. I may have picked up a few tails on my way over. I don't have to time to argue. I'm the one who warned you," she said.

Dina clapped her hands together and hugged her. "What are you doing here, child and alone of all things?"

Melinda lifted the hat off Spence's head. "I'm not exactly alone."

"No. Not him. Get him outta here." Sorcha spat on the ground.

Dina growled under her breath. "Get them inside before someone sees them. And restart those defense wards if she's right."

Sorcha rolled her eyes. "I am not getting trussed up on a lark."

"Seven hours ago, they dropped an engine mount on me. We crashed here after his shuttle's AI got hacked then someone dragged us down here only for him to get aura jacked less than a half hour ago. Now, check those gahforsaken wards or I'll do it for you," Melinda said and winced at the digital feedback through her earbud. "They definitely know I'm here, now. Let's get inside before this gets worse."

26

THE QUIET ONE

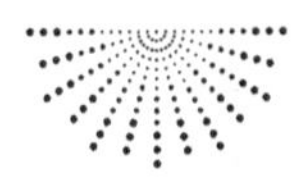

THE CLOAK TENT HAD AN ODD STORY BEHIND IT. IT WAS MORE LIKE A question that went like this: Which came first? The cloak or the House?

Inside the cloak tent was your standard four, tall wheeled, carriage carrier that in the old days would've been harnessed to several four-legged giant beasts that had been seen before or never would again.

Three Witchen drove this from House to House to replenish cloaks when the need arose. Birthdays and Weddings were the highlight because the Witchen while rumored to be child eaters always blessed those on their birthdays or weddings. The cloaks may have been the lightest things imaginable, but they could've and did stop even the biggest of iron laden weapons. Those who wore them came back from the war and so the Witchen became a necessity.

The Houses of Man had never learned how the old Witchen replenished when each season came. Many speculated they came from magical hides of beasts long since extinct. Some even suggested it came from their own bodies. The politics of man always a nest of the shortsighted decided they'd no longer be bound to the Witchen. In their search for these mystical beasts, they discovered newer, easier alloys to make their own cloaks.

The cloak car, the Witchen that drove it and the coat of arms that now tickled Melinda's nose drifted into forgotten legends.

This history lesson came back to Melinda every time her nose wrinkled up at the wind changing and the legends stepped back into memory. The cloak car was just as described, a four-wheeled wooden vehicle that was completely innocent looking. The cloth roof replaced with an iron hard top. But, things in this world weren't never quite as they should've been.

Her curiosity had always been to poke about inside every year, but she restrained herself and waited near the tent flap. It was the polite thing to do and she didn't feel like getting turned into a toad. The inside the tent may have been empty but the amount of size twenty boot prints across the sand meant she wasn't alone. The techno mages didn't use operatives. They used Mechs called Power Armor or PAs and since the ceiling on the tent was nearly twenty feet it was probably three or four power armors covering her to make sure she didn't rush the front door.

Melinda ignored her instinct to geek out over and instead focused on her goggles tagging people come in out of Hairpin Bar.

Her brother was nowhere to be seen.

The wind had changed, it was the only reason she smelled death and it wasn't from Dina's cloak either but instead around the curve of revelers came a phalanx nightmare of coat of arms and edged weapons.

The lightweight revelers clutched their beers and retreated, rightfully so.

Only *him* could cause that much ruckus. During the last war, the houses had called the boogeyman, *him*. Nameless, faceless, no one wanted to summon the boogeyman. Now, he had brought friends and judging from the bone white faceplate, the footlocker had found its owner. His coat of arms had done its job and riled up whatever flyers were in the air. The shadows were no longer full of creatures that went bump in the night. They were on ground with their cursed weapons at the ready.

Spence's head tilted forward and nudged up the hat. He was still half asleep, but his nose sniffed the air. "Who is it?" he murmured.

"Who do you think?" Melinda said. "The boogeyman, two cursed sword carriers along with whoever he had in the bar looking out for me."

"No." Spence leaned back. "It's not *him*. That's something . . . *else*."

Melinda squinted. "Huh, those plated weapons of mass destruction are looking more alike."

"Meylandra Stuk," Sorcha called from the car.

Melinda closed the tent flap and wheeled the barrow over to the side door of the car. The air hadn't moved around her neither had the sand beneath. "What did she say?" Melinda said.

Sorcha descended the car's steps now trussed in several layers of blessed clothing. The gems and embroidery that were stitched into her clothes may have sold the part to the tourists, but she could've stopped a tank shell with her flowered blouse. "My granddaughter, Shevonne has accepted your request for asylum and I would like to apologize for not taking you seriously. They're restarting now and will be fully operational in less than five minutes. If you'd like to follow me as our house guest, you will have a full access to the facilities along with access to a house phone so you can call off your brother and whoever he brought with him."

"You can't smell *him*?" Melinda said.

Sorcha smiled but her aura was a wall of ones and zeroes that shimmered around her shoulders and head that revealed nothing. "Whatever happens out there doesn't affect us until he tries to step through that flap," she said.

"And Spence?" Melinda said.

Sorcha cocked an eyebrow. "Mister MacGregor doesn't step one foot inside until he surrenders unconditionally."

Dina snorted from somewhere within the depths of the car.

"Fine." Spence pushed the hat up, two steps out of the wheelbarrow and onto his knees.

Melinda followed suit and they recited in eerie unison and without prompting, "I surrender unconditionally to your lord and master so our Houses won't be tarnished by this heinous act. I request a liaison of my choosing to defend my rights and well-being until I am returned to my House unharmed."

Sorcha sighed. "You didn't have to do that, Mindy."

"I like to cover all my bases," Melinda said and grabbed hold of Spence's arm before he went face first into the sand. "Point me in the right direction so he doesn't die on me."

~

Melinda passed over the threshold of the car and the four of them were transition from the surface to an underground location. It was the smoothest Melinda had ever experienced. No inner earache, upset stomach or double vision. *Professional to the last,* she thought.

The maze of well-lit corridors hadn't seen a lick of rust meant either the Knoll had spent a great deal of time an effort or it was pre-fabricated. The square design of the doorway arches meant it was pre-war. The old tongue stenciled everywhere meant pre-exodus.

Where are we? she thought. *Everything is shiny and clean.*

"Don't worry, dearie, you're perfectly safe here," Dina said.

That's what worries me, Melinda thought only to say: "Perish the thought."

Several lefts, rights and staircases and the corridor opened so a squad of six techno mages in their seven-foot-tall power armor passed by without either group breaking a stride. Their blessed weapons sizzled.

I really should've waited for Phineas, Melinda thought.

"Don't worry, Mindy. They're just rotating through. Standard house security," Dina said.

"I'd hate to see non-standard," Melinda said and winced.

Dina laughed. "Stukari Holdings is the closest thing you get these days to real security?"

"That and whenever I have to give the Veterans Appreciation Day to the kids about Rushford's days at the front," she said.

Dina grinned. "That man and his tiny suit. I've never seen a farmer go from a pacifist to a full-on jarhead in one tour in my life. He needs to let it go. He runs that house of his like a finely tuned machine."

"He's cute," Sorcha said.

"The cutie that left you at the altar to play war," Dina scoffed.

"It's the uniform and the fact he came home to me." Sorcha grinned.

"I checked his war records, all of his medals were confirmed," Melinda said.

Dina waved it off. "I'm not begrudging him, his trophy or his remarkable feat but the more he upkeeps that claptrap he calls armor the more you kids get stars in yours eyes and the more I need to rotate through freshmen who don't care how much busy work I give them they still want to see the shiny toys." She waved to a door. "We'll let him sleep it off in here."

The doors parted to what could only be the brig. A medium sized room complete with bed, head and shower in dull gray. The paint on the walls had enough iron flakes in it to give Melinda a mild bout of nausea. There was a station inset into the wall, two techno mage guards nodded hello.

She deposited Spence on the bed provided and followed the two generations of matriarchs around.

They descended a few levels and Melinda recognized several underground support beams. "You aren't shifting reality around this is one of the old underground house bunkers, isn't it? This isn't even on my maps. This was one of the first Keeps left over from the first exodus."

"You know your history. I can see why he likes you," Dina said.

"Erik?" Melinda smirked. "He and I share information. Everything is on hold while he figures out who he wants, Benny or me."

"In this day and age, monogamy isn't to be taken lightly," Sorcha said. "Even if that's what your parents taught you."

"Oh, I'm biding my time. The three of us may look sound but Benny's mother isn't to be taken lightly even if she's under supposed house arrest," Melinda said. "He'll figure out what's good for him and choose sooner or later. And I can play the field until someone who shall remain nameless figures out he doesn't need to follow in his father's footsteps."

Dina shot her a look. "I hate you."

"Your sewing circle hates me. I enjoy throwing you off because whoever I decided to cuddle with is none of your concern," Melinda said sweetly. "Besides, you know who I'm going to choose as my first, second and third." She stopped at the support beam and touched the spell scry into it. "Before the D-Genies and the Sword and Shields this is what kept everything out."

"It's a scratch on a post," Sorcha muttered.

"No, you can hear it if you listen close enough." Melinda touched her ear to the plank.

"Oh, please," Sorcha said.

"Get out, this Knoll territory and if I ever see any of you flappy eared, tail draggers so help me I know where all of you live so says..." Melinda pulled herself back. "Wow. She was annoyed."

"Since when can you scry?" Sorcha said.

"I have no idea what you're talking about," Melinda said nonchalantly. "It's why Erik and I had a playdate once. Sure, it pissed off a few people but for all the wrong reasons since the fire breathing witches are supposed to be gone and lo and behold The Silent One decides to show some balls and jump through all the hoops to get Erik a date with me."

"I walked up to your house's front door and asked to use the bathroom. It wasn't planned," Dina huffed.

"Sure, it wasn't," Melinda said and traced a finger down the opposite pole. "Atia Finnegan, the last of the fire breathing witches having successfully battled her way out of her prison cell in The Depths watched her family flee their bonds only to go back to save the other Houses and in doing so brought new life to a dying coil. New Age of Life, Enlightenment, and yawn inducing history. Once she was done ferrying them here she parlayed with the techno mages to build ships to ferry them faster until there was nowhere else to go except into the dark."

Sorcha leveled a look. "Please tell me that epic level of horse piss isn't what they're teaching you in that space station of yours."

"Actually, that is the truth, my sister did things big," Dina said. "Ignore my daughter, she's just bitter . . . but seriously, please tell me you've been teaching them right."

Melinda laughed. "They had me glaze over the death and destruction for the newbies. It was giving them nightmares. By the time her exodus was over, the Stuk had laid down their iron rails from one end of the universe to the other. They gloss over the fact your sister didn't leave because of the Hollow's irregular orbit. Instead, she had the House Knoll build ships on dry docks. The same docks Stuk Expeditions used to build ships to travel to the Outer Coils. The same docks that can't be found because once a ship is built they burn it down."

Dina laughed now. "The lies are almost as bad as the truth."

"The problem is the Knoll Dry Docks can't be torn down because House Stuk indentured House Kincaid to build their ships eons ago to expand their empire. The same dry docks Stuk Expeditions used to venture out. The same dry docks that haven't been seen since the Stukari showed up. So, I'm pretty sure one of the engine mounts from the same docks dropped on my head a few hours ago. It had Spence's shuttle attached to it. Someone was hacking his table," Melinda said and this time both women stopped laughing. "I also experienced what can only be one of two things either: A. The Wailing Seas Test Range's defense grid warming up or B. A compromised resurrection chamber blowing someone up. The network is dead, so someone wants you deaf and blind. So, let's dispense with all this, where's Erik Knoll? Where're the Knoll Dry Docks?"

~

Sorcha looked to her mother and back to Melinda. "We haven't heard from him in six months," she said.

"Months?" Melinda blanched. "Before or after he came back to the Hollow?"

"We didn't pick him up," Sorcha said. "Him and that pin cushion of a girlfriend had a falling out and we haven't heard from him since."

"And where're the Brie? The Emporium makes a killing this time of year," Melinda said.

"The Brie pulled up stakes at Barien Brie and haven't left Goslin Grace in months," Darien said.

"I thought those lines out there are a little thin," Melinda said.

"Leighton, Yashira, Wildes and Ohari didn't show up at the caravan rendezvous point," Sorcha said. "Whittahares and Daires too."

This isn't going to end well for our heroes, Melinda thought and turned back from once they came. The ceiling supports had exit markers every five feet. "And the Freshmen?"

"Half of them are with Alizerin the other half are here. Selene Finnegan and Cherie Leighton got popped for guard duty," Sorcha said.

"They got pulled to come pick me up," Melinda said. "By the way, Roark is alive."

"That's not funny, Mindy," Sorcha said.

"What is it?" Dina said.

"The Brie have been funneling stolen cursed items back into the Test Range for years. Barien Knoll was the biggest find and you're telling me they pulled out?" Melinda said. "No Bries, Daires, Wynns, Leightons, Wildes or Yashira. That's half our shield carriers right there. Swords can't fight without shields."

"Nobody thinks like that anymore. It's all automate this and mech that," Sorcha said.

"What about Roark?" Dina said.

"Someone is fighting old school. The pre-prep crew did this on purpose, that means we don't move until those genies come on-line," Melinda said. "The good news is the bogeyman is here and no one is that stupid to try anything with him here." She turned to Dina. "I need you to interrogate Spence."

Sorcha stiffened. "He already surrendered, Mindy."

"I need to be sure. I need you to get him angry," Melinda said.

"I can do that easy," Sorcha said.

"No." Melinda advanced on the old woman. "I shot him and barely got flicker. Then his brother showed up and barely got a bead."

"Horatio Crosleigh is dead," Dina spat and crossed herself. "Wait. You saw who? Horatio or Roark?"

"Horatio Crosleigh and Roark Knoll are alive. I left Phineas Leighton and Roark at one of the techno mage tents. And judging from that look you don't have a clue what happened at Crosleigh's Caves," Melinda said. "I need him. He's worth more to me compromised then clean. If he has a defense charm, fine, fix it, but if it's worse than we need to fix whatever is wrong with him and put him back on track."

"He's just a Necromancer, Mindy," Sorcha said.

"No. No, he's a Weaver and no one throws away a perfect good Weaver, do they?" Melinda eyed Dina.

Dina stiffed. "No, they don't," she said.

"What's that supposed to mean?" Sorcha said.

"It means I got desperate and need to off load the rest of you when I found Melinda's house. I used Erik as bait and played the only card I'm good at, the wandering Silent One who can't go any further and latched on to her house," Dina said. "As planned."

"What?" Sorcha's voice peaked.

"It's an old trick. You start off as house guests and slowly ingratiate yourselves into a house until you start marrying people and all of sudden you're in charge and the Head of the House is a guest in his/her own house until no one remembers the truth," Dina said. "It's what they've done to Spence, they threw him away and Melinda took the bait, the problem is still down here and not up there." She frowned at Melinda. "I think you're right."

"We need to debrief him and to do that I need to know how they aura jacked him as easy as flipping a switch. I know for a fact the MacGregors and you have never gotten along but I need you to push his buttons."

Dina stared at her. "And just who've you been talking too?"

"The right ones. People I trust. People you trust. We're all after the same thing but I need to nudge Mister MacGregor back onto the path he was supposed to be on six months ago. I'd also like a change of blessed clothes please because these long undies are going to start walking by themselves."

Dina cracked a wide smile. "He didn't think you'd wear them."

Melinda chuckled. "They deflected a full-on aura jacker."

Sorcha sighed. "Thank you, Mindy, he'll be insufferable after this."

Melinda laughed and stopped dead. "You got me off track: first, whatever you're hiding down here, I don't care about it and two: where're the dry docks?"

~

"We aren't hiding anything down here, Melinda," Sorcha said.

"Obviously it's something you don't know about because you weren't gussied up before I got here," Melinda said and narrowed a look at Dina. "Where is it?"

"Where's what?" Sorcha said. "And you don't get to talk to her like that, young lady."

"Whatever she's actually afraid of. There's enough power armor walking around to level an entire city." Melinda thumbed from once they came. "Rushford complained half as much as Erik did getting in and out of those walking caskets. She doesn't know what you've found. Does she?"

Sorcha glared down at her mother. "What is she talking about?"

"The dry docks are here. Probably two doors over," Melinda pressed.

Dina snorted. "Two? Like I'm going to walk."

"Fine, next door," Melinda said.

"We're in an underground Keep, Melinda. Where're they going to hide the docks? Under us?" Sorcha said.

Melinda grinned. "We're only, what, twenty levels below the surface. Want to know what else is around here? A whole lot of nothing and trust me, my scanners find everything."

Sorcha looked back and forth between them. "What?"

"The engine mount. Erik probably used a satellite house to test it before bringing it here. He lost enough of his eyebrows the last time. He learned his lesson quick to use an off-site location before bringing his little find home to grandma. The assault armor is here to make sure no one makes off with it while whoever Erik is working for gets here for the hand off. And then you'll never see it again. I'm guessing when you were doing a room-to-room search, you found something that shouldn't be here and instead of sounding the alarm, you found people you could trust and told them to lock it down. How am I doing do far?" Melinda said.

Dina beckoned her closer. "What's the difference between cute and adorable and being a nuisance?"

Melinda stood her ground. "Stay two steps ahead and not getting caught," she said.

Dina tapped her nose. "Correct. You haven't filed an After-Action Report, have you?"

"They gave you a choice. The network or your house and you chose your house," Melinda said. "Smart move."

"How much does Tommy know?" Dina said.

"I haven't a clue," Melinda said.

"Which means nothing and that's not Crosleigh. His plate may've found a suitable host but that's not him. Who put you on this path?" Dina sighed and rubbed her eyes at the messenger bag. She groaned at the sidearm. "Of course, Zi did. How many days did he give you?"

"Three," Melinda said. "But I can do it in one."

"You're sure it was Horatio?" Dina said.

"Spence recognized him. I didn't have access to the network for facial recognition," Melinda said and scratched her chin. "Might explain that blind contract."

Dina grabbed her by the shirtfront faster than Melinda expected. "What contract?"

"Benny had Spence take back a piece of him from Horatio then he got all dull looking. There's a video tape in my bag. I recorded the entire resurrection," Melinda said.

"You what?" Sorcha said. "Wait, what resurrection?"

"The Mad Stuk. Horatio. Phineas and Terrie Leighton along with whoever is doing a good impersonation of Lauren Daire. I resurrected Roark a few hours ago."

"That's not funny, Mindy," Sorcha said.

"In my bag. Watch it on an air gapped player if you want. But it's all there." Melinda nodded to her bag. "Honest. I'm not playing with either of you and less said about the toothpick carrying belfry and her grandpa the better."

Dina released her and pointed to the bag with one hand, palm up with the other.

Melinda raised both hands. "May I?"

"Oh, just do it," Dina said.

"Tell them to back off and I will, they're crowding me," Melinda said.

"Who is?" Sorcha said. "There's no one here but us."

"There's a squad been following me around since I got here and two belfrys in the rafters have been ghosting us since we dropped off Spence," Melinda said. "Do you want me to target them, so you can see them or not?"

Sorcha scoffed but Dina's silence made her daughter gape. "What is wrong with you?"

"Whatever she found, it's *that* bad." Melinda dropped the cassette into the old woman's hand. "You got an unnamed house camped on your front doorstep and you don't seem to care."

Dina cupped her hands together and a second later of electronica squeal, she returned it to Melinda's bag. She turned to Sorcha. "I need you to get Shevonne. I need to interrogate the Weaver. Give her anything she needs."

"It cannot be that bad," Sorcha said.

Dina straightened up and the old Witchen came nose to nose with her daughter. "I'm going to say this once. This little tiff between us ends tonight. You get your house back and I'm leaving. Take some free advice: I'm very proud of you even if you were the slowest, most annoying of any of my daughters but just for once, just trust me, please."

"No," Sorcha said. "And you're not going off to war when there isn't one."

Dina sighed. "Just as stubborn as your father. It is that bad," the Witchen said and snapped her fingers.

Seven camo cloaks melted out of the shadows and one of the two Belfries dropped from the ceiling. "Anything she needs, you hear me," Dina said and stalked up the corridor with the cloaks falling into formation behind her. A helper peeled off and settled in behind Sorcha.

"And the Quiet One rallies and her swords and shields into battle," Melinda quoted.

"How is it, they banished those novels before I was born, and they just roll off the tongue for you?" Sorcha said with a scowl.

"Mostly bed time stories," Melinda said and turned the helper. "Where's your armory. I need blessings, curses, charms, a weapon-smith and that house phone, right now."

27

NECRO OR BUST

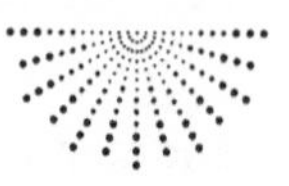

"SAVE HIM."

It was someone else's dream.

Spence stood in a dimly lit cavernous room where candles that lined the walls.

A shuffle of cloth and a crowd on bended knee emerged from the darkness. They wore the cleanest robes he had ever seen. Out of instinct, he covered his mouth; dreams were vague.

However, this wasn't a dream. The stench of death crawled up his nose. Mortal death never rattled his cage this much this was old death. Immortal death.

An old, wooden coffin encrusted with radiant jewels appeared on a raised dais.

Spence had always found it funny how an icon of death radiated with signs of life. He found it less funny to find it flanked by two Necrocloaks. Their quills were short, but their masks had House Daire emblem etched across their foreheads. A jingle tugged at his ears and made his fingers twitch to spin a spell down their throats but the two Necros' quills were still.

The separate jingle belonged to a third Necro with high backed fur collar, a thick layer of quills and to top it off a human skull on the hood. It dragged a bound man towards the coffin.

Once placed atop the coffin the Skull Necro returned to a podium and pulled forth leather bound book from the quilled robe.

The cavernous room grew bright with light; the bound man's mouth opened to scream. "Save him, Weaver."

~

"Not yet," Spence howled and jerked awake to the stench of death.

The stench came from one of two robed people in front of him. One was a flame haired moppet in the white robes of an adept. She wasn't the problem.

The problem was her teacher. A Witchen judging from the death robes. A burden normally passed down from generation to generation. *Normally,* he thought, *except she's the real deal.* She looked to be the same height as her charge, but those death robes were just as bad as his Necrocloak. They deceived weak-minded fools. That made her either old enough to be Spence's mother or worse, great-grandmother.

They're de-hexing me. Ignore the robes. They're not here for you. Spence thought and clamped his jaw shut. *Don't snap at her. Don't snap at her.*

The Witchen pointed a finger and a pressure around Spence's neck tightened. "Who. Be. You. Who. Do. You. Serve." Her old tongue released his jaw.

"Spence MacGregor and I serve no one but myself," he said easily.

The Witchen tugged at the Necrocloak. "Liar."

"I serve no one but myself," he said.

Her crooked finger traced his neck and pulled at an invisible string. A string of a contract. "An old hex for an old war. You're too young to have served me," she said.

"I serve no one but myself," he howled in the old tongue. "No Empress. No Queen. No one has dominance over me. I am free. Unbind and I'll show you myself, blasted Witch!"

She pulled a second lifeless string from his neck. At the end of the string was an iron necklace with a cracked jewel. "Here we are. Almost as old as I am and stop screaming, I can hear you." She patted his cheek. "Even if you are lying to me. The hex around your neck is powerful. But it's just as broken as this defense charm. Maybe... maybe they took you apart?" she gripped the necklace. "You'll need a new charm if you're going to survive." The Witchen turned to her apprentice. "He doesn't leave the house until I come back."

The apprentice nodded and off into the dark the old hag disappeared.

The moppet stared back at him with discolored serpentine eyes that swallowed him whole. "Hullo," she said, a forked tongue passed her under and overbite. She poked his forehead with her wooden, painted sparkle wand. "Bad dream."

Spence ignored her and looked about at the darkened world. *Looks like a privacy spell,* he thought but he heard something, sounded like wings? "Where are we?" he said aloud.

"My house," the moppet said and smiled. A pair of wings sprouted from her shoulders. They hadn't fully matured yet, but her aura was sharp. In ten years, she's be a Shield Maiden or a mage dependent on her keeping the wings and tail. Her tail raised above her head. Longer than she, an iron barb on its tip complete with tiny wheel for tail dragging. This was the final defense if he managed to break free.

"I mean you no harm," he started. "Could you please release me."

"She didn't say not too," the moppet said.

"Your mother?" he said.

"No. Grammy said to watch you." The moppet poked his neck with her sparkle wand. "Burdened," she said.

Spence smirked. "Yes."

The moppet poked his chest then his cloak. "Broken."

Probably, the amount of beatings I've taken. Spence shrugged. "Probably."

"Definitely." She nodded and poked his pocket. "Burdened."

"Very good. You can see my contracts?"

Her head bobbed yes.

"Good, promise me you'll never tell anyone about it," he said.

"Why?" she said.

"Do you like your eyes?" he said.

Her head bobbed again.

"Then if you wish to keep them never tell anyone about seeing burdens again," he said.

She lowered her wand, stepped forward and hugged him.

The world shuddered back into place. His limbs loosened and the medium sized room someone had deposited him came into sharper focus. The chair he occupied needed a cushion. Hardwood floor creaked underneath his feet. A familiar curved wooden design wrapped the room. Defense candles flickered in wall sconces every three feet. Isles and isles full of plastic wrapped cloaks.

"A cloak car. Good idea, Mindy," he said from the vague memories that filled his head.

"Shevonne, be nice to our guest," a warm woman's voice said out of nowhere.

Spence raised his hands over his head.

"Oh, put your arms down," the voice said. "Besides, you couldn't hurt a flee."

"My chest begs to differ," Spence wheezed at the blossoming pain.

"She hugs people too hard, Shevonne, what do you say to our guest," the voice said.

Shevonne released him and bopped her wand across his head. "You are welcome in my house," she said and skipped away down the aisle and out of view.

"Mindy," Spence called out.

"Can't hear you. Shopping" Melinda's voice said from one of the aisles.

"You're what?" Spence hissed.

"Still can't hear you. Shopping," she said.

Spence's head dropped into his hands. "Shopping."

Melinda's singsong voice said. "Sorry about shooting you… again."

Spence tilted his head down and spotted the perfect circular pattern of five rounds stuck in the center mass of his chest. "You aren't shooting me… wait, why did you have to?"

"That's what we need to talk about," the mask said in his ear. "Preferably alone."

"We aren't alone now?" he said with a laugh.

"No dearie, you're not," the woman's voice said.

Spence staggered to his feet. Up one aisle and down another until he looked up. The ceiling was full of people hanging by their feet or in some instances their tails. They were all fully clothed. Different houses' sigils embroidered into their clothes. Arms crossed over their chests, quietly snoring away. Belfries. A magical half step between an old species and a new.

Of course, the belfries relegated to the cloak car, he thought and said, "Wait, her house?"

"My daughter, a chip off the old block," the mother said behind him. "She'll be leading us by the time she gets into the Academy at this rate. But if you must know, we're here because your friend fixed our d-genie like she did with his."

Spence didn't jump and calmly found the moppet's mother wasn't armed as he expected. Instead, she looked to be a techno mage judging from the freckles and red beehive of hair. Slacks, blouse, defense wards glimmered around her neck, wrists and ankles. *Too much defense,* he thought and plucked the stun quills from his chest. "His?"

"That's what we need to talk about. I have restricted files you can only access," the mask said.

"Thank you for taking me in. Would it be possible if I could use the head and/or shower?" he said.

The mother pointed down an isle and stopped him with two fingers to the chest. "And don't try anything stupid. It's her house but I'm still the sharpest knife in the drawer," she said.

Spence raised his hands. "I haven't touched her and never will."

"I don't care." The mother tugged at his cloak. "And lose this until you get it checked."

"Certainly, and if it helps, her brother would hurt me and let's not even go into what her mother would do to me," he said and followed the mother down the aisle into a private bath.

~

Spence emerged from the wrought iron tub proclaimed. "Oh, that feels good." His hands mistakenly pushed hair out of his eyes that wasn't there. He floated on his back all of limbs outstretched. The fact none of the belfries and occupied the tent's uprights above meant he had some privacy but it only meant someone was in the room with him.

Don't care, he thought and dunked himself under, spun about and popped out. Feet firmly on tub's floor and exited the tub. A pair of slacks, a button-down blouse and belt was on the chair next to the tub. The threadbare towel had seen better days but the fact someone had a tub and water meant he had taken it from someone else.

The clothes had recently been unwrapped from storage. They were too stiff to have been left out. The underwear, slacks, socks with iron supports all fit. The blouse was a bit tight, but it was fresh and didn't stink so he didn't stink.

His boots hadn't been shined but the cloak remained unmoved on the table next to the chair. He tied up the boots and eyed the shadows that had pooled too much in the corners of the room. Even with the tent's walls moving the shadows remained stationary.

Glad someone knows what they're doing, he thought. "Read me the file numbers."

"Shadow Chorus Eleven Oh Niner," the mask said.

Shaw Crosleigh. Spence thought and frowned. "He is very dead."

"Not according to several minutes' worth of video before he disabled whatever audio-visual package I had left. Also, you got aura jacked."

"My defense ward necklace . . . which she has," he said. "Not working all this time?"

"And we have to talk about me because the more we talk the more power I'm losing," the mask said. "Sooner or later I'll be a better throw pillow then a weapon of mass destruction."

"You can still disconnect yourself from the cloak?" he said.

"Easily, but restoration won't be possible without me attached," the mask said.

"I'm not thinking of restoration I'm thinking chrysalis protocols," he said.

The mask was silent for a moment. "That may take weeks."

"But with the right parts it'll take minutes," he said.

"Wrong parts and I'll never work again," it chided him.

"First, I need to take you apart to find out what they did because you should be pulling radiation out of the air to charge your batteries and that hit from Mindy probably caused some damage. Full check-up, scavenge the best, burn the rest," he said and turned at the presence of the mother. "Thank you for the use of the tub and I apologize if my wanton needs have burden those in need. If there's anything I can do to repay you, I gladly will." He extended a hand. "Spence MacGregor of the Cross and you are?"

"You always talk like that?" the mother snorted and grasped his hand. "Sorcha Kincaid of the Knoll."

"I was taught to be polite to those who may have unduly burdened themselves by taking me in," he replied without an ounce of annoyance.

"My mother needs to talk to you." Sorcha, on her heel, left.

Spence draped the cloak over his arm and followed. "Would you by chance know of a local Priestess of the Hills or Techno Wizard?"

"First, I'm not yer gahforsaken info booth and secondly you may be welcome here but I'm not helping you," she said.

"Nice to see the reputation of the Kincaids hasn't changed since I've been gone." He dropped down to the Kincaid's old tongue.

Sorcha whipped around and pointed a finger up at him. "Ha! Knew the spoon up yer ass was wooden and thin."

"Not unlike whoever's *You Can't See Me* spells you have guarding me," he replied in standard and stared down the wall of digital auras of ones and zeroes of her aura. "Where are they and I'll be out of your house."

"Where're who?" she said.

Spence plucked out a quill and jingled it around for extra dramatic effect.

The shadows that had been following them down the corridor

froze.

"Have the Brie fallen out of favor or did I misspeak?" he said. "A Priest of the Hills or a Brie Wet Witchen or a Kincaid Techno Wizard."

"If you have one of those gahforsaken cloaks you don't need them, Weaver," she spat.

Color me impressed, he thought and reeled back in his raging aura. "Then may have I use of your mechine shop?" he said coolly.

She parted the curtains to their right and pointed to an empty mechine shop. "Yes, yes you may."

Spence stepped into the shop and the audible click of a tripwire spell was unmistakable. He jerked around and found a gyrating genie keg in the corner. It screamed. He bolted across the room, slid the last five feet on his knees and disconnected the spell from the generator.

The generator ceased only for another audible click to go off in the opposite corner.

Spence repeated the disarming step, thrice more until the room was silent.

What the— he thought but stopped when the genie kegs whined. *Oh, they didn't not separate the kegs, spell by spell.* He rushed back to the first corner and lo and behold, the keg was ripped apart.

Spence picked up the keg, dropped it through the second and after finishing the other two corners he dropped the now fully armed genie keg onto the empty table and re-attached the ripped apart spells.

Ha. Gotcha! Spence pointed at the keg but the noise it made had risen. He unscrewed the top. Inside, the unstable and out of control spell warbled about. He reached inside and pulled it out. He crushed it barehanded and dropped a ripped spell book onto the table.

Spence collapsed into chair and stabbed the farthest corner with his finger. "Happy now?"

"Very." The Witchen pulled back her cloak. Her personal security team of techno mages did the same with their camo cloaks and exited the room. "Explain to me why you've been using this room to build your own Necrocloak."

~

Don't engage her she's just going to rile you up like the last time, Spence thought.

"I asked you a question, Mister MacGregor," the Witchen said.

"I've never been in this room and you aren't my teacher anymore, Murdina Knoll."

"So, you do remember me. Good." Dina pulled up a chair at the table. "For someone who's never been in this room you disarmed that spell rather quickly. Splitting the keg in four takes a lot of work. A novice would've blown themselves up but not for a Weaver. So, tell me, why'd you make it so hard to disarm?"

"I haven't even been in this room before, I don't even..." Spence swiveled about on the chair and spotted another table. He pushed off the seat and ventured closer. It was different then the first, it was metal, clinical. A Necrocloak was pinned down. It'd been crudely vivisected. "Somebody has been playing." He looked past the table to find another one with cloak. This time ripped apart. "Angry too." He passed to the next and the next until after twelve tables, the cloak was laid out and cross-sectioned effectively. "He figured out how to take these apart."

The fourteenth table was empty. The minor exception was a rolled-up blueprint tied off with string. He pulled at the string and the blue print rolled across the table. "These are my notes." He held up the blueprints to the light. "From my private study. What in gahsakes happened here?" he demanded.

"Funny you should ask that. I found the room like this. Your little tripwire notwithstanding," Dina said. "This level is off limits since we don't have the staff to patrol it. It's seventy-five levels away from anyone. The lights, head and air system were powered by a portable genie. Let's not forget the *You Can't See Me* spell on every single emergency exit door. And lifts down here don't work. The only reason I found it was because—"

"The spells weren't three dimensional," Spence finished for her.

Dina nodded. "I come down here to clear my head and the jingle did the rest."

"I got in behind you and stayed there until I was ready then I let you find it as a warning," he said and slumped into the nearest chair. "You swept the place?"

"Didn't find a thing. Tell me, if you're good with that, why do you need to build another one?" she said.

He looked down at his cloak. "Not building another one. Building a fake. Double check to make sure I didn't leave anything behind." He dragged the portable magnifying lens and spotlight over to the table. "I need to know how screwed I am."

~

"Here you are." Melinda's voice pulled Spence up from the guts of his cloak. He had spread out the fabric across the fourteenth examining table and was elbow deep in wires and the occasional misfiring cursed gem.

Melinda had changed into a tan abaya and a lovely gray hijab with black arts defense tchotchkes around her head, wrists and ankles. "Well," she twirled about. "How do I look?"

Like a trojan child horse bride, Spence thought. "How much hardware are you hiding?"

Melinda chortled and waved a finger. "Not telling," she said and joined him at the table. "Whoa. This looks fun and completely out of my league."

"It's fun for a complete fake," Spence said.

"How can you tell?" Melinda said.

"Subpar wiring. The central instrument cluster is a joke. The faceplate and quills are real but that's the only thing keeping it together. The batteries are plugged into the ground power genie, but they aren't holding a charge. If you didn't know what to look for it's a perfect copy."

"How do you know?" she said.

"My father's House built them for his lord and master before the war." Spence tugged at a wire and it came off with ease. "This wouldn't even make it through a sparring session with a mage adept let alone my grandmother. But with the quills and the plate, I can make another."

"I know I didn't shoot you that much," Melinda said.

"Actually, it's the fact you did shoot me," the mask said. "If you hadn't, I wouldn't have run the internal diagnostics to find the problem. My own systems were lying to me."

Melinda scratched her chin and said, "They knew I'd shoot you."

The mask clicked. "Not enough information to form a hypothesis but most people wouldn't run. You didn't and caused me to cross check. Whatever brought us here caused my batteries to fail."

"Restoration is the only option now." Spence leaned on the table. "Someone went to an awful lot of trouble to make this with subpar parts."

"Where's your real cloak and who's wearing it?" Melinda said. "If this is fake what about your book? Someone could've replaced it."

Spence patted the book on the table. "I checked that once I got in here. It's real. But, this," he touched the wire lined fabric. "This doesn't bode well for our heroes."

"Why?" Melinda said.

"Because, taking one apart is the first step to putting it back together again. Took me ten years at the Academy to get mine working properly," Spence said. "And if it's not certified by a Brie Wet Witchen or Kincaid Techno Wizard, you got problems."

"Years?" Melinda blanched.

"You're looking at perfect mix of magic and technology that shouldn't exist. A mage proof infiltrator unit with enough quills you could hack into an enemy's network. You do it wrong and you're looking at explosion or implosion from the batteries. Acid burns. Quills attack you instead of your target. Fabric ignores the central CPU and suffocates you," he rattled off while he paced around the table. "Let's not forget the plate injuries alone. Playing with fire like this isn't worth it unless you..."

Melinda didn't say anything until, "unless they what?"

"Unless you're desperate enough to mass producing them," he said.

"Is that even possible? Why would you do it?" she said.

"Anything is possible until you fail. If it was me, I'd use these for recon before an invasion," Spence said and pointed a pair of tweezers at her. "Which reminds me, what happened with the engine mount foolishness and this supposed aura jacker?"

Dina cleared her throat. "I didn't want to interrupt." She handed over Spence's defense charm. "I think it may be time for you start packing it up."

It glowed correctly, and Spence latched it around his neck. "We actually got a clue to something and we need to leave?"

"I'll explain on the way," Melinda said.

"On the way to where, Mindy? Wait, did you just." He sighed and winced. "I'm not thanking you in front of her."

"See he's back to normal." Dina grinned and skipped out of the room. "And I didn't even have to do anything to that hex around his neck, either."

"Right, we need your cloak operational," Melinda said. "So, show me what to do."

"Wait, where are we going? And did you have her interrogate me on purpose."

"I have no idea what you're talking about." Melinda grinned. "But seriously we're on the clock tell me how to fix it. We've got date with an engine mount."

"Where in gahsakes are you going to hide an engine mount out here?" Spence said.

"Knoll Dry Docks," Melinda said.

"The supposedly mysterious dry docks that no one has ever managed to conclusively prove exist?" Spence said.

"Oh, they exist. They just neglected to tell you how deep they buried them," she said. "Now, seriously, what needs to be fixed because I need both of you at least at ten percent."

"Mindy." Spence pointed the tweezers at her. "Do I look like I'm at ten percent?"

"Constantly. If I must roll you up to another house, so help me," Melinda said. "Now, let's get this weapon of mass destruction fixed, shall we?"

28
TAKING POSSESSION

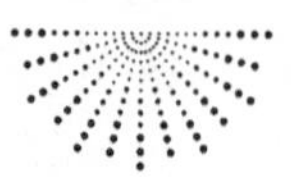

"WHERE ARE YOU TAKING ME? THE SUIT HASN'T EVEN BEEN TESTED," Spence said.

"We're taking a short cut," Melinda said. "Let her warm up, she'll be right as rain."

"Sixty percent and rising," the mask chittered. "Be happy that she did a good job."

"Melinda, where are we?" Spence said and pulled Melinda to a stop.

Melinda raised her torch and illuminated the darkened, metallic corridor they had been traipsing through for nearly an hour. "During the war, the Houses used these sub-basements to ride out the bombardments."

"Which war?" Spence said.

"Every war. The Houses used to be underground because they couldn't breathe the Hollow's atmosphere. They turned to genetics and after hundreds of tests, they got it right," Melinda said.

"To find nothing but sand," Spence said.

"The cartographers went to work and after several years, they figured out the Houses had deposited here for a reason. This area used to be a laboratory," Melinda said.

"No one builds a laboratory in the middle of the desert, Mindy," Spence scoffed.

"Right, which is why after several long nights of hacking the network, I found out they had landed in the middle of a defunct House Weapons Test Range," Melinda said.

"And that's why the Vaults are here," Spence said and released her. "Wait. We're in the Testing Range now?"

"What? No, no, no, no. Stow's End, Goslin Grace, all the cities were built outside the Test Range," Melinda said. "Except, the Knoll dry docks which is where we're going."

"Mindy, you can't just jump an engine mount inside a planet's gravity well," Spence said.

Melinda waved a finger. "Not unless you're using said gravity well as a sling shot."

Spence's jaw opened and closed. "Stupid, stupid, stupid techno mages and bending the rules of physics," he growled. "Wait, how can you tell the engine mount is even here? It could be anywhere by now."

Melinda pulled a palm sized device out of her bag. "I tagged the mount and your shuttle for salvage. So, guess what just appeared an hour ago?"

"You're not 'salvaging' my shuttle, Mindy," Spence said.

"On this planet, I can give you a good price for it," she said.

"No," Spence said.

"Fine." Melinda trekked onward into the dark. "Fifteen more minutes until we reach the doors and I get to strangle Erik."

"Erik?" Spence followed her. "Who's Erik?"

"Erik Knoll, my resident techno mage and one of my ex-betrothed," she said.

"Betrothed? You can't ex your way out of being betrothed, Mindy."

"You and my mother. I can choose whomever I want. Besides, he's just one of them," she said. "The sewing circle can stick it for all I care."

"One of them?" Spence said. "How many people are you betrothed to? Wait, no one betroths anyone anymore. Wait, the sewing circle did this?"

"After the Stukari showed up and paid everyone off, all us war orphans were guests in our own Houses. We were kids and weren't exactly needed until one of the Stukari honchos got vacuumed sealed inside their house. They got out alive and figured out rule one," she said.

"Rule One: Who's in charge," Spence said. "Wait, why not just offer them terms?"

"I did. They declined," Melinda said.

Spence stopped her. "They declined? Those terms always favor the guests."

"They didn't want to be guests," Melinda said. "Who's in charge?"

Spence released her. "Mindy. What're you doing?"

"What does it look like I'm doing?" she said. "We're going to see Erik."

"You know what I mean. This isn't some hair-brained scheme to get your House back?"

Melinda giggled. "No. No. No. No. I don't have a House and I never will. But, some of us are getting a bit antsy. So, no, this isn't some hair-brained scheme I cooked up with the rest of the orphans. If it was, they wouldn't see me comin'." She pointed with her torch. "We're here."

The smooth walls had changed to stone. An iron-pressure hatch complete with a wheel stood between them and whatever lay on the other side.

"You up for some recording?" Melinda said.

"Your repairs to my surveillance system worked. I've been recording since we left," the mask said.

"Good. I don't know what's beyond this door. The Knoll like their security. So be careful. He doesn't know we're coming. Just follow my lead and record everything," Melinda said.

She twisted the pressure hatch, the seals popped, and they pushed through.

~

Spence gaped at the canyon of metal beneath the catwalk. A lattice-work of iron scaffolding lined what were once walls of stone. Now, the metal stretched onto it vanished beneath their feet.

The old scrying on the posts caused his eyes to water. *Gahsakes, she wasn't kidding. The dry docks still exist,* he thought. *Too old. Only meant to last forever.*

Spence craned his neck and spotted the iron doors that capped the roof some thirty feet above their heads.

"Network connection accepted. Updating firmware: complete. Reboot: complete. No signs of life..." The mask clicked. "...correction. Twenty decks below us. aura detected. Movement detected thirty decks below. Type Forty engine mount. Secondary signal detected. Salvage signal detected."

"Unbelievable," Spence breathed. "They closed this off?"

"When the Stukari invaded, you bet I did. This is just the tip. We make it down to Erik and get on board before anything else happens," Melinda said. "It's big enough to fit a carrier down here. It's certainly big enough to hide the engine mount. It was so well hidden the Knoll had completely forgotten it was here. Erik and I found a few left-over diaries. We figured out House Knoll didn't want their children to die on the docks, so they left all this behind and became nomads. We're pretty sure it's the only functioning underground dock left. We kept it a secret for years. Nobody knows where it is," Melinda beckoned and down the stairs she crept.

~

"—they're going to be here in a half hour. I want it cleaned up." A man's voice quickened Melinda's heart and she slowed Spence's decent. In the deepening shadow of the mount, they paused for it was all they could see in any direction.

"I was attached to this?" Spence hissed.

"Your shuttle was." Melinda pointed across the canyon. "There's an umbilical tunnel your ship was attached to thattaway."

One deck beneath them, a man with flaming red hair was

surrounded by a group of auras comprised of ones and zeroes. Unlike most techno mages, Erik liked to announce himself. The flaming hair wasn't real because it was his aura. He was dressed in slacks, boots and a button-down shirt with a tie.

You never got dressed up unless you're scared, Melinda thought and pulled her stunner.

"Get that blasted Foo Fighter off the deck and stowed. Somebody tagged, and I want to know who. The signal from those tagging spikes has been screaming for the last hour." The man pointed to the mount. "And find out why there's an umbilical attached. It wasn't there when I slung her into orbit. Dismissed!"

The auras passed through each other and followed their orders.

"They're dead, aren't they?" Spence said.

"They were never alive to begin with. The Stuk raised their auras because their bodies were too far gone. They're indentured to the Dry Docks until their auras burn out which won't be for millions of years since they aren't building anything." Melinda eased down a few stairs to the next landing. "If we're really quiet they won't see—"

"She did what?" the man's voice cracked over the silence. "Where is she? Well, go find her! She has to be here." The man pulled back his goggles and gazed skyward. "Melinda Scott!" he howled at the top of his lungs. "I am not crawling through that mount lookin' fer ya girly!"

"So, we can get inside," Spence said.

"I would've but I was bit too busy trying not to crap myself because your shuttle had enough stealth tech on it to fill my bank account for years," Melinda said.

"Still not selling it to you," Spence said.

"Mindy!" the man yelled. "C'mon out, I know you're here."

"You have to talk to him before he sends the auras after us." Spence chuckled.

"Fine. No hide and seek today," Melinda said and descended the steps. "Hello, Erik."

The man twisted around. A shocked expression melted to happiness and they embraced. His aura twisted around her and they glowed for the briefest of moments.

They released, and Erik smacked her shoulder. "What're you doin' here?"

She returned the smack and the techno mage toppled to the ground. "You dropped this thing on me, Erik Knoll!" she cursed.

Erik wobbled to his feet only to gape at Spence's silent approach. "Holy shit." He laughed. "Ya got 'em. Ya actually got 'em. Wait. How long have you been here, I just unsealed this place."

~

"— and that's how we got here," Melinda finished. "By the way, there's a dead body with the Foo Fighter."

"The suit's empty. Aura jacker? So, the long undies worked for ya." Erik's grin turned to a scowl. "We gonna need more than long undies if there's an aura jacker on the loose."

"Since when? There's a dead body in that suit," Melinda said.

"See, this is what I mean when I'm around you, things like this just happen," Erik said.

Melinda dropped a duffle bag at his feet and unzipped it. Several swords with glowing gems in their pommels shined. "I brought some backup."

"Backup? Gahsakes, you went to her, didn't you? I warned you not to go to her. They don't know I'm here," Erik said. "Wait, ya told 'em, didn't ya? What is wrong with ya?"

"I need to get on board before anyone else shows up," Melinda said and tugged his clothes. "Who you waiting for?"

"Only you'd try something crazy as like this," Erik said. "And no one you know."

"We do this quick, we'll be on the morning rail carrier, and they won't know a thing," she said and turned to Spence. He had taken up position next to the mount and conversed with several of the auras. "What is it?"

"What's wrong with this picture?" Spence said.

"No one knows we're here. What did you expect—" Melinda stopped mid-sentence when her earbud squelched with feedback.

Erik winced. "Someone just blacked out the internal network and it wasn't me."

"We're not alone." Spence pointed down several decks.

A House-grade camo cloak materialized out of the shadows. The hood pulled back and Wallace Stukari appeared.

"Sonva—" Melinda hissed.

"Hello, Wally," Spence said. "I'll be right back."

"You aren't going without me," Melinda said. "Wait. Someone else is down there, look!"

Wallace and someone else in a pair of overalls and a hat were in mid-argument.

"What are they arguing about?" Spence said.

"Something about it's not here. The ship is supposed to be right here. How can you misplace a shuttle for gahsakes?" the mask said.

"He's expecting you?" Melinda said. "Why is he expecting you?"

"Expecting who, Mindy?" Erik said.

"He was attached to the mount. His shuttle was. They were hacking his table," Mindy said.

Erik turned to Spence. "Hacking your what? Wait, where'd he go?"

Melinda looked around. "I knew I shouldn't have fixed the camo gem on the cloak."

"Mindy." Erik pointed down.

The Weaver's cloak drifted across the uprights until it was directly above Wallace and silently dropped behind him only for Wallace to spin around and draw down on him.

"Oh, you're kidding me," Melinda said. "C'mon. Go do your thing."

"You're not even going to tell me what in gahsakes is going on. Are you?" Erik said.

Melinda pulled him close and kissed him. The little pop between them brought them close. She released him, and he kept smooching thin air. "I was never here." She touched his temple. "Delay them, please."

"Sure." Erik Knoll wobbled about and descended one of the stairs towards the engine mount as if nothing had happened.

~

"Don't expect much for me. My offense package is still regenerating," the mask said in Spence's ear.

That won't be a problem, Spence thought.

Wallace whipped around, gun in hand, hammer cocked at the presence behind him.

"Mister Stukari," Spence said and disarmed him in a blink. He tossed the pieces of the gun over his shoulders.

He plucked three throwing knives as they hurtled through the air.

Wallace unsheathed his cursed katana, but Spence parried it away.

Spence grabbed Wallace's throat and pinned him against one of the uprights. "I.D. him."

"Identity confirmed: Stukari, Wallace," the mask chittered. "Rank: Lord."

The hood's seals popped, and Spence tore it back. "Hello, Wally."

The years had been good to Wallace Stukari. The charming rogue still had a full head of sandy blond hair. His tanned skin meant he had been outside for longer than usual. A few subtle things on his face threw up warning bells like the scars from his jaw to his scalp and his unusual blue eyes were a pale brown.

What's with the plate, Wally? Spence thought.

"How?" Wallace gasped.

"You were expecting me?" Spence said. "They raised to lord, did they?"

"How?" Wallace grabbed Spence's arm to release him.

Spence obliged, and Wallace shoveled air into his lungs. "How?"

"Tommy Scott stumbled across your little plan. Whatever this plan is." Spence gazed up at the engine mount. "I remember when we hustled old farts for a pittance of food but look at what you've done. This is a bit outside your comfort zone."

"It's not what you think. Can't be here," Wallace said. "They'll see you."

"No. You've disabled the network. We can talk freely. Unless you're talking about your associate. Lovely get up. Hides everything. Blends in." Spence knelt next to the hyperventilating lord. "Why're you running, Wally? I already saw the Necro lab. You're manufacturing them en masse now?"

"You are." Wallace coughed.

"I already have one. Why would I make another one?" Spence said.

The boggled expression on Wallace's face was curious. "Wait, which one are you? How'd you get in here? Wailing Seas or the Roost facility?"

"On my shuttle, Wally, when Melinda found me. That's after you tried to explosively decompress—" Spence pointed a finger and Wallace retreated. "What do you mean, which one?"

"What ship? Melinda who?" Wallace grabbed Spence by the cloak. "What ship? You left the ship before it jumped, don't you remember?"

"He's telling the truth. He doesn't have a clue," the mask said. "And I haven't a clue which ship he's talking about, but he believes it. Keep him talking."

"Yes. I remember. They let me go before the jump. They said I'd served my purpose and discharged me. I was in my shuttle when they jumped. I set a course and that's the last thing I remember," Spence said.

Wallace's eyes narrowed. "Shuttle? I brought you home and they—" He slowed. "Oh, they didn't. No. They couldn't have."

"Couldn't have what?" Spence said. "What do you mean which one?"

"You're the spare." Wallace gaped. "You're telling me it's that bad? How long do I have?"

"You've got five minutes to live," Spence said matter of fact.

"You need to get out of there. One of my tripwires just disappeared." Melinda's voice crackled over Spence's earbud. "And Erik is talking to someone I can't see."

"Whoever you're working for hacked my table, and there's an aura jacker on the loose. You can't fool me with this paint job. Which of the Yashira paid you to do this?" Spence growled. "Horatio and Roark are alive, and I'm pretty sure so's Lauren."

"That's impossible. They're all dead," Wallace stammered.

"Melinda resurrected Roark three hours ago, Wally. Horatio was supposed to be the sole survivor but now he's back to being indentured. And Melinda's putting me back together again, again," Spence said.

Wallace sneered enough so the scars around his jaw line and scalp sharpened but receded just as quickly. "Stop calling me that! Wait, why are you red teaming me? You think I'm bent?"

"Check your blessings. They already jacked me. You may be next," Spence said and squinted at him. "That plate looks good on you. Even down to the nose hair."

"Listen to me, someone else is here and they aren't with us." Melinda's voice cracked over the com. "Get out of there. Now!"

"You need to come with me. I can debrief you and wait, where'd you get that cloak? Who's in your ear?" Wallace said. "Horatio Crosleigh is dead; so is Lauren and the rest."

"We'll talk about this later, old friend. You've company coming." Spence sealed his cloak and with a flick of his wrist, he was airborne along with his blood pressure.

~

"Please tell me you got all of that," Melinda said.

"Every single word. But we're still missing whoever was in the overalls and the hat," the mask said. "Thank you for updating my surveillance package. I won't have to do names and faces with them."

"What do you mean 'them?'" Melinda said and squinted down at the group entering the floor. Several squares of pixelated faces flashed across her goggle's lenses.

"Crosleigh, Horatio. He has new friends. Unlicensed Necrocloaks," the mask said.

"Why am I not surprised?" Melinda said, and a hand jerked her around. Spence's glare made her pause. "You okay?" she said.

Spence pointed a quivering finger and dragged her across the deck and into an empty supervisor's office. "Who be you and who do you serve," he hissed.

"We already did this," she said. "Any louder and they'll hear you!"

"No, you asked me and then interrogated me again to make sure of who I serve but I never asked you. You kept asking Lauren and you never told me." Spence pulled off his cloak and heaved it across the room. "I trusted you to fix her without even asking. I just haven't had time to focus. Who be you and who do you serve!"

"Not here, not now," Melinda said and grabbed his shoulder. "The network is comprised. You can trust me."

Spence pulled away. "Like I trusted you since we got down here with a sob story about you getting kicked out of your House?" Spence wheezed. "Why can't I?" He staggered and toppled into a dust covered sofa. "What did you do to me?"

Melinda picked up the cloak and covered him. "I have no idea what you're talking about. I promise you that. I need to get on board and grab whatever I can. You need to stay put. Don't do anything stupid." She turned to the cloak. "Watch him. Give me a five-minute countdown and watch him."

"Good luck," the mask said.

~

Melinda took two steps at a time and reached the top of the catwalk in record time.

The upper deck of the mount lay before her. In the dim light, it was still as big and unending. She edged into a corner. "The network still down?" she said.

"Completely," the mask said. "The model doesn't match anything in my files. The umbilical may be the best way unless there's an engineering hatch."

"Umbilical will be faster." She pushed herself out of the corner and ran down the catwalk. She vaulted over the handrail and across the yellow warning track she sped. She leapt off the track and landed on the mount.

A few auras had clustered around the umbilical, but none of them stopped her.

"Come full circle," she huffed and looked down into the gaping hole. "Why stop now?" she said and jumped feet first.

~

Spence rolled off the couch. A cloud of dust and cobwebs tickled his nose, but he was too angry to cough. "You need to calm down before you get angry at her," the plate chittered.

"It's a little too late for that." He yanked it off the floor and pulled it on. "Where is she?"

"I lost contact with her four minutes ago," the plate said.

Spence barreled out of the office and with a flick of a thrust spell, he paralleled the side of the mount. "Tag everything. Where is she on this thing?" he said.

A yellow triangle popped up on the plate's lenses. It was surrounded by auras.

Spence dropped through the hole and into what looked like a darkened maintenance shaft. A set of metal double doors had been cracked open, and he pushed through them where Melinda was elbow deep in hotwiring the inner set of doors.

"We're leaving, Melinda, and then you're explaining yourself," he said.

"I'm almost there. What part of nothing stupid do you not understand?" she said.

"You did ask for a five-minute warning. This is it," the plate said.

The deck quivered beneath Spence's feet. The quiver rolled into a full-on shake.

"I'm almost done," Melinda said over the noise. "There got it!"

"It's gonna—" The noise of the engines roaring to life smothered Spence's sentence.

The darkened shaft brightened. The swell of zero gravity lifted them off their feet. The rules of reality twisted about. The outside world vanished.

And the engine mount jumped into S-Cut.

PART IV

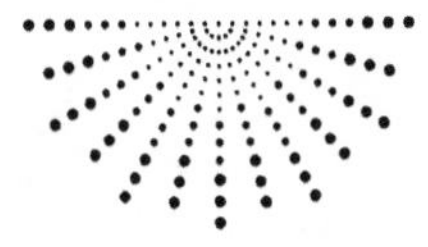

29

WHERE WEAVERS DAIRE, PART II

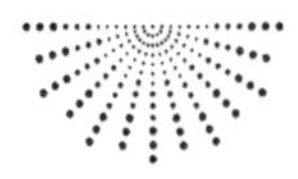

THE ENGINE MOUNT QUAKED AROUND MELINDA AND SPENCE.

The small engineering room they had found themselves just made the bumpy ride worse.

Melinda pulled Spence across the room towards two cushioned seats attached to the wall. An engineering station separated the two.

She strapped the eight point harness across himself then herself.

"Where?" Spence managed.

"I don't know but it's not Erik's math. It's too bumpy. The engine isn't calibrated right." She looked at the flashing control panel next to her arm. "I'll make it worse if I touch anything."

"Let's not do that then," he said.

The G-Forces pushed them back into their seats then to port, starboard, lifted them up and crushed them down.

"I hate S-Cut," Melinda said through gritted teeth.

The shuddering stopped and the tug of gravity left their limbs.

They were weightless for the briefest of times and then gravity returned.

The frame grew still and silence followed.

The console next to Melinda's arm happily pinged.

"That was fast," Spence said.

"Couldn't have gone more than a few feet," Melinda pulled her stunner from her messenger bag and double tapped the eight-point restraint. It zipped back into the chair's housing and she eased herself towards the door.

"Careful," the mask said.

The frame shivered, again and swayed about.

Melinda grabbed a ceiling handhold and the swaying stopped with a jerk.

She opened the door, but nothing rushed to greet her except oxygen.

"Stay here. I'm just going to look," Melinda said.

The glowing sky that welcomed her didn't soothe her frayed nerves. She gripped the handrail with one hand only to stop. "Keep forgetting," she said and pulled a tether line out of her bag. The clamp on the other end locked onto the rail and she climbed the stairs.

Melinda poked her head up to spy the all too familiar peaks of the Stormer Mountain Range. The fires had already engulfed Crosleigh Keep. The smoke twisted into the skies above. The air carrier that hovered directly over the church was a new addition much to her surprise.

Her goggles pinged and speck appeared on the lenses. It was her suit. Less than three miles away.

Any closer and we would've been blown into vapors. Melinda thought. *Wait, they jumped us back across the Range? I'm back where I started.*

The Mount swiveled by an unknown means and a fountain of raw energy came into view. It spewed forth from a resurrection chamber on the ground. Several of them littered the tarmac beneath.

Melinda's goggles adjusted and several Quonset huts and Hangars were tagged. *An air carrier base,* she thought. *They must've tried to transport the chambers when one of them went off.* She stopped gawking at the grounded air carrier silhouettes and tightened the scanning field to find the AV gasoline tanks. The underground tanks had been protected from the first explosion but that didn't mean much if the chamber exploded.

Daire Close. Too close, Melinda thought. "Gahsakes. What've you done?" She said.

A hand dropped onto her shoulder and Spence appeared. "We need to get out of here before they find us," he said.

Melinda tugged twice on the tether and the clamp released. It rolled back up into her hand. She stuffed it into her bag and jingle of quills twisted them both around to sight of the phalanx of Necro cloaks advanced across the roof of the mount towards them.

The leader had a bone white, horned skull snickered. The same amount of quills and fur as Spence's. The cursed gauntlets reminded her of Horatio's. The skull's jaw snapped ad she refocused on the hollowed eye sockets. A soulless gleam appeared. The red electronica lenses had garnered the desired effect. "Mister MacGregor and Miss Scott. What a pleasant surprise. Bring the Weaver to him, the girl can go with the rest," the plate clicked.

"Wherever he goes, I go," Melinda said.

The leader passed by Spence without even looking at him and towered in front of her. It wasn't the cloak, the wearer was a good two feet taller than either of them.

The Skull Necro placed her hands on her hips and leaned down. It's jaws ground together. "Why?"

"Whatever you're going to do, you need someone to read from his book. I already raised The Mad Stuk. You want it done right or you want that?" Melinda thumbed to the spewing energy column. "You're choice."

"You don't know shit," the Skull Necro snapped.

"No. I don't. But my record is better than yours and the last time I checked the Mad Stuk is mobile," Melinda said and stood on her tip toes. "I just want to explain something to you. The whole glowing eyed demon thing may work on the drunk locals but I do know how to put one of these together. So, why don't you stick your ego and take us to whoever's in charge of this mess because sooner or later you're gonna trip over something and it really is gonna blow up in yer face, honey."

The Skull Necro gripped her by the throat, lifted her off her feet and twisted about so Melinda dangling in thin air. "You're still sticking your nose where it doesn't belong."

Melinda shrugged as best she could and wheezed. "Just remember whose got the stunner pointed at your central control processor." She tapped the tip of the stunner through the quills for extra effect. "I shoot you. This thing goes nuts. You drop me and I ricochet off the mount and land on my own two feet while you buddies figure out what to do. Yer choice."

"He's not going to save you?" The Skull spat.

"He doesn't *need* to save me. I can handle myself. Now, what's it gonna be?" Melinda growled.

Spence cleared his throat.

"No one asked you a thing, Weaver," the Skull Necro said.

"You're right. You didn't. But, she's right. The chambers have been compromised. Liches are running around willy nilly and I'm guessing you lost a few of your Liches when the chamber went into overload the first time and now you can't turn it off because you lost your brains when your techno mage or necromancer were at ground zero when it went off," Spence said. "Now, my cloak didn't have to tell me any of that because I do this whole raise the dead thing not as hobby or a job. It's my life because everyone else I trained in the old ways are dead. And guess, what?" he lifted his arms and bowed. "I'm still here so I am telling you," he glanced at the spewing column. "Without a shadow of a doubt, you have five minutes to live before that things takes out a good five hundred miles chunk of this desert. It's time to stuff the ego like she said or do really want to be at ground zero when that chamber goes, I'm really not kidding."

~

The hangar door slammed closed behind them.

"That speech should've worked," Melinda said.

"In about three minutes it will," Spence said.

"That's a bit close," Melinda said. "Showing off up there, eh? I like it."

"Sometimes someone needs to hear it from a professional about how screwed they are," Spence said. "She's going to go back and tell them she found us at which time she will then be told to come get me to turn off the giant glowing stick so they can raise whoever it is they were sent to raise in the first place then we go home."

"You're incredible calm about all this," Melinda said.

"It's not gonna explode. It's just gonna implode then it's gonna explode," Spence said and rolled his wrist over at his non-existent watch. "We've got an hour before we really need to panic."

"They let me keep my bag," Melinda said.

"They don't care who either of us are and they still think those cloaks are the scariest thing out here." Spence walked around the large hangar.

After several hours of the spewing energy fountain in the sky routine more than several dozen desert wanderers had their curiosity peaked. And, like Spence and Melinda had just been, they had been relegated to the hangar. The wanderers didn't give them a second glance and went back to their small talk.

It was towards the back where the manager's offices were that several people had clustered. One of them had been staring them down since they'd gotten tossed inside. He was dressed more casually then the rest of the wanderers. Jacket, shoes, slacks and button down shirt said button pusher. No House cufflinks or tie clip. A basic, brown and boring man. His neck long beard of red and scraggly bed head of brown made him more forgettable than the rest but that's why he'd been chosen as look out because he was *that* boring.

His burnt face wasn't natural. It wasn't from a fire. It was from a curse. The perpetual scowl across his brow and the fact his eye sockets were in constant shadow said a plate but it wasn't.

Spence passed by him and ignored whatever was in the depths of those eye sockets for they were drilling a hole in the back of his head when something old in the back of Spence's brain screamed. "Wait." He spun about and the hangar door flung open.

The Skull Necro bound over the door frame and pointed. "Get the

Weaver and his Apprentice right now. Those two. Ignore the rest." Her voice boomed across the open space.

Spence double timed it back to Melinda and the Necros led them outside.

The Weaver turned back to the boring man only to receive a wave in time for the door to close.

~

"I think I'll wait in the hangar," Melinda said and lowered her goggles so she could see.

"Remember that part when I said I know what I'm doing?" Spence said. "I'm not bullshitting you."

"You've been at ten percent since I met you," Melinda said.

"And I don't need my aura to fix it. My parents built these chambers from scratch." Spence said and stopped at the queue of people at make shift parameter. "What. In. The –" he turned to the Skull Necro. "What in gahsakes are they doing?"

"They're saying good bye to their loved ones," the Skull Specter said.

"The pillar is a beacon. Its summoning all the souls here," Spence said to Melinda and turned to Skull Necro. "What's going to happen when I stop it?"

"You mean 'if', you stop it, Weaver," the Skull Necro said.

"No I mean 'when'." Spence stopped and the Skull Necro stared down at him. "What happens when I stop it."

The Skull Necro's silence didn't bode well. "You both get to live."

"And the rest?" Spence said.

The Skull Necro laugher was worse than it sounded. "They get to live, too."

"What happens after that?" he said.

The silence from the Skull Necro was deafening. "He wants to talk to you," it simply said.

"I see," Spence said and turned to Melinda. "Give her the bag."

Melinda gaped at him. "Excuse me?"

"She let you keep it so when the time comes you'll use it and fail." Spence extended a hand. "Give me the bag."

Melinda glanced at him then the Necro.

"Do you trust me?" he said.

Melinda growled. She lowered her bag off her shoulder and into his hand. "I hope you know what you're doing."

Spence accepted the bag and handed it off to one of the Necros.

"Like it matters," the Skull Necro chittered.

"My cousin, Anji has done far more damage with far less." Melinda said in the mother tongue. "What do you need me to do?"

"Stand there and hold this." Spence handed her his book. "If anything happens, I'll tell you what page to turn too."

"For what?" Melinda said.

"A defense spell that will protect you in case of the worst," he said and advanced through the crowd but she stopped him.

"Define 'worse'." She said.

"You remember when you put the Mad Stuk back together without getting your insides fried?" Spence said and continued through the crowd. "That was 'worse'. This won't take long."

Melinda turned back to the Skull Necro and followed the Weaver.

The chambers has been stacked at the end of the tarmac away for good reason. Items like resurrection chambers, cursed weapons, anything with an aura infused piece was deemed a bio-hazard to anything flammable. The chambers should've been in an ironed up transport crate. This kept the fiery aura pieces from interacting with the outside world like the hot tarmac Melinda and Spence walked across now.

The same hot tarmac that included the AV Fuel at the opposite end of the Air Carrier base.

"What do you think?" Spence said.

"I think we're idiots and our friend wants us dead and that's why she isn't at our heels," Melinda said.

"Partially right," Spence said. "When the big bad can't stand to be near the resurrection chambers it means only one thing. They're really scared of something that's in there." He stopped at the make shift barricades that someone had erected using cargo containers. "When we walk away from this with our heads held high, they're going to shoot me and toss you back in with the prisoners."

"And yer *okay* with this?" Melinda said.

"No. If I don't get killed then they're going feed me to whatever Lich they have left so they'll have their special toy back. The question is: Are *you* okay with this?"

Melinda stared at him. "You mean the part where they kill you or the part where they try and feed whatever's left of your aura to a Lich? Either way, no."

"Good." He reached out and touched her defense charm necklace. "In case of the worst, all of me is in that. Do not fly off the handle and do not shoot your way out of this."

"It's a hot tarmac why would I shoot my way out?" Melinda said and winced. "And that's why you had me give up the bag."

Spence smiled. "Least one of us is thinking, right? No, the reason why is because you aren't Anji and you don't need to take over this entire Air Carrier Base yourself."

"She had help." Melinda said.

"No. She saved everyone with nothing but her bare hands and a crash axe but that's not important, what is important is whatever happens next you have to understand one thing: How far are you willing to go? All or nothing. Stories of glory and the scars to match or sit back while they trip over themselves while you get transported away," Spence said. "Now, let's go see how screwed we are because this entire base should've been glassed when that chamber was cracked."

They turned the corner and Melinda's goggle lenses immediately dilated at the fiery pillar of energy. Like all magical things it threw up errors.

She turned away and gasped at the corpses that littered the ground. All of them were fused with the rocky terrain. There were only two chambers. The first was the cracked one with its pillar of energy. The other was untouched.

The cracked one had a pile of mage corpses around it. One of them sat cross-legged on the ground, his back to it.

Once her goggles corrected for the pillar's energy the facial recognition immediately threw up a familiar pixelated face.

"Unbelievable." Melinda pulled down the goggles.

Spence MacGregor sat there against the cracked chamber. A blessed sword across his lap.

"I should've known it was going to be you two," he said with chortle.

~

The Weaver ignored his doppelgänger and eyed the other chamber. "Melinda, do me a favor and get the other chamber out of here, " he said.

"Once we get the chamber closed. Yes, we will push the chamber back into its cargo container, together," she said.

"Melinda," the Weaver said.

"What?" she retorted. "I'm not leaving you two alone. Gahknows, what will happen."

"You're the original," Spence MacGregor said. "Mister MacGregor gone then?"

"Sucked into his chamber," Melinda said.

Spence MacGregor nodded. "That's one way to do it. You can't even look at me, can you?"

The Weaver seethed.

"That would be a 'yes'," Spence MacGregor said. "Where'd you find him, Mindy?"

"Your shuttle in a stasis chamber, exactly where he was supposed to be," Melinda said. "Roark landed us three miles short."

Spence MacGregor laughed. "Lord Know-It-All alive?"

Melinda bowed.

Spence MacGregor's face dropped. "She's going to insufferable after this, you know that."

"Which one are you?" the Weaver said.

Spence MacGregor nodded gravely. "I see. Wally spilled, eh?"

"Yes, Wally," the Weaver said. "There's no body, there's no voice. It's just my sword."

Spence MacGregor shrugged. "Hey, auras have rights to ya know. How long do I have?"

"Hour or less," the Weaver said. "What did they do to you?"

"Nothing. Family bought me at an estate sale. I kept my head down while their kid went through the Academy. She finished top of her Necromancer Class. I was her good luck charm. I thought we were doing good until this happened. She listened to me until the end. You would've liked her. They couldn't have cared less about us. Didn't even know you were here until you came around the corner," Spence MacGregor said. "How bad is it, Mindy?"

"Ohari Brothers are cleansed. Roark and Phineas are getting sorted, I hope. Aura jacker is on the loose. *He* is around somewhere and so far we're it. The rest of my back-up is out following a lead." Melinda said.

Spence MacGregor sighed. "She's got your bag so that means it's a no win scenario. Can't shoot your way out. If he gets any closer, the radiation is going to finish him off. I thought it through there's no water source nearby."

"You're holding the energy back," the Weaver said.

Spence MacGregor nodded. "Too many innocent people and the AV gas tanks are too close. Why do I see smoke on the horizon?"

"Some idiot in an air carrier is pummeling Crosleigh Keep to rubble," Melinda said.

"They're not that innocent," the Weaver said.

"Remember: Always take the middle. Never the sides," Spence MacGregor said. "Melinda."

"No," the Weaver said.

"We merge and she wields. It's that simple. We protect her until the end," Spence MacGregor said. "I've already marked the bad circuits. Only she needs to do is to re-wire it. I know, I hate these mind games, too but it has to be done."

"Protect me from what?" Melinda said.

"Once you close the breach in the chamber. The Liches are going to come back to finish me off," the Weaver said. "Unless there's nothing left of us to take. The sword will mask my aura for the time being until it replenishes and then I'll be a lighthouse."

Spence MacGregor tapped his temple. "There's the ole Weaver I missed."

"Doesn't make sense. Why two chambers? They didn't split the chambers." Melinda said and tweaked her goggle settings. "I can't see the other one. It's displaced. Time is bending back on itself trying to close the hole. I can't save her. I can't save either of you. But, I can save the chamber and then let them have the rest of you."

Spence MacGregor and the Weaver stared at her.

"I like her," Spence MacGregor said. "Please tell that defense charm around her neck is all of you."

"It is," the Weaver said.

Spence MacGregor clapped. "All good."

Melinda reached out for the sword but the Necromancer that had been *under* the mages bodies since the beginning jerked awake. Her gloved hand, the one not still clutching the Lord Spence MacGregor's blessed broadsword grabbed Melinda's hand.

"I've got this." She coughed through cracked teeth and bloodied face. "All or nothing."

Melinda retracted her hand and looked for either Spence MacGregor or the Weaver but they were gone. She picked up the errant cloak off the deck. "Just follow my instructions . . ." she said and calmly guided the Necromancer through the final instructions and the pillar of energy sputtered to a stop.

The two chambers merged into one and the Necromancer howled at the success. She unbuckled the sword belt and held it out to Melinda. "He's your burden now." She whispered and struggled to stand. "Announce yourself and be welcomed into my House. So decrees His Imperial Majesty Hilal MacGregor bids you welcome, Xio Ohari."

The chamber did as promised and the healing spell enveloped the

Necromancer's battered bits. They snapped back into place and the dark haired necromancer smiled.

The jingle of Necros came next.

"Where is he?" the Skull Necro demanded.

"She's not dead. Wonders will never cease," Melinda said.

"There was doubt?" the Necromancer laughed and extended a hand. "*Xio Ohari.*"

"Who?" the Skull Necro said.

"Your necromancer," Melinda said and grasped her hand. "*Meylandra Stuk.* Xio here actually fixed your problem."

One of the security guards sprinted around the barrier and hugged Xio. He had a vague family resemblance, probably Xio's brother. "You're alive. Gahsakes, I told them to come get you but they wouldn't listen."

"I'm fine," Xio said and kept her hand extended. "I'd like my sword back, please."

Melinda returned it and turned to the Skull Necro. "We're done here."

"Where is he?" the Skull Necro said.

"Dead. Now, take me back to the rest. I need a House Liaison and a phone to call my brother," Melinda said and tagged the chamber with her goggles as Xio pushed it past.

~

The Hangar was a buzz with overlapping voices until the door opened and Melinda stepped back inside. The lack of the Weaver didn't get noticed by anyone.

The door closed behind her and she walked the length of the Hangar until she reached the group that had been there the longest.

K. D. Stukari had done a good job hiding herself. Her sword was nowhere to be seen.

It was her father that had set off the alarms on Melinda's goggles. A bearded man so boring and basic shouldn't have sent off enough biohazard warnings that even the goggles recommended sheltering in place.

"Where is he?" Dinah asked in a low voice.

Melinda flopped into a chair. She dropped the cloak into her lap and scratched her neck only to confirm her necklace was still under her abaya. "He didn't make it," she said.

The beard next to Dinah dropped his head and said a prayer for the lost.

"What happens now?" Dinah said.

"How far are you willing to go?" Spence MacGregor's voice rang in Melinda's ears.

"She's got the sword and his chamber. I've got all of him," Melinda said. "If they want the Weaver, they're coming to me."

Dinah sucked in her breathe through her teeth. "Keep it down."

"No. They've got the entire place bugged. They already know I have him *and* his book," Melinda said.

The Hangar Door heaved open and the crowds scattered at the clack of heels echoing across the floor.

"Ladies and gentle souls." A woman's voice jerked everyone around. "My name is Bernadette Bedriskah Brie, House Liaison and I'm here to expedite your return to your Houses. There's a ship that will be taking you home. Please gather your things and we can all be home for dinner."

Benny Brie stopped in front of Melinda. Clenched hands on her suited hips. Three hair quills now, not just two. "Twice in one day, Mindy. Twice." She growled and tossed her an encrypted House Phone. "Now, call your brother before this gets worse."

"They get released immediately," Melinda said. "And I want to talk to whoever is in charge of this mess or they get nothing."

"Someone actually pulled your House file and called me in," Benny said.

"Careful," Dinah's sotto voice said.

"No. It's time to make them care," Melinda got to her feet and turned to the beard. "Don't do anything stupid. You'll be released in five minutes, as planned."

The beard laughed. "As planned?" *his* warm voice said.

Melinda followed Benny out the door. "As planned."

~

The sound was quiet at first. A background hum in the air. The hum grew louder. It wasn't the air recycling units in the ceiling, either. It grew louder until it halted any conversation.

"What is that?" Dinah said.

Her father tilted his head back and listened. "Good ole round Cross Runner Engines." He said. "Can't mistake'em anywhere. Worse than boots on the ground is that sound. It's from an air carrier. Probably one of mine."

"Why're they coming back?" Dinah said.

"Oh," he turned to the exiting Melinda. "I have a pretty good idea of why."

Another howl rattled the hangar and everyone jolted about.

"*Itty Bitty,*" he said. "I thought Junior was grounded."

Dinah wandered over to one of the windows. "She's not landing," she said and grabbed her bag but her father reached out. "No," he said.

"Why?" she said.

"Junior just got waved off. He doesn't buzz the tower like I do," he said. "He's not picking you up. They are. We are not getting on the ship."

"Duchess Stukari," the Skull Necro jerked them out of their conversation. "If you'll follow me, your appointment awaits."

Dinah stood up while her father stayed seated.

"And your father, too," the Skull Necro said.

Dinah didn't turn around but the quills quivered when her father stood and came nose to nose with the Skull Necro. "Lead on," he said.

30
WHERE WEAVERS DAIRE, PART III

"WHO'S THE BEARD?" BENNY SAID ONCE THEY WERE OUTSIDE.

"You really don't want to know," Melinda said and followed Benny across the tarmac.

"Where's Spence?" Benny said.

"You really, really, don't want to know," Melinda said. "Where's our ride?"

Itty Bitty's engines howled through the night.

"Junior can't land. The air-to-air defenses are all jacked up. I tried to get them out with him. You have to trust me on that. But they would barely listen to me," Benny said.

"Because the air carrier isn't supposed to be at the keep," Melinda said.

"Tell me you didn't lose him," Benny said.

"Not exactly," Melinda said. "Wait, where are you taking me?" She stopped and squinted at the night sky at the flying silhouette that stalked towards them. "What've you done?"

"It's not me," Benny said. "This all you."

"It certainly is," the Skull Necro said from behind them. The group of hostages followed her along with Dinah and the beard. All surrounded by the phalanx of Necros. "To ensure your safety. No quills."

Benny dropped her three quills into the Necro's awaiting hands.

"You really need to learn not to be so accommodating," the Skull Necro said.

"I don't need them," Benny said. "Duchess doesn't need her sword just like Mindy."

The running lights illuminated across the silhouette until the graceful form of an air carrier appeared. Melinda's goggles measured from bow to stern at five hundred meters long. A combination thruster powered VTOL engines and maneuvering propellers kept her in the air. Several halogen beams of light from her belly spotlights danced across the tarmac. Eight pairs of long legs extended from either side of her curved undercarriage. Pairs of large blocky feet at the end of the legs touched down onto the tarmac. Her engines slowed to an idle. The loading ramp extended from the hull letting the interior light beckon.

Yes, I see how a dozen these landing on beach head with hundreds of Power Armors spewing forth, Melinda thought. *This is why Rushford never talks about the war.*

The Necros nudged the hostages forward, except the beard.

The Skull Necro blocked his path onto the ramp. "Tell me something," it's plate jawed. "Why you."

"We all get to vote," the beard said. "If you'd read the House contract you didn't sign you'd understand that."

"You were banished for thirty years. You don't deserve a vote," the plate snapped.

"In the end the blessed, cursed and the plated all get a say," the beard said. "Even the banished. You'd learn more if you listened instead of arguing."

He side stepped around her and re-joined the rest.

"You're nothing without that stupid plate," the Skull Necro said.

"I would agree with you," the beard said and jerked a thumb to the rest of the Necros. "But they beg to differ."

"They're for the chambers," the Skull Necro snapped.

The beard nodded. "If you say so," he said and followed the rest deeper into the air carrier's innards. "If you say so."

~

The groups were split into three. The hostages went to the balcony state rooms. Melinda, Xoi and her brother were escorted below deck twenty and Dinah along with her father were escorted above deck twenty. Each deck looked the same. Plush red and gold carpet with the day of the week. The brass and wood reminded Melinda of the rail carrier.

"Is the Baroness enjoying her stay?" one the women magess droned.

Melinda turned at the voice and the hooded magess was the shortest she'd ever seen since it was actually Cherie Leighton. "I most certainly am," Melinda said.

"I'm to escort you to your quarters." Cherie turned to Benny. "Excuse us." Once they were out of sight, Cherie poured on the speed. They were down three decks and across to the port side suites. "I brought everything," she said once she was inside the brightly lit suite.

"How much do they know?" Melinda said.

"Nothing. I've got six months of escort duty," Cherie rolled her eyes. She chucked her magess robe on the bed.

Cherie put on an identical abaya and matching jilbab. She pulled the goggles down around her neck. "Keep the Weaver's cloak and book. I've made some spares."

"Thank you," Melinda said and hugged her. "Defense charm and tethers."

Cherie patted her hidden neck. "Tripled checked. The charm works and I got my waist bag matches yours. I have no idea where anyone else is, the onboard wireless network reeks."

"Completely out of position. Junior is probably paralleling us," Melinda checked her bag one last time. "I'll swing by the closest maintenance closet and set up a private server. You'd better get out there before Benny starts combing the place for me."

"Good luck," Cherie said and out the door she went.

~

The red landing lights on the wall of Gregori Ohari's suite pinged to green. He double tapped is eight point harness. The straps zipped back into his wall seat. He pushed himself up and lazily kicked the seat back into the wall. *This is my last voyage,* he thought and his bones agreed with him wholeheartedly.

His suite door chime ringed and he acknowledged it. He smiled at the return of his grandchildren, Xoi and Jai. His air carrier suite was big enough for a half dozen and had been empty for far too long. The resurrection chamber they pushed in front of them slowed his heart. "You recovered it," he said. "We'd heard rumors someone tried to open it."

"They did," Xoi said. "But, we closed it."

Gregori's smile faltered. "What do you mean, 'we' closed it?"

"She got lucky. They had a specialist on site," Jai said. "We can present it at the vote and get on with our lives, finally."

Gregori walked around the chamber. "Why did they open it?"

Xoi shrugged. "By the time we got to there it was already opened. Half of their Liches got vaporized and the rest, well, are dead. I should've ask them for a head count but it took a lot out of me."

"Chamber's defenses wouldn't cause that much damage," Gregori said. "I need to tell you both something. Kaare and her sons are alive."

"Since when?" Jai said.

"Since they made it to Crosleigh's Caves and came out the other side, they're onboard," Gregori said. "And completely healed from what I've been hearing."

"Healed?" Xoi said. "They're Liches, you can't heal that. Unless there's another Necromancer running around."

"I've been hearing it was Weaver and his Apprentice," Gregori said.

Xoi grimaced. "That girl," she said and rubbed her temples. "Everything is still fuzzy."

"She didn't look like much," Jai said. "I think she's on board with the rest of our guests." He turned to Xio. "And I'm prescribing bedrest. We can handle the vote."

"Guests?" Gregori said. "What guests?"

"Small group of wanderers showed up because of the lightshow," Xoi said. "Between that these fools blowing up the keep I'm surprised no one has thrown a fit." She wandered over to her room. "I'm going to get some sleep."

Gregori pulled Jai close. "Blowing up what keep?"

"Crosleigh Keep. You haven't taken a look outside have you?" Jai said and grabbed the handles on the chamber. "I'm going to go store him and I'll be right back."

It's time then, Gregori thought. He waited for Jai to leave. *Her sword was meant for him but his sister has earned it.* He pulled the sheathed sword from his footlocker. "Xoi, I need to talk to you about something," he called out to her.

The door chime buzzed.

"Enter," Gregori said "Jai, what did you forget?"

The darkness came next knew his name.

~

Jai pushed the chamber into the freight elevator and stabbed the down button. The doors closed but a gloved hand stopped them and a somewhat familiar face mostly obscured by a lovely rose color jilbab. The matching air filtering bandana was a bit much in his opinion.

"Just made it," she said and Jai stared into her lovely eyes.

"Hello," he managed.

"Level please," the elevator intoned.

"Where you going?" she said.

"Where ever you're going," he drooled and coughed. "I'm sorry."

Her eyes grinned. "Portside cargo hold."

Jai stabbed the cargo hold button repeatedly. "Absolutely."

"I think we met," she said. "Your sister is the necromancer."

"Yes, she is," Jai said. "Who you with?"

"I'm apprenticing at the moment," she said and extended a hand. "Melinda Scott."

"Jai Nibbons," he grasped her hand and shook. "Apprenticing with who?"

"The Weaver," Melinda said.

Jai coughed and jerked back his hand. "What?"

"I'm the one who helped you barely alive sister finish her task which should've killed her but the Weaver's sword saved her," Melinda said. "I'm here to make sure he gets resurrected in time for the House vote."

Jai pulled his eyes away from hers, down to the chamber and back to hers. "Are you going to kill me?"

Melinda laughed. "You're too cute to kill. Besides, I made a promise I wouldn't shoot anyone . . . anymore . . .today."

Jai laughed. "And that's a problem for you?"

Melinda's eyes swallowed him whole. "You have no idea, Mister Nibbons."

The doors whooshed open and Melinda stepped out into the under lit cargo bay.

Down the aisles they walked until they reached a secure area for magic items. The cage door was ajar and several defense magi were sprawled across the deck.

~

"What happened?" Jai said and pushed the chamber in line with the rest.

"They're all barely alive," Melinda pulled the magi away from the chambers. She pulled the hood down over his face and checked his gauntlets. "His defense gems are bone dry."

"That's not a good thing, isn't it?" Jai said. "Sorry, I never understood the whole defense magi bit to be honest."

"The gems are filled with a defense spell. The spell is supposed to impenetrable. The magi guard the chambers against raiders," Melinda said. She pulled the magi's sword from its sheath and walked around to the rest. "One of them I can't read. The rest say Leighton. Those six aren't Leighton but this one is."

"Those are horrible odds," Jai said.

"Someone passing as one to get as close as they can," Melinda said and dragged the magi farther away from the lone open chamber. "Grab his staff we can wait for it re-charge."

Jai picked up the cursed bo staff off their chamber and it's gems glowed happily.

"Do that again," Melinda said.

"Do what again?" Jai said.

Melinda grabbed the bo staff and leaned it against the chamber. The gems dulled.

She picked up the staff and stepped ten feet back. The blessed gems glowed happily.

Melinda stepped closer to the chamber and the gems darkened.

"What're you doing?" Jai said.

"It sponges," she said and stepped ten feet back. "Open the chamber."

"Are you insane?" Jai said. "There's someone in there."

"Yes, I know," Melinda said and checked the staff, again. "Trust me."

Jai sighed and knocked on the lid. "Housekeeping," he said.

The lid parted and drenched man pulled himself out. His tan suit didn't have cuff links. The interior was just as damp as he was. He toppled to his knees and shoveled the air into his lungs. He didn't look like Spence in fact, Melinda didn't recognize him at all until her goggles pinged with a facial ID.

"He belongs to House Lir according to his ID," she said and knelt down. "I don't speak in the high tongues, do you understand me?" she said in a lower tongue.

The shaking man nodded.

"My name is Meylandra Stuk, Baroness of the Wailing Seas," she said. "Who be you and who do you serve?"

"Alastair Lir and I serve no one but myself." The man coughed. "May Crosleigh is dead."

"Yes, and Meylandra Stuk, my grandmother rose in her place. I'm burdened with her name, titles and land." Melinda said and raised her tongue to standard. "Tell me, what are you doing in a Lord MacGregor's chamber?"

Alastair coughed. "Which one of you has the gahforsaken defense charm on? I'm drowning."

Busted, Melinda thought and eased back.

"I do," she said. "I've also been burdened with raising Spence MacGregor."

Alastair didn't look at her and instead pushed himself to his feet. He staggered over to the chamber and opened his mouth. The roar of the ocean filled the room while water exited his mouth filled the chamber to its edge.

"What. The." Jai couldn't finish the sentence.

"The Lir sponge off other auras. They're the original Liches. Something they can't turn off," Melinda said. "There's a few kegs worth of heavy water in that chamber for one person and one person alone."

"He's throwing up water," Jai said.

"Some Houses are space borne, others are planet borne not all of us used to breathe oxygen," Melinda said. "Spence must of switched chambers before they were mailed out."

Alastair nodded and gave her a thumbs up.

"Why'd they try to crack his chamber then?" Jai said.

"An ounce of my augmented blood can kick start a civilization. A Lir is ten times worse. No offense," Melinda said.

Alastair stopped hurling and wiped a sleeve across his mouth. "None taken," he said. "Where is Horatio?"

Indentured but alive, she thought.

"Around," Melinda said looked down at the opaque water that filled the chamber. She unlatched the charm from around her neck and dropped it. The water boiled and the lid slammed shut. "That'll purify the water in time for me to resurrect him." She turned to Alastair. "I've got a ship ready to get you to a safe house."

"Not without the rest." Alastair said.

"Melinda," Jai said.

"The situation is fluid and you're the first bit of good news I've had," Melinda said.

"Melinda," Jai said.

"I need to find the rest before we move." Alastair said.

"Meylandra." Jay said.

"What?" Melinda snapped and followed Jai's pointing finger to one of the unconscious magi bodies.

The after image of an aura jacker wasn't too happy.

~

"Huh," Melinda said and shuffled behind Alastair and turned him towards the after image.

"What are you doing?" Alastair said.

"My defense charm just went into the drink. You're all I got unless Jai has another on his person," Melinda said.

"Actually, I don't have one," Jai said, sheepishly. "I never needed one."

Melinda reached out and pulled him close. "This is what we're gonna do. Jai, push the chamber. It's defenses should ward off the aura jacker."

"That's what that is?" Jai said.

Alastair squinted. "They de-funded that project years ago. There's a defense necklace in my back pocket that should work."

Melinda patted down his pocket and found the necklace along with his House ring. "Ring." She said and handed it to him but he returned it.

"Not mine," he said. "She'd want you to have it."

"Who?" Melinda said.

"It was your grandmother's," he said.

"Oh, that lost House ring," Melinda said.

"Where're we going?" Jai said.

"The starboard side cargo hold. It's where all the rest of the chambers are," Melinda said. "We don't stop for anyone."

"And him?" Jai nodded to the after image.

"Someone sponged all the aura out of his gems," Alastair said. "They can't aura jack him without an aura. I give him an hour before his aura re-lights. There is one little problem."

"You mean besides you being in Spence's chamber and the aura jacker?" Jai said.

Alastair laughed. "Yes, since I wasn't in here to begin with so I didn't drain the magi."

"Someone else did," Melinda said. "So glad I came prepared."

The trio silently pushed past the unconscious magi and back into the lift.

~

"What makes you think he's in another chamber?" Jai said.

"Unless he's hiding out in a room somewhere," Melinda said. "The other chambers are ironed up for shipping and pre-loaded before the ship boards the passengers."

"Mailing yourself," Jai said.

"It's not as bad as you think it is," Alastair stretched while they walked through the lower deck corridors where passengers were forbidden but should've been filled with maintenance crews but instead it was empty of any traffic. "It's felony to open and considered a pox if you do."

"Except the poor bastards back there that were drained and unconscious," Jai said.

"Defense magi know the risks. But having your aura drained by one of us is unfortunately part of the job description," Alastair said. "Not to pressure you, Mindy, but who else is here besides you?"

"You're looking at it." Melinda adjusted the necklace and the warmth from the House ring calmed her heartbeat. "I've got his book, the chamber, we just need his body."

"And his sword." Alastair said. "It'll keep the Liches away and stop drowning me."

"How does that work?" Jai said.

"Imagine a giant, bottomless ocean and you have to keep treading water," Alastair said.

"That doesn't sound so bad." Jai said.

"Also imagine there are several beasties in the ocean protecting their lord and master who want to eat you," Alastair said.

"You never do things small, do you?" Jai said.

Melinda stopped the chamber short of the cargo bay's maintenance lift door. The wide open door didn't catch Jai's attention until Melinda unzipped something he couldn't see and out came the biggest rifle he'd ever had the mis-pleasure to see. "You two push the chamber. I'll be on point," she said.

"That's not a stun gun, Mindy," Jai said. "What else are you hiding?"

"Actually, that's a Granger stun rifle. Nice to see you're not as blood thirsty as your brother," Alastair said.

Melinda waved a finger at Jai. "Maybe if you're good I'll show you," she said and tossed Alastair an earbud. "Secure channel one."

"What did the carrier's innocent wireless ever do to you?" Jai said.

Melinda smirked. "Get it out of your system now. We're in complete agreement this thing doesn't get off the ship, right?"

"Absolutely," Alastair said. "Any of my deranged family gets off ship and I'll never hear the end of it."

"Good to know we're on the same page," Melinda said. She pulled down a hood along with her goggles and promptly disappeared from sight.

Alastair laughed and pushed the chamber onto the lift. "There's parts of this job I didn't miss like being bait."

~

The lift stopped and Melinda pushed up the door. The goggles wireframed everything in the two-dimensional pea green. The twelve foot tall gates hadn't been touched but the door leading deeper into the bay swung back and forth. The two unconscious magi that should've flanked the door on the deck like the rest.

Melinda shouldered the rifle and pulled their bodies onto the lift.

"It's clear," she said and Alastair bum rushed the door faster than she'd expected.

Jai double timed it to catch up and dove through the door. She closed it behind them and the rifle was in the crook of her arm. The scope appeared in her right lens, normal view in her left. She ignored the crates and found the tether line against the wall. *Not this time,* she thought and with a muffled snap her tether cord was attached.

The goggles pinged movement. And, not from the two hyperventilating idiots, either.

" . . . you don't have to do this . . ." a familiar woman's voice echoed.

"Back of the bay," she said and moved at quickly as she could. The borrowed camo cloak flashed warnings that she wouldn't be invisible for too much longer if she kept the pace but she chanced it because of the dimly lit room.

Alastair and Jai quietly pushed through the aisle until she nudged Alastair.

"Hold here. Jai stay with him until I clear the area. Don't do anything stupid." She said and advanced down the aisle of ironed up crates.

She quickly reached the back of the bay. The lenses snapped a blurry photo of movement and immediately, Gregori Ohari's face and House affiliation pixelated into view. He stood next to a chamber, a Daire broadsword in hand and Xoi collapsed in front of him.

Well, this can't get much worse, Melinda thought only for him to raise the sword in her direction. *And, then again.*

31
DAIRE CLOSE

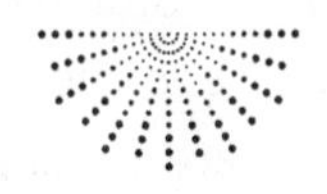

THE SKULL NECRO ESCORTED DINAH AND HER FATHER TO ONE OF THE conference rooms and closed the door behind them. The medium sized room had an oval table, six chairs and a lovely spread of fresh food laid out.

The emptiness was punctuated by the snores of an old man with frazzled graying hair. He was dressed in the livery of a House Mister, a male liaison and judging from the crispness of the slacks and coat, it had never been used. The lovely red flower in his lapel was real.

He was sprawled out across the couch that occupied the fall wall. The wall was made of glass to go along with the balcony.

Dinah cleared her throat and he cracked an eyelid. "Well, look at this," he said. "I won."

She filled up three glasses of water and placed one of them in front of the old man. "Dinah Stukari," she said and extended a hand.

"Oh, my name doesn't matter. Just that I won," he grinned with a full set of upper and lower white teeth.

"You won what?" she said.

"I bet them I couldn't get you two alone and on the ship without forcing you," he said.

"Where're the rest of the prisoners?" Dinah's father said.

"Prisoners?" The old man laughed. "They weren't prisoners they were us. After the stupid idiot just had to tweak the chamber we sped up the timetable and waited. Somebody always calls a liaison, we're picked up and repatriated just like we should be. No one knows the difference."

"Except for us," Dinah said and turned to her father. "Who is this?"

"We were the ones who were brought in when Melinda dug her heels in when the Stukari showed up. We're the ones who sided with her only to be benched when the Stukari cried loud enough to bring down their lord and master. We're the ones who were supposed to have been retired by now but here we are, playing our part." The old man sipped his water. "There's no one at the wheel of this thing anymore. The last of them left on Kirkus' train when he managed to get into Stow's End without so much as a whimper."

"If that's the case, they probably rigged this thing to blow," Dinah's father said.

Dinah glanced at her father. "If no one else is here, we can re-take the bridge and land."

"No. We let Melinda finish this farce then your father can land us back at Stow's End," the old man said with a wink, "as planned."

~

"Oh no." Jai's face slackened at the scene. "What've you done?"

"Stay back she's been compromised," Gregori said. "Aura jacker got disconnected when I knocked her out."

Melinda pulled back her hood and Gregori refocused on her. "Is that the twin that goes with one in the Ohari Vault?" She said.

"And what if it . . . wait," Gregori squinted. "Yer the apprentice, aren't you?"

"Yes, I saw Kaare's sons regain their auras," Melinda said. "If that's the twin it's beacon to the jacker. Give it to me."

"Why?" Gregori said.

"You can't aura jack a woman," Melinda said. "It's only the men."

"What?" Jai said.

"Daire Empresses used their crowns to control the men to do their bidding since none of them had daughters. What do you want?" Melinda said.

"She's the one who tried to kill me," Gregori said.

"No, you can't aura jack a woman. I think you two were in the middle of having a polite conversation when someone came to the door and jacked him with the sword still in his hand." Melinda said. "Probably Cherie or her handler."

"What?" Jai said.

"Your sister is an Ohari necromancer. It's rare, so rare, you two have been hiding on the Hollow because of all the ruckus going on at home. Selene was probably assigned to watch over you but when Xoi went to the Academy things got shuffled out of position. The sword is hers for a job well done. She wields it and survives, she's a Daire. It's how weapon burdening works," Melinda said. "Now, what do you want?"

Gregori sneered. "Know it all, stuk witcha!"

Melinda smiled. "I was read in along with everyone else and that's probably where the leaks started. The Hollow is used for two things, dumping ground for the worst and a training facility for the next generation of Houses. All of which had been going swimmingly until the Stukari showed up and demanded to be trained for things they couldn't even pronounce. So, yes, I am a know it all."

Xoi stirred and crabbed walked away. "What is that thing?"

"'Thing'?" Jai said.

"When you get jacked your mirror image gives you away," Melinda said. "Unless you're touched the right way and she can see the jacker. Who're you here for, me or them?"

"Those idiots didn't listen to me and jumped ship early." Gregori hissed. "We could've taken down all of you at the same time. But, not after the idiot tried to get in the chamber then everything went to shit."

"Aren't those protected for that same reason?" Jai said.

"My my, when Mister Crosleigh sends you all on a chase he

certainly knows what he's doing, doesn't he?" Melinda said. "Drop the sword and I'll walk you in myself."

Gregori cackled, actually, cackled with glee. "You think I'm coming in with you?" He snorted. "You think I'm going to scrape the floor for six months and just start singing your praises. Is she always this naïve?"

"Naïve or offering you a job because so far you've done a very good job of almost getting my family dead, the Weaver, his hacked ship and then all of sudden this idiot tries to crack a secure chamber all the while I'm three miles away from it all. I going to go out on a ledge and say your friends stumbled across Roark's chamber and played with it first. It was empty except the burden and his sword. How am I doing so far?" Melinda said.

~

"And he thought he could just resurrect himself." The old man said. "What is it with resurrecting yourself anyway? Immortality isn't all it's cracked up to be."

"On that we completely agree," Dinah's father said.

"See, you got it good. You disappear for a few millennia then come back. Why?" the old man said.

"To see my kids," Dinah's father said. "And to see if it's time to rise."

"I think it's more than time. They're down in starboard cargo bay," the old man said.

"I know," Dinah's father said.

"Of course you do. Always spying on people you need a new line of work," the old man stretched.

"It's his ship. He had eyes on everyone the moment we boarded. Funny how they missed that, Uncle Joshua." Dinah said.

"How does she know, how does she know." The old man demanded.

"Your cufflinks are your fathers, the tie clip belonged to your son and the flower was her favorite." Dinah said.

The old man lowered his glass to the side table. The bluster deflated. "I surrender."

"Until he says it in the old tongue don't take your eyes off him." Dinah's father got to the door only to be kicked across the room and into the wall.

A cloaked Leighton magi flowed across the threshold. His four footed, two ton, feline animus growled at Dinah.

"Was that really necessary? I swear you always take things to seriously. He wouldn't hurt a fly." Uncle Joshua pushed himself off the couch and bowed in front of Dinah. "See ya around, kid. No heart feelings about all this."

"Says the one whose running," Dinah said.

~

"'Says the one whose running.' Get a load of her. The shuttle?" Joshua Crosleigh said.

"In the rear hangar," the magi's cursed gems said.

"That kid of his is smart. Didn't even bring a weapon on board." Joshua said and depressed the lift button. "They told me to kill you all. I may be an backstabbing *stukarree* but I'm not an asshole."

The magi and his animus were silent.

"Tell him I'll be gone by dawn. Your house will be yours again and you two can stop hiding. I think this night has gone on long enough," Joshua said and the lift doors parted. "I don't need to be walked down."

The magi and his animus joined him in the lift.

"You really don't trust me, do you?" Joshua said.

The animus growled.

Joshua laughed. "You're right, I wouldn't trust me, either."

The doors re-opened and Victor Stukari waited at the shiny and chrome private air yacht.

"Here we are." Joshua said. "Victor, please give our friend their reward."

Victor handed the magi two leather bound tomes and a small

wooden box. "You are relieved of your burdens to me. He is relieved of at least one of his. He will no longer be nameless." he said.

The magi grasped each of them but Victor didn't release them.

"And in return," he said. "He gives me three days to get off this planet. We both know how he works. My debt to him is over."

The magi nodded and Victor released the items.

Victor and Joshua boarded the air yacht. The engines spooled up. The bay doors opened and the ship disappeared into the night.

~

Dinah rushed over to her father.

"When you mother asks," he managed to get to his feet, "there were ten of them."

Dinah jerked around at movement at the door where the magi and the animus had returned.

"I told you to stay in the hangar," The magi said, he pulled back his hood and Grainne Stow appeared. "I didn't hit you that hard, did I?"

Dinah dropped her father back on the floor. "When were you going to tell me?" she huffed.

"We weren't," Grainne and her father said.

"He let you go?" Dinah's father said.

Grainne waved her tome contract and box. "Our contract, keys and your name. He also requested three days to get out of here," she said.

"Good luck with that never happening, That's three days too long." Dinah's father said and staggered to his feet. "Don't open anything until we're on the ground. I deserved that punch."

"And a lot more for making me wait this long." Grainne smacked his shoulder. "Those minders they sent didn't have brain cell between them. They didn't check to see if that Gladys Stow mannequin had a pulse. We need to get that plate off you."

"Not until we're on the ground. They may have rigged it," he said.

"I haven't felt the deck move. I think we're still on the ground."

Dinah said and the family hobbled towards the door. "Mindy should've talked him down by now."

Grainne's animus growled at the door across the hall. The wall indicator blinked busy.

"Now what?" Dinah said.

Benny poked her head out the door. "Go away, we're busy."

Dinah squinted and pushed open the door. The rather busy room was filled with people and one of those people was Melinda. "Hold it. You're down in the cargo bay."

Her father and Grainne entered, too. "What is this?" Grainne said.

"What's it look like," Melinda said. "I'm getting my house back, there's paperwork to be signed."

"Hold it. Whose down in the cargo bay then?" Dinah said.

~

"No," Gregori said. "They're just leaving?"

"It's over," Melinda said. "I give you all the credit for making it this far but we both know none of these chambers are rigged. The Liches would've been all over them by now. And, really the only thing I came for was the Weaver's chamber so I can put him back together."

"This isn't about you." Gregori said.

"Right, it's not about me. It's about the fact things have gotten so out of hand that even the die-hards are leaving the sinking ship," Melinda said and tugged on her tether. "I just need you to disconnect from the rig and let Gregori go. He didn't do anything to you."

"They left us to die!" Gregori said. "They left us on a barren world with nothing."

"They freed you. Yes, I know," Melinda said.

"What is he talking about?" Jai said out of the corner of his mouth.

"Those gems," Alastair said. He and the chamber were closer now. "My family figured out how to curse and bless weapons by binding souls to them. Many of them didn't go willingly."

"None of us went willingly, the lir liar knows all about that." Gregori snapped.

Alastair sighed at the nickname. "I'm guessing they followed my instructions to leave you on a barren world and release you," he said. "If you're back I'm guessing someone found you, didn't they?"

"And gave us purpose again!" Gregori said.

"No. This isn't purpose this is exactly what my family wanted you for. They don't get their hands dirty and you get, what, blown up?" Alastair said. "Listen to her. She's not like the rest. Her brother would've blown you up three times over by now and the less said about her cousin the better."

Gregori hesitated and Melinda extended a hand.

He flipped the sword around and everyone sucked in their breath but Melinda accepted the weapon handle first.

"Thank you," she said and handed it back to Xoi.

The audible click froze everyone in place.

"I didn't touch a thing," Jai said.

"Alastair, where's the chamber?" Melinda said.

"Um," Alastair said. "It's gone."

"I won't go back." Gregori lowered his hands to the drum fed carbine in his lap.

A gentle breeze passed by and chamber next to Gregori jerked up right. The lid pulled back.

Gregori twisted around and unloaded the entire carbine into the empty space.

"Always with the guns," a deep male's voice echoed.

A shadow dropped from the ceiling's cross beams and knocked Gregori across the deck.

A soaked Belfry rolled back his wings, curled his tail up where in a blink they were gone, and a fully dressed Spence MacGregor remained. His aura bubbled around his shoulders and eyes brought a smile to Melinda's face.

"Yours," Melinda handed off his cloak to him.

Spence winced and pointed at the pooling after images around them. "Jackers. Where's my sword?" He said.

"Forget the sword, you've got me." Alastair stepped forward and the after images hesitated but more arrived through the walls. "Actually, Xoi, where'd that sword go to?"

"Mister MacGregor, pleasure to see you back amongst the living." A familiar mechanical voice echoed along with the jingle of quills.

Spence pointed at the advancing Skull Necro that wielded his sword. "Who be you and who you serve?"

The Skull Necro hood seals twisted and Diedre Yashira appeared. "Sorry, I used you as bait but I had to get you all in the same place," she said and with a flick of the wrist Spence's sword landed in his hands.

Her bow slid out of one sleeve, her sword from the other.

"You don't have to do this," Melinda said to Gregori. "I'm going to be taking back everything they took from me. Anyone who is chained to those rigs or war tables are getting tossed out on their asses. You don't need to be their toy anymore."

"We're no one's toy," one of the auras wailed.

"The log out of the rig and walk up to the Sys Admin and tell them you're done. It's that simple. You're in control, not them. Take it from someone who used to be a rig runner. I was chained to my chair for years until one day I was fed up and broke free. If I can do it then so can you."

The cluster of auras swarmed about.

"This isn't working its making it worse. Which one is it?" Jai said.

"What?" Melinda said.

"They're clustering together it has to be one of these," he pushed over the empty chambers one-by-one and got to the bottom where one wouldn't budge.

The one that had power going to it. The one the noise was coming from.

"Is it supposed to be making that noise?" Jai backed away.

Melinda grabbed Gregori by the shirt front. "What've you done?"

"No escape from any of this," Gregori slurred and his head sagged. A ring dropped onto the deck and he jerked awake. "Whaaa, happened?"

Spence grabbed the ring off the deck and tossed it to Alastair. "Iron that up, please."

"What're you going to do?" Jai said.

Spence rolled up his sleeves and turned towards the screaming chamber. "What do you think I'm going to do? I'm to stop this stupid thing before we blasted into vapors. I need a tool kit and Cherie next to me."

"Whose Cherie?" Jai said and Melinda's face shifted about.

"Sorry," Melinda said and pulled back her mask to reveal Cherie Leighton. "Mindy was double booked." She handed the tool kit to the Weaver. "Tell me what to do."

Spence triple tapped his ear bud. "Whoever else is on this channel. I need to talk to the bridge. In case this doesn't work I need you to gain some altitude."

"We're working on it." Dinah's voice replied.

~

The conference room across the hall was full of people. It's why Grainne's animus had stopped and pawed at the door. The room full of people surrounded one person: Baroness of the Wailing Seas Meylandra Stuk. Much to everyone's surprise, they didn't know the carrier had landed or the prisoners had gotten off. Instead, they were celebrating the fact the war was over and to do that Meylandra Stuk needed to be there in person.

Zi Stuk and Vernon had sequestered them in the hallway while Dinah's father calmly explained to them the situation.

"I was told they relinquished all command to you." Zi said. "It's the only reason why I got on this ship in the first place."

"I need you all the stay calm and remain here while we sort this." Dinah's father said.

"So, I should or shouldn't call the fire brigade?" Vernon said.

"She needed more ground ops. This is more ground ops," Melinda said.

"Putting Cherie in the thick of things doesn't count as ground ops," Benny said.

"They're supposed to recognize the fact it's not me since the place hasn't been shot up yet," Melinda said with shrug. "The bridge is that way."

The steady run up three flights of stairs came to halt when the blast doors to the bridge were welded shut.

"I don't think they're welded shut," Dinah's father said. "Any command deck doors are biometric." He turned to the box in Grainne's hands. "I need all of you to get back one of the blast doors."

"What're you doing to? Shoot your way in?" Melinda said.

"No, I'm going to trust by backstabbing uncle and put my plate on." Dinah's father said.

"There's another way," Grainne said. "We can circumvent the door and get in from outside."

"All entry points to on this level are triple sealed, biometrically sealed and the outer deck is electrified," Dinah's father said. "For obvious reasons."

Melinda innocently whistled.

"In case those jackers come back, get behind the blast doors." Dinah's father said and popped open the box.

"If it helps, I saw a plate in a footlocker bounce it way out a tent." Melinda said.

"Probably my war helm. Good to know." Dinah's father pulled off the melted face plate and for the briefest of moments the corridor was filled with storm of darkness. Unlike every mage Melinda had ever encountered, his aura was a frothy sea where a pair of aura pupils rested.

He lowered the face plate onto his face and it clicked into place. The storm resided and Nathaniel Stukari, Sr. stepped into the light.

"Hey, you were the one in the tent," Melinda said.

He stopped them and counted off on his hands to ten.

"Well?" Grainne said.

Nathaniel grimaced and his green aura eyes flared to life. Dark hair and shortened beard sharpened. "I think we're okay," his fake lips moved properly with his voice. "Computer, recognize, Stukari, Nathaniel, Captain. Heiden Corps License Number: One, One, Five, Three."

The bridge doors opened to a wail of klaxons and acidic smell of smoke.

"Or then again maybe not," Melinda said.

Nathaniel waltzed onto the bridge and flipped switches on the captain's chair. The air circulation system kicked in and the smoke cleared immediately to reveal every single of the five command consoles had been crushed in.

"Emergency Auto Destruct activated," a dull voice said. "Two minutes to self-destruct."

"Not again." Melinda crowed and immediately pulled up a temporary deck plate and jumped down a half level into a sea of wires. "Gimmie two minutes to fix this."

"Grainne, fire control, Benny, coms. Dinah, damage control." Nathaniel said and tapped his ear bud. "Cargo, Bridge, ignore the alarms we're working on it."

"We're not going anywhere, all the consoles are slagged," Dinah said. "Including the pilot's well. No fuel but we're on ground power at least."

"Cargo bay, Bridge, how bad is it?" Nathaniel said.

~

"Both control panels and the back-ups are dead," Spence said. "I can't stop it."

"How high do you need?" The distorted voice over the com said.

"You don't get it. We'd have to be in orbit to get rid of this thing," Spence said.

"Hang on," Cherie said. "We don't need to gain altitude. It does."

"Bridge, Cargo, we may have an idea," Spence said and pointed a light into the inner guts of the whining chamber. "I don't see an altimeter sensor. But we've only got the shell off of it. We'd need something to attach it to. There's a map on that wall."

~

Melinda pulled herself out of the floor. “It’s disabled.”

“Evidence?” Nathaniel said.

Melinda dropped an innocent looking, small, smoking box into his hand.

“Mindy,” he groaned.

“Look I pulled it out and it popped itself.” Melinda closed the decking. “He can’t stop it?”

“It’s a no-win.” Nathaniel said and dropped himself into the captain’s chair. “They need you down there. They’re going to launch it manually.”

Melinda laughed. “Seriously, they’re going to do what?”

“Cargo Bay to Bridge. We’re Oscar Mike to starboard side weapons bay three have Mindy meet us there,” the intercom box squelched.

~

Nathaniel cycled the bridge’s airlock and everyone wandered out into the cool night air. The air carrier was still on the ground. Her fuel reserves as Dinah had found were already drained by constantly being in the air.

“So, Uncle Joshua gets to live and he tells them he blew us up and no one is going to check?” Dinah said.

“Oh, they will, but by then he’ll be long gone.” Nathaniel said.

“You going to chase him?” she said.

“Absolutely.” Nathaniel said and the rest of the group joined them. “Mister MacGregor.” He extended a hand and Spence’s punch landed him on the deck.

Grainne’s animus growled but Nathaniel stopped her.

Spence extended a hand and pulled him up off the deck. “You know what that was for?” The Weaver said.

“Marrying Panya without your permission.” Nathaniel said and rubbed his jaw.

Spence nodded and hugged him. "Thank you, my friend," he said.

"Here it goes," Melinda announced.

The missile bay's door slid back and a small carrier-to-carrier missile launched. The plum of exhaust engulfed the gray phallic weapon of mass destruction then it shot skyward.

"Since when do air carriers have carrier-to-carrier missiles?" Grainne said.

"Other way around. Since when do star carriers mascaraed as air carriers?" Nathaniel said with a wink. "When the war ends and both sides are selling their war toys for cheap only for you to come along with a king's ransom and buy them all up."

The sky exploded in colors, hues and sounds that weren't natural.

"Mindy," Spence said. "Call your family. Tell'em you passed."

32

AN ENDLESS EPILOGUE

THE NEXT MORNING, SOMETHING WONDERFULLY HORRIBLE HAD happened, the sun had risen. A feat that surprised many because the land had been damned to eternal darkness for thirty years until the heavens exploded last night.

Melinda rolled her eyes at how fast the rumor mill had turned the explosion into the reason why the sun was out. "A chamber blowing up doesn't cleanse the land," she said.

"I would generally agree with you but some chambers do lich into the soil and the rest, well, isn't pretty." Spence sipped the warm coffee and watched Benny gussy Melinda up to be presentable. "I think someone tried to smoke the town out but the villagers just got used to the eternal darkness."

Nathaniel paced up and down the corridor and when he wasn't on the intercom barking orders to have Erik re-check the ship's systems again. He'd been roaming of the halls with his camera since the sun came up.

"At least you're getting a formal introduction," Spence said. "I just signed a piece of paper and got stamped. I owe them money for my unlicensed weapon of mass destruction and paperwork fees."

"They here, yet?" Melinda asked Nathaniel.

"Freya, Jainey and Thom are here," he said and fired off a few wide angle shots from the door.

"What about junior and the rest?" she said and turned to them when she received silence.

"*Itty Bitty* hasn't checked in yet," Benny said and fixed a hair pin. "Dinah is working on it."

"They should've been back by now," Melinda said.

Benny snapped her fingers at Nathaniel. "What're you doing?"

"For posterity," he said and snapped off several stills before Benny kicked him out.

The conference room was over capacity. Her family sat on one side of the isle while Spence and the rest sat on the other.

"Baroness of the Wailing Seas," Zi Stuk announced.

Melinda jolted awake and hopped out of her seat. Accepting her House Marque of Intent along with her newly created House ID Key on board the grounded air carrier in an empty conference room lacked everything she had built up on her mind like accepting it with the rest of her crew but this was more secure Zi had told her.

Melinda stiffly walked up to the podium. She grinned at Cherie and Jai closeness.

"Thank you," she said. "I want to say this has been a long time coming. I promise to keep my pledge to help those wanderers who ask my help. I promise to protect those on the road between Wailing Seas and Crosleigh Keep. And I promise to be a calming presence even in peace and war. But, let me say one thing, for those who feel the need to test me, my name is Meylandra Stuk, Baroness of the Wailing Seas. Don't run."

"We're retaking that video," Zi said.

"Nope, that's perfect propaganda footage, thanks!" Nathaniel said and disappeared before anyone could catch him.

~

Victor Stukari waited with Joshua on a hill top five miles away from the air carrier base. The launch of the carrier-to-carrier missile silenced them while the detonation made Joshua whistle low.

"It'll take them a year or longer to put two and two together and figure out that wasn't me." Joshua sniffed. "I think we better get while the getting is good."

Victor kept his eye on the radar even if the ride was without incident. The ship diverted past Stow's End and instead towards a region north of it. It was here where the crowds of families' personal air carriers filled the skies.

The ship shuddered when the landing sequence finished. The airlock popped open and he waited for one of the volunteers to bring the stairs over. Joshua was already out the door, down the steps and wandering around families.

You're running. Crosleigh's never run, Victor thought absently and tossed the keys onto the pilot's seat. He grabbed the go bag from the overheads and descended towards the crowds.

The air and rail carrier station was in the middle of nowhere. The grass and fields surrounding it used to be something, but no one remembered its name, only that the views were spectacular. The grounds bustled with parents dragging their suitcases through the grass. The world was warm, and the future was bright to everyone just for today.

Victor passed through the families when a Leighton magess blocked his path.

"Excuse me." He clumsily looked elsewhere as to not intrude on her privacy.

"Hey, Victory." The magess turned his chin towards her. It was Terrie Leighton. "My father is over there." She nodded over to the rail carrier stop's gift shop. "Don't look so glum."

Victor walked into the shop. It was wall-to-wall, lacquered wood. It was cute for the children's sake and that's what made it so unbelievable to him. He used to like the cute and now his teeth ached because of it. The hand-painted mural on the wall depicting Crosleigh's Aviation pilots drew him close. *It's all such a lie,* he thought.

"Mister Stukari," a warm voice said from behind him, and he winced at not checking his corners.

Somewhere, I just failed Entry One oh One. Victor thought and Alizerin Leighton passed through the doorframe. The Magi would've blended in at Stow's End. A foot taller than he, dark, mahogany skin, the khakis, boots, light jacket, and a duffel bag over his shoulder but with no children doting behind him said would-be prospector. No one would've recognized him as Alizerin J. Leighton the war mage.

"Successful then?" Alizerin said and idly spun one of the postcard holders.

"Yes," Victor said. "Nathaniel has his name back. *Itty Bitty* hasn't reported in yet. Once he finds out what's happened he'll assemble them as planned."

"Very good. My friend is back on the merry go round." Alizerin smiled.

"There's a seventy-five percent chance that Phineas will go with him," Victor said.

"As he must be. Balance. Leighton will rise with him." Alizarin nodded. "We must prepare to greet my friend." He gripped Victor's shoulders. "Thank you for doing this. I see why my daughter likes you."

She didn't give me much choice. Our kids are on your rail carrier. Victory bit back. "Friend of the family is a friend of the family," he said.

Alizerin laughed. "Just like him, you're just like him. When in doubt, always compliment while you grind your teeth." He held out a locked tome. "If you could leave this for him. We'll be on our way."

Victor turned the tome over: *When Riders Crosleigh.* His hands quaked at his family's name and placed it on the counter. "What does it mean?"

Alizerin grinned and led him out the door. "It means my friend is going to come find us in his own time. It means our Houses will be one, again. It means a Cross will rise."

I don't like the sound of any of this, Victor thought and, with every inch of his will, boarded the rail carrier and found his children's arms welcoming.

The whistle sounded, and the families waved goodbye to their children.

Onward, the rail carrier chugged across the horizon towards a new adventure.

CALL TO ACTION!

You!

Yes, you!

Thank you very much for reading this book. I know it was long book to read and it was longer to write it.

To that end, leaving a review on your favorite retailer would be greatly appreciated!

And if you wish to join my no frills mailing list please visit:

www.rkbwrites.com

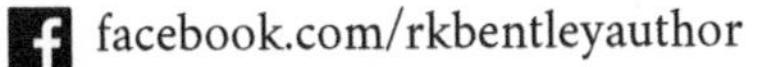
facebook.com/rkbentleyauthor
twitter.com/rkbentley
instagram.com/rkbentley
goodreads.com/rkbentley
bookbub.com/authors/r-k-bentley
pinterest.com/rkbentley93

ACKNOWLEDGMENTS

A History of this Book

I started writing on my father's TRS-80 laptop. The first thing I wrote was an adaptation of The Transformers Generation One television pilot.

I kept writing through Junior High School back then I didn't know what self-insertion or fan fiction was so myself and few people occupied the lovely world of *Robotech* on 3.5 discs that only worked in Appleworks on my family's Apple IIGS.

Fast forward a few years and in college the now defunct Amateur Creators Union had some feedback for me: create your own universe.

By this time, I'd taken a Creative Writing Course at Rhode Island College and discovered their fledging graphic design department. I became fast friends with Paul F. Chabot. He was an artist learning this thing called Photoshop and was patiently waiting for his Power Mac to arrive. We hit it off with creating a comic strip for Rah-CoCo's Comic and Collectibles entitled Rah-CoCo the Kilted Berserker, said lovely Berserker can be found on http://www.rahcocos.com

Paul and myself created a comic book called Totems and managed to self-publish four issues in total and ventured forth to different cons like Project A-Kon, Katsucon, Megacon and the biggie: SDCC.

We decided it was time to try something else that didn't drain our credit cards.

During the Totem's years, I hadn't really been writing that much of my own until NaNoWrimo (National Novel Writing Month - http://www.nanowrimo.org) appeared in someone's Facebook timeline and I joined up.

I dusted off the old universe, stripped away the copy-written material and wrote.

A few years later, during a NaNoWrimo TGIO party (Thank God It's Over), we critiqued each other's stories and I asked the Rhody Wrimos as we called ourselves if they wanted to do this monthly.

The Rhody Writing Group met the next year and I looked at the half finished collection of stories set in this Universe and said: I'm gonna finish this story so it can link to the rest.

While I went to work, one of the Wrimos told me about Association of Rhode Island Authors, http://www.riauthors.org, a group of local authors who go together once a month to listen to speakers and talk about local events. One of those events was the Rhode Island Author Expo, http://www.riauthorexpo.com an annual event held in December that has grown so much now the author's tables are selling out within hours.

ARIA helped me a great deal with learning how to present yourself and your table at local events which were thankfully many even if we did live in the smallest state. It was during the ARIA years that I said: I want to finish Weaver so I can sell it.

The monstrous beastie of a first draft that came in at 147k words was like all first drafts: crap and thankfully, I was told to revise it by everyone.

The monthly Newport writing crew stopped asking what I was working on over burgers at Mission knowing full well my answer.

In the meantime, members of the Rhody Writers Group, Matthew Cote, Bennett North and Kristie Claxton had short stories published while Matt Keffer and Janet Parkinson had each published a collection of short stories / poetry.

The high point of this adventure was having myself, Matthew Cote, Bennett and Kristie go on the Writing Excuses Retreat Cruise in 2017. The week across the Baltic Sea was great, the sights wonderful (*when boat docked properly and the buses were on time*) and getting writing advice from Peter Newman among others was just what the story needed.

It's seems fitting to write this on the one year anniversary of the cruise.

Thank you for reading and enjoy the ride.

R. K. B.

Rhode Island - 7/22/18

ABOUT THE AUTHOR

(Photo by Matthew Bentley)

R. K. Bentley was raised in New England on a steady diet of 80's Cartoons, Tom Baker Doctor Who, Babylon 5, Star Trek, Star Wars, Buffy: The Vampire Slayer, comics books & movies.

CPSIA information can be obtained
at www.ICGtesting.com
Printed in the USA
FSHW010116081021
85287FS